When They Lay Bare

Andrew Greig is the author of six acclaimed books of poetry and two books chronicling his Himalayan expeditions of the eighties. His first novel, *Electric Brae,* was shortlisted for the McVitie's Prize and the Boardman-Tasker Award. His second, *The Return of John Macnab,* was shortlisted for the Romantic Novelists' Award.

by the same author

poetry
MEN ON ICE
SURVIVING PASSAGES
A FLAME IN YOUR HEART
THE ORDER OF THE DAY
WESTERN SWING

mountaineering
SUMMIT FEVER
KINGDOMS OF EXPERIENCE

fiction
ELECTRIC BRAE
THE RETURN OF JOHN MACNAB

When They Lay Bare

ANDREW GREIG

faber and faber

First published in 1999
by Faber and Faber Limited
Bloomsbury House, 74–77 Great Russell Street,
London WC1B 3DA
This paperback edition first published in 2000

Typeset by Faber and Faber Ltd
Printed and bound by CPI Group (UK) Ltd, Croydon, CR0 4YY

A CIP record for this book
is available from the British Library

ISBN 978–0–571–20121–1

2 4 6 8 10 9 7 5 3

In memory of Anthea Joseph

The support of a Scottish Arts Council Writer's Bursary
during the writing of this book is gratefully acknowledged.
Special thanks to Iain B for the wee Mac.

To the Queensferry Mafia (plus Shirley) – love and all.

When They Lay Bare

As I was walkin all alane
I heard twa corbies makin a mane
The ane unto the ither said
Whaur sall we gang and dine the day?

Oh in ahint yon auld fail dyke
I wot there lies a new-slain knight
And naebody kens that he lies there
But his hawk, his hound, and his lady fair

His hawk is to the hunting gane
His hound tae fetch the wild fowl hame
His lady's taen another mate
So we can mak oor dinner sweet

O you'll sit on his white hausebane
And I'll pike out his bonnie blue een
Wi ain lock of his gowden hair
We'll theek oor nest when it grows bare

Though many a one for him maks mane
Yet nane shall ken whaur he is gane
Oer his white banes when they are bare
The wind shall blaw for evermair

Plate 1

The story waits in painted plates that years and many hands have scoured till nothing is for sure. This bright speck off-centre could be the flash of a coin or a blade. That greenish patch below might be bracken or a discarded cloak. The hurrying figure could be a tall woman or a long-haired man, so worn is the outline. And this one at the centre, head back, mouth open, limbs askew, may be falling or reaching for love.

Take the only comfortable chair and one by one pick up the plates. Stare into them as though they were windows out of a place where you have come to stay for as long as it takes. (This is a kitchen, cool and bare. The windows have small panes that leak wind and the creak of crows in the trees outside. This cottage looks over a tumble of pale wintered fields that fall away to the Border, and it has been empty for years, until now.)

Think of the Willow Pattern plates that gripped you as a child. You were fascinated how stages of the story were painted alongside each other – the lovers, secret trysts, discovery, the elopement, pursuit, death, the dead returning as birds of the air – as though they were really all one time. As though in the lovers' first meeting their death was already standing at their side on the bridge with a whip, and the white doves are rising even as she first turns her dark head his way.

So it is here. You start to realise the many figures are just the same few recurring, and these multiple scenes are often the same event recast. The novel element is that these plates, helpfully numbered on the back from 1 to 8, are not all the same but form a series, and their worn, uncertain pictures yield a story in a darker and more northern light. They are called Corbie Plates and their setting is the badlands, the ballad lands, those debatable Borderlands where two countries join and separate in some rough and pungent mating.

It's a very old story that has come down to you.

This first plate is so worn only the essentials are beyond doubt. You sit at the table in a dwam of pale March sunlight, looking first at the plate then out the window as if to compare the views. A metallic taste rises in your mouth as it often does these days. Perhaps you are being poisoned by mercury fillings. Then something quivers up your legs, arcs through your groin – it's like coming suddenly to the edge of a great drop, and you sway between wanting to move back and stepping forward to get it over with.

But the truth is you have nowhere to move back to, and that is what brings you here. So tilt the plate to the light.

The faded blue-grey is sky, the brown below is moorland. Beneath that is green, a patchwork of fields sloping down towards a silver brushstroke river that must mark the Border. (Impossible as yet to say which side of the Border we are on, or whether it matters.)

Look closer now and find a crumbling wall of turf or stone. Behind that dyke there's a faint grey road curling round the shoulder of the hill like smoke from an old man's pipe, and this tiny smudge – scrape it with your nail, it does not come off, it isn't someone's food – is something on the road.

It is a young man travelling. On horseback or foot or wheels, there is always a young man travelling. Usually he sings to keep his spirits up as he moves towards his unknown but certain destination.

Peer more closely now. That darker green below the dyke, half-hidden among the skeletal bracken, is surely a cape, and there's the hunch of a shoulder and legs folded up to the chin. There is someone behind the wall, and it's not a new-slain knight. It is a woman, waiting. (There is always a woman waiting.)

Now look out through the window at the old wall and the dirt track that runs by it. The road is empty, but if you went outside and waited, certainly someone would come.

These plates are very old, passed on from generation to generation and finally to you, but their story is ever present as the air. Already you suspect it will touch you as if it were your own. And you are needing to be touched, aren't you, or you wouldn't be here.

All day the cack of crows and the yearning wind have been at you, gusts tugging at dark hidden roots. Watch and listen now till you begin to go behind the wind, and the light hawk hangs steady in the violent air.

She has been so long behind the wall, the corbies no longer protest. It's chill and the wind is strong here, high up the dale. It blows dark hair across her eyes but she doesn't blink as she hugs the cloak around her and stares out over the rough pastures that fall away down to the Border. There's no sign to mark it, only the river and a grey haze around the trees, but it's there just the same. On either side the long bare shaven ridges horse down in a pincer movement and head off the glen in a choked valley, a narrow bridge, a frail road skewing east towards the village and a wider world.

She's not looking at anything visible. The corbies skirl above her as she shelters behind the old dyke whose grey-green lichen blends with her rough woollen cape, and her face is hard and pale as the trunks of the beech trees that soar above the darkness of the cleft away to her left. A fine spray from the hidden waterfall has webbed around her hair.

She is so still she could have been there for centuries.

The crows cack louder, their wingtips clap the air like worn black-leather gloves. Her head tilts slightly, long white fingers stroke a heavy clasp that holds the cloak about her shoulders. She twists to stare along the old drove road. A puff of dust, a flash of light on glass. A faint rumbling like a stone running round and round a bowl, and somewhere along the rim there is faint music.

She bows her head, her fist tightens on the metal clasp, and it begins.

*

Tilt this first plate better to the light and find more guessed-at detail. Down in the bottom left, what looks like the same green figure is emerging from a mist that hangs over the river. She – if it is a she, and you prefer it to be – has something on her back, and a pale shim-

9

mer going before her, perhaps a companion now worn away completely.

This is her arrival. For that's how these plates work: events apart in time are held alongside each other in one frame. (These bare yet oddly secretive hills, with their steep dales, narrow passes, towers and ruins and grassy mounds, vanished forests and forts, if they had memory, everything in it would be simultaneous.) These arrangements say whatever has happened, happens always. It is for you to settle on an order and live it.

Shift in your chair then look again and see what you hadn't seen before: a short brown smudge by the edge of a patch of trees. A witness. A watcher. He's on nearly every plate, at the edge of things, near where the lovers meet in secret or hard by the dizzying waterfall or the great stepped drop where someone falls.The voyeur, he has a part in this. At the very least he is eyes and a voice.

Be still. Listen behind the wind. His voice comes through, light and throaty.

I kenned it a man, even without binocs, the first time. Something about the sure gait of yon distant figure walking out of the haar that hangs by the river, swinging a leg over the first stile then louping down and pressing on without pause. Something in the bold, braisant way the head swivelled left then right as though checking everything was where it should be, then jinked surely across the bog and up the brae as though he owned the dale itself.

He veered closer to the trees and the dark hidden waters that split these long braes and riggs. This was no tourie out for a daunder. Nor a loon from the village – I knew the walk of every one of them, poacher, loner, or spunkie lad.

I eased back into the shaw of birch behind Ballantyne's Farm. There was no cause to hide nor watch, yet I did so. I was puzzling where the mannie had come from. There'd been no one on the river bank when I'd scanned it minutes afore, just the road into the village and not a car on it at that time of evening. Then a drifting mist closed over the water like a fist, and when it opened again the walker was there. At first I thought there was another went ahead of him, smaller and a woman forby, then the wind blew and there was but one moving strongly up the brae. It was as if he'd just walked out of the river or snouted like a mole up out of the land itself.

I lit a wee cheroot and tasted again the rightful bitterness. My mind, such as it is, was working fine yet just in behind the low ribs, I felt now as at all times, like a cancer in reverse, some dwindling inside.

The stravaiger moved on steady through the chill gloaming of what passes for early spring round here, following the trees up by the dark heuch, past the byres of Crawhill Farm, and pressed on for the cottage at the top of the lands. But Elliot had cleared and locked up the place once Patrick Johnstone left with the bairn after the trial, never sold or rented it. Once or twice a year he'd send me or Annie to paint the window frames, repair the roof, generally redd up inside, but no more than that. Daft, I told him often enough, get rid of it, man. And he'd look at me with eyes black and empty as the windows of that abandoned house, till I learned some thoughts like some loves are better left unspoken.

Now I let smoke slip like a wraith from my lips and lifted the glasses. My walker bent forwards, as if slightly humpie-backed or under a burden, stepped up on the stile and stood tall there a moment.

Then two things became clear. He was a she. For a moment I thought maybe a long-haired young man, one of the new travellers maybe, but no. Tall, upright and bold like a man, but solid in the hips as if the world spun round her hurdies – that and the other usual female appurtenances. She wore breeks, boots, some kind of moorit-coloured material round her shoulders. And as she jumped down the far side of the stile, I saw she was carrying a sack, a bag, something heavy slung over her shoulder that weighed her down.

I palmed my cheroot and began to shadow her up the brae.

I am not Sim Elliot's man, though I defend him against the blether and clash of this valley. I am not his spy, though it's understood I keep an eye on every coming and going around the estate. Nor his protector, though whiles I carry the gun to affricht craws and vermin. Whatever they say in these parts, I am not his shadow nor his confidant. Though I do the accounts for what's left of the estate, and ken something of certain payments which never appear on those accounts, I could not say we are close.

I wouldn't want to be close to a man to whom I am so bound. Who is so bound to me he flinches if our eyes meet. And if Elliot gives me the house and the pay that allows me my passions and still puts food in the mouths of me and Annie and the bairns, it is not for my silence. That has been long secured.

After my bairns were born I had a greit to myself in the hospital car park because I knew then even they weren't going to put me right. A nurse passed me my first cigarette. On ye go, Tat, she said, and I accepted, needing then as now some sort of friend touching my lips. But Annie and me are a good team, she does her job at the big house as I do mine on the estate, and she never speirs about what went before. Far as she's concerned, it's just an old scandal, a bit local clack best laid aside with the dead. But ever since then I've kept sooking smoke from time to time. When all else fails, there's aye habit.

So I shadowed this woman out of habit, and a bit curiosity. I couldn't jalouse where she might be headed as she louped another fence and picked up her burden again. I followed her because I was in no hurry for hame, and late air helps me sleep nights.

I used what cover there was among the hillocks, scrags and burns, just as I had twenty years before as a young laddie burning to find out what men and women did when they met secretly. Were it not for my curiosity I would sleep well of nights, far from here.

She never looked back till she came at last to the dyke that borders the moor and the old road. Then she put down her satchel and took a long look back down where she'd come from. I didn't hunker down, for she was the one on the skyline, not me. I just kept still, and have no reason, then or now, to think she saw me. Yet that long stare made me shake and grue. A man's look, I would have said, quite unlike Annie's sharp sideways keeks in my direction when she thinks I am about to 'go strange' as she cries it. Strange it might be to her, but it's the only honest thing I do though I have to go to the city for it.

She sclimmed the dyke and crouched on top, agin the sky-line. The colour had drained from the sky and mirk was seep-ing from the ground. The corbies were silent now, only wind twitched and reishled through the long grasses of the windlestrae as her shawl blew up and hung a moment like a dark wing over her head.

She jumped down and disappeared.

I followed, shaking the shiver from me. Because for a bit moment, most like water raised in my eye by the snell wind, again I'd seemed to see another, a smaller, light-footed woman standing just ahead of her, but that was impossible and the lass long dead.

This one walked strong through the failing light, puffs of dust biffing from under her boots, along the old drove road where for hundreds of years men, women and beasts have passed. You'd not have to be fanciful to see them still, the sheep and kye heading for the market towns, goods coming north on the hobbie ponies and on the backs of the dusty-feet, the peddlers, tinkers and Romanies. Vanished tribes, the si-lenced Picts and the lost legion, all strode down that road. And the reivers, the armed men moving even as she did, fleet and silent, to do fell business on either side of the Border, seeking cattle or bloody revenge. And the lovers hastening from for-bidden trysts.

I could see them all as I followed her through that gloaming, close enough to wonder at the muffled clink from the load over her shoulder.

It was near dark as she passed the last of Ballantyne's byres. I thought perhaps she'd doss down there, for surely to God she had to lay her head somewhere. Could be she had a tent and a man waiting for her up on the moor, that would be it. But she pressed on towards the Liddie gorge and the woods. A low dark rectangle against the last of the light. The roof of Crawhill Cottage. No lights there, of course, there hadn't been in over twenty year.

She stopped hard by the door. I ducked down ahint the dyke and heard the faint clink again. Her muttering to hersel. A creak, a tinker's curse. I didn't have to keek over the dyke to know what she was about. Well the lassie could struggle with

that padlock half the night – the key was on the board at Elliot's and though the door was old as everything at Crawhill,
it was secure enough.

A rattle then a different kind of creak, a long groan. I was
hunkered down with my mouth open like a simple. I'd
changed that padlock a month back at Elliot's word – he'd
been getting right timorsome of late, in a way I'd not seen of
him before. Another creak then thud as she put the door to.

My heart was beating the retreat on its side-drum as I
looked over the dyke. The light of a candle – no, a mantle lamp
– bloomed in the side window of what used to be the kitchen
all those years back, when Jinny Lauder waited by it for that
wee tap at the glass, and her man Patrick away at the tree-
planting, and her secret hurrying across the wooden brig over
the falls. I minded it as I minded the laddie who crouched
where I did now, his heart shoogling like a pheasant gripped
in the hand.

I'm not a fanciful man and have no truck with superstition.
Though I ken something of the bogles that lurk in the mind,
they have no life outside it. She was only a lassie come from
nowhere to bide a night in an empty cottage. Nothing to be af-
frichtit by, and she had no business there. I raised one leg high
on the dyke.

She was singing, I could hear it faint but clear, the tune and
the half-murmured words. Perhaps that stopped me. Or the
notion that her and me, alone inside that place at night, it
wouldn't be wise. It could be taken wrong. And maybe Elliot
had given her permission and the key, and didn't think to
mention it to me. No point making a right fool of myself till I'd
checked the facts.

I lit again my short bitter smoke then hurried down the
braes for home and Annie, John and Laura. All good reasons
for turning away from that door. But the strongest and worst
reason, the one that clutched in my gut like a man going
down, was the song the unknown woman crooned. I never
wanted to hear a woman's voice sing *Barbara Allan* again, and
for sure never there, not in that place where I'd crouched
below the sill, a tremmlin loon of fourteen, and heard Jinny
sing it as she waited for Sim Elliot coming one more time

across the wet and narrow bridge that spans the torrent of Lid-dieburn, twenty-plus years syne.

*

You are intrigued, uneasy. Perhaps you have other things to do, and this story is not quite what you expected.

Yet it insists as would a lover. Let the watcher and the woman's arrival fade. Look back again to where she crouches still behind the dyke in the morning light. She is alert to something happening on the old drove road. It is what she, and you, have been waiting for – the young man in ignorance, singing as he travels on. In the silence behind the wind, it's not hard to hear him yet.

The wind is strong from the west, and the sound of his father's Land-Rover and then his voice arrive long before he does. She stays hunkered down behind the dyke. Where have you been my blue-eyed boy, where hae ye been, my darling son? *His voice is bold enough but uncertain in tune and accent. She almost smiles to hear it.*

The story runs a cool hand down your neck and turns your head till you hear tyres crunch, brakes squeak, a dog bark. Then the clunk of the door closing, his boots scuffing the dirt, and somewhere a stone slows inside a bowl and rattles to the bottom.

David Elliot stopped up short of the cottage, not sure why. He swung the keys from their stone disc as Hawk flowed past him and peed up against the wall. The dyke. He'd never wanted to call this dale home, but still the words came back when he did.

He stood in thin sunshine, not knowing what had brought him here. Through the trees past the cottage was the waterfall, the ravine of the Liddie Burn, the wooden bridge if it hadn't fallen yet, and the short-cut path back to his father's house. Up on the moor were the lochans he'd come to fish, he should be on his way there, needing to pass time till the water-glint brought peace for a while.

He looked down to Ballantyne's Farm, the Tattersall house below it, and the long falling-off to the river, the Border and the hills rising beyond. Then at the cottage. Not a pretty one, something secretive in the bland way it hunched back into the brae, the dark line of its low roof. It was empty, of course it was, no smoke or washing line, the garden gone back to long grass and bushes though the cottage itself seemed in good enough condition.

He hesitated. What was to be gained by poking round such places? This was where the dead woman had lived. Let it be, Davy. The dead are too many to take on. But this was his father's estate, what little of it remained after the settlement, and he could sniff around it if he wanted. His father never mentioned the place, the talk swerved round it. He knew without asking Elliot wouldn't want him to come here.

So he called on his dog and began to walk carefully towards the cottage. The name came to him: Crawhill. He took in the raised mound behind of the original building, the tall pale twisted beech trees rising over the ravine – heuch, that was the word – the old privy out the back. He walked so slow now he'd almost stopped, feeling the cold sweep over his palms as the dog circled round him.

He checked back the way he'd come, another look down the dale, then up on the moor. No one watching. Of course there wasn't.

He shook hair from his eyes and let the wind at his back push him on. A volley of rooks exploded through the trees as he put his hand to the little rotten gate and stared at the empty windows either side of the door.

He did not much like such windows. Without curtains they minded him of his mother's eyes, open and empty as her last glass on the table by her bed. The furry ridges of her eyelids under his thumbs as he closed them. One would think the dead would close their own eyes, like switching off the lights when you leave the house, but we must do it for them. Someone will do it for me some day, he thought. I hope they will be kind, as I hope my Redeemer liveth.

He crouched down at the gate, gripping the dog by the collar, reassured by the rough silky warmth on his wrist, its unquestioning affection. No smoke from the chimney, but in the side window was a paint-streaked jar, and pale flowers, daffs most like, leant against the rim. They looked fresh, and the cold sun gleamed on a new padlock lying in the grass by the door.

He could just walk away. When he'd shaken off the big house that morning, his father's white face smeared to the window, Annie Tat gesturing him to stay, he'd wanted only silence and clean air, to fish a lochan in the hills till he could face going back. Company he did not need, nor mystery.

Then the privy's corrugated roof creaked and lifted, dropped with a little thud and squealed again, and he had it. Years and years ago, when he was wee, before the deaths and changes: a summer picnic, or just a casual visit, he cannot say. The garden well kept with raspberry canes taller than himself, dreels of tatties, roses, some plants like green limbs sticking from the ground, his father . . .

Maybe this long overgrown memory is what's brought him here, if here was where it happened. He cannot say. But as the roof bangs again he glimpses a woman smaller and slimmer than his mother, a long fringed skirt, laughing down to him from long ringleted hair against the sun. He likes her but feels they shouldn't be here. He senses a wee girl, a toddler, gurgling somewhere off to the right, but maybe he's made that up. He sees his father's eyes spark as he lights a long cigarette, bends backwards and exhales with a great phew into the sky. And that's all and it's over. Only a background sense of high trees, some corrugated roofing like on the privy here, and a sound of wind, crows and waterfall, suggest it might have been here.

Let it go, Davy. Walk away. You want nothing of this. Everything you want is in the peaceful flatlands and soft woods of Southern England, in the woman who even now is decorating the house you will both soon live in.

He looked back at the dead windows, the fresh flowers leaning in their jar. Jo would come soon. They'd do the formalities with Dad as she'd insisted. Make peace of a sort though there was disgust still there, then leave and drive back south to the life that waited for them. Make a marriage, make children, make a life. No more greed and vacillating. No more walking with darkness like it was the only way to be true.

A red-haired woman with the sun behind her, a toddler gurgling. Not his business. His father exhaling at the sky, glowing with guilty energy, huge with his secret.

Just one quick look round. See where she lived, where it

happened, then let the dying bury the dead. There is nothing to fear here. Actions based on fear are invariably stupid.

So he reached over the gate for the rusty latch. Then as his hand came down, another hand brushed quickly over his, long and white-fingered as it flipped the gate open.

Don't be shy, come on by!

He birled round like a late falling leaf and she was standing close, her outline dark against the light that burned like new-forged steel over the Border.

*

The coffee's cold but it's too soon to take a break when you've only just begun. Instead let your eyes slide back to the watcher at the edge of the scene. Find his voice behind the wind that oozes by the window frame. Soon he'll have a name and then you may come to know his part in this.

Like cloud-shadow over the glimmerin lochans that lie like blades among the muir, my heart grew dark when I saw the Land-Rover stop by the cottage. It had to be the laddie, for Sim Elliot hadn't come this way for years. My elbows shook on my bedroom sill and jiggled my binoculars as the woman rose from behind the dyke.

She closed on him by the gate. *Leave. Leave, you fool!* He seemed to hesitate as though he heard me, then his head dipped and her arms waved like she was casting nets, and he stood back, then she moved closer, and all the while the dog ran circles round them.

When he bent and dragged the hound to the Land-Rover then came back to her, I put my passion carefully aside on the work-bench, sheathed the tiny blades in rubber, then bent to lace my boots. Not my business, you might say, and I'd agree. But it's my nature or fate not to mind my own business, and on account of that for many years Sir Simon Elliot's business has been my own, and so his son's is too.

I left a bit note for Annie in case she got back early from the big house, then I was out the door heading up the brae at a lick.

As he stands at the gate, the road winds away over the young man's shoulder. It kinks round the side of the hill, reappears lower down the painted plate, and you can follow it as it twists past other scenes. In it are the roads that have brought him here. Follow back down them – you have seen her arrival, now it's time to trace his. And you have time, for this moment of meeting will still be here when you get back. After all, nothing here can start without you.

Now look until you see and hear him well.

I watched once a time-lapse film of a small farming village being flooded for a reservoir. The dammed stream rose, thickened, broadened, then the fields flipped from dark to silver. The wind blew and what had been solid went choppy with small waves. Then the road into the valley went under. Next the dykes of the fields disappeared one by one, the lowest first, as though someone was levelling a rule over the valley floor. The people had left their doors open, the water went in and vanished, then began to pour out the windows. Then the windows were gone, debris floated on the water – old cushions, a chair, biscuit tins and newspapers – and then all that was left were three roofs. Then one roof, then its ridge like a dark log, then the waters closed over and it too was gone and the whole valley was water, bonnie enough in the sunlight but empty, empty.

It came back to me the long day I sat watching my mother die. As she talked and haivered I felt the waters rising in her brain. The fields of her memory disappeared one by one, boundaries and divisions crumbled as she talked and slept then woke and talked more, and all the while the waters kept rising.

I prayed, of course, and knew my companions in Faith prayed too, but the waters were strong and her liver and kidneys long gone, and by the last afternoon I was praying for something other than her survival. The rank smell must have been because her organs had packed up, and the only way out was through her sweat.

So when she woke again and asked for drink, I put one in her hand and held her hand to tilt the glass to her lips and she almost smiled and I almost ceased to drown inside. Then all that was left was the last citadel, the roof and chimneys, the core memory she could never let alone.

Those images will not let me be. Her skin by the end was yellow, her body and brain and spirit made thick and coarse by two decades of cigarettes and alcohol, bitterness and querulous lust. She haivered on and on about my father and the woman who died. She called it Justice, then she called it Murder, and challenged me to read the newspaper reports of that time, but I won't because the truth is not there. The truth is in our hearts or nowhere.

Make him pay, she whispered. I stared at the far wall and saw it was not smooth at all. I tried to tell her about forgiveness, the Mercy, the anger that is broken glass in our heart. She muttered some blasphemies. Her eyes were grey but red round the edges, like a sunrise through Borders mist. Her grip slackened on the glass. She dribbled from the left corner of her mouth. *For her he'll pay,* she said, and smiled, and let go. Her smile uncreased slowly like a wave smoothing out, and she was away.

These images will not leave me be, and the reservoir is filled up to my throat, even to my mouth so I must stand a little taller before I dare speak with friends. When I proposed to Jo after the funeral and she accepted, water came from my eyes. Now I can see the way ahead and know it is good. I see the future smooth and shining.

And yet as I drove north through the flatlands, and then through the industries, all I could see was the flood that will cover it all. And the roads merged and grew wider and spread over the plains through the March rain. Turn-offs came up and receded, the cars flooded round the cities and gushed into their canyons, but I drove on, feeling yet the boundaries, the fields and houses, hopes and harvests drowned within me.

I would pray but while driving it's inadvisable, like using a mobile phone. The radio poured static so I switched it off and I crouched forward peering through the segment of visibility that opened and shut with my wiper blades. The rain was coming down in rods. Monstrous trucks in front sluiced mattresses of water into my way, and in my rear-view mirror I watched great walls of metal, blurred and buckling, close on me. Boxed in I drove for miles sandwiched between what was up ahead and what was behind, knowing either could kill me in a flash, and I could not find a holy name when I needed it, only long-forgotten ballads, only *Johnny Armstrong's Last Goodnight* and *Young Lochinvar*, just sweet deadly *Barbara Allan* and *Lord Randall*, bawled defiantly as the great current carried me north. They alone kept the waters from closing over my head.

Beyond the Lakes the deluge stopped, the wide road narrowed and the traffic drained away west and east, and in time I took my own tributary, the one that runs back to my source.

The road played tig with the railway lines for a time, coming near enough to touch then running away. I sat on that train every school holiday for years with a frozen or heavy heart, on the way to see that stranger my father, or ashamed at my dread of returning to that wearying drunk my mother. I hated holidays. Boarding school was cold, fascistic, stupid, but after my parents it was easy, almost a home. Odd now to see those curves in the river, that hill rising and sinking, the familiar names scrolling back.

Going home is more than a physical journey, and to marry a Canadian, as my dear Jo points out, is surely an end to history. Let it be so.

The lands opened like a book I'd read often enough to anticipate what comes next, but not so often as to know exactly what till I see it. The mist clagged in as the road rose higher, but even wrapped in shawls the Borderlands are hard and clean. I stopped at the top of the bar, smelled damp moorland and heard two curlews go pirl-pirling into the cloud, and felt them fly through my chest, as though I belonged here. But really I belong only with Jo and the Mercy, so I walked up and down swinging my arms and from my legs kicked off the feeling.

I said a brief prayer and felt near satisfied, then got back in the car and descended through thinning mist. In a patch of sunlight a slight woman with tangled red hair stood at the roadside with her thumb held out. She lifted her hand and waved as though she knew me or would like to, but I recognised the mixed motives that made me slow, so I signed to her I was turning off soon and drove on.

I found the crossroads and the sign, then twisted along the

tight curves following the river. Trees bare, land bleached at the end of winter, a scattering of blasted flowers along the edges of mixed woodland. Hard right over the narrow bridge across the river and I know I've crossed the Border, though of course it looks just the same as the other side. It doesn't matter much to me.

Then onto the B-road, winding ever more obscurely, all hemmed in by banks and branches. Something always happens along this stretch after the village. Signs disappear, everything is a one-off as it is in childhood. Even the air seems to change and distances aren't the same. Winding up the valley it's as though I'm passing through an invisible gateway, leaving the known world behind and entering an estate where leaves are sharp-edged, thoughts unpredictable, the few people and houses loom larger like they're coming out of a mist. Looking in my rear-view mirror, I'm surprised there's anything at all left behind.

Then the unmarked turn by the lightning-shattered hornbeam, up the pot-holed drive and I'm home, not that it's that. Park round the back, switch off and wait a moment. The window frames need painting, the sheds have slumped against each other like drunks, the silver birches are being strangled by ivy.

Not my problem. I don't want what's left of the estate, he knows that. I've told him straight yet he doesn't hear me. He says I have no choice. Hundreds of years, he says. You can't walk away from that. No one can.

Watch me, Dad.

He can give it away for all I care, or will it to Tat and Annie. I have come back one last time to be free of it all. To be free above all of the long hollowed man glowering down through his study window at me like I'm some kind of assassin come at last.

I get out of the car. Hawk grovels at my feet, I kneel and smooth his head and try to stop my hands shaking. He's standing at the door. His hair's greying so fast. The ponytail is an embarrassment. For all his height he looks stooped and dark, his very face seems to have darkened and died back to cheek and jaw bone. He's burnt out. I remind myself to have compassion but I'm glad he looks hollowed out, burned out to his jutting eyebrows, haunted, and I am a young man about to be free.

He walks from the door, looking round suspiciously as though he believes there's a rifleman hidden somewhere in the trees. He glances back to the door. I can feel his longing to be back in the safety of the house. *He's no been right since he heard the news about your mum*, Annie Tattersall wrote on the card. *Best come soon.*

He comes towards me. I stand up straight and we're nearly on a level. His eye-sockets are craters full of dust, and the hand he holds out is shaking.

David, he says.

Dad.

He still has a grip on him. I slacken my hand and brush the moisture onto my jeans.

Where's the fiancée woman?

Jo will be a few days yet.

He stares at me. His eyes are moist black rabbit droppings. I think he's stoned already.

Wants to keep it short, eh?

My father looks round for the hidden marksman but there is none except his conscience. Whatever the verdict of the courts, he destroyed three lives, and it's hard to find the Mercy though we must.

Bring your gear in, he says, and hurries back inside the house, leaving me with the dog whining at my feet.

I lug my case from the car. We needn't punish each other further. I will try to be civil till Jo comes. Then she will charm him, for the old goat still likes women, I've seen his eyes swivel the few times we've been in the village together and a bonnie one crosses his path. We'll get his blessing then leave.

Annie Tat is in the scullery. A cloud of feathers swirls round her feet. The one friend of my childhood wipes her hand on her apron.

Welcome back, Davy, she says.

*

Time for a short break before your concentration blurs. Lay the plate face-down on the table and go over to the camping stove. Open the valve, sniff gas till the nausea starts, then flick the lighter and jump back laughing. On with the blackened kettle. Invisible flames turn blue on its base, yellow where they lick up the ancient crud on the sides, burning it off in flares.

Go into the bedroom, kneel on the mattress on the bare clean floor and pull a little radio from the backpack. You wander through to the kitchen, birling the dial to Friendly Meaningless, turn the volume down and leave it by the window. Soon the coffee drips slow and heavy through its own silt.

Sit down at the table and pull the first plate towards you again. Two people in a room lean slightly towards each other as though invisible strings pull between them. They could be negotiating or arguing or falling in love. Perhaps all three, they are not always so different. And somewhere nearby, a smudge where the watcher hides.

But that surely comes later. Return first to the meeting by the gate, the young man turning, his arms coming up, and the woman who stands close enough for him to smell moorland and river damp in her.

As he turned, his right hand went up inside his jacket as though to protect his wallet or his heart.

Well, my first visitor, she said. Or is it the eviction committee?

He blushed then, he took a redder like a laddie while yellow hair blew over his face in the snell wind. She looked direct into his eyes and thought him surprisingly young and fresh for all his standing and southern education. So she smiled before he could recover and said, Kettle's on. You'll surely take tea with me.

She thought his eyes an excision from the sky above, pale blue-grey and far away. He hesitated then smiled his long-mouthed Elliot smile, not without danger.

May do, he said, if you tell me what you're doing here.

His hand lifted hers off the gate latch and she cursed the old grip that made her dip her head to him. She saw the grey-green lichen gripped to the wood of the gate, the blood-red stone clasped in the clunky ring on his right hand.

Come by, David Elliot, she said, and opened the gate wide.

I'm sorry, he said, do I know you?

She stared him back.

And why should you?

You're not from round here?

She shook and nodded her head as if to loosen her neck of something. The dog gurled closer round her ankle, then flashed its teeth by the hem of her trousers. He grabbed it by the collar and hung on as it slavered. The collar was finished with silver and on it his father's crest. The hand that twisted the collar was broad and tanned, his arm was trembling from the strain or the wind.

What brings you by here? he asked.

You could say I'm taking time out, she said. Her smile was for herself alone. And could you get the dog off me?

He started dragging the hound back to the Land-Rover but never took his eyes off her. When he came back he stood differently, chin high. He's remembered who he is, she thought. The son and heir. He was better before.

This cottage is supposed to be empty.

Well it isn't now.

So I see.

As his head turned away she saw the corner of his mouth tilt like a lapwing in flight, the white of an eye-tooth. Then he looked directly at her and for a moment she felt the force of him.

Leave you to it, he said. But best not stay here long.

He turned. He was going. The hound was barking like crazy in the cab.

I'm pleased you've come by, David, she said quickly. I like my own company but I needed a visitor. As he hesitated she added, And I've got almond slices.

Oh well, he said. That makes everything all right. But he ducked his head and came through the gate, and the world fell like an apple into her hand.

Look out the window and think back to a morning visitor. You think you remember but perhaps you just imagine. Then pick up the plate again and read into its ghostly lines. You think you imagine, but perhaps you see what's in the air.

The radio burbles, the coffee is run through, and you have thoughts, feelings, words and pictures in your head, some of which may not be your own. You think yourself an original source, a transmitter, but perhaps you are just a receiver.

Outside, cold wind through dry branch and dry stone whines like a child. Somewhere in the great distance a dog barks itself hoarse. Chill light on rough pasture and slow drifting clumps of sheep, pale glitter of the distant river. In time dusk will come and then night, that much alone is certain.

David Elliot followed her into a cool bare stone-flagged kitchen. A wooden table, two chairs, a recessed press cupboard, a cardboard box full of groceries on the floor. Two notebooks and a pen by a squared-off pile of books. A little black radio. On the main window sill, a saucer lined with moss, some early primroses, and one tall black feather stuck up like a mast. A slightly open door into what must be the bedroom. Slim bunch of daffs in the paint-streaked jar by the side window that looked back down the drove road.

Very spare, almost monastic. Impossible to tell whether she has been here for weeks or just arrived. He'd expected the cottage to smell damp, unused, musty, but the air was fresh, smelled faintly of moorland and outdoors. A clutch of bog myrtle hung head-down in the corner.

There's a lot he should ask her, but he hates it when his voice goes cold and officious, and now he was inside he felt quite different, light and almost young. So he perched on the edge of the table, swinging his legs and watching while she quickly put away some plates and chattered on about the wind, the view, the mice in the roof at night. For the first time she seemed eager to please and uncertain, as if now she'd got him in here she didn't know what to do. Her dark eyes moved about him like flies around meat, landing for a moment then away.

Your hound will get hoarse, she said. What's he called?

Hawk.

She stopped then, hands poised over the old stone sink.

I'm sorry?

His name's Hawk. When I was a boy and my parents – well, I desperately wanted to have a hawk of my own. But Dad wouldn't have it, said he didn't like wild things tamed.

She stared fixedly out the window at nothing he could see. Did he now? she said. I've some sympathy with that.

So do I now, he admitted. I was just a boy.

And were you angry?

I suppose. Yes. Aye.

So now you've a hound called Hawk, she said. Very good.

He shifted on the table and waited. In no particular order he registered large pale hands, dark hair cut short and loose, fringe swinging across her forehead as she turned away. Grey wool trousers tight around her hips, loose linen shirt, straw sandals she kicked off. *She dressed in clothes of other times*, he thought. That was a ballad, but which one? Something to do with hats made of bark. *It fell about the Lammastide, when nights are lang and mirk.* She paused to undo the green shawl and hung it on a hook by the door, and he saw again the glint of a heavy brooch pinned to its throat. *The Wife of Usher's Well*, that was it. When the dead come chapping at the door.

He stood and looked out the front window. A fine outlook from up here. Beyond the dyke a patchwork of fields, getting greener and more hedged in as they descended into the valley where the sheep multiplied. The upper headwaters of the river were burning threads of platinum wire. Big sky, steady clouds and breaks of blue. One could spend a lot of time just looking. He had a feeling she already had.

Her hand came past his head and pushed the window open.

Have a good look, she said. I expect it'll all be yours soon.

He stared at her. She stared straight back. Eyes dark, very dark, the colour and sheen of wet peat from the bottom, densest cut of the bank.

You have a problem with that?

Do you, my Lord Elliot?

Cut it out. My father's title is nothing to do with me.

Sorry, she said with no effort to sound it.

How do you know my name?

She crouched over the box of groceries, sorting through jars and tins, bread and at last the almond slices as she talked back over her shoulder, so that much at least was true.

The sudden return of the son of the lord of the dale to make peace with his reclusive father isn't the least discussed news in the village, she said. Apparently the prodigal is tall and tolerable-looking, fair-haired, beaky-nosed, near thirty. Need I go on?

Her accent wasn't local, in fact he couldn't place it at all, yet there was a tinge of the Borders about it, faint and unmistakable as the myrtle. He put his hands in his pockets to get them out of the way.

This place is supposed to be empty. He tried to sound authoritative but it just came out grumpy. He sounded like his mother, uselessly complaining. Girning. That's what came of trying not to sound like Dad.

Is it now? She rose fast off her knees, then smiled in a way that made him glad and wary. So I'm curious as to why this prodigal should come so furtively to a cottage he thinks is empty, and that Sim Elliot, after all, owns. An assignation, maybe? Local girl? Bit on the side?

The contempt in her voice was bad enough, its casualness worse. He made for the door.

I'll pass on the tea and almond slices, he said. Goodbye to you.

Davit!

He stopped dead, one hand on the door knob. No one had called him that in twenty years.

David, I'm not very used to people at the moment. I get a bit nippy because I forget how to act. Sorry.

He hesitated. Her mouth had softened, her lower lip

swollen out towards him like she'd been biting it. She held out her hand, palm up.

I apologise, she said. Nothing's your fault.

He thought that an odd way of putting it, but his hand dropped from the door.

Well, just for the slices, he said, and got a smile that left an afterglow like whisky or heartburn. Look, I'm not much interested in conversation as jousting.

Her eyes moved slowly over him, much more carefully than before.

And conversation as conversation is boring, she said. Such a waste of energy. Maybe that's why I don't see people much.

He laughed quietly, recognising the feeling. Sometimes Jo complained he'd rather talk to the trees than people, and it's true they disappointed him less.

So what possibilities are left? he asked.

She grinned as if he'd said something funny, then twisted again the single tap at the sink. The jet pummelled into the heavy black kettle. She tightened the tap abruptly. All her movements were like that, powerful and decisive. She nodded at the gas rings and he flicked the clicker then put the kettle on the flame. No doubt she is deeply strange and . . . unaccustomed, like she's just dropped by from somewhere else. And yet there are moments when he feels to have known her most of his life, knows the very lift of her elbow and anticipates the dip of her mouth when she talks.

He peeled off his old Barbour and hung it on the hook next to her cloak.

Can I borrow your knife? To cut the bread and that.

He took the fishing knife from his belt, held it carefully by the blade and set the handle towards her. Her fingers wrapped round the wood and brass and ivory.

Nice one, she said. Very sharp. Too good for fishing.

I found it in the back of a drawer in the big house, thought I'd best use it for something.

Inheritance . . . she said vaguely. Can be a mixed blessing, I suppose.

She had her back to him again, sorting among the shelves of the press.

You get the bad stuff along with the good, she said over her shoulder. Bad debts, bad genes, old feuds . . . Old hauntings. Bet you'll get a lot more than the big estate from your father.

You're out of touch if you think there's much of the estate left. And I don't believe in haunting or inherited characteristics – they're an insult to my reason and free will.

So you have free will. Gosh.

He blushed, believing she was putting him on, but he couldn't stop.

Yes, he said. I do. So do you.

Her eyes turned away from him, her strong shoulders dropped and left her white neck long and vulnerable. He felt he'd pushed into a painful private place. Maybe that was why he found himself saying there's bad things – lust, betrayal, murder even – said to run in his family. And he can't believe that. It can stop running right here.

You're an only child, aren't you? she said. So if you die soon, that really will be an end to the family.

He paused by her cloak, thinking about children and Jo. Wait till we have sex first, Jo had laughed, then we'll see. But you know how I feel about it.

He fingered the big heavy brooch. Pewter, he thought, or an oddly pale bronze. His thumb ran over the worn silver disc mounted in its centre, feeling something cold come through the gap left by his mother's death. He didn't know how they'd got here, why they were talking like this, or what on earth they were really on about.

The Borders have long been wild and lawless, she said as she cut into the bread. Badlands. Fire, lance, sword, hangings by the score. Rustling and revenge. Murder most casual. Elliots and Grahames, Nixon and Johnstone and . . . Lauder.

His fingers lifted from the brooch like it was molten, he looked to her but she was bent over the kettle as the steam rose.

Sure, he said, trying to sound casual. Blood feuds to outdo the Sicilians. Kidnapping – and more rape than you could shake a stick at, though they don't like to talk about that.

She coughed. Some dangerous women too, she murmured. They were no softies.

He sat back at the table. Probably just chance, he thought – Lauder is a common enough name.

Anyway that's all by with, he said. Nowadays this is a prosperous douce wee place where nothing much happens, and the Borders have been settled these four hundred odd years.

Really? she said. I look at some of the faces in the village and it seems like yesterday.

She stretched and reached up to the top shelf and her shirt pulled out from her waist. Pale skin, thick and white. A trace of hairs in the hollow of her lower spine. The same hair that catches in the light below the line of her cropped hair. For a moment he's tracing that powder trail from the base of her neck to the base of her spine, connecting head to hips.

He blinked and stuck his head out the window, needing cool air. He felt right strange, not quite himself, as though normal had been suspended the moment he'd come in the door. To the left were the high twisted beech trees he can just remember. Above them, rooks rose and fell like soot from an unseen conflagration. A faint path tunnelled into the woods and disappeared. As the kettle began to hiss, down some long-overgrown pathway words stumbled and emerged. *Creagan's Knowe. Lauder Brig. The Liddie Falls.* He felt dizzy and strange, like the words were coming in a voice not all his own.

Lauder Brig. The narrow hanging wooden bridge over a crash of water, planks green and wet from spray. His father waiting halfway across, urging him on. Dripping black rock, moss and ferns clinging above his head. Roar of water and the gloom. Some drunken farmer going home was said to have skited off the bridge. It may have been Lauder himself, or maybe a Lauder had owned the estate, or swum in the pool at the bottom. Nothing more corrupt than folk memory.

But give the man a name and say one dark night a long time ago, coming home with a head full of whisky and a bag of silver coins, taking for some reason the short-cut path from the big house to the cottage, Lauder fell from the bridge. The money was never seen again, though plenty looked. Some said Lauder was pushed. Murdered. How that word ran between them in the village, thrilling and wicked as *ghost, rape, divorce*. Then another – the Ballantyne kid – said that was haivers. Everyone kent Lauder had jumped. Jumped into the black heuch. Why? Debts, some guilt, a black mind? Whatever. Deid Man's Brig and the falls that rushed by it . . .

David Elliot turned away from the window, saw her head dip as she went back to buttering, the dark hedge of her hair brushing her pale ear.

Sounds scary, she said. We must take a look sometime, see if we can find the silver. Interesting detail that, isn't it? And you can call me Barbara.

She stuck out her left hand behind her, her right still holding the knife. Her head turned, he hesitated then held out his left hand. She grinned as if he'd finally got something right. Her hand was hotter than he'd expected as her fingers tightened across the back of his knuckles and squeezed on his ring. He tried not to wince.

You still have the advantage of me, he said. She raised a very dark eyebrow but he knew she knew perfectly well.

Second name, he said. Surname.

She hesitated. Allan, she said.

Barbara Allan. Oh sure. Born in Scarlet Town, I suppose.

The knife smeared the same jam over and over. Her shoulders rose round her milk-white neck, then dropped again.

Well all right, she said. It's really Mary – though I always wanted to be Barbara. Honest. And Allan's my . . . adopted name.

Let me guess – you're hiding out here under an assumed name from an international terrorist organisation.

She turned and levelled the knife at his chest.

You're winding me up, but I'm not a clockwork toy.

He stared back at her, then nodded.

Absolutely, he said. No one takes the mickey out of Mary. Mickey-taking is strictly one-way traffic, yes? And I don't take jam before tea-time. Cheese would be very fine.

Her lips twitched. Very fine hairs at the shadowed corners of her mouth.

I had it changed for me, she said. And I've no cheese so

you'll either have to do without, or change the habit of a lifetime, or . . .

Or?

She looked up and smiled. He felt ludicrously gratified, like
he'd done something unexpectedly right.

Or come back tomorrow, Lord Randall.

So you can poison me?

She tossed the knife clattering into the stone sink.

My cooking's no that bad.

He had to laugh then, feeling raised and foolish and alert.
The brightness outside, faint caw of the rooks, kettle sputter-
ing, the square of light that fell across the pale wood table and
stone floor, it was all very clear. Smell of jam, and lavender –
from her shawl, he thought. Or maybe her hair.

He plucked two tea-bags from the box on the floor. Found a
second mug in the open cupboard and rinsed it out, standing
beside her at the sink. The lavender was definitely from her
hair. How old-fashioned.

He hummed *Where have you been, my blue-eyed boy?* He'd a
notion Annie Tat used to sing it. Another song of sex, jealousy
and murder. Then she sang back, unexpectedly high and clear.

Where have you been, my darling young one?

They sang through the first verse till he clutched his heart and
staggered against the sink.

I'm weary wi hunting, and fain would lie down.

Take a seat then, she said. You might feel safer making your
own tea.

I will that, he replied and stood guard over the kettle. She
was on his right, still humming to herself as she rinsed the
knife under the tap, her fingers turning the blade to flick sun
into her eyes, and for the first time since his mother died his
belly felt spacious and soft.

*

The kitchen is cool and the rusty stove stays unlit though
there's wood and a bag of coal by the grate. She doesn't seem
to feel the cold and her long-toed feet are bare on the stone
floor. He licks his fingers and dabs up cake crumbs from the

table as he talks. The low sunlight picks out tiny hairs by the corner of her mouth, then spreads a square of light on the floor hard by his chair. Her mouth – wide, level, strong – tugs to the left as she talks. They seem unable to stop talking. The streams of their words interrupt and intertwine.

He doesn't know where the words flow from, only that they must come. They are talking about times of fear and it's his turn.

The child clings to the handrail, his thin bare legs shaking and his face wet with spray. His father walks on across Lauder Brig using no hands like he'd done it a hundred times. His father waiting at the far side, calling something but David can't hear, not above the spate that skooshes under his feet, hits a ledge and bounces out into space. It hangs then smashes on another outcrop, streams out in a dim peacock's tail of fractured light. The broken river rushes together again at the bottom, foaming yellow and brown at the edges then settling into the stillest pool he's ever seen, black and radiant as the centre of an eye. That was where Lauder had been found, bits of bone and skin and not a shred of clothing left on him, and the silver coins gone for ever though you can see them glint yet if you look down on a moonlit night.

He clings to the rail. He can see his feet sliddering across the planks, slipping off the edge leaving him hanging by the rail over the drop, above the pool a hundred feet below. He looks back the way they've come, but it's too far away, he can never make it back. He looks to his dad who is waving him on, looking impatient now. But wee Davy Elliot can't shout or scream. He's starting to greit and he can't see properly. He can't move. He knows, absolutely knows, he will die here.

He begins to slide one foot forward, then the next. He daren't lift them. He inches forward, hand over hand along the slimy rail. If his dad would come back for him, he wouldn't die. They'd go and see his mum and she'd come back. But his father won't move, and his mother is in another country.

Slicing pain in his left hand. A long skelf of wood from the rail sticks from his palm like a dagger. Blood begins to ooze. He glances up at his dad, whose mouth isn't moving now. He isn't even waving, he just stands on the far bank, waiting, so tall, so dark, unmoving as the rocks by his head.

The child stops. He must pull out the spear of wood but that would mean letting go with his other hand. He can't do that. He looks down. He'll let go and fall. Then they'll be sorry for what they've done to him. He feels the tug of the water, the fall pulling his chest as he sees himself slide down into the centre of that black eye.

He slowly lifts his damaged hand to his mouth and grips the wooden skelf between his teeth. Tastes the blood as he jerks it out and spits and the huge splinter drops into the fall and vanishes. He turns to face forward and feels enormous as he half-runs along the rest of the soaking planks.

He jumps off the last plank and hugs the nearest tree. He feels a big hand on his shoulder, but he ducks under Elliot's arm and runs on. When he comes out into the light at the end of the trees he shouts his rage till the corbies skirl in the sky like a black snowstorm.

David sat on the other chair and sipped lukewarm tea through his nausea.

I can't believe I've told you that, he said. I've never told anyone. It seems so . . . weak.

It sounds a scary place for sure, she said. Thank you. Her hand rested on his shoulder for a moment as she went past to close the window. And your father shouldn't have done that to you –

One quick thump then the door scrapes open. The short man is framed by light that leaves him dark. A wind comes in behind him, the shotgun hangs in the angle of his arm.

Tat, David says. Long time.

The man nods. His elongated shaved head turns, takes in the groceries, the cloak, the gas-rings, pauses at the myrtle. His head twitches, he glances at the half-open door into the bedroom.

Saw the Land-Rover, laddie. Elliot never comes up here.

My father doesn't go anywhere these days.

Heh, true enough.

Tat knows how to wait. He looks at the back of the woman who has not turned to face him. Her shoulders are raised like a hawk. Dark hair short and coarse as a boy's, matted across a white neck. He checks beyond her again to the green shawl and a glint from something hanging in it.

She got permission?

David puts down his mug. His hands lie flat on the table. He looks across at her but gets no cue there, only her knuckles white around her fork as she turns at last to stare at the factor.

Got a message for me, Tat?

Heh, no.

His long thin head is full of angles. Hooked nose, high cheekbones, sunk cheeks. Eyes a very pale grey, like the sky nearest the horizon. For the first time David sees Tat is not that much older than him, though it's hard to imagine he ever was young. He could have been his father's younger brother, or adopted son. Or shadow, or conscience. In fact he doesn't know what Tat's role is, only that he's always been there and for some reason his father is beholden to him.

Tat opens his fist and lets a length of chain slip and dangle a brass padlock.

There's twa keys to this, he says. One's in my pooch. The other's in the big house. So I'm wondering how she got in.

David stirs.

Does my father tell you everything, Tat?

A smile flickers across her mouth, a swift undulation like a weasel flowing under a fence.

Is she your wee secret, lad, or his? Or is it squatting?

David pushes down on the table then reaches out and lifts the chain steadily from Tat's hand.

She has permission.

He pours the chain, clinking clattering onto the table. The two men stare at each other while she watches.

Fine, Tat says. All righty right. I'll leave you two to it.

He's at the door. His skull tilts.

I'd step canny, young Elliot, he says, and is gone. He moves like that.

A long silence in the kitchen. He looked up in time to see her

36

tongue brush along her upper lip then vanish inside.

Thanks, she said. I appreciate that.

He shrugged. I've known Tat since I can remember, and he's always got up my nose. Something sleekit about him. David nodded at the padlock and chain. As a matter of interest, how did you get in?

The usual way. She lifted the brooch from her shawl, flicked the pin and diddled around inside the brass padlock. It clicked open.

Easy-peasy, she said.

Where did you learn to do that?

A school for Very Bad Girls.

She shrugged and dropped the subject. He picked up the brooch and looked at it more closely. Its centre was surely a coin and on its worn silver he could just make out the remains of a pattern. A head perhaps.

This looks old, he said.

It is, very. Her voice had dropped way down. It's family.

He looked at it more closely. What he had thought scratches round the circumference were the remains of an inscription. Not in English. Latin, maybe. At the centre, worn almost flat but not quite, was a silhouette, he could see that now. Hooked nose and some kind of halo round its head. He wondered just how old it was. Her eyes clicked onto him like round black magnets.

My real family, she said, then turned away.

She turned back to face him. Fair's fair, David, she said. So I'll tell you one of my scary places.

Her head is turned away to look out the window. His arms are folded. It could appear they are trying to get away from each other. But between them there run barely visible lines – which could just be scratch marks where a knife has come down too hard – and these lines connect them. They could be talking about anything as fine wires multiply between them.

Stranded between midnight and dawn she clung to the freezing rail of the iron bed. Up to now it had been possible to believe she'd been pretending. She'd felt bad, a little rocky for sure, slightly besieged by impulses not her own, but nothing she couldn't out-face. She was still in her right mind though it wasn't a very pleasant one. Still fighting, still in control. It wasn't that she couldn't cope, she'd just needed a safe place to rest and hide out a while – and where better than the ward, the soft-slipper shuffle, the slop food, the therapy groups. How restful to have the burden of choice lifted for a while, to be told when to get up and go to bed! The individual sessions with the man with the white socks and slip-on shoes and no irony whatsoever. How could a man with such tastes know anything of her? Him she could take anytime.

The other inmates? At times it had been possible to feel moments of affection as she pretended to be one of them. But now they slept, now it was for real and her night terror was in full bloom.

The clock on the wall ticked, paused and the world stopped. She fell into the chasm between one moment and the next. The clock ticked again and she was back. Then the silence and she began falling again, terrified at her existence. Anorexic Billie whiffled in her sleep in the next bed. Tick. Back again.

If she let up for a moment she was gone. The night was too long. At last she really was cracking up. This wasn't a game or a fantasy or a try-out. It wasn't even the times she'd had to be restrained as a child. Thoughts split, fragmented, split again. She was locked inside her own head with a crazy. She whimpered and stuffed her knuckles in her mouth to keep silent.

She couldn't hold out all night. She had to let go. In the morning they would find her in the bed, but she'd be gone, gone even from herself. Let go, then. Fall out of your mind for ever, for it's too awful a place to remain.

She coughed, her throat swelled till she began to choke. She mustn't throw up, not here. On her feet. Cold floor. Find the handle. Into the dim-lit corridor. The loo third up on the left. But light under the door of Rosie the night warden. She couldn't go in. She'd never asked for help ever, not even in the worst times when her only love had been sent away.

Clinging sobbing to Rosie's knees. Hands on her back, clasping and stroking her head. Smell of vanilla. Soft warm stomach she clung to. Spray of hair tickling her face. It's all right, it's all right. Her name over and over. It's all right, I've got you. Let go, it's all right.

She let go and though it felt like dying it didn't kill her. She came to herself clinging to Rosie's breast, a pink nightgown wet with her own tears. She looked up, stripped bare. Rosie's face above her, eyes sure and gentle. Her lips slightly open.

She strained up and kissed. She sucked and hung on. Human warmth, Rosie's mouth, tender as a mother. They both wanted. She needed Rosie, needed these kisses, tongue in under her lips and the long-forgotten warm softness of breasts against hers as she kissed. Look down and see the nipple rising, bend towards it. Hear Rosie groan quietly. Feel strong.

Hand in her hair. Tightens. Pulls her head gently back. Rosie smiles down at her like a regretful madonna.

We'd better stop there, Rosie says. My partner is very jealous and I have to tell her everything. And I need to keep this job. This is not what you need.

A finger to her lips. Shush, Rosie says. Cry all you need. And holds her, carefully, to her shoulder till dawn.

Was it the, ah, gay part scared you?

Oh no. That . . . She stared out the window as if that night was still out there. I'll always be grateful to Rosie, she said. Wherever she is now. It was the letting go.

Silence in the kitchen. Cawk of the crows, sporadic distant hoarse barking of Hawk out in the Land-Rover.

It's safe with me, he said. Promise.

She looked across the table at him, soft, expressionless. Then her mouth tightened as she leaned forward. Excite you, does it?

His lips parted but nothing came out. He shook his head then quickly stood up.

Look, I must be getting back. Expecting a phone call.

From the lady fair.

What makes you think there's a lady fair?

There's always a lady fair. She shrugged. Anyway, I picked it up in the village with the other talk. American?

Canadian.

She stretched and stood up. Would you show me that bridge before you go?

He lifted his jacket from the hook. Another time, maybe, he said.

Meaning never, she knows. She's scared him off. Too intense, too confessional a session. And he's not the one she's looking for. He's not guilty. So let him go.

He felt in his jacket for his keys. Looked baffled. She dangled them in front of him, her fingers through the round hole off-centre in the black polished stone disc.

Interesting, she said. Unusual.

His mouth went like he'd been sucking something sweet and bitten on silver foil. Used to be my father's, he said. He gave me it on my 21st like it was a big deal.

So you use it as a key-ring to piss him off.

He shrugged. Seeing he won't tell me what's special about it, yes.

So it is special?

To him, maybe. But all that old stuff . . . I'm not interested.

So it seems, she said. I'd better let you go.

Yet she gripped the stone a while longer, felt the metallic taste rise in her teeth, and knew what she must do as if it were already written. She dropped the keys into his hand and led him out into the light.

*

Parts of this plate are so faded it's like looking at the world through mist. Half-drowned trees stretch out to nothing, headless men hold conversations. The animals weaving through the scenes and round the circumference could be weasels or frantic dogs, so uncertain have scale and distance become. You have to invent as much as you make out.

There's a space dead centre. It may be the picture has worn away completely, or perhaps it was always so. It's the one spot where you may rest. You lean forward till you feel the coolness on your lips and are comforted.

But what you did with your visitor was so very unwise.

She pulled the cape round her shoulders against the wind and followed him to the Land-Rover. They were nodding and talking while inside the cab the hound scrabbled on the glass. In the trees corbies skirled as a hawk circled overhead. A peregrine falcon, David said. That at least my father got right, they're better wild. Then they gabbled about birds and falconry and he laughed, so full of ease and confidence and decency she could have hated or loved him. She was creaking inside. She needed him gone, then she caught him glancing at his watch.

Thanks for the morning, he said. It seems the world's still full of surprises.

She slipped her hand from under her cloak.

The world is as it's aye been, she said. She laughed. But life's most interesting where the border's up for grabs.

He pulled a face and reminded her the Border had been settled a long time now.

On the maps, maybe. Are you that settled, Davit?

His eyes flicked down at her clasp or her breasts.

My father used to call me that when I was wee. Davit. When he was being affectionate or light-hearted, in the time before . . .

He looked back at the cottage. He looked everywhere but her, and she glimpsed what had to happen next.

So it's odd to hear it from your mouth, he said.

She looked away. He wasn't simple but he was guileless. It was hard not to feel her hands at his throat.

So am I too familiar, my Lord Elliot?

Piss off. He hefted the keys in his hand, the hound barked again in the Land-Rover cabin. But you do feel familiar, he added.

The things we've said – you'll keep them close?

On my life, Mary Allan.

But there's some have wildness yet, she said then and put her hand behind his head and pulled him down.

She opened his chill mouth and found a soft ridge inside his long upper lip. She opened her lips to him and a little gasp bubbled in his throat as her tongue came in. Then she stepped back before he could, smiled like it was foolishness, a nothing, and sent David Elliot on his way.

You fabricate. You embroider. You make stories and surround your-self with foam till you are the bug hidden safe in the heart of cuckoo-spit.

There has been fact and invention but till now you have always known the difference. There's a border you move back and forward across, like a needle stitching up a life. And you've always known which side of that border you're on at any one time. You are just wandering a while in these debatable lands, embroidering a story, still confident you can find a way home, even in the dark.

But when you pulled his head to yours and kissed him, you were on the wrong side of the border and what comes of it will be hard to tell.

When the rattle and girn of his Land-Rover and the yowling of his damn hound faded in the wind and the road was empty again, she dropped her hand and stood vacantly on the brig-giestane. She had meant to think doorstep or maybe threshold. Briggiestane – where has that word surfaced from?

She looked over to the woods shrouding the gorge where a boy was terrified and Lauder fell or was pushed. And over to the west, in the next dale, was another fall, closer in time, clos-er to home . . . She felt again that metallic shiver forking down the back of her legs, the same as when she'd first looked on young David Elliot, when she first saw his ring and the gleam of the gutting knife at his belt.

She stands on the doorstep, half in and half out of the cot-tage, and feels herself stepping in and out of two worlds. Back and forward, past and present, real and pretend. She could rock like this for hours as a child, especially when she moved to new parents.

This place is ravelling and unravelling her. She knew it the first evening coming up from the river in the half-light, carry-ing the plates in the leather satchel because she didn't trust the man from the village who'd dropped off her gear not to break them. Maybe it was the half-light that had her moving be-tween two worlds.

But she has always been that way. She has woken with a

man's skin as her own and smiled with pleasure and recognition even as it peeled away. There have always been daydreams from which she would return with the taste of someone else's mouth in her mouth. Sometimes whole sentences heard in her head that she didn't know whose thoughts they were. And since her first lover moved in her, she has never been certain what is truly hers. She lacks boundaries. Perhaps that is why she is so often solitary.

Standing on the briggiestane, she opens her eyes and for a moment can remember nothing. She feels herself radiant and calm, as though she has been born anew. Scraps of a possible past spin away, none of them very convincing.

She steadies herself on the door frame, feels the wind stroke her face and her breath caress the inside of her nose. She is alive now, whoever she is or was. That's all that's certain. It's such a relief to come back to this, unchallengeable and full of secrets as the bare ridges that ride against the grey-blue lift on the other side of the Border.

A dreamer, Rita and Jim called her. Our little dreamer. They said it kindly. They were, they are, kind people. And when they found her standing at the bottom of the garden saying her name over until it emptied of all meaning and became a sound empty and forlorn as the wind and she was disappeared, when they brought her back to herself she saw the glance that flickered between them. Her last parents, the best of a long, bewildered line. The rest just called her liar.

She shrugs. Sometimes her thoughts amuse, but now she's hungry. She goes inside and gets busy, boiling another kettle and washing the cups and plates in the big sink. She switches on the radio to hear some friendly voices. As she leans to adjust the volume she says a name and it goes out on wavelengths Marconi never dreamed of.

Plate 2

Like a set of divining cards, laid out where you might read what has happened, is happening, will happen to you, these plates are in several senses a service. As you wait for the kettle to boil, lay them out round the table as though for guests who have not yet appeared.

Take this second plate. At a glance it has outlines and scenes you recognise from the first one – yellow hair, shaven-headed man, mystery woman, the waterfall, cloak and coin and shining blade – in different combinations. But also some new places and characters. Good, you like some novelty to draw you on.

Take your tea and the plate to bed and let the day begin again. You like to think of yourself as an active agent, but you could be only a resonator, and your soul but a wind-chime hung in another's draughty hall.

A new day seeps through a curtainless window on a rising tide of light and smoothes away tracks on the sand. Dreams of fights and lovers, the usual. She opens her eyes, rolls her head and checks the little framed photo on the floor beside the mattress. She picks it up, the silver frame cool and smooth-greasy between her fingers, inspects it at arm's length like the passport it is, then drops it on the duvet and rolls up and out.

Today is colder. The stone floor makes her shins ache, her numb fingers chap off the stove, and she needs to slow down as she hacks kindling with the gutting knife he left behind.

She sucks sluggish salty blood from her knuckles and recognises she's furious with someone. That really was very unwise.

Or maybe not. She stands in the kitchen with the knife in one hand and her shins turning blue, run through by a notion sprung fully armed from the shadowy woods.

But she wants to get back to the plates, to lose and find herself there. So many ghostly selves, like so many voices slipping from one into another on the radio's spinning dial. She's not unusual, she believes, she just notices it more. As the kettle boils she lays the plates out on the table, selects number 2 and decides to take it back to bed while waiting for the stove to make a difference.

The bedroom is cold but the duvet is warm. She lies on her back, tea at her side and the second plate held against her chest. Closing her eyes she focuses on the wind – fainter today – and the scuttering of mice playing football in the ceiling. Then outside the window a whistling bird – blackie by the sound – starts to scream. A hiss and a little thump and the screaming stops.

Her heart is punted like a rugby ball up in her chest. Really, she doesn't need reminding this is a murderous place. It is also home, for however long. As she lies with the plate resting face down on her chest like a book, the whole valley and dale is stirring about its business. It isn't too hard to hear voices in the wind behind the song of birds as they proclaim the necessity of mating and territory.

*

I spent the morn round the village speiring after our new arrival. It's a wee place and she wasn't someone your eyes would slide by, not dressed like yon and with such proud gait. Some said she'd come off the bus, others that she'd jumped down from a truck, others that she'd stepped head high from a great black car.

But when I speired more closely, the truth was none had actually seen her arrive. One minute she wasn't there, the next she was walking into the hardware shop with a leather satchel and pack over her shoulder, and spending money in her hand. She might as well have stepped from the stoor that blows over the fields for all the name and history she had. Even our courteous and inquisitive bobby MacIver had got nothing from her, she just near-smiled and let our best gossip's questions bounce off her and gone on asking for what she wanted.

She'd bought or borrowed double mattress, bedding, gasstove, kitchen gear. Coal. Enough food for a week, they said in

48

the store. Then she sat on the high stool at the bar with a pint, friendly enough yet no one dared tell her whose seat that was. And when Neb Nixon came in he glared at her but she looked right back till that crabbit loun took his drink and sat himself by the window, muttering into his fist.

Byordinar, was the verdict, not a common sort – and having set eyes on her I would agree. At the bar she heard some of the local clash about old and young Elliot, for there is still plenty of that talk in the village. Then she rounded up her buys and engaged Nattie Kinloch to take the gear to Crawhill Cottage. She named it, everyone agreed on that, and that vexed me more than I let on. She was no ordinary squatter. And Nat was sore taken aback, for all folks knew no one had bided there since Patrick and the wee girl had left after Sim Elliot's trial was done.

Crawhill Cottage, she'd insisted. *You'll find the door open.* And Nattie took it Elliot must have changed his mind at last. *You'll be a relative?* he speired as he loaded up his van. The lass nodded and shook her head both and repeated *The door's open. I'll be up later. Lock up after you.* And because I was away in the town and no one spoke to Elliot anyhow, he took the money and did as he was tellt.

It was plain to see I kent nothing about her, and they teased me sore I had lost my grip on the old man. I drove away from the village vexed and bothered. Most likely I should have overridden young Davy the day afore and sent her on her way, for I was sure he lied when he'd said she had permission. But I didn't want to cross him and I didn't know my ground. So I went home and spoke with Annie and she didn't like it either, though her reasons were different. Annie sees far, and she had it in her head this was about the estate. And me, I see wide and don't like what I see at the edge of my vision.

So I drove Annie to the big house for her work, went through the passageway but the door into the tower was bolted behind. I banged on it a while, though I doubted Elliot wouldn't hear up in his bedroom. So I left word I had to speak with him soonest, and went back home again to sit up here at the work-bench with my rack of knives and rasps and diddlers.

I pick up my latest half-carved hobgoblin – an ill-natured wee creetur – and turn him over and over in my hand, looking for the best way to set him free.

*

The kettle judders on the stove. The wind keens in the frame of the window that looks down to the Border from this place you have come to be alone in, and sometimes you hear in it her voice close as your own . . .

You turn the radio down, then off. You sit on the wobbly chair with the plate in your hands and listen to the wind till you begin to drift and go behind it, as you learned to in earliest years.

Behind the wind there are stories without end. The Border wars, raids, skirmishes. Family feuds, rapes and burnings, chains of betrayal and enduring loyalties. Cattle-thieving and summary justice. And revenge of course, hot trod or cold trod.

Anyway she always wanted to be Mary. It's a fine plain name.

It's good to be busy, to build up heat in the old stove and with full attention slice up the neeps, potatoes, onions. Add the stock then loads of pepper. Mushroom ketchup. Good to lean over the rising steam as the day creaks forward like a slow cart.

She could say to herself this place is doing her head in, and perhaps that's what she's come here for. To be done in. To be resolved. She stands with David Elliot's knife poised. *To make a just end,* she hears the voice murmur. Shut up below, she whispers. Be quiet.

She turns on the radio and carries on chopping. Soon it will be time to do some research. She could go to the town, where the newspaper office would be a good place to find more detail on Jinny's death. And the County Court should have transcriptions of the Elliot trial. Keep busy, stay solitary. Hear the voices but stay on the right side of the border.

She brushes the back of her knife hand across her lips. They can't be swollen from one kiss. Her knuckle slips under her top lip, she begins to rub against her gum. He didn't back off, not at first. Davit Elliot liked it, he wanted it till he remembered who he means to be: a good man, an honest man faithful to the lady fair, anyone but his father.

That first evening she'd yomped uphill at a lick, even with the load over her shoulder, up through the twilight towards the darkness of the trees around the gorge, towards the cottage she knew was there. Then she heard that long pirl-pirling cry. A shadow tilted in the dusk then disappeared like a thought had and lost. But she'd glimpsed the long curved beak and a word tilted from the back of her mind to the front: whaup. Curlew. How differently they taste in her mouth though they refer to the same. How different a father and son can be, and yet be the same in the end.

She'd felt like an arrow homing in. Her laughter sent a clutch of rabbits scuttering through the lea. The words were coming back and they fitted the place and the place fitted her as a sheath fits the knife it was made for. The deep-cut ravine – heuch – and trees up on the right, the cottage on the skyline, the long ridges sailing down so bare and sleekit, they were all present and correct.

And as she got nearer and put her foot to the crumbling dyke – again the word's jumped out of somewhere and she giggles, light-headed, reminding herself that's a wall not a common sexual orientation – the rooks clattered from the shaw of trees and the word came to her, *corbies*, and then the threads of this dreaming pulled tight around everything she carried on her back.

She thinks a counsellor once told her she had a weak sense of reality, but that's so wrong. She has too strong a sense of too many realities. Like her radio late at night, she receives too much.

By the time she'd arrived at the cottage in the gathering dark, diddled the lock again and stepped across the briggiestane with a sense of returning, the stories had already begun. About a woman walking out of the river valley mist. About a factor who watches and hides. About the only son and heir with his hound, his ring, and a polished stone disc whose value he knows not. Who comes calling though he is actually being called. And his father skulking in the tower of the big house with whatever it is that connects him to the payments that have sporadically appeared in a trust account over the years and now stopped. Soon it will be time to get closer to him. *Go canny. All will be well, you'll see.*

She shakes her head, stands at the side window looking down the drove road. It's empty, of course it is. Just a pair of corbies that bounce and strut along the dyke, their beaks grey and cold as chisels. He will not come today, she has frightened him away. Just as well, she has not come here for that.

*

Up there among the hillocks and sudden mounds, the rickles of stones and unexplained dark outlines, root around and you may stumble yet on a corroded haft of a Pictish dagger, or pick up a worked stone from the time before metal, or clean the dirt off a Roman coin. Set among the stones at the base of the dyke is a carved altar to the god with the hammer in his hand, and his ravens at his ear. They are Rumour and Memory, and between them they tell him everything he needs to know.

Pick up the plate again. Turn your eyes away from the high painted bluff with the two tiny figures clinging to each other at the brink, for you aren't ready. But a thin gold line runs direct from it to a room with casement windows. A bearded man with long dark hair pulled back sits staring out, his eyes like black arrows, his cheekbones taut as drawn bows.

Sim Elliot sat knees up in the window seat on the back stair between his study and his bedroom. His territory in the big house had shrunk to this by degrees insensible as the beginnings of arthritis in his knuckles. He felt safest here in the old peel tower, but the news Annie had given him an hour back had penetrated even its walls. A young woman had moved into Crawhill.

The pain started at the hinge of his jaw then jumped to his chest and zig-zagged through it like lightning seeking earth. He gasped and slumped back against the wall, willed himself to relax, breathe deep while his fingers strayed down the side of the seat and lifted the little panel. He drew out a short fat joint, slightly bell-mouthed like a miniature blunderbuss. He put the match to the touchpaper and lit up. Jinny had taught him to roll, among so many other things.

Draw deep, Sim. Relax. *Be cool, love. Live in the moment.* They said things like that back then, when the moment was all they had. Now the present is where he lives least.

He exhaled, felt his head expand then steady. The window was a bit open and he heard David's voice drifting up from below. He must go down and talk to him, find out about the woman. Probably it was nothing. He inhaled again.

He could and sometimes did go into the kitchen to pass some time slicing vegetables with Annie, or sit cross-legged on the draining board in the yellow scullery watching her pluck pheasants, the small reddish clouds of feathers tumbling to the floor and drifting around her blue tennis shoes in the draught under the back door. He found it soothing like a memory of childhood, his mother perhaps not pictured but felt as a presence, young before death had kept her always young, a humming and a calm busyness, a glimpse of yellow hair and piano keys tickling in the corner of his mind. And at such times, with the rain tick-tacking on the little panes as Annie's hands dived in and out of the birds, he felt nearly at peace and a child again – the child who doesn't yet know what it has been born into, or how many people have yet to die before he too can cease. Then soon enough everyone who has known him will be dead too, and all personal memory of him will be gone from the planet like last summer's leaves. Sweet relief.

He exhaled that musty earth smoke over the window pane, stubbed out the joint and stashed the remains in its niche. Then he took a deep breath and went down to talk to the laddie.

*

The plate blurs. Perhaps you'll strain your eyes like this, or your mind. Blink, and see the kitchen is full of steam and the condensation drips on the cold china. Push the soup pot to the edge of the stove, wipe the plate with your sleeve and look again. (For the hammer god, all events are simultaneous. Flames jump from flint arrows to bronze axe to steel lance.) The dark man and the yellow-haired youth are face to face.

53

David stood munching toast at the dining-room window thinking sometimes weather is more than weather. Today everything is suspended and waiting. Cold too, the hoar frost steaming off the pear tree branches in the lemony sun. It must be freezing in Crawhill. He wondered what the woman was up to this morning. Maybe she'd cleared her few things and left. That would be smart.

He sucked his bottom lip, feeling her bite yet.

So who is she, laddie?

Elliot stood in the door, head lowered under the lintel. However wasted, he was still a big man with a power about him. Or maybe that's how a father will always look to his son. David took his time.

Who?

You ken fine – the lassie in Crawhill.

He glanced at his father then away. It was hard not to take pleasure at the anxiety in the old boy's voice.

You should know. It's your estate.

His father grunted, tapped his boot into the side panelling as though testing it for rot. He seemed unable to come further into the room. David wondered if he was stoned again, though it seemed kind of early.

In the village they think she's your bit on the side, he said.

Heh – I thought she might be yours. His father giggled, tapped the wood again. Disgusting phrase, he added.

David nodded. About as pathetic as the reality, he said quietly.

Simon Elliot's head came up quick at that.

You don't do that sort of thing, do you?

No. Because you did.

Elliot produced a roll-up from his palm, lit it and looked back up at his son.

I sometimes think, he said, self-righteousness might be worse for the health than smoking. You've an awful big intake of it these days. Have you never slipped up with the fiancée woman? With anyone?

David turned back to the window. His lip was definitely swollen. Odd. It hadn't been that much of a kiss. Nice. Uninvited. Over.

Slip up, he said. His voice sounded thick and odd, and his heart was much too fast. Of course he had, often, in the London time, but that was over. So you call an adulterous affair with your neighbour's wife which lasted – just how many years? – you call that *a slip-up*?

The silence went on and on. Somewhere in the scullery a clink as Annie Tat moved around. At last his father's head turned away.

No, Elliot said. He looked round the dim dining room as though the true word for what it had been lay there, muddled in the curtains or buried behind the panelling or hidden within the portraits of his ancestors. No, he said again. It was not that.

He looked so weary David took the first two steps towards him. His father looked straight at him, just for a moment, and what David saw in his eyes was a fall that had no end.

You've never been there, Elliot said. Love? You may be marrying this lass but I think you havena been there.

David turned away sick at the longing he'd seen, and for the first time wondered just what and who his father had silently mourned for twenty-plus years. He wished he could spit.

Your idea of love isn't mine. His voice wasn't steady. His father took a long drag and stared at him mockingly. I suppose you'll tell me it just happened, you and the woman.

His father's foot swung back and stirred in the air an inch or so off the floor.

It happened, he said. But believe me, there was no *just* about it.

He dropped the fag end and watched it smoke on the wooden floor. His foot came down, squashed, turned.

Some of us still believe in free will, David muttered.

Some of us ken damn all, laddie. I married a woman I knew could never break my heart. And that – he lifted his boot and peered at the evidence – was my real crime against your mother.

David stepped back, turned away, turned back again.

You've a fucking nerve. Your real crime –

His father put his hands out like trying to stop headlong traffic.

Davy. You hate, loathe, despise, whatever, me. Dinna blame you. I've let you down all my life. But listen to this. Listen. He frowned, looked out the window. You thought about it long and chose to marry Jo?

Glad she's got a name now. Yes. That's what I've chosen. We chose.

Then don't. If it felt like a choice . . . Anything of weight is fated, David. It's inevitable or nothing.

Marriage guidance. Who'd have thought it? Save the hippie haivers, Dad. I'm out of here.

Elliot's arm shot out, braced against the door frame. David stopped with the arm against his chest.

My bad timing, son. I've forgotten how to act. Maybe I should get out more.

Aye, take a daunder over to Crawhill yourself if you're so curious.

His father shook like a dog throwing off water.

Canna do that. No Crawhill.

His voice was thick in the throat.

Why not?

It's ower far.

Take the Land-Rover. Or the short cut across the Liddie Burn.

Elliot's face had gone white. David thought he was going to faint, and put his arm out.

You all right, Dad?

Yon way is no wise. Don't use it. Please dinna use it.

He was leaning heavily against the door frame. Christ, the old bugger's fried his brains. His voice keeps changing register. It's pathetic.

What's she doing there – the lassie?

You really don't know? David shrugged. Hard to say. Reading and writing things. Pottering. Looking at plates.

Plates? Elliot's head jerked forward. What like plates?

I didn't really see them. Big ones. Old-fashioned-looking with bits of picture. She put them away, we ate off plain ones.

She had painted plates . . . What's her name? Did she say her name?

What is this, Dad?

56

A fierce grip on his arm, face up close.

Name.

Dad, she's doing no harm. Maybe she's getting over something. I don't know, honest. Look, she'll only be a couple of weeks. She's tidy and that. Why not leave her be?

Her name. Tat didna get her name.

Mary, if it matters.

Mary . . . He said the name slow and long, dragged it out like the setting sun on broken water. You're sure it was Mary?

That's what she said.

His father grunted.

Surname. *Family name.*

Allan. Mary Allan.

His father's breath hissed out as he leaned back on the door frame. Then he looked up and grinned like it was nothing.

If she's no doing any harm, she can stay. Two weeks most. I'll send Tat.

No, I'll tell her.

Stay away from there, Davy.

Maybe she'd rather hear it from me.

You hear?

David turned away to look out at the track that ran from the end of the garden towards the woods and the Liddie and the mirk there.

Why do you still keep Crawhill empty? he said over his shoulder. Why not rent it out – or just sell it?

I told you – just have nothing to do with it. I'll talk to Tat, maybe get more sense out of him.

Again that terrible longing that made David want to belt him one. He took long slow breaths and let the rage fade.

Did you and . . . Jinny . . . meet there?

Silence. When David turned round, his father was gone.

*

You cross, uncross your legs, and feel that old heat rising. Lock ankles tighter round the kitchen chair, prop elbows on the wooden table and stare down the glen to the distant grey threads of the headwaters

of the Tweed. Most of the time you like living like this. You feel se-
cure alone with books or plates or voices. They are – be frank – easier
and often more interesting company than real people, whatever they
might be. Only once in a while do you think perhaps you are too
much alone, and wonder why.

It's been a long day with only voices for company. My choice,
I know. Still I almost regret sending David Elliot away. Even
the damned factor would do as a visitor. With only the plates
and reference books to anchor to, sometimes they become
light too and I start to float away from who and where I am. As
though I was just another option on the radio. But I'm back
now.

My lurking watcher crossed the fields this afternoon,
glanced up my way but went on by, so it seems for the time
being I'm allowed to stay. *So what does that tell you about Sim El-*
liot? Wheesht. Tat's an odd one, right enough, looks between a
convict, a dancer, and a monk. That light body and elongated
grey shaven head like a bullet, such quick eyes, and the way
he moves from one spot to another without anything inbe-
tween. *He'll need attending to.* Be quiet!

David Elliot and I did talk, overlapping, for the entire time.
He really was here, I didn't invent that. And he doesn't look so
like the young man on the plates, just one of those partial
rhymes we call family resemblance. But we heard a lot about
each other that seemed significant but which neither of us remembers a fraction of. Still, interest flew down, grasped its
perch and never took its raven eyes off us. It's my only atten-
dant now as the light greys.

Ah, blethers. He's not the one I'm after but there were invisible strings between us. And as we talked and our hands
passed each other mugs of tea and toast and biscuits, I was already constructing my story-lines. I haven't quite decided
whether the damaged academic Canadian fiancée – I can see
now her big eyes and skinny nervy sickly body, and understand how honoured he feels by her trust – is to be my rival or
my ally in whatever my purpose turns out to be. *I've known*
your purpose since the plates came to you.

I am too much alone. I shall lie down a while in the room

where Jinny and Patrick lay. These hands, this blanket, that tiny photo by my head, these are real enough. Though no one sees me or holds me, I am real. Tell me what to do and what I must not.

Wait for the breeze to shift and change the whisper in the window frame. I is just another voice, don't be too taken with its insistence it's the only one. Follow instead down the plate till you come on a casement window, a man and another woman, leaning together, so faint now it's hard to say what she's doing with her strong elbows either side of his neck. Notice too the neighbouring panel is that high stepped cliff again, and this time there is only one person standing at the top. The other is halfway down, a tiny reddish splotch with thin limbs or feelers, like a mosquito squashed on a white wall. But look away, you are not ready yet.

When she judged the time right, Annie Tattersall came up the back stair. She stood behind the big hunched man with the long grey ponytail who leaned his head against the window glass and screwed his forehead round and round as though trying to wear a hole through to the other side.

Is your head bad, Sim?

Aye. Very bad.

He turned, looked up at her. His pupils were huge, taking in too much light.

Most of all I see her falling. My arm goes out and she spins away, loose soil on the ledge spurts from under her foot, I see the red stone beneath. Then her head turns back to me, speechless for a moment before she falls. She looks and then she falls, and my soul waits to be judged by the expression in her huge eyes, her parting lips, her silence as she disappears.

Annie put both arms out, lowered them onto his rigid shoulders. A puff of breath came out of him as his head dropped onto her chest. Her strong thumbs reach down the back of his neck. She gets in under the ponytail, sets her feet and begins to work.

*

In the time of the reivers, when cattle or wife were stolen, house burned and men kidnapped or hanged according to their worth, there were two distinct kinds of revenge: Hot Trod or Cold Trod. When a force rode out hot trod, signalled by a smoking turf at the point of the lance, no one could stop or impede it. (See also: red-handed). That was the law in all the Marches, both sides of the Border. One even had the right to call on assistance. And if the perpetrators were found, all reasonable force could be employed to obtain justice – which commonly came from a sword or rope. Hot trod revenge had to be commenced inside a week – unless there were reasons making quick pursuit impossible. Otherwise it was adjudged cold trod and normal process of law – often unreliable owing to the complex allegiances and political factors involved in the Borderlands – applied.

It was most important to be wary when riding out on hot trod revenge, because the original wrong could be a ruse to lure one into ambush off home ground, as many a Borderer discovered too late.

These were a ruthless, passionate people of quick temper but long memory. To be hot-headed was dangerous, and those who lived in the Borderlands adjudged that time spent on reconnaissance is seldom wasted . . .

I drop my book, roll off the bed and go through to the kitchen. As I lace up my boots, I say I'm just going for a daunder into the woods. Take a look at that bridge over the falls that frightened him so. Check out the source of that distant continuous rumble and spray and see where old man Lauder went down. I've put that off since I arrived, like a bairn saving a treat. Now it's time.

On with the cape, its dark green will be hard to make out in the woods. Close the door and click the padlock. In my position it's not good to have folk wandering in and going through my things. A mild drizzle hisses down through the air, shifting, cooling, continuous, like stories told to oneself. At the far end of the bridge must be the short-cut path on to the big house, though that would not be wise, not yet.

*

Just keep an eye on her, Tat, Elliot said to me, and on the boy and all. Do nothing for the whiles.

Sim Elliot's a fool. To my mind, he's letting her stay to impress Davy with his generosity, and maybe to allay his mind, as though so small a thing could bring redress.

The way I see it, the woman's a fence-louper trying her luck, though I'll admit she's no ordinary squatter. I see again her shadowed eyes fixed calm on me in the kitchen, and I grue a little. While I baited young Davy, she fixed on me and never blinked once that I saw. That's not an easy trick – the only man I kent could do that wasn't right in the head. For a full minute she sat stone-still with her white feet bare on the floor, as though she was one who came from the place where leaves never fall and rain never hits the ground.

But her name is Mary Allan and I can't see Jinny in her. She is not the one Elliot has waited for all these years. Or so I tell myself as I carve and hollow out my wee netsuke man.

All the whiles I'm looking up across the fields to Crawhill and nothing happens till afore the gloaming and I see a flicker of movement. Now I've got her in the glasses, coming out the door and walking east towards the Lauder Burn, and I'm on my way, Simon Elliot's man, with an ancient half-truth drilling holes in my conscience.

*

She crossed the dyke and took the narrow track into the woods where the silver birch trunks glowed dim. Her fingertips knew coarse sycamore and rough-barked oak, and scratchy pine plucked at her cloak. She followed the muddy track into the deeper dark, ducking silently under branches as she moved closer to the falls.

At first it was just fine damp on the trees she touched. Then moisture on her face making her eyelids twitch. She hesitated a moment. The path was faint now, for it was only an old and tricky short cut between Elliot's and Crawhill and the Ballantyne place. Easier now to take the car and drive the long way round. She guessed only Tat came by here, and a forester now and then. Not often either, these woods were falling into decay like David Elliot said, badly needing someone to thin and clear all the rotten clutter.

Her head went up at a faint snap behind her. A dark bulk through the trees, slow at first then plunging downhill. A deer. David had said the woods were full of them. She moved on until she couldn't hear her footfall above the growing roar. She saw the white gleam through the trees and hurried on. Moss happed the trunks and branches, it slid off easily against her thumb. She looked at her hand in the gloom and saw her fingers green but steady. Then she turned the corner and looked down on the drop.

She stood head bowed awhile on the near side of Lauder's Brig where the gorge was black, streaked with green slime and lit by murky rainbows. Then when she was ready she set foot on the slimy planks, her right hand on the thin wooden rail, and began to cross.

It was a suspension bridge, sagging towards the centre. On her left was the black rock face where she could almost lean and touch water brown and yellow hurtling down through the gloom. Hard not to be drawn towards that blur, hard not to overcompensate and lean away too much. Hard to walk the middle way. To acknowledge the danger, and its draw, and keep on walking.

At the lowest point of the crossing she stopped, gripped the rail in both hands, turned and looked down. At her back she felt the chill draught of the fall as she looked until only the smash told her there was motion. Only the odd quaver and variation told her time was happening.

She looked into the eye of the pit. Cool bottomless black pool. In its deep iris she saw the Lauder who had fallen or been pushed from here with his missing bag of silver. Then David Elliot as a frightened boy, and his father waiting on the other side. Then when she was ready she at last let herself think on another fall, the one that ended the life of Jinny Lauder, and left Sir Simon Elliot standing alone at the top of Creagan's Knowe.

This place had been waiting all her life. She felt her own fall, saw a husk turn and tumble, the last outstretched hand, the end that was never the end. She stood till she was gone from herself and there was nothing but the endless crash and the stillness.

Her neck cracked as she finally looked to the far side. The trees there became liquid and swam up the cliff. That's what came of looking too hard too long.

She should go back now. Yet her feet followed her hands across the bridge and at last onto the solid ground on the far side. Without looking back she hurried on through the thinning woods towards the big house in the last light of day.

*

She hit the first ledge and lay still. Then she twitched, jerked as though hit by electricity. She was on her knees. Then standing again. Her head turned away, he saw the blood bloom on her temple. She sidestepped to the edge of the drop, her arm came up like a salute, and then she fell again . . .

For a while now there's been banging on the door at the bottom of the stair. Young David's voice calling up. God knows what the loon wants now, but whatever it was Sim can't face him. Some folks you've nothing against but that they make you feel guilty from the moment you meet them. He'd felt like that since he looked and saw this wasn't the baby girl he'd somehow expected, and he didn't feel the big thing he'd been holding out for, and the bairn looked straight back at him then started to greit in anger. Some things are so from start to finish, and there's nothing to be done but thole it.

The watery thump as Jinny hit the next ledge. This time she lay still. She stirred. She jerked onto her knees, twitching and jerking as the damage came home. Then she was standing swaying like a waltzer lost her partner, and he couldn't speak, couldn't think anything other than She's not deid yet, *as her head rotated and seemed to see him. Her mouth opened then she pivoted away and stepped off*

*the edge and dropped from sight. But he heard the sounds drifting
back up, each tear and crack and rattle. But no word of speech, not a
cry, nothing.*

Elliot lowers his head to the cold glass. The knocking has
stopped below but his other visitor won't leave. These last
years Jinny hasn't been vivid, more an old deep ache, a vague
willed recollection, but recently she won't stay away. Since
Fiona died, and now this woman at Crawhill . . . He thumps
the side of his head against the stone wall, feels pain and sees
some flashes, but the pictures don't stop. They won't till his
heart does, and by God he hopes that won't be long.

*

She crossed the end of winter fields all pale and scraggy with
die-back, ducked under a fence, eyes fixed on the big house in
the distance. That way she nearly fell over the remains of a
caravan in the middle of some silver birch saplings. She
stopped, puzzled, and looked it over. It was derelict, maybe
burnt out, had once been blue, had nearly entirely been en-
veloped by rust and ivy and wild clematis. The door was
locked. She stood on a rusted wheel arch and peered in the
broken window. Just a strip of ancient carpet, water and leaf-
mould on the floor. A bunk bed with a grey mattress growing
some kind of fungus. Two tiny doll's-house-size curtains in
orange.

She winced, jumped down and hurried on. She crossed the
river at the bottom of the garden by hauling herself hand over
hand under the little bridge. The light was failing fast, the
colours were draining and she should be safe enough. She
worked up along some trellises, closing in past the rockery on
the downside of the driveway.

She should stop but there always seemed more cover.
There was the main house, an extended three storeys of mel-
low stone, various outhouses, trees hemming it in round the
back. A couple of lights on, then a third and curtains drawn.
But it was the stone tower at the side she crouched and
crawled towards. God it was grim, a squat mass of blackened
stone without ornament of any kind. A low rampart at the top

and single window on each floor. Elliot's study, then the landing, then the bedroom, if she remembered David rightly. Only one way up, and a massive door at the bottom that Elliot bolted on the inside when the mood took him. It seemed he virtually lived in the peel tower these days. In the village they'd said he hadn't been seen for months.

Taking a chance she ran across an open space and crouched in behind a big clump of bamboo. Now she was right opposite the windows. She wiped the drizzle off her face, hunkered down again behind the fronds and looked up. A pale blur of a face at the middle window, looking her way.

Sir Simon Elliot, in her sights at last.

She swivelled, checked behind. Something not right. Just a feeling. She saw nothing but a slight stir in the birch across the burn. Maybe Tat, maybe not. *Something must be done about that one.*

She mustn't be caught here. The time hadn't come. Keeping low she drifted sideways behind a screen of young willows, pushing up the twigs tenderly as she passed underneath, receiving the drops shaken on her face like blessings. At the gap before the fence, she knelt in the beech-leaves mulch, looked back and waited. Patience. Wet leaves sticking to muddy knees. No one there, no unaccountable movement. Then a yellow light snapped on in an upper room – the study she thought, from what David told her. She should have asked more closely.

She flowed across the gap and under the fence and was caught by a clutch at her throat. She fell sideways and lashed out with her boot. Hit empty air. Her cloak had snagged on a barb. Giggling and cursing both, she unpicked it, crawled a short way on sodden knees to the short-cut track. Reconnaissance over.

She stood up in the last light and turned for home, for the fire to be stoked and the night ahead.

The plates circle high above their story like the hawk that patrols over this dale, implacable, hungry for detail. It hangs above the cottage as dawn comes and in the bedroom a lamp light finally goes out. Then it cants and rides the breeze on the upslopes of the moor for an hour before its shadow flickers again over the rough green pastureland running down from the dyke.

From up here, the outlines of the past are much clearer. Here are the old field boundaries, there the darker green marking the forests of oak and elder that used to cover the lower slopes. It was those woods as much as the steep-sided sinuous glens each side of the Border that made it such fine raiding country, an auspicious place to hold an ambush or a secret meeting.

With an upward flick of a wing tip the hawk drifts equally over the dark circle of a Pictish fort, a longhouse that once had in its hearth the altar of the hammer god, the greener rectangle of an Empire camp where the last remnants of a legion were finally overrun and left for the corbies and this hawk's ancestors.

The hawk tilts away from Ballantyne's Farm because scowling Smiler Ballantyne is already out and about and his rifle is never far from his hands, especially now during lambing. It circles a long time above the brick two-storey house where the Tattersalls live. It drifts unconcerned in and out of Tat's binocular sights, the two are old acquaintances. Annie Tat goes out back for kindling and on her way scares a frog from the shadows near the pond. Annie goes back in. The hawk side-slips down. The frog turns its head and makes for the pond some four yards away. It never gets there. Then the head comes off.

That's what the plates are like. They circle and wait, watch from a distance, then move in.

A smear of rain on the windows, the fading stump of a rainbow across the valley roots in by the Iron Age fort. A dislocat-

ed fogginess in the air, breath on the window, everything in-
distinct inside and out.

Right about now, David guessed, if she's on schedule and
her health's held up, Jo would be starting on the bedroom. But
he needs her here. He's restless and bored. The house is op-
pressive, even Annie has been giving him funny looks. When
they talk his own voice sounds echoey as though bouncing
back off the invisible screen between them.

He must go out, find someone interesting to talk to. He can't
go to the village where there are only more muttered words,
eyes sliding away from him, a hint of laughter as he walks
past. Not Crawhill. Mary Allan comes under interesting. Make
that challenging. But a challenge he could do without. Be
frank and say she was irritating and downright peculiar. Yet
there'd been moments of ease, of sudden kinship and confi-
dences. He wants to talk with her more, explain his life and
discover hers. Her life discovers his, they're like mirrors facing
each other, the other way round but the same. What's brought
her here, how does she live, what about the school for very
bad girls, what exactly is her sexuality?

No. He palmed his own mist off the window and tried to
think of something useful to do round here.

*The hawk tilts and side-slips down like a falling sheet of paper away
from the big house. It slides until it hits the updraughts rising from the
burial mounds. Men and women lie there yet, knees drawn up to the
chest, a little jar by the skull facing east in utter darkness. They have
waited some four thousand years and the light hasn't come, except in
one where the jar lies broken, and the skull is separated from the rest of
the bones. Light came once to this tomb, a spade broke in and a hand
jerked a stone amulet from the vertebrae, took fright and was gone.*

*The bird's eye drifts down the burn that runs into other burns. It
soars over the red stepped bluff of Creagan's Knowe and makes another kill there. It wipes its beak on the branch of an old Scots pine
then spreads its wings and swings back west until it turns high and
silent again over the solitary cottage.*

Simon Elliot reached into the window-seat niche and lit up,
thinking about Tat's report. It wasn't good. Crawhill Cottage,

of all places. Tat had agreed without meeting his eyes, it was not good nor canny, the way she'd appeared and gone straight there, knowing its name. And she was about the right age, Tat admitted, but nothing else was familiar.

She doesna look like . . .?

In no particular.

The bairn was but wee when she left.

She's not familiar, Tat had repeated, that's all I know.

If it wasn't the child, Sim wondered, who was she, and what the hell was she doing moving into Crawhill? And if it was her, what had she come back for, why had she not come to see him? Instead she'd taken up residence in the cottage and waited. What did the lassie want with Davy?

He gasped at a jag of chest pain as he looked out onto the garden where his son was stubbornly hacking out hazel roots, heaving and slashing like they tied him to everything he despised. The righteous prig had been out there half the morning, first howking leeks and now this.

No, it wasn't possible. This is paranoia. This is Banquo's ghost. A thing of nothing but conscience, and you owe it to Jinny to keep your mouth shut to the end. That's your penance so bear it, man, thole it.

Just go see her. Go to Crawhill. One look and he'd know, surely. But it couldn't be her. The administrator for the trust fund was quite clear: she was going to emigrate. She'd cleaned out the fund and was going to the other side of the world. Or so she'd said.

Sim had another drag and eased the window open to let the smoke out. Not that Annie was so fussed, in fact on occasions he could never predict she would silently reach out as she passed by the window seat, reach out and pluck the joint from his fingers, stand beside him and have a couple of deep drags as a formality of sharing, then tutting to herself she'd carry on up the stairs with it still stuck in the corner of her mouth, leaving him gasping in the vacuum of a woman's departure before he'd pad after her, calling out for what he'd lost. But she did insist he was discreet, she ran an orderly house, she'd say, we'll keep your nasty wee habits between ourselves.

We find such comforts as we can, he thought vaguely. He was looking at his son's long angry back. How can a back reject so? God knows what had led him to Crawhill of all places. Like Tat said, it wasn't canny.

A root snapped and Davy jerked back as if hit by bullets, stumbled and fell among the last of the sprouts. Sim sniggered, then stopped as the boy's head turned his way straight off, looking up at the very window. Elliot put his right hand to the glass and waved slowly like bored royalty. David Elliot jumped up, whacked the dirt from his breeks and walked smartish out of sight round the corner. A moment later, the back door scraped. Then thumping on the locked inner door to the back stairs.

Simon Elliot stubbed out the joint and stuck his head out the window but the thumping continued. He felt it in his neck and put his hand there, twisting it slowly. There were words yet to be said between them, and a furious laddie determined to confront a man as good as dead.

He swung his legs down off the window seat and went down to unbolt the door. It would be best, as always, to start on the attack.

You might have told me she was deid, boy. Christ, I shouldn't have had to read it in the papers.

Mum didn't want you at the funeral. She had the right to that, so I promised her.

Sitting facing at either end of the window seat, they stared each other out. It was the first true eye contact since his return.

You don't think I have rights and all? Man, she was my wife once.

Aye, once. You lost your rights when you shagged the Lauder woman.

His father's big hand twitched then was still.

That's awful coarse, boy.

I try not to be. He looked away. Ach . . .

Silence. Hail rattled like handfuls of tacks on the glass. Brisk footsteps on the stair below that hesitated, stopped, then padded back down again.

Davit . . .

He slid off the window seat and stood looking down at his father.

I'll tell you this. He waited till he knew better what he wanted to tell his father. When Jo and I marry, we'll make a better fist of it. Your lot had everything and laid it to waste because you were greedy. And now I know what I most want to avoid being. You.

His father's face was white but David couldn't stop the words shaking from his mouth like burning dice as he backed towards the stair.

You're greedy. Adulterous. Murdering. Unloving . . .

His father was on his feet with his arms coming up and mouth red against the whiteness about his cheeks.

You think I killed her? You daft wee shite, I loved Jinny.

Why couldn't you love us!

There it was, raw and bitter, scooped from the bottom. It stopped his father dead. It left nothing to say so David turned to go.

What's happened to your religion of forgiveness? Elliot called.

At the turning of the stair, David paused and looked back.

Dad, go and talk to the dead about forgiveness.

He pushed through the door out of the tower and away. Simon Elliot looked a long while into the smirr of rain. At last he reached a shaking hand under the seat and drew out the remains of his joint. He lit up and drew deep and waited for the smoke to wrap like a duvet about his brain.

Talk to the dead, son? I've never stopped. I see Jinny laughing, turning, frowning, stirring asleep under blankets by the window as I dress and leave the caravan before dawn. I see her helpless with joy in my arms. I see the flash of her anger like a portcullis clanged down between us. I see her look down on me as I rest my head on her belly. Most of all, I see her falling.

*

He chapped once at the door then walked in.

Hi, he said. How's it going?

She put a notebook down on the pile of plates then looked up at him neutrally.

70

Greetings, Master Elliot.

She was sitting where he last saw her, bare feet on the stone flags. Her hair, even thicker and darker than he'd remembered, curled in and hugged her ears, brushed by the pale back of her neck as she turned to look at him. He held out the bulging carrier bag.

I thought you needed some greens, he said. You looked a bit peelie-wally and I was taking out the last of the leeks . . .

She opened her mouth. When she smiled she wasn't so scary, just another struggling mortal.

Thanks, she said. You're either a true Christian or a devil for punishment. Sorry I was a bit nippy the other day.

I was being stuffy, he replied.

He crossed the room and put the leeks and cabbage in the cardboard box she used for veg. His back was turned but he heard her put the big plates away, the ones his father seemed so twitchy about.

You could stick the kettle on, she said. Seeing as you're staying for lunch.

Got some good news for you.

She grinned.

I know.

*

In the cool morning kitchen they are telling stories in fragments. The low sunlight comes through the window to lay a bright rectangle across the stone floor. A page of light curls at the edges of the uneven flags as it inches through the morning towards him. The same light falls across his forearm and shows her under the yellow-gold his hair is red. As he cools off, the hairs rise and stiffen. And when he talks and becomes excited, when he talks about another argument with his father, or the lady fair coming soon, those hairs fold and lie back flat along the nap of his skin. His bundle of keys lies on the table by the polished stone disc she tries not to look at.

Stories in fragments. She is making soup and salad as she talks. Her long fingers pluck and shred leaves. She slices tomatoes, peppers, quick and decisive on a wooden board. He is held by such rapidity, the absence of hesitation as she uses the side of his knife to sweep the veg into a yellow bowl.

You prepare like a pro, he says.

She nods. Had a lot of practice.

Restaurants?

The knife stops. Her eyes flick to the window as though an out was there.

Sometimes when I've needed the money, she says. But I did a lot of food preparation in the homes.

The blade flickers and the mushroom falls in slices.

Children's homes, she says. Times when I was between families.

They are telling each other stories. They are tracing the roads that brought them to this pale, cool kitchen high in the dale. The potatoes steam in their pan, she lays out plain white plates and sits across the wooden table from him and waits.

Homes, he says. Two is one too many, isn't it? Trying to explain, he puts his hand flat on his chest where the ribs divide. It leaves a space here.

She nods, pauses. Was it after the trial your folks separated?

He stares at her, trying very hard not to fight or flee. He stares till he can see a tiny disc of himself in her pupils. Then she looks down.

People talk in the village, she says. I'm sorry.

He could ask whether this is an apology or sympathy. He could ask exactly which from a range of options she is sorry for. Instead he swallows and tries to look across the table at this very pertinent person.

After, he says. It all came out then.

I think Not Proven is a very useful verdict, she murmurs.

Her face won't stay still to be looked at. It deflects his inspection like a shield reflecting the sun. The light bounces back off her, there's a constant subtle shifting as he tries to memorise her. Long black eyebrows straight as hawks' wings. He blinks and she looks young and unlined, scarcely out of her teens. Then her head turns and he sees broad cheeks, dark lines at the drop of her mouth, and he feels like a gangling boy next to her. Her face, even the shape of her head, won't stay still. It must be the play of light coming in the window. She looks slim then she looks solid and powerful. And he can't let his eyes settle on her mouth, not after that kiss.

Were you in many homes? he asks.

Her face flickers between child and adult as she talks, turned sideways to him, clasping her knee like she's giving a recitation of some old lesson, and he has to look away from the rise and fall of her chest as she talks.

The green home. Then the stone home and the brick home and the pebble-dash. The wallpaper house. Single rooms, shared rooms, dormitories. The darkness when the lights went out and the small sounds as she lay awake clutching the metal bed frame. Whispers, giggles suddenly cut off. Someone choking, someone sobbing through a fist jammed in her mouth.

Night-walkers. Girls who talked in their sleep. Girls who peed the bed. Feet padding across the floor, a creak of springs under the extra weight. A pale girl who would take anything without a sound except a soft huh from her throat. Girls who kept splintered biros under their pillows for protection.

Someone lost an eye once, she says. Her name was Veronica. She'd come to the wrong bed and put her hand in the wrong place, and the biro stabbed and went in somewhere squishy. Then the squealing, Veronica jerking her head into the floor, and before the lights went on she put the red biro in the secret place inside the bedframe but someone told on her.

An accident. One of those stupid, fated things. And then the Bad House, and a reputation to defend. A file that got thicker. Bruises that mended and bruises that didn't mend.

She holds up her left hand and he sees the little finger is squint above the joint. We used to practise torture, she says. The nail on her next finger is small and bent and dark. You can't imagine.

His chair scrapes loud in the quiet room. He fills his glass at the tap and sits down again. He sees another self lean over her and put his arms around her shoulders, cradle that erect head. He sees his shade gently wipe away tears that haven't even been shed.

He's been here before. He knows where such feelings lead. He's engaged to Jo, and it was her illness and courage that first touched his heart. So he sits again, drinks his water and sees the sunlight has moved across the floor towards his feet. If he stays much longer the sun will reach him.

He says nothing. There is absolutely nothing adequate to say. He wonders about Veronica but daren't ask. Eventually she looks down, nods like he's done something right. Then she shrugs like it's just a story that once happened to someone else.

We grow up, she says. Those years have awful bits for everyone, I'm sure. Anyway, in the Bad House I met my bestest friend.

Who's that?

She hesitates. She swallows. He sees her throat thicken like she's got a potato stuck in it. His phantom has already enfolded her. He feels her eyes pricking at the corners of his even as she looks away.

Carol, she says. She says it like she was offering a title to a song he ought to remember. Her name was Carol Anderson.

Was?

We don't . . .

His hand has reached across the table. Her broken little finger curls round his ugly family ring.

We're not in contact often, she says.

Her finger strokes the ruby stone then lifts away. There's no accounting for this sense of suffocation. He feels like the clumsy gladiator who has had the net thrown over him and now waits helplessly for the sword.

She's standing at the back of his chair. Her hands fall on his shoulders. She bends forward and over, kisses him from above.

Her mouth is full and hot and swollen. For a moment he responds. His hand is shaking as it comes up from his lap. He puts his palm across her forehead and gently pushes her back. Her hand trails across his neck, his throat, then her damaged fingers slip between his lips.

His fingers close round her wrist to push her hand away. For a moment they both use all their strength and with her leaning over him they're evenly matched. Then she laughs and draws her hand back.

It's only a kiss, Davit – no harm in that. There's something so strong here.

He swallows, draws his fingers across his lips.

I feel it, he says. But I can't.

A kiss before marriage, she says softly, like a kiss before dying? I'm sure your fiancée would understand.

He seems to consider this. He nods.

Maybe. But I wouldn't. He laughs quietly. Anyway my Faith won't let me.

What's faith got to do with it?

He spells it out as she stands behind him with her hands now resting loosely either side of his neck. He can't kiss her again. He can't make love to her. He doesn't make love even to his fiancée.

Never?

Not till we're married.

Bet you tell them all that. She looks at him, then shakes her head. No you don't, do you?

He grins and flushes, looks down, unable to conceal.

And does she share your Faith?

She accepts it's part of me, he says quietly.

And the celibacy – she likes that.

It starts out as a question and becomes statement. He nods.

She'd had . . . a difficult time with a couple of men. And she's got this illness . . .

What illness?

It's called lupus. She calls it her wolf. It comes and goes. She could die of it. When it comes it's serious and leaves her very weak and not exactly feeling like very much. So maybe the celibacy was a relief for her.

Was?

He looks up at her and laughs.

Now it frustrates the hell out of us. Well, me at least.

Her hands drop from his neck. I bet it does, she says quietly. I couldn't stand for it.

Then she briskly sits at the table again and draws her chair in. So tell me about your conversion, she says. Was it sudden?

75

Flash of light on the road to the pub? Are you saved, oh my brother?

Forget it.

No, really. She leans forward across the table and for once her mouth is unambiguous. I'm not mocking. We mightn't be so different.

He looks down at his hands then spreads them like a hand of battered playing cards, face down on the table. As he talks, hesitant at first, his fingers shuffle across each other. He looks up once in a while to check but she isn't laughing. She seems to be listening for something behind his words, the sound of his voice or the wind perhaps. He can't believe that he's telling her. He's learned not to talk about it much outside the prayer group. You can worship fire or mighty Pan or be a Zen Buddhist, and few bat an eyelid. But say you're a Christian and people back off like you're HIV positive. Perhaps it's possible to be this earnest only with a stranger.

They lean towards each other, studying his hands as he shuffles and deals his life.

A nearly young man feeling old was walking weeping through the streets of London. That morning, about an hour ago he reckoned, his married sort-of girlfriend had had their would-be baby aborted. The night before she'd looked up from the asparagus flopping into her mouth and said there was no question about it. His. No doubt, no blame, no debate. A fling (he winced, stopped in the street half-bent over, converted it into a coughing fit so no one would look at him), a fling was one thing but she couldn't deceive Harry with a child. There were some things one didn't do.

Apparently abortion was not one of them. He'd looked at her looking at him, then neither of them could bear to look at each other. Their great glamorous original adventure, this giggling secret of passion, of remarkable sex and awe-struck guilt and tender allowance in hotel rooms, friends' flats and Forestry Commission Leisure Amenity Woodlands, was revealed truly in the length of time it took her to lick her fingers and pick up a napkin. He pushed his plate away and that was the end of a life.

As when she walked away outside the restaurant with a vague backward flip of her hand and her head down into the drizzle, he knew they both knew it wasn't even tragic, and that was the only tragic thing about it. It was so *little*.

And he was so tired he had to sit down but there were no seats and the kerb was wet. He believed in nothing and nowhere was home, except a flash of hillside mottled green and yellow sloping down by a big house wrapped round with trees. But inside was a man he could never walk past. A man who had destroyed three lives by his greed and lust, a man who might have killed. A man who was his father.

He clicked off that picture in his head, as he had thousands of times for years. He closed it like a window on the computer screen in the Forestry office. That revealed another picture that had been hidden behind it. A yellow face, aged before its time, the mind and liver rotted. His mother before she moved into the private nursing home, still calling for justice and gin.

He clicked that picture closed and then there was nothing. He was leaning like a drunk against a shop window full of blank-eyed dolls that never blinked. There was a baby who would never be, and he had no say in it and in the end he wasn't a free spirit but another greedy lost soul. He had become the man he most wished to avoid.

He put his hand to the glass window and pushed himself back into the street. A huge woman bumped into and past him, muttering. Bastards, she said. You're all bastards.

He had to sit down. There was a red-brick church coming up. The door was open. He went up the steps with his legs so heavy and chest feeling like a balloon filled with water. He went into the dim, and slumped onto the first hard wooden seat. He could go no further.

He opened his eyes when he felt someone sit beside him. A man about his own age. Longish hair, no dog-collar, thank God. The man looked at him and nodded.

Life's bloody tough, eh?

David bowed his head. The simple statement got under whatever defences he had left. Life was tough, that was all that could be said, the final wisdom. He felt water prickle from his eyes.

I suppose you think this is where it's happening, he muttered.

A long silence.

The church? the man said. I doubt that. It's only a building.

David looked at him then. He wasn't clean and shiny. His skin looked older than the rest of him and he wasn't smiling.

Still, the man went on, if this place helps you should try our group. I was a wee shite once and all. The power of prayer is amazing and the Mercy is a much bigger hit than smack.

Prayer, David muttered. I haven't got one and I don't believe in it.

No, but we do. I'm Chris. He held out his hand. Have you got any better ideas?

The Mercy, David says to Mary Allan. Have you ever felt yourself forgiven, completely? Forgiven yourself? When it finally happened I felt it from the crown of my head through to my toes. It shook me like a rat on an electric fence. I couldn't pretend it hadn't happened. So . . .

So you're a Born Again?

David shrugs. Evangelical, he says, if you have to call it anything. It doesn't mean fundamentalist, though I did go a wee bit overboard that way at first. We meet in folks' houses rather than church, so I guess we're dissenters. He pauses then laughs. Aye, we do quite a bit of dissenting among ourselves. But the prayer and the love, that's real enough. End of sermon.

So what's this Mercy? she asks.

It just means you have a conversion experience. Feeling the Mercy is like . . . He pauses, looks across at Mary Allan. For once she won't meet his eye. He looks past her, out the window at the trees moving.

It's like *seeing the wind*, he says. I don't normally talk about it. Don't worry, I won't try to convert you.

Thank Christ for that, she murmurs, but still she doesn't look at him. She seems to have gone way back inside herself. Her left hand is brushing small circles on the wooden table top.

I'm burning in Hell, she says, so quietly he's not sure he's heard her right. That's how I breathe.

What?

Slowly her head comes up. The black discs of her eyes punch into him.

Nothing, she says. Then she begins to nearly smile. I don't normally talk about it much, she says.

She gets up quickly and stands over him again. He can feel her heat, and smell it. The world has clicked off, leaving only her body and his in a small room. Time has gone strange as her hand moves towards him. It descends slowly through the air, the long pale fingers opening. She grasps his shoulder, he feels her fingers burn through his shirt.

I'm sorry, she says, then abruptly lets him go. She bends over the soup pot and stirs while the flames flare blue and yellow.

He clears his throat of something swollen there. For what?

Uh? She sort of chuckles like it's nothing and already in the past. I don't know yet, she says. I hope you're hungry.

He manages a nod. This morning's talk has been even stranger than the last. He's no idea how he got here, only that he feels so alive it's uncomfortable. Her shoulder blades flex like wings beneath her T-shirt but he can still feel his shoulder burning where her hand came down.

Spook, she says. That's what I believe in.

What?

She pulls more onions from a drawer then stretches back for his knife.

Sometimes I live in Spook.

She says it with a capital, as if it were a place.

What happened to you in that prayer meeting, that was Spook. People say they don't believe in the dead or hidden purposes or invisible connections and forces – yet they believe in subatomic particles and curved space and electrons going backward through time, which I personally think is completely away with the fairies.

He laughs. She turns and points the blade at him.

We both have that in common, she says, then goes back to slicing. We both believe in Spook, the invisible. We're surrounded by the dead and the past and the future. It's all there while we sit here. In its way it's solid as these hills, and without it nothing means anything.

He wants to protest. Her ideas have nothing to do with his Mercy. He does not want to be claimed by her like this. But she hasn't laughed at him. She too believes in the invisible. She has glimpsed the wind that bends before it. In a way they're kin and if she's deluded he may be too . . .

So he leans back, his hands clasped at the back of his neck, and he sings for no reason he knows of as the blade flickers through the onions and the distorted rectangle of sunlight moves over his boots: *In Scarlet Town where I was born, there was a fair maid dwelling.*

He feels charged, alert, giggly, almost strong. Reflections from the knife flick across the ceiling, into his eyes. *And her name was Barbara Allan.* They sing it together. Her singing voice is light and high and sweet as her speech is low and throaty.

She sweeps the onions into a blackened pan. It's good to have some company, she says, though that's not what I came here for.

What did you come here for?

Her hand stops. Her hips push against the sink.

I promise you'll know soon as I do.

He dries the last of the dishes and is about to put them away by the painted ones he's still curious about.

Does it still bother you? she asks as she takes them from his hand. The trial and . . . everything.

No, he says. He flips the drying towel onto a hook. Or at least, a lot less than it did. Now I'm moving on, got a new life waiting once I finish up here.

He looks round the kitchen one last time. He feels he's been here before yesterday, though so far as he knows he hasn't. But there was a picnic, the tall woman in a patterned skirt, his father, a toddler on the grass in front of a cottage. Maybe he saw it in a painting or a film.

Thanks for lunch, he says. I must be getting back.

Give my regards to your father.

I don't think that would be a good idea.

You're right.

She laughs, quite easily, as she covers the painted plates. He

80

looks around, feels in his jacket pockets but finds nothing there.

You keep mislaying these, she says and opens her fist on a glint of metal and polished stone. The keys to the kingdom?

He picks the keys from her hand. The keys to his father's Land-Rover, his own car keys, the Yale for the new flat where Jo should be. She needs him, she accepts him. She trusts him to look after her when she's ill and not to hurt her.

He holds out the Yale.

This one is, he says. Believe me.

She looks at him like she's unexpectedly found something from way back she'd forgotten about, and the finding makes her glad and tearful both.

I envy you. Goodbye.

She says it to the shelf above the plates. He wants to hug her or something but she's not making any moves that way. When he turns at the door to look back, she is still staring there. He takes a breath to say something but chokes on the tide of isolation that has risen round her.

I think it's okay with my dad for a week or two, he says. Tat may be back but I reckon you can deal with him.

She smacks her hand on the table, a hammer falling when the auction's over.

Surely, she says. Bye.

He looks back from the door and can see the waters that have grown around her and they are so so cold.

He stands outside and gulps in the bright blowy day now that the drizzle's cleared. The trees, the corbies, the Land-Rover, Hawk waiting patiently this time. The real world. Something happens when he's inside that cottage, he starts to drift and lose himself, but she can't work that spell outside.

He says a short prayer for her as he gets into the cab. Hawk sniffs his hand doubtfully, licks it once then curls up in the seat. David drives along the rough track without looking back. It wouldn't be a good idea to go there again, he can't help her even if she would let him. He can't save everyone, he can't put the whole world right. Only the Mercy can do that.

The wheel twists and jerks in his hands as he drives fast along the drove road. He'll not be back. Crawhill Cottage bounces small in the mirror.

*

Here on the plate the same bird in the sky reappears above the building in the lower left. A window and a thin bald man with something glinting in his hand. A knife? you wonder. Coins? You stare and stare till your eyes water and blur. These plates like the ballads are so corrupt it's hard to be sure of anything. Yet the light shines back as though from a mirror, and now you guess what's in his hand.

I set down the binocs, lit a cheroot and had a wee think. A second visit, a long one. The laddie came out alone and no canoodling at the garden gate this time. Perhaps they'd done that and more inside.

No. It's not possible. It's just my clarty mind. The boy's a bit of a stookie, but honest. An evangelical these days, Annie says. With his fiancée woman coming, he'll not be fooling around.

Yet he is his father's laddie, however much he kicks agin it. The same cottage. When Ned Lauder came off the brig last century, he went down like the Nixon men from three hundred years afore him, pricked onto the bridge with hands bound then used as targets till they fell or leapt.

I locked my workroom, picked up my gear and gun and louped past Ballantyne's Farm towards Crawhill with muckle on my mind.

Old Elliot knows in his bones it's not right. She's called Mary, Tat, he said this morn. So it's not her. And he'd looked at me like a dog waiting for a clap.

Mary is a bittie nearby, I said, but not close enough.

So it's coincidence, man.

Yet she asked for Crawhill by name, I said, tormenting him. And she's the right age.

Did you recognise her?

Dinna be daft. Marnie was a bairnie then.

All the same.

I shook my head. But he could see I wasn't right with it, and he speired some more. I admitted there was a feeling about her that wasn't canny. Maybe it was just seeing her in yon place, standing at the window where Jinny had stood. And the bare feet too.

Old Elliot went darker then. Bare feet? he says. Like Jinny.

Aye. And your boy spoke of pattern plates.

A long long silence in his study.

It's not possible, Elliot said at last. You say yourself she doesn't look right. And why would she stay there and not call on me? Eh? Makes no sense.

He was right enough there. He should stop fashing himself or throw her out. I told him that to his face. In the old days he'd have bawled me out. Now he shook his head slow like it was a bucketful of mucky water.

Let her stay, he said. But keep an eye on her. I don't want her getting closer to the laddie.

Aye, there's surely been enough shaggin in Crawhill.

He came from his chair to swipe me. I shimmied back and he caught thin air. He sat down, panting. The whacky baccy had done for him.

Before God, you've a dirty mind, Tat.

I didn't deny it. Nor did I say the lassie had been checking out the big house. The man's paranoid enough as it is.

Now the cottage door swung open. I leaned back into the shaw of trees and put the vision on her. She walked to the fence yon braisant upright way, looked about like the place was hers. Then she leaned on the gate. She leant over the gate looking down to the river with her elbows on the top bar and her big hands hanging down loose. Her feet were bare.

That did it. I stubbed out the cheroot and put away the binocs. I waited till she went back inside then got to my feet, a bit cramped or maybe shaky from minding the summer evenings I'd seen Jinny Lauder hang over that same gate in the same drop-wristed way. This was a strongly built woman, and Jinny a high-spirited midge with her long red hippie hair, but I wasn't having it. It seemed an insult to her memory.

Sim Elliot aye said I should use my initiative with regards to the estate and it's time I was doing just that.

*

So, Davy, Annie said as he came in the scullery. The lassie like leeks, then?

It seems so. And you don't have to look at me like that.

If you say, dear. Your fiancée woman will be here soon?

He stopped and grinned.

She will indeed. Couple of days maybe. Can't wait.

He stroked the brace of pheasants hung from the hook. One cock, one hen. Cold, stiff, beautiful, smelling faintly of coal dust from the shed where Tat always hung them. Whenever he hears the word 'dead', that's what it brings to him – the whiff of coal, the head lop-sided and the black eye empty. What will pheasants know of Resurrection? What will he?

I'll be roasting these when she comes.

She doesn't eat meat, Annie.

Oh aye. Her head cocked like she was listening to something, then she bent to the washing machine and began pulling out damp clothes. Sensitive, is she?

Her hands pulled underpants from the grip of a shirt.

You could say that. Jo sees a roast and thinks of the animal being slaughtered. She's got an active imagination.

That must make life hard, eh?

He hesitated. It does sometimes. Of course I've no imagination at all, so maybe we balance out.

Annie nodded, her back still turned. He folded his arms and leaned back on the counter, comforted by her presence. He watched her flip socks into one basket, shirts into another. He recognised his father's shirts, mostly faded and plain. Couple of pairs of jeans peeled apart by her reddened hands. He couldn't say why that felt odd, watching her hands pick apart the clothes his father wore next to his skin. Her solid hips in stretch pants as she crouched. Something pale, cream-white wrapped round the jeans. Her hands didn't hesitate, they peeled away the slip and what looked like French knickers and flipped them in with the socks.

He must have made a sound, something like a laugh.

The old man's had a visitor?

She ran her hand round the drum to check it empty then stood up.

Times I do some bits and bobs of mine and Tat's along with Elliot's.

Uh-huh. He reached for that basket but she got it first, propped it on her full hip, the other basket gripped by the rim.

I look forward to meeting her, she said, and for a moment looked him in the eye. Life's better when you don't imagine too much, Davy.

Sit back with the sun glaring in your eyes off the pale plate. When you look around, your surroundings are dim and bleached, much less solid than before.

So get up and walk around, stretch and make sounds out loud, not meaning anything by it but I exist, I am here. More than ever it seems to you there should be a place where nothing fades and all things co-exist. In comparison everything here is fleeting, narrow and quick as the stroke of a blade over the skin.

We do not live in that place, she hears herself think, yet we glimpse it whiles. Maybe that's why we're so seldom at home here.

She tilts the plate again, trying to separate the story from the shine off the surface. What colours remain are grey and green, moorland shades. Instead of white doves cooing, we have fell black corbies. No elegantly weeping willows, but pale high twisted birch and beech. In place of a rising bridge over the pretty lake, we have rotting planks strung across a chasm. And the charming summer house is a sparse cottage, yellow-stoned, slate roof gripped green by lichen. And in its bare kitchen the young woman is holding a plate, and in that plate a fatal, mysterious young woman grips the plate she stares into as though it were a warped mirror.

She feels dizzy. Her feet ache on the cold hard stone. Did she have breakfast some hours ago? Share lunch with David Elliot? There is no one here to tell her. That is the hook and danger of solitude, she thinks – no one to correct your stranger notions. The few dishes are clean on the formica by the sink. She cleans up after herself. She covers her tracks. At times she isn't sure what of her past is real and what she's invented.

That's silly. Of course she knows, if she could only concentrate. She has been here before, to this place out on the edge. She has looked down into that series of drops where the mind can fall. She has looked into it two, maybe three times in her life, and always she has been able to turn away and come back to herself stronger. It has always worked in the past, unless she has just invented that past.

She is her own ghost. She is shining, empty, a nothing contemplating itself. I am not here, she hears herself think. I'm not here.

The door scrapes open. She drops the plate, grabs for it as it falls but it hits the stone floor and smashes at her bare feet. Widening light as the door is pushed open. She turns, wide-eyed.

Right, whoever you are – out .

She stares at him. Blood is tickling her toes where a shard has cut her.

You're a liar, young lassie, Tat says. He lays the shotgun across the chair where David had sat. You have no one's permission. Elliot knew nothing about you, so in my book you're squatting. The boy's no the factor of this estate – I am. And I say you're out tonight.

He walks up to her and stands, hands on his hips, exactly at her eye-level. She doesn't move. She stares back and lets the blood flow from her toes. For a moment, Tat hesitates. He knows what he is afraid of, and this place gives him the creeps. So does this motionless woman who stares into him as if into his secret soul.

Her lips open with a faint, unsticking sound. Her eyes never waver.

No, she says.

In fact, she adds, fuck off back to the organ-grinder.

She wipes her bloody toes across the hem of his trouser leg and smiles.

*

Sim Elliot leaned his forehead on the cool mahogany desk. His head was worse than usual today, whenever he bent forward the pressure slid down over his eyes and the world went dark for a moment. If he kept absolutely steady it could be all right.

He opened his eyes and looked out the window. At the end of the garden, the line of tall stripped willows shivered by the river in hard light. It was better in summer when they formed a solid screen against the rest of the valley. The original peel tower and then the house had been built on the rise and all the trees for a hundred yards cut down so enemies could be seen ways off. Even as a child that empty ground had made him anxious. He'd rather not know what was coming his way. When he'd inherited the title and the estate descended on him inevitable as a headache, first thing he'd started planting trees in that gap. Without mother or father or siblings he felt exposed and alone, as if there was nothing between him and the enticing, dangerous world.

How else could he explain his failure of nerve then? Marriage to Fiona Grahame had made him feel more protected. Hedged in. Settled. Dull but secure in his raised position. Like him, Fiona was semi-posh but local. Elliots and Grahames had been intermarrying for generations when they weren't at feud. She knew the limits and what was owing. When in the course of a fumbling night they became each other's first lover – he flushes still to think of her wincing silence and his clumsiness as he laboured like a cack-handed safe-cracker to find the right combination to open up her desire – among what was owing was that he married her. And it had seemed to work so long as he kept his head down to detail and accepted he'd now never go to China or design bridges or take part in the riot of pleasure and joy that seemed to have broken out all round them towards the end of the sixties. And then Jinny came stepping through the saplings in bare feet with her man, slipping through the screen like it wasn't there.

Surely he must have invented the bare feet. Could she have walked shoeless across Lowfield, then short-cutting through the new willows? That's not the way to come asking favours of the man whose land you'd parked your rusting caravan on. But it was Jinny's way, when she was still young and careless of the world.

Sim almost smiled. It had been from this same window he'd

seen them first. He'd been boxing his father's old papers and weapons, the photos and mementoes of the Malay rubber estate, the kukris and gaudy plaster Buddhas, and wondering if this should be a nursery or his study.

His life was certain and clear and fortified if prematurely resolved, and he was lifting the heavy blades from the wall when he'd seen the movement by the willows. The girl bold, alert, daring someone to take her up. Long dyed ringleted hair – the first time he'd ever seen henna – vivid green print dress brushing the grass, belt of beads cinched round her neat waist, huge eyes ringed in black. The husband bearded, long dark curls, patched jeans and best sweater, trailing a couple of steps behind her as he looked truculently up at the house. The husband catching up and taking, almost grabbing, his wife's hand, and she'd turned and pulled him on like this social call was a game, as if living itself was a game, not a burden to be shouldered. She'd put her other hand up on his shoulder and walked backwards like they were dancing, and the young husband had suddenly smiled as if he heard the same music, then arm in arm they tacked across the lawn towards the door of the big house.

Even then he'd felt a twinge of jealousy. Jealous, he thought, of their freedom, their lack of burden. They weren't twenty-seven going on fifty with all the major decisions of their lives made and their son and heir already in place. They hadn't missed out on the sixties in a single-sex boarding school. The girl moved light as blown seed while the husband was a supple jaggy thistle. He'd heard the door open, looked down from the window and saw Fiona, sensibly shod, walk towards them, uncertainly drying her hands. Wee Davy toddled out behind her, stopped and stared at them.

He'd sighed and put the kukris on the desk. Better go down and do his lord of the manor bit, tell them they had to move on. He'd even help get their ancient Humber going again. Then the young woman had tilted her head from Fiona and Davy and looked straight up at his window, and though she surely couldn't see him she had smiled as if entertained. And as he went down the stair sucking the finger he'd knicked on the blade, he felt not like lord of the manor but like a man on his desert island seeing with exultation and dread the ship finally sail into the lagoon.

He blinked and took out his stash from the little drawer. So easy to look out the window and see those ghosts still. Some days, days like today, conditions were such he could see the shadows on their faces, the fate-lines on their palms. Jinny had believed that the past and the future were all laid out just beyond the range of our sight. Like the undulating line of hills on the horizon, from where he stood he could see it all, see how it connected, but when he was there walking he could see only the short strip by his feet.

Jinny, Jinny. He crossed to the cupboard, reached behind the estate files and pulled out his secret journals of that time. As he blew the stoor off his fingertips, he wanted just to flick through and check if Jinny really had been barefoot as she so often was, as though she wanted to feel the planet close to her as possible, and grip it confidently with her toes.

Barefoot, Tat had said. And in Crawhill Cottage where Jinny and Patrick had moved to have the baby when winter made the caravan impossible. And David had said something about a stack of plates the woman had with her. It wasn't canny. It wasn't possible. The right age, but nothing else fitted.

Everything disappears but nothing ends, she used to say. *It all comes back in time. I certainly intend to.*

Charming nonsense of course, she scarcely believed it herself. It was just one of those kid-ons, a let's-pretend. Lovers' talk. Not like the real and powerful magic she could work between her body and her eyes, strong enough to astonish them both at the time, and leave her later shaky in his arms.

He opened the old blue cover, put his nose down to the page and inhaled a gone time, the only time he'd truly lived. With eyes shut he glimpsed his younger self crossing to slide the bar across the door before settling down to painfully confess to these pages that his world, his title, his morality and his responsibility were not worth saving. That was the worst ghost of all, the young man he'd been before he'd lived or loved or known himself, before the fall.

Jinny falling away from him, small hand moving away from his outstretched arm, bright head already turned away to look down

Creagan's Knowe, saying nothing as she went.

He took a deep toke and began to read the old words, the faded ink, the young shaking hand of a man who had always acted right and still knew nothing about anything that mattered a damn, a young man whose life was about to end so it could finally begin.

*

For a while Tat gawps at her. His right arm comes up too late. She has grabbed it in both strong hands then leans her face within inches of his.

I lied, she says. About my name. It's not quite Mary.

He blinks. He closes his eyes and the kitchen is very quiet but for the wind outside. The strength goes from his arm. When he opens his eyes she seems to have swollen and distorted as though he was looking at her through glass that has run by reason of its great age.

I don't think I have to say it.

Tat edges back from her. He looks round the kitchen as though seeing it for the first time. And at last he starts to think. He lays his hand across the shotgun.

Anyone can say a name, he says. It's common gossip round here. I kent Jinny Lauder and saw the bairn many a time. You don't look like either.

So long as he doesn't look at her, he can think. He glances towards her then away towards the half-open bedroom door.

Reckon you're a chancer, lassie. Out with you.

His hand is small, sinewy and brown across the shotgun stock. She looks at his shaven averted head, the small runty bones and the quick jerky moves of his shoulders. She'd thought him a sparrow, now she sees he's a sparrowhawk. She sighs and swoops to pick up the biggest shard. She holds the long fragment in her hand, extended towards him like a blade.

Now she has his attention. She steps forward carefully over the broken bits, feels blood slippy under her feet. Standing very close to him and looking into his eyes, she smiles and opens her hand.

In the jagged shard Tat glimpses tall trees, two lovers lying in their shade, a small figure hiding watching them.

I think you'll recognise this, she says. My mother must have shown you.

He nods, unable to lift his eyes from the remains of the plate. Jinny lying on her side in the garden outside the cottage, twenty-odd years back, long red hair tickling across his arm as she talked him through her plates. Family heirlooms, she said, a few hundred years. Teasing him about the lurking watcher, making him red and sweating. But if she had known he'd watched her and Elliot at it, she could never have sat with him like that, surely to God.

The rest are over there, she says. All seven. She nods towards the press. He can see the pile stacked up. Heh, you look like you seen a ghost.

He shakes his head till his tongue comes loose.

I dinna believe in bogles.

She smiles like she doesn't either but that's not the point. Then her smile is gone and she's looking at him in that distant way that makes him feel one of them isn't all there.

What d'ye want?

She nods towards the sink. Pass us that cloth, eh.

She sits down and starts to caress the cloth over her bloody feet. She cocks her head, raises a heavy eyebrow at him.

Left alone for a start, she says. And then some justice in this world.

Tat finds himself at the door. He tugs it open.

And, Tat. He stops. Tell Sim Elliot I'm Marnie Lauder and I've more besides plates to prove it.

Plate 3

Today a smirr of rain and mist shawls down across the window. Stove hisses, feet are bare, radio murmurs and the chair is comfortable. Everything is happed up, inside and out. No one will call today, you've made sure of that.

In a while you may take a walk, just a little stroll. But for now the first plate is laid aside and the pieces of the second are wrapped in a polythene bag in the corner, and this one has '3' written on the back. Turn it over, trace a finger over its pale icons until one stirs and the yellow-haired man enters the dark wood.

David folded away Jo's letter and looked up into the arch of trees. A grey yet shining day, very Borders, light drizzle swaying in from the west. Her letter – hassles with builders, progress on the bathroom, her paper on aboriginal land struggles nearly complete – began and ended with her loving and missing him but seemed to come from a long way off. She had gone dim on him.

He might just call in briefly at the cottage, have tea and see how Mary Allan was doing.

He hesitated at the edge of the wood, recognising that quickening in his chest. Temptation was always an open doorway and whenever he passed it he heard his name said soft and low.

David Elliot turned away and set off uphill, willing himself deaf to everything but the sound of his heart and the rain.

*

She smirks down into the void, runs her hand through her hair and flicks the spray from her fingertips into the falling smash of water then walks steadily across the bridge. She isn't scared of drops, she's fascinated by the quickening of water just before it falls, and the end of motion when it does.

She comes fast and whistling out of the far side of the woods. Halts, blinking at the light. It's a day of weak sun and drizzle, a silent manufacturing of rainbows. There's one hung over the river. Another melts into the green mound of what her Border guide-book identified as an Iron Age fort. She shakes her head and a pair more are lowered over the standing stone leaning squint on the brow of the moor.

She notes how the outer bow reverses the colour order of the first, with a dark gap in between. This may reveal something about generations, how they repeat by reversing qualities but the shape is always the same. Old Elliot and young Elliot . . .

And then she sees a tall greenish smudge moving up by the stone. She also believes she saw the face turn away. If it hadn't been for the rainbows she never would have noticed him. If he hadn't turned away she wouldn't have set her feet uphill after him, into the spooks of sun and rain.

David Elliot sat back against the standing stone and let it shelter him. It was quiet up here, just the hiss of light rain and wind over acres of heather and shorn land, a faint endless tearing sound as if the winding sheet of the world was being slowly ripped open.

He shook his head, cracked a chocolate bar and pushed it with his tongue into the roof of his mouth and waited for the sweet dissolve to trickle down his throat. He'd escaped up here often as a boy home for the holidays. He looked down the dale to the battlement of the peel tower over the trees, then out over the whole Borderlands fading into uplifts and downfalls of grey-green, knowing he might well never come back here again, except for his father's funeral. Sell the big house, give the estate to the Tattersalls and walk away.

He leant back on the worn grey stone, bare of Celtic knotwork or Pictish symbols. It had absolutely nothing to do with the Covenanters. It was just there, from some much older time. He'd once spent days digging round its base, taken fright when the stone began to shift, quickly shovelled the dirt and small animal bones back and left in a hurry. Now he cupped and shifted his balls inside rough tweed. Something about high lonely places visible only to the sky, and the thick earth smell, always made him randy and alert, ready for action of some kind.

But he wanted to disown all that. Disown too the displaced boy who'd been the hero of countless rescues of violated maidens, had rescued, tended, held one when she wept, accepted gently her grateful kiss then led her away on his short-legged hobbie pony over the moor. Sometimes they were on the run and had to sleep nights in hollows on the moor or in the thickets, and as they cooried together for warmth she would slowly, shyly, offer of herself to him in thankfulness and eventually love. Fugitives and comrades by day, then at night inching towards trust . . .

He sat up, following the thought. In Jo he'd found a hurt, clever, sickly woman whose trust could heal him, so long as he was always gentle, never too sexual, never passionate and raw. Not making love with her made him feel good about himself, and he was touched by her acceptance of it. Her sexual past was varied enough, she'd hinted, and she welcomed a break from all that. She almost seemed relieved. His Faith had nothing to do with it. He was celibate because it was safer.

He stood up, kicking the tingle from his knees and the devil of doubt from his mind. He saw a flicker of movement on the lower moor. It dropped from sight, then reappeared. Someone coming this way. Not Tat. Not Dad. *Her*.

Fuck. He really did not need this. He turned and set off up the brae. At the top he'd cut left and drop down into the Langwast. At the far end was Shankheid Pass. Let her follow him into that if she dared.

She came over the top of the moor and looked around. Not a tree or bush, just desolation of heather and cropped turf, dips and hollows and boggy oozing. No sign of him, and up here columns of mist rose around her like the dead. She had no compass and this wasn't her territory. She should turn back while she knew the way.

Then she saw him half a mile off, almost loitering before he dropped into a declivity and disappeared. She pulled the damp cloak tighter round her shoulders and hurried after.

The plates never discuss the causes of love. They never explain. They just show, and even that ambiguously. They are concerned with actions and events, with the patterns, the inevitable. The shape of things past and to come.

But one thing you could learn from them is the danger of pursuit. You could for instance have hurried in anger to recover what's yours, then stop, look round and know yourself lost.

She'd heard the stories, she'd read about it in the book. She knew now where she was though not how she'd been led here – and looking round trapped in the throat of this lost valley, unable to see out in any direction, she was sure she had been led.

She hesitated, stepped and pulled up onto a flat-topped boulder and lay chest down in the middle of the pass. Despite the absence of cannon, horses, and screams, the place reminded her of a childhood illustration of the Valley of Death from the Charge of the Light Brigade. A tight valley, steep and loose with scree on either side. Blocked off ahead with the turf and boulder terrain of a terminal glacier moraine. She squirmed and looked back. The mist was already drawing across the way she'd come through a maze of choices and channels, old stream-beds and swires, drawn on by his yellow head that never turned to look back. She doubted if she could find her way back from here.

A rattle of stones up on the left. She cowered down, squinting across the rock. She saw no one, but a little run of stones pushed down the scree, slowed and stopped.

There was so much cover up there among the eroded outcrops. The valley was scored with stream-beds. At the head of the glen a black path twisted between two mounds like giant ant-hills. No doubt now – this was Shankheid.

SHANKHEID PASS: Here five Lomax men in over-eager hot trod pursuit were ambushed and cut down by a group of Kerrs. It had been feud and the reiving had been a ploy to bring the men out – a classic Border manoeuvre. The one survivor had his tongue severed at the root, was sent home tied to

his hobbie with a note in his mouth and the business end of a pike lodged you may imagine where.

In a subsequent episode more reminiscent of
Romeo and Juliet than the Wild West, two young
lovers made the attempt to defy their families' long-
standing feud. They disappeared together at the
end of a market day in Carlisle and headed for a safe
house across the Border. Unfortunately Jenny
Lomax had confided in her elder sister Margaret,
who had strong views on the subject of the Kerrs of
Westholmeford.

So after Jenny had eloped (or been abducted and
raped, depending whose family you were allied
with), and the lovers were found, the notorious Meg
Lomax had her men bring the young man to
Shankheid Pass. His name was Wat, or Wattie the
Beau, and it was said he had once unwisely rejected
her advances, which may account for the action she
took now. He was strung up from one of the two
mounds at the head of the pass (the Black Yetts), his
hands tied behind his back as Lady Meg primed the
big-bore pistol known as a dag, rolled in the ball,
put the muzzle carefully to young Kerr's groin. According to local legend she looked up into his eyes
and smiled before pulling the trigger. Revenge hot
trod for rape and abduction, she claimed. The
Lomax family had powerful allies and she wasn't
prosecuted, just a resigned sigh from her cousin the
Warden of the Middle March.

These are just two of the episodes that give this
desolate spot its particular atmosphere . . .

Shankheid Pass – even reading about it in her warm bed, she'd
shivered.

Then at the corner of her eye, to her right, a flicker of grey. A
shoulder and arm turning and vanishing into the boulderfield.
The wrong side of the valley, the wrong colour – young Elliot
had been in his tatty green Barbour jacket.

Two of them, then. She gripped the rock as her insides went

liquid. She'd thought she was pursuing but she'd been led here. Who was the other? Tat? Sim Elliot? One thing for sure: this was a wicked place and they could do anything. She was unarmed, in the wrong place, asking for trouble. She was a fighter but without a knife or even a stick and without surprise on her side, she hadn't a chance.

Out of here. She wriggled backwards and down off the boulder, pretty sure it was useless. Still the two were ahead and she could maybe lose them. Crouched and crawling and panting with nerves, she worked her way back into the boulderfield she'd come through. A sharp bang on the inside of her knee brought water to her eye. She knelt, panting and nauseous for a moment, then set off again. Glancing behind left and right. No sign, no movement. If she got out of this, she'd bloody kill him. Nobody did this to her.

Sharp crack up ahead. Perhaps she'd imagined the puff of stone but the rattle that followed was real enough. Three of them, then. And a rifle? She was sealed in.

Her legs had the strength of wet newspaper as she crawled deeper into the boulderfield then turned down a stream-bed, knowing it useless. Blood on her hands, her knee aching, water running from her hair and eyes. Easy to forget what physical terror is. It feels like someone has pulled the plug on your being.

Three men could do anything to her here. They probably would. And she'd asked for it. She'd been insane to give Tat the name. That's what this was about, she was sure. Simon Elliot knew who she was and what she'd come for. He'd killed once. And yes, she had been threatening him. She'd enjoyed being at the cottage, making sure he knew she was there, letting him stew. Then Tat with his darty eyes, tiny ears and long shiny head . . .

A rattle behind, left side. A low hooting whistle off to the right. She was too scared to look, that's how bad it was. Davy had liked and fancied her. Likely he was a parfait Christian knight in normal circumstances. But this wasn't a normal place. He was in the end his father's son. She'd glimpsed in him flashes of another much more forceful and unpredictable man. She'd even played up to it. Stupid stupid girl.

She jumped from the stream-bed, ran crouching round an outcrop, tripped and rolled down into a pit of loose stones. She gripped a jagged quartz rock in her fist as she pushed up onto her knees. She'd hurt the bastards before they did for her. After that it didn't matter.

She was rising to sprint for the path out when the hands came over her eyes, the strong expert grip round her shoulders and neck. She went absolutely still.

So how do you like being followed?

His voice. David. Amused, not-amused.

Not much fun, is it? You should have left us alone, Marnie.

So he knew. Of course he did, Tat would have told him. She said nothing but twisted her head away from his hand so she could see the slopes on either side.

Looking for my friends? he asked.

Bastards, she said.

Drop the rock.

He squeezed tighter and she did. He gave a piercing whistle. She waited, shivering. Let it come. Let it be brief. He whistled again.

She looked round but no one was emerging from the rocks or hollows or stream-beds. No Tat. No gaunt dark Simon Elliot.

It's an old trick, the voice said behind her. Tat taught me when I was a laddie. She felt herself released. She turned. He'd reversed his Barbour, grey side out. He was grinning.

A rock lobbed here, a stone there . . . Very effective, isn't it?

You had not bargained on this when you began. At this point it would be good to break away but that isn't possible now. You must let this run and continue to believe you of all the people in this story cannot come to harm. After all, your soul, you must believe it, is your own.

She went for his eyes.

He was quicker but only just. He turned his head and her nails scraped over his eyebrow then he had her by the wrists. For a moment they were staring into each other, then as she went to knee him, he pressed in close. She stumbled back. He followed her, held her close and tight so she couldn't get her knee up.

She struggled to free her hands. Twice her nails went by his eyes. Already a red trickle was coming down his cheek, mixed with rain. He was unexpectedly strong and for the first time she felt the heat of him. His father's son all right. His eyes were sparking like mica, she could see the separate flakes of blue. Her breasts were flattened against his chest. His legs were either side of hers as they swayed and struggled.

She folded at her knees then head-butted where his ribs divided. He stumbled back and fell among the stones, was up in a flash as she grabbed a rock in her right hand and came forward.

Are you really her?

She hesitated. He hadn't picked up a stone but his eyes were nailed on hers. His voice was hoarse.

Are you Jinny's daughter? Is it true?

All her life had circled round this moment. She had no choice.

Yes.

He leaned back on the stony bank, put his hands on his knees and she heard his breath go out. The rock dropped from her hand and clattered between them. His head came up, the yellow hair plastered to his forehead, some of it catching the blood from his cut. He looked as though seeing her anew. She could feel herself being recast, felt her identity waver.

I can only just remember, he said. I think we played together. I think I liked you. Maybe I was jealous too.

She looked down at her hands then stuck them in her pockets to stop them shaking.

My, how you've grown, she said. Can't say I recognise you.

Me neither. Not really.

She cleared her throat.

I've this feeling . . .

She looked away as she spoke. Her voice didn't sound her own. It was some ancient longing, a bit of history that never aged.

Marnie . . . He came towards her. His hands were open, palms up. She looked him in the eyes before her hand came up to wipe blood from his forehead.

Come back to the cottage and I'll show you us together, she said.

*

They came over yet another crest and there was the valley below, the cottage, the forest, the distant river. She flopped down onto the turf and lay out straight. He sat down beside her, took out chocolate and handed her half.

You're a pal, she murmured, popped it in her mouth and closed her eyes.

Beyond the trees by the heuch that split the brae, he could just see the topmost chimneys of the big house and the battlement of the peel tower. Off to the west, at the furthest outpost of the next dale, the sun lit red on the prow of Creagan's Knowe. He looked away. There were some things he wasn't ready to talk about, and he was hoping she wouldn't ask.

Your friend Carol at the home, he said – what happened to her folks?

Her eyelids flickered but stayed closed.

Why are you asking? she said at last.

Because she seemed important to you.

She sat up abruptly and hugged her knees. The moorland over her shoulder was full of diffused refracted light. He waited until he realised she wasn't going to offer more, and he stretched to go.

The short version, she said. Her voice was flat as ice. Carol's father was a piss-artist alcoholic, mother epileptic with severe depressions. She had delusions, sort of religious ones. Old Testament with her own extras. Who knows, maybe she believed in Spook.

She nearly laughed but it was more the hiss of a stone sent skirling over a frozen loch. Then silence, damp air sizzling quietly into the heathery land.

But she was all right most of the time, Marnie went on. Or so Carol said. Anyway, her father announced he'd fallen in love or at least in bed with the woman next door. Then he moved out. So a few weekends later her mother gave Carol and her sister – she had a sister, did I say?

No. David sat with his insides dropping, wishing he hadn't asked and not sure why he had.

So she takes most of a bottle of pills and gives the kids the remainder, ground up in their juice. Then she locks the front and back doors, takes them into the kitchen with some toys for them and the old man's whisky for herself. When the kids start getting slow, she opens the oven door, turns on the gas and says they'll have a sleep while waiting for the invisible man. Her sister falls asleep, then her mum does. But Carol wants to stay awake because she really wants to see the invisible man, and she crawls over to the window where there happens to be a draught . . .

So her mother and sister . . .?

Uh-huh.

How could her mother *do* that?

Again that low skidding laugh.

I suppose she wasn't in her right mind. Marnie shrugged. Not her fault.

Not her fault?

Oh no. At the edge of his vision he saw her head turn his way. Her father was the one to blame, she muttered. He's the one who left them. He's the real murderer.

David felt a dark stone fall. It fell till it settled somewhere deep, sending up clouds of mud and his vision dimmed. He turned his eyes away from the red-lit knowe and for a moment saw a pool of black water surround them, peaceful and still. Slowly it faded back into heather as his vision adjusted.

Still, Marnie said and stretched, I'd say Carol's quite well, considering. Though she never really got over losing her sister.

Maybe that's why . . . you two were so close. In a way you *were* her sister.

Yes. She sounded as if this had never occurred to her before. I suppose I was, among other things.

They stood up at the same time and faced downhill for home.

I don't know what you've heard about Dad and Jinny, he said. But best not jump to any conclusions.

You weren't there.

Nor were you.

Neither of them looked at the other. She was pale and motionless, just the breeze lifting hair from her forehead. His head was bowed and his heart going much too fast.

He's guilty, David said. Of plenty. But I cannot think he killed Jinny.

Most folk round here do.

Since when did you set store by what most folk believe? She shrugged, but looked away, point taken. If you want to know more – I suppose that's what you're here for – you should talk to Tat.

Tat?

She sounded genuinely surprised.

He was living here then, must have been in his teens. He's a distant relation and my dad kind of took him in.

Interesting. Maybe I will.

And she set off down. He caught up, opened his mouth to say more but she shook her head. So he walked home beside her, still wondering.

So, ah, you and Carol?

She was ahead of him, he heard her voice in jerks.

We lost each other . . . years. Often . . . men. She managed to find me, and then . . .

He stumbled over the ground till he was at her shoulder.

And then?

Her head went down and he wished with all his heart he hadn't asked.

And then she left.

Where is she now?

Carol? On the dark side of the moon. Marnie stopped dead, swung her arms out wide. On the other side of the world!

Then she ran, and what came back to him sounded like laughter.

*

You tell him you once lived in a cave for three months, a cave above a raised beach looking out to a rocky coastline and two barren islands like battleships anchored on the horizon. The nearest neighbour was ten miles away. It had suited you well, for solitude feeds your spirit.

So why did you leave? he asks.

I could have been going mad and not known, you say. That's what scared me away. (You were crouched over a clear clear rock pool, watching the life down there, and then nothing was out there, the contents of your mind and the pool were the same, and you sat back with sea anenomes waving in your eyes, and wondered for how long you'd been addressing snatches of your skull to the air. And you couldn't know, not without someone to correct you. You picked up the biggest boulder you could lift and dropped it into the pool and left that cursed perfect place.)

What you want and what's good for you aren't always the same, you say, and see his hazed eyes come clear and sharp, and then he nods, and then he blushes, and then he looks away.

There's no more talk about his father, nor Jinny, nor Patrick. Neither of you is ready yet. But louping down the last of the moor towards the drove road you're both laughing and bumping into each other easy as if family or old friends, though you're not, though in ways you are. And for that time you're happy, all present and correct, almost like a real person.

*

She came out of the tiny bathroom towelling her hair as he moved around the kitchen, never too far from the door. She'd changed into a man's red shirt that hung loose but forced him to see she was not a man.

You said you've some proofs to show me.

And so I do. I do.

She stretched up, slowly and deliberately and almost insultingly, to hang the towel over the pulley. He moved back slightly as though the kitchen was already too small.

Don't worry, she said. I'll not eat you.

She stooped into the press cupboard and turned.

These were Jinny's picture plates, she said, and put them carefully on the table. You'll have heard about them?

He shook his head, leaning over them with his eyes jumping from panel to panel.

They meant plenty to Tat – and to your father, I bet.

And now they've come down to you.

Yes, she said. Down to me.

These must be Border Ballad plates, he said. I've heard of them but never seen a set, not even in a museum. Amazing . . .

His fingers drifted lightly as though he could brush the scenes into life, then he glanced up at her.

It's *The Twa Corbies*, right? Only longer and more complicated.

I think it's the original source material, probably in a real incident. Perhaps between the Lauders and the Elliots – at least, that's what I was always told.

He nodded again. Figures, he said. They were aye at each other. These lovers . . . This looks like someone . . . This waterfall's almost like . . . He shook his head then looked up at her again, his pupils big and blue irises flecked and radiant. Marnie, these are magic.

She shrugged. I thought you weren't interested in the past.

But these are recent too. I mean . . .

He tailed off, looked round the kitchen as if seeing it for the first time.

My dad was here with Jinny. He must have seen these. Must have touched them. They must have . . . Here . . .

She swiftly lifted the plates and put them on the shelf.

There's something else, she said to distract him. He shouldn't look in the plates too long. He might riddle them out. He shook himself, something between a shiver and a dog throwing off water.

Show me.

She held out her hand. He hesitated then took it. She led him into the bedroom as that morning's plate had foretold.

He looked round the bare room, curious and uneasy. Double mattress on the floor by the window, a few books, a backpack. Flowers and a lamp on the sill. His father and Jinny, in this room, on a bed like this?

She nudged him. Here's my other proof, she said and handed it to him.

He gripped the silver frame and stared at the photo. The woman in the garden laughing to camera as she moved from light into shade. Long ringleted hair, feet bare, fringed hippie skirt and black crocheted cardigan buttoned across her small chest. A wee boy with a sword, and behind him the toddler pushing herself upright. The photographer's shadow in the foreground was long and black. Right enough, in his memory the day was very bright.

He looked at her. This is Jinny?

Yes, she said, very quietly. That was her.

I mind that plastic sword. The feel of its handle . . . There was a seam on it that rubbed my fingers. And that's you?

In a right bad temper, by the look of it.

Who took it?

She looked straight back at him.

The invisible man.

His hand shook slightly. They were standing very close beside the mattress. He felt the heat come off her, the scent of lavender and long gone summer.

So they were here, he said quietly. My dad and your mother.

They are here.

Her words stirred dust in the corner. Her hand came up to touch his cheek, she turned his head towards her and he didn't resist as her dark eyes came closer. His mouth parted. This time they wouldn't break away till it was done.

She put her fingers to his lips. She bowed her head.

You're not the bad man, she murmured. Then she looked up. And if your heart was your own, perhaps I'd steal it.

She took the photo from his hand, knelt to place it carefully beside the pillow.

Time to go home, Davy. She looked back over her shoulder. Now. Please.

*

The book is heavy in my hand tonight.

How solid everything has become – the sink weighs tons, the tea-pot flatly gleams like lead, the trees above the gorge are weighted down by moonlight. Real and solid too is the young yellow-haired man kissed out of mischief. Tonight he is surely in bed thinking of his true chaste love, due in a couple of days he said and seemed full of joy.

Close the book, stack up the plates, put away my notes. Time surely for bed. I've been spending too much time on other people's lives, real and imagined. Tonight I can lie and tell true stories of my lover, to mother myself to sleep.

A long time ago but still ever-present there were two girls, near-children really, who placed themselves in each other's care. In the desolation of the children's home, the one with green paint everywhere except the shower-torture room, they were each other's only family. They told each other the very small everything of their lives so far. Especially they told each other all the cruelties and betrayals, and made solemn, fervent compacts for revenge, sealed in thumb's blood.

By day they stood back to back, the tall strong one and the light quick one, and fought off all comers. At night after punishment they clung together, and if there were tears they came then, smothered into the other's shoulder. (Her little ribs melting into mine, I felt her going in, rib of my rib.)

They became interchangeable in their hearts. Marnie-and-Carol, Carol-and-Marnie. Sometimes waking in each other's beds with no memory of how they got there. Or creeping barefoot across cold linoleum, the hand outstretched, then chill feet on warm shin. (Learning to wake and creep back to separate beds before first light has left me this poor sleeper.)

After Veronica lost her eye, it was very bad though nothing was proved because they were each other's alibi. (She clung to me all night long, her head in under my chin. We swore to each other for ever, the kind of promises that can wear thin but remain, however faint. As though the soul was a sheet washed over and over then held to the light.)

They were moved to the place for very bad girls, many of them older, and then it was a matter of survival and time was very short. But in those last months, between the beatings and the torments, they found the source of pleasures inside their skinny bodies. They were too close to need kissing, but the pleasure they learned to uncork and open like phials of streaming light, and with their fingers split the spectrum over the skin.

They were caught one grey afternoon when they'd sneaked back to the dorm to make the sun rise yet again. (Believe me, there is no place for love in places like that.) The sheets were pulled back, they burrowed into each other and hid their faces till the Director and the Matron came to prise them apart. They were split up, sent hastily out to families with no forwarding address allowed. For good measure they were sent to different sides of the Border.

But they took their revenge. The clever one worked out how before they parted, and they wrote the letters and spread the stories, and at the enquiry spoke so quietly and broken, and their evidence was so convincing along with the medical inspection which suggested repeated penetration (the sad experts of the body cannot distinguish pain from love and pleasure) that the Director and the Matron never worked in homes again. He may have gone to prison, I can't remember. Useful to learn early the power of the powerless, and just how much can be done with sex and accusation. There was the loutish son in one foster home, the pinching bullying daughter in another – both snared, netted, dragged down from their high place.

But after the first love there is no other. Not for some, in any case. Not for me.

The moon is heavy and pins me to the bed where I lie slowly wriggling. Love is not in question when sleep is not the answer.

She woke at first light feeling not quite right, a slight pain nagging behind her eyes, and a dull ache in the lower back, the kind of symptoms one might get from sleeping badly after wrestling with something bigger.

Yellow hair, golden hair – she thinks how often those motifs recur. She pulls out a book from the loose pile by the bed and flicks through it crooning *With ain lock of his gowden hair / We'll theek oor nest when it grows bare* till she finds what she's looking for: *The Lament of the Border Widow*.

> *But think na ye my heart was sair*
> *When I laid the mould on his yellow hair?*

Maybe the yellow hair, the golden hair, isn't a simple detail about colour. It could indicate gold, preciousness, dearness to the beholder. In the way that black meal, the black rent of the reivers, is black in nothing but heart.

> *No living man I'll love again*
> *Since that my lovely knight is slain.*
> *With ae lock of his yellow hair*
> *I'll chain my heart for evermair.*

The finality of it makes her gorge rise. She wonders if the pun on 'lock' is intended. In one ballad a woman kills her man with yellow hair, in another she mourns him for ever.

Perhaps it is possible to do both.

The thought drifts round the chill room for a while like stoor raised by a passing broom, then settles into silent corners. She bends over the plate, thinking about meetings and yellow hair and love and murder. As love it might have been. As murder it might be.

There must be some movement today, some certainty. Time to go to the town and do some research.

*

Close my eyes and the blow in the top nest of the birches is the sea breaking below a sunny headland I'll never revisit. The sound of my own heart as I pick up a stoat's skull and hold it to the ear.

In lower Crawhill Woods the ravine broadens and the burn shallows into flat pools (linns, I think). A few shrunk crinkled leaves lie still on the surface. Only at the far end do the leaves and twigs begin to spin and look as though they're going somewhere.

Tall pale smooth shining beech trees by the linns of the Liddie, how may I ever forget them? The grass soft around, strewn with shells of nuts like rough brown empty chalices. This is where lovers come, hasty and silent in the shade on hot afternoons, or wrapped in a travelling blanket on a hard freezing night. Jinny Lauder and Sim Elliot lay here as many before them.

Soft tearing hiss of wind through hawthorn, knotted and scraggy. Wizened haw berries like very old blood, exactly that shade.

*

Down by the road as she turns to follow it to the village, the river after rain is brown and swollen, lipping over the banks, white froth and yellow scum along the margins. Across the road, fields widen and shine. It is hard for her not to remember times when banks gave the river direction, times when her life was shaped by a lover's walk. Times before her earliest friend and lover walked onto a plane and left her carrying the past and a chestful of water which she must find some way to shed.

Her oldest friend, the only one to whom she'd ever entrusted herself and curled around in the dark so often like a blind, white root, had hugged her again, told her to bury the past, kissed her for the last time before Departures. I don't want these things any more, she'd said. I'll send you a card.

Her earliest friend waited for her to say something but there was no breath left to speak with. Have a life, lover, her only love said. A swift Judas kiss on unresponsive lips. Goodbye now. Then lover walked through the squealing arch of the metal-detectors, one backward wave and was gone. Leaving her standing with nowhere to go but here.

In the fields across the road, the floodwater is retreating. She squelches through loops of baler twine, scum, a fertiliser bag blown in from somewhere trying to raise itself and falling back again, twitching in the breeze.

A drowned skinny cat. White teeth, little grey twisted tongue. The hoodie crows stand on fence-posts, staring below their grey judges' caps. She briefly wishes for a shotgun, or that she was a dead-eye with a catapult.

She heads towards the village, walking parallel with the road but some way off it. She sclims a dyke – and where did that word come from, so antique and so right? – jumps down and almost falls on a sheep lying on its back. It must have been there for days, unable get up. A pool of sheep-shit round its rear, some bloody. She tries to wrestle it upright but her back hurts and the sheep is wet and heavy and unable to help itself. Then she sees it has no eyes. The crows have been at it already.

She stands over it, sick at heart. The legs wave slowly, the head turns blindly, uncertain if she's foe or friend. She looks away down the empty road. Where is Tat when he could be useful? Where is David when she needs him?

Leave it, she thinks. Walk away. It's all cruel and hopeless. The best we can do is put each other out of our misery. Even murder's almost an act of love.

The hoodie crows stand their ground, the rain does not relent and the wind is beyond indifference. It's just wind. Stone is just stone. The dead are just dead and will remain so. There is no Spook, nothing means anything.

She looks down at the black head turning, the worn green-stained teeth, blackened tongue. Something hesitates in her. Her chest is waterlogged but she cannot weep. She has not wept since the airport, and that just a small angry dampness stinging her eyes as she'd stumbled into the concourse bookshop with no idea where to go next.

She is so angry at the sheep. Why doesn't it die and be done with it? Kill it, then. How do you kill a sheep? With a big stone? Strangle it with baler twine? She should carry David's knife at all times. Again she wonders how a woman is supposed to kill a full-grown man behind a dyke when she can't even work out how to kill a blind dying ewe.

She looks around. Still no one on the road. She goes over to the wall and with a grunt lifts off the heaviest stone she can. She staggers towards the sheep and stands over it. Twenty yards off the corbies are still waiting.

She positions herself over the head. She sways, hesitates, then her hands open. Her eyes are shut tight but she hears the crunch. Then she walks past the crows and stumbles on towards the village, unable to see for all this water everywhere.

*

In the big house David takes a bacon roll upstairs and sits on the end of his bed reading Jo's letter yet again.

*So what's the matter with me? I know you need reassurances
but I just want to tell you things like the latest academic gossip
and how there's bubbles under the wallpaper that I can squeegee
around but not get rid of . . .*

You should get out more – isn't there anyone you can visit?

*I want to share things I see, like the tadpoles for Christ's sake,
I want you to see their little legs. I want to update you on the
land struggles of aboriginal peoples – is that you? Or are you,
historically considered, one of the imperialist oppressors? And
are the oppressors themselves oppressed more by the sheer weight
of history or by their ignorance of it? Are we?*

Oh and I think my eating's getting better . . .

The creases of her letter are getting grubby and frayed. His eyes move over the words but fall into the space between the lines.

He puts the letter between the pages of *The Screwtape Letters*. Someone cares more about him than he'd ever thought possible. He reminds himself of that. God is good. But what if He's not? What if He's just a power that moves through everything, the one that equally pushes the cloud across the sky and the woman from the cliff-top?

He cannot afford to think this.

He stands at the window watching the rain. He could take a

walk, but there's only one way he'd end up going. The photo has locked them in the same frame. They're connected, he feels it down in his belly, like shared breathing. They rise and fall together.

He stands possessed by the certainty that somewhere Marnie is breathing.

He coughs and blows her out of him.

He can hear his father upstairs, walking up and down. He's singing now. David pushes up the window and sticks his head out. Now he can hear better. Same bloody song as yesterday. And the day before.

> *I loved a lass and I loved her sae weel*
> *I hated all others that spoke of her ill*
> *But now she's rewarded me well for my love*
> *For she's gone to be wed to another . . .*

The house is empty but for the nutter upstairs. Annie's not due in today. Tat's off to some carving class in the city.

> *The clerk of the parish he gave a great cry*
> *If you've any objections then please bring them by*
> *And I thought tae masel great objections hae I*
> *But I hadna the wish tae affront her*

Great objections hae I. He has had great objection to something since he was tiny. At times even his Faith is mostly quarrel with the world as it is, with himself as he is. But Jo's illness, her intelligence and courage call out his tenderness. To hold her when she needs it is to be at rest.

But someone has raised tarn-black eyes and leant unasked to kiss him and that kiss has lifted a lade-gate and set the current through him. He feels the great stones clunk and grind in his chest as the wheel turns and he can't stop it.

> *The men of the forest they ask it of me*
> *How many strawberries grow in the salt sea*
> *And I answer them back wi a tear in my ee*
> *How many ships sail in the forest?*

How he hates daft questions that have no answers. Like why doesn't his father *do something*? Why doesn't he visit his lover's daughter? What's he waiting for, why is he frightened?

David pulls the window down and sits to write back to Jo.

He stares out at the drizzle. It's been days now. His hand moves. He writes *Rain like love feels forever till it stops.*

He stops. He can't say that.

*

Where is the watcher today? He wasn't in his usual place at the margins of the scenes. This morning on rising you noticed something odd and different in the top left curve: high ghostly verticals, and between them are many round blobs. Like a basket of eggs you think. No, it's heads. People in numbers, streaming forward, glancing but not talking. A cathedral spire, a citadel, distant hills.

The city, then. And leaning closer you saw one blob has his back turned away, the crowd parts round him like he was a stone in the river current. You think you recognise this one. He must always be accounted for. Your thoughts follow him as you move through the day.

The ballads are drooned in the city. Streets and pavements, shops and tenements cover the earth, the burns are piped out of sight, the wind is baffled and dies in multi-storey car parks. The only birds are tuneless starlings.

Man, I love it.

One of the scraggie travellers, your modern stoorie-foot, told me the city was inhuman. Did you ever hear such thoughtless blethers? The city is human, every bit of it is our work. It's the perfect lover, the one that never quite delivers. It's a drug ten times stronger than anything Elliot kens of. Most of the time I resist it and don't allow myself to come here often.

Folk know I seldom stir beyond the valley and the village. They assume it's because I've taken a scunner to the city but they're so wrong.

I turn my eyes from looking out the art college windows, away from the human tangle of spires and wires, roads and monuments, the deep sough of traffic and the people moving like corpuscles in the circulation of the blood. Whiles I've felt the city like a breathing body wrappit round me, and my gasps are its own.

But I turn back to the still world, the wee and the cool. Bone, ivory, jade, boxwood and my soft metals. My skeelie fingers poke and prod with blades and rasps, and like my hairt was a charcoal-pit I smoor its fires awhile in this work.

*

You lean over paper, reading and remembering. Sometimes you take notes, for it's a complicated story with no clear boundaries. One voice side-slips into another, a push becomes a fall when witnesses disagree, lovers become birds, men become women and women are as men. Everything is debatable.

You turn another page and hear the rain shush in the distance like a librarian's sigh.

You're too far in to back out now. You dream of clarity and charity, but this could take some time.

By late afternoon the rain had passed over and clear light returned over the town cramped at the meeting of the valleys. She accepted she'd missed the bus back to the village. Carrying bags of shopping and her notes in the satchel on her back, she left the last stone houses behind and lengthened her stride.

Cars passed. Her right hand dangled. One or two slowed, unsure whether she was wanting a lift, interested in a woman walking the road alone. But something about her – the fierce set of her shoulders perhaps, a purpose and indifference in that dark, alert head – made them swerve and carry on.

She walked on, damp squeaking in her boots. Plenty to think about. A session among the back numbers at the newspaper office, glaring at the curious secretary. No photo-copying, so she'd made pages of scribbled notes. The trial had been in the central market town but now the transcripts were held in the city. Still it had been written up in detail, this local sensation. She knew the verdict, had known it since childhood. It could as well be branded across her high forehead: Not Proven.

But the detail was enough to make her hands shake. She stopped, mouth open, outraged when at the last minute the prosecution reduced the charge from Murder to Culpable

Homicide. Meaning he killed her but didn't really mean to. Meaning the prosecution were losing confidence. Their adult witnesses – a man on a tractor, two brothers walking back from the pub that afternoon – were becoming less conclusive. There were discrepancies. It had been a long way off. Drink had been taken. And they had clearly, like most local people, already made up their minds.

Maybe he hadn't meant to kill Jinny. Maybe he was trying to persuade her, stop her from telling, asking her to run away with him, and she'd slipped over the edge. If Sir Simon Elliot pleaded guilty to that, he could get off with two to four years. Not bad for a human life.

But he hadn't changed his plea. Thrawn bastard, or in full denial. Perhaps he knew what was coming next: the stuttery, nervous testimony of the adolescent Kevin Tattersall – malnourished urban reject, distant nephew taken in for the summer, part-time shadow of Sim Elliot, full-time voyeur.

She pictures him in Elliot's cut-down clothes giving evidence. Knobbly knees, thin white arms, sweating in his pants. She can feel for him as for herself, the outsider dizzy with the power that's been given. Glancing nervously between Elliot and a catatonically drunk Patrick Johnstone with his daughter clutched in his arms. Tat with one sharp eye on the recent past, the other on his future. Then making his choice. Or maybe just telling the truth as he saw it, frightened into stammer by the formality but refusing to budge.

Sir Simon and Jinny were very close together at the top of the cliff. He had an arm out, she pushed and some earth came loose and she fell. She hit the ledge and got up and fell again, and it was like that all the way to the bottom where she tumbled down broken and bleeding, opened her mouth and died. Did she say anything, Kevin? Did she say if Sir Simon pushed her? Sir, she just said *Ah*. She said *Ah* and the blood came out.

It didn't look much in transcript – patchy, incomplete, but enough to undermine the more distant eye-witnesses. Enough to introduce doubt at the trial, to make the other witnesses hesitate and admit that from that distance they could have misunderstood two figures clasped together on the edge of Creagan's Knowe.

She splashed grimly along the verge, letting the passing cars spray on her while two new items burned between her ribs. The prosecution began by establishing how long the affair between Simon Elliot and Jinny Lauder had gone on. A few months, Elliot admitted. They had meetings in Crawhill Cottage after Jinny had moved there with her husband and baby. Again, Tat confirmed he'd seen their trysts when he was staying during the holidays. There were no other witnesses, but Elliot's admission of the affair and Tat's corroboration had ended that line of questioning.

She slowed and stopped, for the first time wondering just how long . . .

She stood for a moment at the roadside, letting the possibilities fork and streak down like rain across a pane. Then she took some deep breaths, straightened her shoulders and walked on with only the slightest tremor at her knees. She had to get the story straight before . . . Well, before whatever action she took.

And something else to be considered – her notes had gone shaky, she'd had to print the few words before giving up – at the end of the pathologist's report on the deceased: *Pregnant, approximately three months.*

Sure as eggs are easily broken, defence argued she could have jumped and Elliot had been trying to stop her. They argued no man would deliberately kill his own unborn child. Understanding nothing about Jinny or the times. Cretins. Pregnant Jinny meant divorce, losing the estate in settlement, losing his son. Public and private shame. That was cause enough. But come on: think. If he thought the baby was his surely to God . . . Then again, if he thought it *wasn't* . . .

Up ahead, a car had stopped. It began to reverse towards her. Battered green estate, mud on the sills. She flexed her free right hand and kept walking past it.

Marnie? Marnie Lauder?

A woman's voice. She stopped mid-stride. The window came down further. Full open face, weathered and lively.

Uh-huh.

Would you like a lift to Crawhill? I'm going that way and it's an awfy walk.

She stared at the woman. Plump hands on the wheel, wedding and engagement rings. She wanted to be left alone to think. But she also wanted some normal company and this woman had normal stencilled across her old purple anorak and tartan woollen beret. It was starting to drizzle again, remorseless as a girning child. She'd done all the thinking she could stand. She mustn't compromise herself. Accept no favours.

The woman tugged the handle and swung the door open.

I stay down the brae from you. Jump in.

You're Annie Tat. Sorry, Mrs Tattersall.

Got it in one, dear. Put your bags in the back with the dog food.

*

So I fettled up my kit and lowsed early from the class. Anyway I'd been foutering about the last hour, jalousing ways of setting silver into bone but it was aye melting or peeling off. In truth my hand had a tremmle on it as the blade and solder iron moved in and out of the wee smooth valley. I saw the ancient cleft and Elliot's white shaft sinking in.

Fuck off back to the organ-grinder.

The lassie had shoogled me up right enough, wiping her blood onto my breeks and smiling. She wasn't natural.

Standing out on the pavement, the West End rush-hour pouring by me, I felt myself a finnock in the burn, waggling its fins to stay still. I should be heading home. But the key to Elliot's flat was hot in my pooch. I could take a daunder around, maybe see a few kent faces in the part of town I know best, then head off when the traffic had run dry.

I'm a great kidder. I'd no more choice than a bitch in heat nor the dog that sniffs her. So I jumped on the bus wi a fiss in my wallies and my tools and gear for overnight in the bag over my shoulder, then went up front to watch as the driver swung toward the dirty part of town.

*

Consider these ghostly meetings at the circumference. Dogs chasing deer, hawks pursuing doves. Below them, what looks like two women in a clearing. The one with her arm round the waist of the other is strikingly thin, fair-haired. Are they sisters, lovers, dancers? Or perhaps the thin one is a boy, a youth. Really the detail is so faded and corrupted, you can only guess by what feels right. In any case their faces are turned to each other as though in sudden recognition, or they have heard their names called a long way off. But surely, by this long line of ivy that runs from one scene to another, they come later. It's a foreshadowing. Let it be so.

Hiss of tyres, murmur of radio turned low, the laboured beat of wipers. Warm in the car, windows steaming up, and for the first time in a long time, a safe feeling. Something about Annie Tat's old blue cardigan under the anorak, or the stretch pants and flat slip-on shoes, or her loud and cheerful voice. Safe. Cuddly. David's second mother.

Have a boiling, dear.

Annie held out a tin labelled *Berwick Cockles*. Marnie fumbled inside the tin, struggled to hold onto a sweetie and still get her wrist out. The cockle was striped pink, oval, rough. In her mouth she remembered: mint sweetness puckering the tongue, the kindly woman who once gave her them, another life ago. So many lives . . .

Did you know her when she lived at Crawhill?

The car swerved slightly as Annie put the tin away.

Poor Jinny? No, I'm not from round here, can't you tell? By the time I first knew the estate well, your mother was a year dead and all that was left was talk. How they loved it round here.

For a moment Annie didn't sound very mumsie. Marnie glanced at her, saw the line of muscle under the plump jawline.

Remember your mum, do you?

Uh. She sucked sugar through the air pockets of the cockle, rubbed her tongue on the coral roughness. I think she gave me these sweeties. Apart from that and her red hair and a feeling . . . I mean I was very wee when she was – when she died.

Annie's hand dropped onto her arm, squeezed.

I'm sorry, dear. And about your father. Terrible that was.

Yes.

The road began to wind down into the village. She sucked then crunched the last of the sweet and felt her fillings dissolve.

It was hard for Tat then too, Annie said. Cos he was a wee city tyke and had nits which didn't help and a bit stammer from being hit by his dad. After Jinny died, lot of folk had it in for him because he gave evidence for Sir Simon. But all he did was say what he saw.

What he thought he saw.

Tat has sharp eyes, dear.

He must have been very grateful to Elliot, taking him in and that.

He was grateful to Simon and Fiona. Annie Tat leant on the 'and' briefly like a quick peep on the horn to warn an animal off the road. They were both good to him. And – a quick glance her way – he was very fond of Jinny. A quick conspiratorial between-women grin. I think he was a bit sweet on her.

He wasn't the only one.

Annie Tat said nothing as they drove slowly through the village. It was a place where people looked to check who was in each car. Annie waved a couple of times. Marnie saw the curious glances linger, heads turn towards each other in their wake. She sensed patterns interlocking outside her mind, in the few folk on the street and the bare trees and the shining fields. Something she couldn't stop now even if she wanted. For all the chill weather, the first hint of green on garden shrubs. Call it spring, the movement unstoppable.

No denying it was a wrong thing they did, Annie went on. Jinny was a married woman for all she was a bit of a hippie. She knew what she was about. Maybe they called it free love in those days.

It cost her life. And . . . my father's with the drink.

And the divorce and the break-up of the estate. And Davy – you can see what he's like about his dad. Sim Elliot's not a bad man, and he's paid enough.

Uh-huh.

The field with the dead sheep was coming up on the left. She hummed to herself to drown out the crunch of the stone.

So you were adopted, Marnie? We're awful nosy round here.

She blinked something away then reached for another Berwick Cockle.

In care, then fostered out after Patrick . . .

Where did you live?

Here and there. How long have you been at the big house?

She'd only asked to change the subject, but Annie Tat looked at her closely.

I've been working at the big house since my kids were old enough to go to nursery.

She said it clear and deliberate, like a statement made on record, and held Marnie's gaze a moment longer before looking back at the road. The car slowed for the turn-off up to Crawhill. Marnie reached over the back seat for her bags.

Why did you come back here? Annie's voice had hardened, not even pretending to be casual.

(In the airport bookshop, unable to leave till her love's plane had taken off and in any case she knows not where to go from here. She's looking over the shoulder of a woman in front of her, who is flicking through a road map, her loose red hair curling over the pages. And it would have meant nothing but for the page she stopped at. A finger brushes by the name of a town, then a village, and at the back of her head a sound is ringing from a bell no human hand has struck. Then the petite woman turns as though angry at this invasion of her space, thrusts the book at her and is gone, leaving a daze, a direction, and a faint sweet smell.)

The car stopped.

Are you here to see Elliot?

Silence. The empty whump of wipers. The car moved on.

I'm not having you walk up the hill in this, dear. You'll come in for some tea.

Bouncing up the rough track they passed a tall slouching man with a dog and rifle crooked on his arm. A toot on the horn, brief wave answered by an even briefer nod.

Is that Smiler Ballantyne?

Aye, my dear. Annie Tat laughed. Except he never smiles and he's not a Ballantyne.

Huh.

Plenty of things here aren't what you might think.

The car lurched to a halt outside the Tattersall house. An old cottage extended in breeze block with an uneven patio and conservatory tacked on the side. Mud up to the back door and a satellite dish below the eaves.

Well, I hope a cup of tea is still hot and sweet, she said.

Two women talking together: two hedgerows meeting at a boundary. The shivering tops, the sides with their ancient wizened berries and crimped leaves rustling together. In behind the thorn-protected centre, the hidden nests, wool and feather-lined.

Two women talking cannot be simple. You realise you had thought lazily about Annie Tat if you'd thought at all. You had her down as a stock figure, the housekeeper and country wife. As you prepare for bed you'll still weigh the last thing she said today, the story about the crows. She was telling you something but you're still not sure what.

The kitchen was reassuring and as it should be. Wood-burning stove, chewed-over rugs on linoleum, a pulley with drying clothes hoisted up by the ceiling, microwave and the usual collection of terrible children's drawings mostly in purple and green. Underlying animal smell, dog and cat with a hint of guinea-pig from the cage in the corner.

The kids are round at their pals, Annie Tat says. Tat's away for his classes, so it's you and me. Put on the kettle, I'll just be a minute.

Annie crosses the kitchen to switch on the radio, glances then goes out the door opposite.

Leaning to fill the kettle, she hears another door close quietly. She twists the tap and finds herself thinking of that last appraising glance. Something about the way Annie left the room. The unnecessary radio. The insistence she came in for tea. Above all, the tell-tale forking quiver at the back of her knees.

She noisily filled the kettle, clunked it on the stove then edged out through the yellow door. A hallway, a rug, a child's anorak lying on the floor. Black binoculars hung from a brass hook. A small table in the corner and a white telephone lead running round a closed door. A faint murmur of Annie Tat's voice. She put her head to the door but still couldn't hear enough.

She pushed open the door. Annie's head came up, she stopped speaking. Left hand cupped over the mouthpiece.

Sorry. I was looking for the loo.

First door up the stair, dear.

She went loudly up the stair, humming to herself. She'd not caught a word Annie had said but she was sure it was a man she'd been speaking to. Something about the way she sat, and her tone of voice. It's one of those evident things.

She had her pee, ran the tap and eased the frosted window up. The back of the house looked past Ballantyne's up the grazing land towards the moor. The dyke, just a darker wavy line at this distance. Follow it along to the cottage. Then the woods. And through the woods and across the burn, out of sight round the corner, the big house where Elliot sat twitching, hugging his Not Proven like a cancer in his chest, waiting for news from his spies. And Tat's in the city, so . . . So it's Annie on spy duty today.

She eased the window down, turned off the tap and clumped down the stairs.

She looks back smiling at Annie Tat then sieves more tea through the cake crumbs. The two women talk in the cluttered cosy kitchen. They talk about the cold and the wet.

My Tat says there'll be a change soon, maybe an early spring after a last frost if you're staying that long.

I've no plans but I'm pleased Sir Simon seems to be letting me stay a while.

You have some work to do here?

Some loose ends to tie up.

So this is a sentimental journey?

Yes, you could say that.

And will you be calling on Elliot?

I will have that cigarette, thank you. She lights up and smoke rises between them. I've no plans at the moment, beyond recovering myself.

Annie dips her cake in tea and sucks.

Have you been unwell, dear?

My last mother died a few months back. And . . . a close friend emigrated recently.

Annie nods and leans forward. Maybe it's best to make a fresh start like that, she says. Yes, I could fancy emigrating. Leave the past and begin again.

She balances her cigarette on the ashtray's rim and watches the smoke unkink.

That's what David says. Just walk away and start again.

Does he, now? But the estate will surely be his soon enough.

I don't think he wants it. I mean, would you?

Me and Tat? Annie leans back and laughs loudly. She seems to shake with laughter but the cup in her hand is entirely steady. More grief than it's worth, dear. There's not much left but the fishing and that's on the slide. And the big house is falling apart. She pauses, fills her mouth with cake. You'll see if you come visit sometime.

I might if I was asked.

I could mention it to himself. Elliot doesn't see many folk, but in your case . . .

She drinks more tea and puts up a cloud of smoke and lets it pass.

So Tat works as factor and you're the housekeeper?

More or less, ever since the kids were old enough to go to nursery, like I said.

You do all the cooking and cleaning for that house – must be a lot of work.

Part-time, dear, and my duties are . . . flexible.

She watches as Annie gets up for more tea, and sees from a fluidity of movement that the woman's actually quite young. Maybe only ten years older than herself. Plumpness doesn't necessarily mean soft nor in any way past it. At the back of her head something more ratchets into place, a distant rumble as the grinding-stones spin.

I'm sure they are, she says. This tea's running through me.

Out in the hallway she lifts the binoculars from the hook and clumps up the stair. She opens the bathroom window. Now the cottage is quite clear. So too is the car parked on the track

126

outside it. And now in the shaky binocular circles, an impression of grey, hesitating at her door. The door opens, the man ducks inside.

She leans on the window sill and considers. Sim Elliot himself, seen first through a window at the big house, now through these glasses. Next time it will be face to face.

She slides the window down, flushes the loo and goes downstairs.

Annie Tat pours more bog-brown tea. With a glance to her guest, she adds a slug of whisky to both mugs. She talks about money for a while, about how it's a bits-and-pieces economy these days. Like Tat has his carving hobby, makes some cash from that when he can bring himself to sell a piece. Sir Simon has a wee business up in Edinburgh, a share in some rented properties, a framing business. And what about yourself, Marnie?

Bits and pieces, she says. Just like you say. Sometimes I cook, sometimes I nurse people, but mostly I develop storylines.

They both look at the last piece of cake. Annie divides it with a knife, clean and decisive. Hands it directly to her. Their fingers touch for a moment.

David will take the estate when it comes to it, Annie says. His father never wanted it either but once his dad died early . . .

They seem an unlucky family. Always dying early.

Annie doesn't quite glance at her watch as she swings her feet up across the chair and passes over another cigarette.

Bad hearts and bad luck, dear. Anyway, the estate's not something to sell or give away. You're a Lauder, you'll understand that.

I don't exactly come from the land-owning classes.

Your mother did. What d'you think she was getting away from, coming here with her caravan and her man?

She lights up and tries not to cough.

She and Patrick lived in a caravan before the cottage?

Annie Tat opens her mouth and lets out three perfect zeroes. Well I don't know, she says. It was all before I came here. Annie chaps her cup into its saucer. It's a right pity when you think of it, she says. If Sir Simon hadn't already been married when they met, he and Jinny could have finally ended the whole thing. United the families, eh? All that 'at feud' rubbish meant nothing to them, it doesn't to anyone these days, does it?

You'd have to have a very long memory, that's for sure.

Of course whoever David marries will share the estate. Annie stubs out her cigarette and swings her legs down off the settee. He did say he's getting married, dear?

All the time.

He does seem set on the lass, doesn't he? She's arriving any day. Ah well, there you go.

The two women look at each other.

*

Sim Elliot stood at the Crawhill doorway, waiting till he could breathe properly again, resting his forehead on the lintel. He'd once nearly knocked himself out on this, hurrying to see Jinny. She'd summoned him to the bridge and told him over the roar of the waters she was so low she wanted to die. Perhaps it's hormonal, after the baby, she added. But I must talk to you again soon. I can't hold on much longer. And of course he'd come next day, so het up with anxiety, excitement, and some residual anger from when she'd ended the affair and he'd almost got resigned to it and now she'd called him again, that he pushed open the door and forgot to duck. Bam! A great dunt on the head and the world black and white for a minute.

That was how they'd started again. A dreich afternoon, Patrick working or drunk at the hotel in the village, the bairn sleeping in the cot by the stove. This same stove, same smell of coal and woodsmoke and . . . lavender. After she'd cradled his head, them both laughing and crying, more despairing than glad. In the bedroom, not on the bed but pulling blankets onto the floor by the window as though that softened the betrayal. The shock of her belly on his after nigh two years.

He went through to the bedroom, pushed the door open. The bed had been against the wall on the right. This woman who said she's Marnie had only a mattress on bare floorboards but it was right under the window, exactly where Jinny's head had rolled from side to side as she cried out. He'd felt her roughened soles scraping on his thighs as she'd pulled him deeper. It was a wonder the wee girl had slept through it, if in fact she did. And now it seems she's come back.

He stared at the duvet rumpled on the mattress. *I've got you. Don't worry, I've got you.* And then five minutes of unrecoverable peace lying like cooling meteors in the rough blankets with fading memories of their flight. And then the rain on the window, checking of the watch, the awfulness starting again. The alibi. The cover story for the welt across his forehead. Washing away guilt at the kitchen sink, rinsing their hands, drying on the towel. *Part of me will always be here,* she'd said.

He sat heavily on the mattress. The chintz settee had been here. The planks on bricks that held her and Patrick's books. The little altar for the plaster Buddha and brass incense-stick holder. A smell of lavender. Dear God.

He flipped through the books by the bed. Border histories. Border families. Accounts of the reivers, their stratagems, their brutality, boldness and queer honour. All tacky and bent from much reading, the tops of pages folded back.

> ELLIOT: One of the largest, most powerful and most quarrelsome families, with bases on both sides of the Border, the despair of the Wardens of the Marches. Quick-tempered, passionate and cunning, bold yet capable of being underhand when they judged it necessary, the Elliots were born for the reiving life. When things were quiet, they could be depended on to stir up action and, in the phrase, *shake loose the Border!*

The last phrase had been underlined three times. He put the book back carefully on the pile. *The lass has been doing her homework.*

I've done nothing so right and wrong as this, Jinny whispered.

Why do they call it falling when it feels like soaring? he'd replied, still dreamy.

Her giggle. *Well I'm sore. Oh, why are our jokes so sad? What happens now?*

Then he saw the little photo frame on the floor in the shadow of the mattress. Carried it to the window, smooth and cool in his palm. Tilted it to the light. Jinny. Wee Davy. Marnie. Outside the cottage, summer, a foolish impromptu picnic. Her crappit little camera. *I want something to remind me.*

She is smiling across at him as she crosses from light into shade. She looks so present yet so fugitive. The toddler is pushing herself up from the ground, not looking at him. She's turning towards David who's waving a plastic sword. He's grinning, pleased with something, but she is so serious. Marnie Lauder aged two, rising between him and Jinny.

He'd never thought to see this photo again. From all their times together which crowd his mind of late, this is the only evidence he has of her apart from the one scrawled note. Patrick must have kept it when the cottage was cleared before the trial. After his death it must have been passed on to the child in care.

He put the photo down, trying to reproduce the angle at which it had sat. Think, man. Work out what she can know. What she believes she knows. What she's here for. If it's to look him up, she's taking the long way round the mountain. Maybe she just wants a free place to stay. She can have it, because this must be Marnie all right, she can have whatever she asks for, though he'd be disappointed if it's just more money. For years he's been waiting, hoping, dreading. He's imagined a dozen ways in which she'd reappear to accuse, to embrace, to sit opposite him and talk through Jinny's mouth and eyes . . .

But her just arriving at the cottage then sitting there doing nothing, not even giving her right name at first, that squeezes his stomach so tight and triggers the zig-zag jag across his chest.

He glanced out the window to check she wasn't coming up the fields towards the cottage, then hurried back through to the kitchen. He found the plates as he knew he would. That's it, then. It's her all right. He just glanced at the top plate, it was the third one, the one of intrigues and ambush and a rare city scene. He remembered it well enough, though Jinny never liked to take the plates out often. *They're not to be played with, Simon.*

Then he couldn't breathe in that room and had to get out. Crack on his forehead, the world went black and white a moment. God damn it. Damn these repetitions. But this time there's no Jinny to laugh and cradle his head. Her lips rising to him, white teeth and eyes closing, both their eyes closing as if that would stop it. If it hadn't been for that crack on the head, they might never have started again. She might be living yet.

He hurried out shaking water from his eyes, clicked the padlock and made for his car and the safety of home.

*

Tat in the city – on fire, in heat, bright hard grey eyes chapping like a flint off the eyes he meets, looking for a spark. He comes from one place he knows, where his name could be Kevin, and sets off for another where he's Ian.

Charcoal makes the cleanest blaze. For all its darkness, there'd be no stoor at all, no residue, just pure heat.

Whisky is fine but couthy – I'll take a dram with Elliot but never touch it here. In this place I experiment among firewaters. This evening it's tequila slammers with my forcie friends, banged down on the formica then down my thrapple mixed with lights and laughter and a bitter cheroot. Catching an eye here and there, the promise offered in a wide-set mouth or hurdies leant forward at the chair's edge. I stick the promise behind my ear like a smoke for later as we spill out onto the street, well lit, and head for the action of the evening.

And if I stay away for months on end, it's not because I'm fickle. It's because I love it too much, this illdeedie stirring in my belly, this hunger I see in folks' eyes at the onset of Saturday evening as we step onto the street, me and half a dozen braw callants, and a sprinkling of hoors like early stars already coming out above where the footbridge crosses the canal, and sweet guff blowing from the breweries as we head into the random trysts of the night.

Annie Tat glanced at her watch and picked up the tea things. She must get on, the kids would be back soon.

This carving you said Tat does – could I have a look?

I don't see why not. She sort of laughed. No big secrets here. Thanks.

She followed Annie up the stairs past the bathroom. A low brown door, more stairs up into an attic workshop. The dormer windows looked straight up to Crawhill Cottage and the moor behind. Another pair of binoculars on the window-shelf. A brass telescope on a stand in the corner. Likes to look, Tat does.

A long trestle work-table in front of the window. Small heavy work-bench with a vice off to the side. An expensive adjustable chair on rollers for moving between the two. Two racks of knives with bone handles, some of them so small. Some curved, some straight, some pointed. All very sharp. Tiny jars of paints. Rasps, files and emery paper. Brushes, tweezers. Everything in order. A pile of exhibition catalogues. Tat's secret world.

She picked up a catalogue as Annie hovered. Sniffed it, opened the contents page. Found his name third down and turned to it. Full colour photos, quality art printing.

Kevin Tattersall brings a unique style to his mastery of quirky detail. He specialises in powerful imaginary animals and grotesque, sometimes erotic, spirits and hobgoblins of the Borderland.

At a glance they were gorgeous and indeed grotesque. Annie shifted beside her.

It's called netsuke, she said.

I thought that was something the Japanese ate.

This is simpler than me explaining it, Annie said, and held out another catalogue.

Netsuke: the Japanese craft of carved toggles, originally for the cords by which money pouch, pipe case, medicine case, writing set etc, hung from the girdle (eboni) of the kimono. (The kimono has no pockets.)

*Netsuke are roughly thumb-sized and carved most commonly in wood,
bone and ivory, though sometimes in jade and other semi-precious stones.
Further decoration by stain and lacquer, paint and inlays, is permissible –
for uniquely in Japanese art, there are no clear rules or conventions govern-
ing netsuke. Designs include mythological, legendary, historical, contempo-
rary and satirical motifs. Katabori are figure-carved netsuke. Birds and
insects are common too, along with hedgehogs, mice, grasshoppers, rabbits,
crows. Also mythical beasts and quasi-supernatural spirits.*

*In Europe there is now a small but dedicated band of practitioners and
collectors. The finest netsuke are expensive – gram for gram, nearly as costly
as gold . . .*

Sounds like one for the obsessives.

There you have it, dear, Annie replied. Still, it keeps him out
of mischief and I dare say he's very good at it.

Arranged on a black velvet cloth in the corner ledge were
half a dozen miniatures.

May I?

Annie looked doubtful.

I suppose.

She picked up the nearest and held it to the light. Turned it
round. It was cool and rough and perfect in her hand, roughly
the size of her thumb. Bone, she thought. A weasel, perhaps,
emerging from rosehips. This one was a hawk's beak jerking
after a rabbit twisting away in undergrowth, cold and slip-
pery. Here, on top of an ivory stump a beast that never was
crouched like a guardian or a bad conscience. Delicate silver
inlay, all the eyes were tiny rubies.

This is beautiful.

She looked at it one more time then put it down exactly as
she'd found it. She picked up a stained ivory one that reminded her of a chess piece. A rook you might say, except the long
heavy-duty beak and grey pate were all too familiar. She
pushed away the dying sheep, the crunch of rock into bone,
and ran her thumb over the corbie piece. Like all the others it
had a hole bored through it for the cord. The hole went
through the heart. Witty, perhaps. There was something about
all these pieces, something strange and glittery and wounded
. . . She stood silent a moment, trying to feel her way into Tat's
world, it might come in useful.

I must be getting on, dear, Annie said.

Yes of course. On the way down the stairs she asked, How on earth did Tat get into netsuke?

Annie stopped, holding the banister with both hands. Oh, Jinny, I think. Tat said she had one hanging in the window of the cara – I mean the cottage. Her mum had been out East . . . You don't know much about your family, do you?

Thumps and shouts downstairs. John and Laura back and starving. Both had thin brown hair in pudding-bowl cuts and Tat's pale eyes. They seemed unburdened and natural and Annie reverted to country-mum mode.

She stood by the doorstep, in a hurry for the off, made uneasy by happy families.

Do the craws bother you? Annie asked. I couldn't be living with that din all the time.

I like it, she replied. It must be one of the first things I ever heard.

Is that right? Annie stood with hands on her hips, looking up the fields towards the cottage. They're very intelligent, you know.

Mm, I suppose. Thanks for tea and the lift.

Yes, I came round the corner the other week and saw a flock of craws fly across the road and into a tree. On the road was a dead rabbit, and lying beside it was a crow. They must have been run over, I thought at first.

Both of them? Not very likely.

Exactly.

Poisoned, then. The rabbit must have been poisoned and the crow ate some.

I'll tell you what happened. The craws had a good long look, peering and jooking and cawing. Then of a sudden, a clap of the wings and they're off.

That's intelligent of them, she said, and made to go.

That's what I thought, Annie said. She put one hand up on the door frame to block the passage. Then when they'd gone the craw on the road jumped up and went back to tearing away at the dead rabbit.

Now that *is* intelligent.

Learn something every day, don't you, Annie said. I'd keep it in mind.

She nodded like nothing special had been said. Thanked Annie again for the lift and the tea. Said cheerio to the kids and cut up between Smiler Ballantyne's barns before the blood came back to her face.

She yomped up through the tussocks, muttering under her breath. She sang the ballad where one sister drowns the younger and bonnier one. *The Banks of Binoorie*. The drowning sister, who like Ophelia seems to take an awful long time to sink, begs to be rescued. *Give me your hand. Sister o sister, but give me your glove* . . . But she is younger and bonnier and has the man, so the elder sister turns away and lets the water do its work.

The song is remorseless, wicked, bleak and beautiful. She sang it through twice and felt better. Annie Tat was no pushover but she'd over-played her hand. And Tat's netsuke . . . She came up loudly across the fields in the brief gloaming, pushed open the gate and went up the path. The padlock and chain were back in place. She picked the lock with her clasp pin and went in.

The air had been subtly displaced. A faint sweet earthiness that hadn't been there before. She checked the plates, wondering if Elliot had noticed the missing broken one, the pieces still in the carrier bag under the sink. That'll give him something to think about.

She went through to the bedroom and knelt by the bed. No doubt he'd held the photo in his hand. She wondered if it had shaken. He'd called secretly when he knew she was away, he'd left no note – yes, she had him on the run. She reached under the mattress and felt for her journal. If he'd found and read it, her future here had a sudden ending. It was still there, felt undisturbed.

> *But you were fair and I was thin*
> *So you'll droon in the dams of Binoorie-o.*

In the ballads, that was motivation enough.

*

135

The posters we pass tell me to Just Say No. We laugh and carry on. I was thinking whiles we hurried through the streets with the fire in us how fine it is to be burned like this and be delivered of that scunner, choice. I can't lay a hand of judgement on Elliot and Jinny. What they were about was wrong but when I surprised them that first time how their eyes shone. And I saw it in the eyes of the lassie in Crawhill. May be she saw it in mine.

Later I'll not feel so grand and canty, but right now I'm up for the whole clamjamferie. For I've the key to the flat in my hand, and my click sliding a fist into the pooch of my breeks even as we climbed the tenement stair.

My need leans back against the door, grinning cockily.

So what's in the other room, Kev?

Never you mind.

My affliction rattles the handle then gives up.

Got a drink in here, my man?

I find the bottle and pour two shots, my hand dead steady yet. I never hurry this sulphurous moment. This is the best, the last drawn pause before the rammie and the tummle.

Bottoms up.

That'll be right.

My curse drinks with one hand, winks and puts the other straight to my crotch, feels around and squeezes exactly where. They aye ken what I'm about. I back against the wall, my knees shaking as my click undoes the first buttons – my craving, my tart, my fine rough justice.

*

For those who lived around the Borderline, 'at feud' was a most deadly state of affairs. It could start with the stealing of a horse, an accusation of cheating at cards or in love, and quickly become an implacable vendetta between families, one of quite Sicilian longevity and ferocity. For the argument was extended beyond the guilty party to include his entire family and descendants, and pursuit of this vengeance – and violent reprisal for it – by man or woman was considered a matter of honour, almost a sacred duty.

Such quarrels could go on for generations – as between the Maxwells and Johnstones, the Scotts and Kerrs, Grahames and Irvines, the Elliots and almost every name either side of the Border. Sometimes the feud would die down for a generation then, like a below-ground fire in a peat bank, break out again into the light of day.

'At feud' was ended, if it ever really ends, with Union – the union of crowns or the union of marriage . . .

I put down my book and in a daze look round this little room. It's late, late, the time of strange voices on the radio. Woods and wild seas are silent and all good citizens are in bed. Only weasel, owl, lover do not rest. The plates are full of need tonight, or perhaps it is me – so hard to know just where that border lies.

Soon I'll to bed and take myself in hand till sleep comes. I do not think Sim Elliot will sleep well, not once he's phoned Annie Tat and he's learned of our conversations and my visit to the newspaper office.

Into my head slides an image of Elliot pricking through the trees behind the point of his shaking torch. He's heading on down towards Ballantyne's. He'd be going to see Annie. Yes of course, Tat's away in the city, and he doesn't want David to hear the Land-Rover. That's how the story-line goes. So, yes, he's walking, taking the short cut through the forest and over the bridge. That would be hard on him. His need must be great.

He wouldn't pause in the middle of the brig though his head yawns wide as the night and the spray blows upwards, dimming his torch. He would think of Jinny and stare straight ahead as he clutches the rail and inches along the slimy planking. He doesn't believe in ghosts, he would tell himself that, though his breath hisses with each step like a sword being drawn from its sheath.

You cross your legs, uncross, improve your posture but soon enough it returns to its bad old ways. You tilt the plate a little and see yourself reflected back. In this world what you see is what you are. You tilt again and see Elliot on this side of the bridge, coming your way with white torch juddering.

Time to lie down and take yourself in hand.

*

David wakes in the bedroom where he was once a child. The ache is back in his right leg again, above the knee. It could just be from that stupid struggle with Marnie on the muir, but it feels deep in the bone. At this time of night, it feels like bone cancer.

He turns on his left side and tries to think about something else. They say thinking about cancer lets it in. Think about Jo. What would she be wearing? He's marrying a woman when he doesn't know what she wears in bed, if she sleeps on her back or front or side. He knows her entire medical history – the sexual he opted not to hear too much about – but he doesn't know how she sleeps.

He sees Marnie, lying under the duvet on the mattress on the floor. Her shape is stretched out long, one arm extended past her head as though swimming side-stroke. He can lean in to kiss her neck, settle in at the curve of her back and kiss the neck by the dark hairline, smell the faint lavender and feel more certain about this than anything ever.

He turns onto his other side, sweating and sick. At this superstitious hour of night, with the bone-cancer ache in his leg like a weight pulling him down into his grave, for a moment he feels Marnie is doing this. She believes she can project herself. She believes people constantly pick up each other's desires and thoughts, and think them their own. Spook. A world of invisible forces, processes, powers, hauntings.

He turns again, his erection rising as though some mouth was already tugging at it. He must not think about that. He is sinning in his heart. This is ridiculous. He's being given oral sex by some succubus. Sick mediaeval claptrap. There is no kingdom of the invisible. Except one. Why only one?

138

The quiet voice is clear, mocking, high: *In Scarlet Town where I was born . . .*

He jerks onto his back and opens his eyes into the darkness, his heart thrashing in his chest. Marnie's voice, clear as waking.

Then, very quietly, *There was a fair maid dwelling,* then her laughter, not unkind, just sharing the joke she's played on him. He turns his head to the sound. She's actually in the room, by the open window, looking at him and raising a glass of water to her lips. She has her cloak on over jeans and sweater, her feet are bare. She toasts him and raises a dark eyebrow like a tilting wing.

So, my Lord Elliot . . .

Cut it, he says. Cut it out. How the hell did you get in?

Through the window, how do you think?

She steps towards him. The soft thud of her feet on the wooden floorboards. She has weight, this is no spirit and no dream. With each footfall the ache in his leg is worse, his desire closer, his death more imminent. He falls onto the floor in a twist of shroud sheets.

When Annie Tat comes to make up his bed again, the way she did when he was a feverish child, he knows perfectly well where she's come from and what's been happening upstairs. She puts her fingers to her lips, winks. *Wheesht,* she says, *no need to wake up now,* and leaves.

Even as he struggles upright to pray for help, a voice whispers he is only dreaming he is praying and so it doesn't count. His God cannot hear him, the night sky is empty, Spook is coming his way.

*

I threw the duvet off and let myself cool awhile. Always I feel lonely after.

I got up for water, the stone flags cold on my feet. I glanced out the window and nearly dropped my glass for a yellow-white light was going by on the other side of the dyke. The torch bobbled up and for a moment I saw the head of Simon Elliot, his face set and grim as any carving, before the light turned away and headed down towards the Tattersalls'.

Now for the first time since my arrival I'm truly frightened. These were meant to be only imaginings.

The Lovers' Plate (Rose)

Were it not for a similar border – a frieze of hawthorn and bramble, birds, dogs, beech trees, leaping fish – at first you might think these next two plates come from a different set altogether. What colour remains in them is pale rose and red, not green and blue. They're not numbered on the back. No weapons here, no hanged man, no burning towers nor mounted riders. They are perhaps more lyrical. There's secrecy but no death, not yet.

You think of this pair as the Lovers' Plates. For it isn't pain that contorts and spreads these bodies so. You may feel that old heat rising as you dream over them, for some of these scenes though sketchy are explicit. You do not think that is a red squirrel he's feeding by hand in her lap. She could be lowering her head to nibble from a bunch of fruit, but on the whole you doubt it.

She jumps up, breathes on the window and writes her name against the valley below. These plates are near four hundred years old and so is their story, but the lovers that pass through her today are the last generations, very close to home.

The windows rattle like a drum roll. The wind is high this morning, blowing one weather out, bringing a new one in. She reckons spring will be here in a matter of days, and wonders if she'll be here to see it.

She clenches her hips, relaxes, holding the glow inside as she sits again. What goes on in these plates is quite sickening as well as quickening her breath.

There's treachery and betrayal aplenty here, frequent enough to make it impossible for her to always blame the man. She can see the woman standing in a clearing of mountain ash, arms raised to the sun as she pulls a shift off over her head. Look at what remains of expression there – there may be pride, fearful joy, or self-disgust in that dark twist of her mouth as she stares across at her lover sliding down from his horse, but she doesn't look a victim.

Jinny was young but scarcely a child. She'd been married for two years. She must have wanted this, she must have chosen Elliot.

Down in the valley she sees a tiny figure leave his house, cross the yard holding a stick or a gun more likely. Sun flashes on his binoculars, then he's into a shed. It's tempting to go down and talk to Tat, there's much she needs to know. About the caravan, for a start, and just when the baby came.

But her boundaries are too thin today to talk with anyone real. She could dissolve in conversation with anyone but ghosts. She doesn't want to dream up something then look out the window and see it happening. She doesn't want to look up from the plates and see Sim Elliot going by in the night as though she wasn't running the story, the story was running her. As though she were helpless and fated as the others in its grip, held like the bloody stone in David Elliot's ring.

If you play spooky games you must expect to raise the dead.

No, this is coincidence and too much solitude, nothing more. David will not be back and in any case her business isn't with him. So she turns again to the plates, the rosy and the red that must hold her attention now.

In scene after scene she sees the pain of that affair, but worse, she feels the lovers' joy. It reaches her intimate and dizzy-making as a whole summer crushed in one handful of myrtle held to her face and breathed in.

*

In the topmost arc of the first Lovers' Plate a tall young man is bending to tighten the girth of the saddle, one arm hugged around the neck of his horse. You like that arm, it's strong and full of juice. The phrase The morning of the day *drifts in from somewhere.*

His dark head is turned away, pressed to the horse's flank. He hasn't yet seen the woman standing behind him, her hand on the gate leading into the yard. She carries something glinting in her other hand. Her hair is ringleted, her long skirt is green. Bend closer now and see her feet are bare. You catch your breath for you know now who she is, and what bare feet signify.

Something about the way she hesitates suggests they haven't kissed yet, nor even know that they want to. You sit back, close your eyes a moment, still feeling that long forearm wrapped round the horse's neck. You run on four and a half centuries from the story in the plates, then skip back twenty-plus years, and you could be there to see it begin.

Simon Elliot bends in green overalls over the Land-Rover engine, working on loosening the starter motor with a spanner. The angle of his back and his elbows as he reaches for another spanner to lock against the first says to the world *I don't want to be doing this but seeing I am* . . . She closes the gate and crosses the yard quietly, not sure why.

His shoulders tense. Something slips, a clang, a curse *Oh fuckin hell,* and he's nursing his knuckles in under his armpit. He bends silently over his pain, squeezing it in to himself. She sees him nod to himself, feels the breath forced back into his belly. Then he slowly reaches for the dropped spanner and in that gesture she sees everything about him that matters. She sees the pain and his acceptance of it, sees his patience and his disappointment – in himself, the resistant nuts, the uninspiring world, man's estate. As he wipes blood from his knuckles onto the overall, she sees his temper followed by his acceptance of the way things are, and the sadness in that, the lack of consolation. Above all she knows before the thought has even arrived, the way lightning arrives before thunder, she knows that he has not ceased to be alone. He has never been comforted and yearns to be and does not expect to be. Though he has a child, his life hasn't really started and may never. This is what he's struggling with.

He settles again over the engine. The sunlight is yellow in the yard, the day hot and still. The shadow cast by the barn falls across her feet, her shadow falls across his arms. His head turns.

Do you need a hand, Simon?

Jinny! He smiles, his dark eyes radiant. Heh, right now I need a mechanic of genius.

Whatever they say now is just grit on a threaded bolt. It will only delay the giving way, the unlocking. She takes his hand, the bloody oily one, shaking slightly with pain or something.

She looks at it more closely. The skin's scraped back and when she wipes away blood there's a deep notch at the side of his ring knuckle.

When did you last have a tetanus jab?

When I took over the estate.

She nods. That was wise. Better clean this up though.

And because the way she says it is not bossy or reproachful like Fiona but just a simple concern, he nods, puts down the other spanner, reclaims his hand and speaks.

If you're looking for Fi, she's in town.

She shakes her head. Patrick's away at the tree-planting so I've been busy about the caravan, she says. Thought you might like this. Elderflower. She holds out a cloudy bottle. It's still a bit young, but it's got a fizz to it.

Simon Elliot puts his head on one side and grins. So let's have a go at it afore it gets any older.

As they cross the yard together she seems so at home he understands better that she belongs with something like this too. The way she sidesteps horse-shit, rests her hand on the pile of fertiliser sacks as they turn the corner, looks up instinctively for the martins' nests in the eaves of the barn. This is her world, for all that she was brought up in the suburbs of the South. The big house and the estate have been as long in her family as his. They have already talked about this and their families' history of feud. She has already warned him not to stand in front of her on Lauder Brig in case her ancestors take her over. And he has informed her – on the lawn, as Fiona passed the sandwiches and Patrick muttered that property wasn't just theft it was also boring – that her people had taken the Elliot lands by treachery so she should stay away from high places . . .

She looks up at him, sparking flecks in her eyes, pupils wide and black despite the brilliance of the day. It would be so natural, so human to drop his hand onto the curve of her hip-bone under the long green cotton skirt. But he isn't human, he is a position and a place. He is Sir Simon Elliot, a married man and father and minor landowner, and what he wants doesn't come into it. He has been told that all his life and he believes it. Without that he fears what he would be.

She steps sideways, picks up a rusty bolt from the dust, bowls it overarm into the long grass then comes back to him again. He glances at her and sees through her skitteryness and almost frantic light-heartedness. He sees she is an untethered balloon. She is looking for something binding and weighty, and Patrick isn't it. Patrick just goes along with her. She's still alone.

Then she passes her hand over his and gently rubs away the blood again.

That must hurt, she says. Let me fix it.

If he had said something, the moment might have been disarmed. Some kind of repartee, or a politeness appropriate to his class, even a flirtation would have unmade it. But he was speechless and she said nothing either as he opened the back door to her and they ducked out of the glare into the cool dim scullery.

*

The images and voices follow each other like one gust of wind pushed aside by another. You lie open, dreaming, and feel them blow through you. You see Sim Elliot turn in his morning bed and reach for his secret journal. You feel the pulse in his wrists, sense the quickening of his heart as he journeys to meet Jinny again. It is as though you and he have become porous to each other, the way lovers do in their brief season, till you do not know what's his and what is yours.

You look up quickly and in the blinking almost see Jinny standing at the kitchen sink. Her long hennaed hair – only a man could think that copper-red natural – her calm wide eyes as she holds her hands out either side, palm up as though she was balancing something not visible to you. You shake your head and she's gone, her hair becomes the red dish towel at the window's edge, and you are puzzled because she did not seem angry. She was demanding nothing. She seemed content at the way things are developing.

You shrug and return to your story, for you are used to these flickers at the edge of your eyes and mind – some foolish, some murderous, some obscene. You assume this happens to most people but we choose not to mention it, and rightly, for it's best not to dwell on them.

*Lay yourself open again to the voices of the lovers' season. What-
ever direction they come from, they are all one wind coming from the
same place blowing over the same land, and each raises the hair from
your skull.*

It happens whiles at the netsuke, when my blade speirs out
what manner of man or beast is emerging before it's clear to
me. I blink a few times then let my hands carry on and only
later do I see what's shaping here. So it was the first time I
clapped eyes on Elliot and Jinny together.

I was lying up in the hay-byre ahint the big house, nursing a
bottle of skoosh Fiona had put my way afore she went off in
the car with wee Davy for the shopping. The last thing I saw
was the bairn's anxious blue een as the car rounded the house
and was away.

Like a pup-dog to its master that summer I liked to keep Elliot in eye-shot wherever I stravaiged. I went to find him in the
yard, hoping he might have time to work with me on the tree-
house, or come down to the river to spy out the trout or even
take a dook in the Ruickle pool for the day was that hot. But he
looked up from the Land-Rover and said he'd promised Fi
he'd get it sorted that morn. But we'd go onto the muir and
count the whaups' nests in the afternoon.

So I climbed up among the bales where I could see him, dug
a nest and opened the fizz. The day was flat calm but buzzing
a summer silence. A cushie-doo was moaning in the sauchs
down by, and up through the roof-slats a laverock was bur-
bling like a leaky spigot. Elliot had been learning me the right
names of the birds, beasts and fish thereabouts. He spoke
more stiff and proper in those days, and he aye looked surprised when the Scots word came from his mouth, like he'd
turned on a tap and it had run not water but rust and blood.

I footered about some in the scratchy hay. Hidden up there
I had some magazines with photos of lassies' bubbies, but in
truth they were beginning to deave and bore me. I got more
het shinning up the poles of the byre and feeling the rub
atween my legs. I needed to see it for real. The week afore –
and it makes me black-ashamed yet to mind it – I'd crept along
the passage to keek through the bathroom keyhole and see

Aunt Fiona strip for her bath. Yon was a let-down, just a swift keek as she turned away, and I was more affrontit than aroused. I needed to see the real whole hough-magandie. I had to see Elliot go in.

So I was full of fizz and fidget that day, feeling keisty as I rolled on my belly and saw Jinny Lauder come in the gate. Elliot hadn't seen her, being bent over the engine, but I saw how she paused there, one hand on the gate and the hot breeze stirring her skirt about her shins. I saw how she saw him, the man entire. The virr and the sorrow, gentleness and the sonsie humour that peeked out once in a while from the laird's part he was born to. Her red head dipped then came up like a chaffie's down by the linn, and she came silently across the yard towards him.

I learned early how to watch well, and the trick isn't in the eyes. It's in the mind which needs be blank and open, without opinion. Then you can see under the surface, then you hear behind the clash and babble. I learned that in the city among the family I never wanted to go back to, and dodged many a beating that way. So I watched the angles of her arms by his, the way his head turned, the shift of his hurdies and in response her small neat arse back off then sway forward again.

I kent fine who Jinny was. I'd spied out her and her man's caravan in the trees. She'd waved to me across the river and I'd taken a redder and run off. Her and Patrick had been twice to the big house and I'd kept hid. The second time they'd all sat out on the grass with Davy toddling about. There was laughter and some crack, and she had taken off her shoes and chased after the laddie bare-foot.

I'd watched like my life hung by it. I saw the stiffness in Aunt Fi but also that she was glad of company. I saw the black-avised near-silence of Patrick as Jinny skittered about like a midge. I saw for the first time Sir Simon with a cigarette at his lips and how Fiona keeked at him then. I saw Jinny's hand go down to David and him hesitate then grip her fingers tight. For a moment I'd seen strings run between them all, crossed and looping, like a skeelie spider was at work.

Now her man was away at the tree-planting and she was in our yard. I could hear the laughter but not the words. He leaned back against the bonnet and fankled up his sleeve, keeked sideways at her then away as she came closer to look at his bloody hand. Then the two of them crossed the yard through bits of straw like splintered sunlight, the stoor kicking up from their feet. He was about to go first through the open scullery door then paused and stood aside for her. He said something and she went in first and his arm came up behind her, and though there was no touch or music it was like at the dancing as he followed her on.

I gave them a few minutes as I pondered the matter. I looked round at the dale, the river, the road, the high riding of the Border hills that clasped us fast and siccur. I never wanted to go home. I wanted to bide on here, close to Sim Elliot, the only man who had ever given me time and tenderness. Now this new lassie, this hippie Auntie Fi cried her, had brought some new business. It was the top of summer, soon I'd be sent home to the city, back to the old battlefield. There must be a way to make them keep me here.

I slid from the barn and came in very douce. Truth is, I kent before the kenning. I kent afore they did.

They were laughing over a pile of records. Square, she said, you're so square. And he looked gey pleased though he pretended not to be, and then together they moved apart as they saw me.

Tat, this is Jinny. She's staying in the caravan across the river.

The tall man, the lively woman, the sweating youth, stand in the sitting room of wood panel and sun-worn chintz covers. She is shaking the boy's hand but they're both looking to the man standing at the wide-open window as though something were now up to him.

Half-way to his mouth, his glass has stalled. Life has ceased to be something that just happens to him. The hot breeze spreads elderflower through the room, sweet and perishable, and Sim Elliot feels as though he is standing at the top of a great drop with untried wings strapped to his back.

Long skirt ragged and stoorie at the hem, her hair shivering and springy as she held out her hand to me though I was just a laddie. I feel yet her fingers slide into my sweating palm and run along my life-line. I see her eyes light on me and open wider as though I was yet another welcome by-blow of the day, as though I would bring her only good. Now in my long dwams at the work-bench I smell above the acrid scorch of solder a calming whiff of lavender, or the earthy patchouli that folks used then to hide the guff of hashish beneath a harmless imitation, in the way we might hide growing love beneath jokes and easy friendliness, and for all that I smile yet.

I ken, I said. Are you a gypsy woman? Are you staying?

That depends on his Lordship, she said. Elliot grunted but didn't disagree. Then she prised my fingers open and asked for a keek at my hand. If she'd asked me to stick it in the oven I'd have done it.

Well, Tat, I see you're not going far from here in this life. She tickled her nail along my life-line. Any travelling you do will be inside, and I see loads of it.

Her eyes were the shifting green-grey of hazel twigs at just this time of year, and a wind blew straight through them from her to me.

*

Simon Elliot lies on his side in bed with the sun blinding on the pages of his old secret journal. *I regret everything except these hours.* He looks up, thinking he has heard Jinny's voice inside again the way he used to, and the room is faint and silent and insubstantial.

She's dead for certain, he thinks, but she does not sleep. She stirs red-gold in my mind each time I pass through the trees by the river. She is wide-awake in dreams where I lie sweating. She flutters these mornings between my ribs like a goldfish. Patrick's long dead and all, but he's well rotted in the acid soil. No one seems to hear from him and maybe that's what he wanted by the end: silence. But Jinny was burned and her ashes shaken over the Liddie Falls to drift into the piny woods. Perhaps that's why she gets about the world more . . .

Simon Elliot screws his knuckles into his eyes till black spots explode, then turns a page to meet her again in a day long dead and living yet.

She stepped quickly from the trees beyond the village and into my car. Warm day, a polka-dot dress, gym shoes, arms brown where her freckles grew that summer. There was a drive, my hands on the wheel and hers on her lap, our hips shifting as we tried not to look or be seen looking as our voices entwined. She was talking about family rows as we drove through the heart of the debatable lands. *Some days I regret everything except, perhaps, being born*, she said of a sudden, and I had to leave the car to walk in tears up and down by the road. Summer at the roadside with hawthorn-stink thick and sickly as she walked close by me but we still didn't touch.

For this was the day of being sensible. This was the day we'd agreed we had to stop while stopping was still possible. She recited again the arithmetic: once is a one-off. It's wrong but excusable, just. The second time is to check the first time wasn't a fluke. It's stupid but understandable. But one more time and you're having an affair, and that's just sordid and predictable. And destructive. Unforgivable. There could be no one more time. Agreed.

We got back in the car and I drove on through the outlaw country till we came out by the pewtery firth, and called into a wee café and bought sandwiches and walked by the flaming gorse that edged the dunes that gave down to the sea. And I was dazed by the pewter light that edged her shoulders as she said she'd thought she believed in free love but this wasn't free. It was costing her everything, including her opinion of herself, and of me. She couldn't be who she thought she was. She'd never been unfaithful before and she didn't like it at all.

And I agreed it was miserable and desperate and over, but our words went one way and we went another like the boats out in the firth moving against the breeze. When she turned to me again, Jinny looked filled out as a sail by an invisible power, and I stood waiting with a certainty I'd never known about anything before as she moved towards me and placed her hands flat on my shirt. I looked down and saw her hands lift and fall on my chest, and as I flattened my hands on the small of her back and felt her hips sway in, she said *You know, desire isn't wrong, only very very painful*. And when we broke from kissing, she stopped being clever and said only what was needed. *Here, now.*

Flat radiant light over empty beach, sea beyond the distant trees above the dunes. Turmoil lies down and lifts her dress. Panic turns and unbuckles my belt. *It's my period, do you mind?* Are you kidding? I may have said that. I hope I did.

At last my weight on her. Beautiful to us both. Oh help.

Marram grass scraping my legs as her hips rise off the sand. Her face over me becomes plastic, I see her flicker as a child, a girl, a woman. I see how she will look when old, and for pity on us all my head dips to her wee breasts. As I suck her sweetness out and she takes me in, a current fizzes round and round, faster and brighter with each sweep. Her words are panted at my ear. *Open your eyes! Look at me!* Her mouth opens, we feel the powder-trail fizzing up our spines and can't speak as something crosses between us like a white diver leaping and I feel my very self go into her. *I've got you, I've got you!* she cries. Then *Don't worry, Sim, don't.*

Simon Elliot lies back on his pillows. He knows the rest by heart. He hears again her murmur in his ear as he turns another page and looks out blankly over the garden where the winter is being blown away: *I regret everything except this hour and anything that comes hereafter.*

Jinny Lauder is dead and not gone. She lies wrecked on the low dunes by the firth wrapped around her lover who rests his head on her sweating shoulder. For she has leapt into him and will never leave as long as he lives and breathes.

Peace for minutes on end. A dog barked above their heads, she wriggled back into her dress as the unseen walker scrunched by.

They dug the hole with their hands on the beach, slow at first then faster and deeper, saying nothing. At first the hole was dry, then water seeped up and the sides began collapsing. They scooped the water out but always it filled up again. The deeper they dug the quicker it filled. Aye, that's life, he said. Shore is, she replied.

She sat back on her heels and laughed till she put her hands up to his face and began to weep into his chest.

That's how she lives still, he thinks as he turns the page. We dug down to a level where there's no separation. She'll seep into the mind of anyone who goes down far enough.

He closes his journal and lies out again on his bed. No matter how often he scoops these memories out, she always comes back. Now someone is living in Crawhill Cottage again. She has the plates, the photo, Tat has seen the clasp with the silver coin at the centre. So it must be Marnie. He's long hoped this day would come when he could see Jinny's only living remnant, and now it's here he's weak and black afraid.

Laughter in the garden comes clear through the open window. He's on his feet at the window to see a woman coming through the bamboo grove towards the house. She stops and stands where Jinny stood but she is not Jinny. She turns and holds her hand out to the man coming up behind her. The man who stops and glares up at the window isn't Patrick but David. He hears a light accented voice.

Hey, you didn't tell me you were loaded!

We're not, his son replies.

So let's go meet the ogre.

It's the first time he's set eyes on his prospective daughter-in-law. She stands hands on hips of her jeans. Thin, too thin, he thinks, for that mouth. Short spiky blonde hair, red-rimmed glasses. He can see the angle of her cheeks and hip-bones. As she looks up he sees her angular hause-banes rise either side of her neck and he shivers.

He moves back from the window, he doesn't need to see any more. She's the wrong woman and he cannot go downstairs yet to greet her for he cannot empty himself of the sand dunes and Jinny's hips rising, the threat of rain and the flat pearly light, her parting lips and shattered eyes and the light over the firth where yellow reeds bustled to wind's change.

As they walk through these woods or lie in the bracken under the wall, give the lovers their season, carried yet in the breeze sifting through the windlestrae. As they drop from sight into the heather like shot grouse, let them breathe in the hollows where the need to be wanted wars with the want to be needless. Let them have their time, for somewhere it lies hoarded yet, and you may run it through your fingers like coins unearthed, tumbling into your heated lap.

The moor was right hot, baked and shrunken that afternoon they first met above the dyke. A shimmer of heat and bugs drummed over the heather-heads, there was a background hum in the earth and air. She wore her husband's jeans, cut ragged above her knees, cinched tight around the waist with a black leather belt. A faded check shirt knotted up. He was trying not to look at her belly-button or the bright coin winking in her buckle as he stumbled, put out his hand and skinned his knuckles on the dyke.

Accident-prone, my Lord Elliot, she murmured.

You know I hate that Sir nonsense, he said.

So why keep the title?

It's not exactly something you can get rid of. He sucked his knuckle and the sun was crushed in his ruby ring by the corner of his mouth.

They didn't touch. Nothing irreversible had happened between them yet. One way was back down to the settled lands, grazed and ordered, what folk mean when they call the Borders pretty, though creepy had always been the word, far as Sim was concerned. Or on their side of the dyke, the open humped moorland, the unaccountable standing stone and the burnt mounds drowning under heather, the wild lands shawled in peat.

I was going for a swim in a lochan on the moor, he said.

Fiona's off with Davy to her county pals.

I got fed-up with making wine and it's too good a day to get stoned, she replied. Patrick's at the pub again.

In those days whenever they opened their mouths they said more than they were saying. He tasted his blood, the sun was crushed in her belt-buckle. She told him the silver coin set there was Roman, an ancestor had dug up a number of them up on the moor in the days when they still cut peats. The others had disappeared with Lauder when Elliot's henchmen had pushed him off the brig.

Nonsense, he said. The man was a notorious drunk and womaniser. He was on his way to see a lassie with some money for her, and he fell because he was pished as usual.

Your lot got our estate by sooking up to Dacre after Flodden.

Aye, and how many did you kill to get it back?

That was marriage not murder, though sometimes it's hard to tell the difference, she said and laughed. Anyway, we lost it again.

It was an old flyting they'd carried on since that first day he'd come down the stairs after watching her from the window, walked blinking into the light knowing he was supposed to get rid of her, and she'd stood in front of him barefoot with Patrick, Fiona holding wee Davy off at the side, held out her hand and said bold as anything *I'm Jinny Lauder, I believe you own my estate – can we park our caravan?* Even Fi had smiled at her nerve, and they all had tea out on the grass, and the caravan was still in the corner of the field with nettles and dockens growing tall about its wheels.

I wonder if there's more treasure up there, he said. I should get one of those metal-detectors.

I heard great-granddad Lauder had a by-blow daughter by an Elliot girl and that's who the coins were for . . .

They were talking about anything as their feet turned them up onto the moorland.

High up there, beyond the grey salmon-pouted lip of Shankheid Pass, past where the heather peters out and moorland studded with the moraine of retreating glaciers becomes so barren even sheep are few, there are no ruins, no habitation visible in any direction. This is the trackless moor.

The man and woman who veer over the horizon seem to be tacking on hot invisible winds. They are still talking. Sweat runs down the fine gingery hairs on her bare arms, his eyes sting with salt. He is trying to explain that life is not a game, that he accepts his responsibilities as husband, father, the owner of the estate. In a few years, unless she chooses to drift on and be a waster, she will know what he means. There comes a time to grow up. That means turning our backs on all the doors we haven't gone through and never will. To make that decision and live with it, he says, takes courage. And courage and sacrifice move him more than anything else.

She rubs her palm over her belly and tacks away from him.

But surely we're born for joy? she says. Otherwise what's all this sacrifice for?

The slope falls away and they come together again in a hollow. Joy? He admits the whole Sixties thing passed him by. Perhaps ten years ago her words made sense. Perhaps he had dreams but he knows now it was fantasy. Now he is an adult, or trying to be. He has put childish things aside. As we must.

He stops then, looks down at his feet as though seeing them for the first time in years, and he doesn't intend the words that come now.

But whatever happened to the things that mattered?

The words leap from a cage he didn't know existed and he is suddenly quite close to tears. She glances at him and for all his size she sees the unconsoled child he once was.

They're still in reach, Sim, she says. If you've the nerve to grasp them.

He explains he is very ordinary. He could never drop out like her. He must accept that nothing extraordinary will happen in his life, unlike his passionate, bloody, devious, reckless ancestors. Sometimes he wishes those times would come again. Something, anything . . . But those times are past, yes? And it's as well they are.

You don't sound very sure.

Don't you ever get scared, Jinny? Are you always brave?

She laughs. Only when I've no alternative. I couldn't bear

college or my family. Visions of years of the straight life ahead. So I grabbed Patrick, told him we had to marry and cut loose, drift till we found the right place. She stops, looks at him. And this is the right place, she says. I don't want to leave now.

They are climbing the far side of the hollow. From up here the breeze tugs a few faded grasses and that is all. Heather is stunted, the peat worn to sandy earth and bedrock. They look back but all signs of that old life have disappeared. Even their names are wearing away as they veer onward. She is beginning to tell him about her mother's death, how it left her beyond fear yet wanting so much . . . Her voice trails away, her feet hesitate then stumble. He sees himself wrap his arms round her small body to keep her from hurt, but of course he does not.

That's when I changed my name back from Nixon to Lauder, she tells him. My mother's people.

And I suppose you want the estate back?

She laughs. I'm no bread-head. Just a bit will do.

How big a bit?

She stops, looks him up and down as if measuring him. Then she flicks her head aside, her tongue peeks over her lower lip as she smiles, and in that moment he knows his life will be wasted if he doesn't kiss her once in it. And he knows he won't so he walks on ahead of her. Her laughter and lightness both he and Fiona have enjoyed, but now he knows she also aches and has sorrows no one can put right, that knowledge runs him through like a lance.

He is walking away but not fast enough. She is level with him now, chewing a dry grass. They seem to be slowing up. The words are running out. She has been haivering something about insects.

Are butterflies insects? she asks. She drops a black caterpillar onto his palm, he feels the crawling tickle travel inside. Or are they related to birds?

He stands back from her, swaying slightly as something rises in his chest. He swallows and it stays down. She looks at him with something like concern. They are standing at the edge of a black tarn that has appeared out of nowhere, one he'll never find again. The bubble expands like marsh gas behind his ribs as her lower lip swells in his sight. He truly believes he might faint.

Don't you know?

I know . . . The bubble rises and burbles like blood over his lips. I know if you don't kiss me my life will be unlived.

She grins. Sure, she says.

Jinny, I mean it.

I said sure, you big daft gowk.

She takes a step forward then tilts up her head to him. He sees it all slow as he lowers his head.

She kisses him. A slow brush of her lips. That was all he wanted, just to have felt her once. But she doesn't step back like she should. Instead he feels the flat of her hands press hard on his back, and her lips begin to suck on his.

They stand swaying at the edge of black water. Then they are kneeling, her small hands working at his belt. He tugs at hers and the coin flies from the buckle. Minutes, slow-time minutes later, after the touching and learning her mouth, his hands down her man's jeans, the soft crackle of her sweating bush, he waits for her to tell him to stop. Surely she will stop this.

Wait a minute, she says. Her fingers grip the head of his cock through his trousers. Her other hand goes into the back pocket of her jeans. Put this on.

He gawps at her. She looks down a moment.

I may be faithless but I'm no daft or donnert.

He blinks at her language then he is passive as she unrolls the condom and settles onto him, her face frowning and intent as she starts to rock.

Close up her eyes have tiny tobacco-coloured threads radiating out. His dark eyes were like the tarn, she said later, mild and bottomless. Somewhere between sky and land her warbling cry ascends in stages like the unseen laverock, higher and higher.

He opens his eyes. She is lying across him, her red hair sticking damp on his shoulder. Her head shifts, her eyes open and look into his. There is no holding anywhere, nothing to be said. Then she reaches down and slowly pulls him out. He notices the scratchy heather on his back, the ant tickling across his leg. Normal service is being resumed. She sits up and looks around.

Gosh, she says. Golly.

What happened to the tarn?

You saw it too? And the burnt grass?

They are lying on the barest moor. There is no water, no black grass. They look at each other, something crawls across his chest and it can't be flicked away.

Spooky, she says. We both saw it.

Must have been the heat – blood running from our heads to . . . other parts. Some kind of hallucination. There's a scientific explanation.

She laughs and coughs, he feels the shake of her inside his ribs. As she speaks the vibrations move in his own throat.

Is that what you call it?

You were speaking Scots. I didn't know you could.

Nor did I. By the way, what's a laverock?

A lark, he says vaguely.

She puts both hands on his chest and pushes down hard to lever herself up. It hurts, feeling her go. She pauses as she hides her breasts away inside her husband's shirt.

I can feel other words coming on.

Wheesht, Jinny.

She grabs the finger he's put up to her lips. She grabs it in both hands and twists as her head comes down. He lets the pain go through him then slowly pulls her down to him again.

Five minutes, Jinny. Five minutes of peace then we can go back.

We can't go back. Let's not think about it yet.

A long silence. Her hair tickles the side of his nose. Her cut-down jeans are still round her ankles. He rolls her over onto her back and has a good look because this won't happen again. His hand traces where he's been, the bright open lips, the brown squashed crinkly hair.

So this must be a burnt mound.

Her hand closes round his balls. He feels them shift inside her palm. They seem to move of their own accord, creeping off elsewhere.

This must be man's estate. Doesn't amount to much.

I ken, but it's all yours.

She looks right into his eyes, squeezes gently. His fingers curl inside her. This time there's no dark circle, no black tarn lapping.

Can you find a way back from here?

He looked at her then around at the horizon in all directions. He shook his head.

I've never been here before. Never like this, I swear.

Me neither. Closest is the first time I got stoned. Everything was expanded, brighter, sharper.

I'll start smoking your dream tobacco if that's what it's like.

She began to laugh, sort of.

I doubt if Fiona will like that.

I doubt if Patrick would be that keen on this.

Let's not start, Simon.

Right. He looked round again, thought about the position of the sun. Must be this general direction, he said. Ready?

As I'll ever be.

Hand in hand they tumbled back across the trackless waste. On the downhills they were running, colliding, and it all felt light and easy, like born again without a history. When the slope turned up they were exhausted, weak-kneed, silent. They came to a lochan he thought he recognised, and they knelt by the bank and washed and sniffed each other and washed again. The sun was low and the hairs on his legs rose and quivered at the cool. They came over the horizon, knew where they were again and they dropped hands.

This can't happen again, Jinny.

Don't talk about the future.

She pressed so close she felt inside his ribs.

This feels like the only true thing I've done since I was a boy, he said. He felt very tired and his knees were beginning to give. So why is it the worst?

Then there was no end to the possible saying, so they set off downhill on different old paths, he to the east and she to the west. He stopped for one last look but she was gone into the land, so he hurried on with his mind blue and empty as a blown egg and the coin from her belt-buckle still slippy in his right hand. And when he came finally through the trees behind the house preparing his story for Fiona, trying to concentrate and look ordinary and care-worn instead of ecstatic and exhausted, the sun was splintered low and red in his eyes so everywhere else he looked but at it was dark and vague, washed-out, unreal.

Simon Elliot looks up from the pages as he lies in bed, hand coddling his cock for the comfort. There are still threads of grass in the spine, pale sweat stains on the paper where he stored his secret life, the only real one. He puts his nose to the page and imagines he can still smell her. Lavender and patchouli and earthy hashish and the juice of her. He hears laughter faint up the stairs from young love down below as they talk with Annie Tat. Soon he must go down and spend the evening with them, eat and make conversation and not drink too much. But it's not love just sanctuary Davy and the girl are chasing, and there is no sanctuary in love. He knows that now as the light begins to fade.

*

Surely I've no special powers. Seeing Elliot's torch go by outside last night after I'd imagined him doing just that, it does not bear much thinking of. I cannot have caused it, surely I didn't foresee it. The event went by the door of my invention as he did, not stopping, on its own course.

I'm just too much alone, though it's by choice. Now evening silts up the valley below and I've spoken to no living person all day. I walk up and down and talk aloud to remind myself who I am.

I don't believe in the supernatural. I've never met a ghost. But Spook, I do believe in that. It's hidden science, the connections we can't quite grasp that tilt our lives one way rather than another. It's the huge web in the corner of the window, glimpsed for a moment when the sun is low. Science and Spook agree: everything is fated, everything is connected, nothing truly disappears, everything bears the address of everything else. So when a small woman in an airport bookshop abruptly thrust a map into my hand, into my head there slid an image of a place I'd always known about. A place where all events are moved by the same force. A place, a destiny, a role at last. At the very least, a free lodging. A place of silence and voices. Crawhill Cottage on the Elliot estate.

The evening star rests in the topmost fork of the tallest tree, it will grow brighter as the dark comes on. Some days your life's a letter written by the one who delivers it, and some days that one is you.

Propped up in his bed, Sim Elliot groans and drinks the tea Annie has brought up as he waits for the paracetamol to cut in. He's been bad, he's been a damn fool. It's the pressure emanating from Crawhill. He can see her lying on the mattress staring at the wee photo by her head, or reading too much into the Corbie Plates. If she meant him well, she would have called straightaway. She knows who took the photo of her mother, herself and Davy. She knows everything, or thinks she does. She must come to him, that's all he knows. He needs that.

He ate with Young Love last night. Shaved and unstoned and on best behaviour till the drink caught up, he talked and listened and watched. The lassie had a high laugh and voice but was right bright, no doubt about that. Something hectic about her said she wasn't too well, the way a power-saw engine will race just before the fuel runs out. Whiles she seemed angry, at other moments she eyed Davy like he was a lifebelt in a gurly sea. Her hips are too narrow, he'd thought vaguely as he raised his glass. She'd slip right through a lifebelt.

She ate very little and drank less. But she laughed and was lively and sought his opinions. When he talked he felt his mouth obscenely big and fleshy.

She told him their plans and made plenty eye-contact. Once she was married and had citizenship, she could stay on and chase another lecturing job. If her new book did well, she might even get tenure. David would stay with the Forestry Commission at first but look to go freelance as a consultant. And the boy had nodded and agreed, drunk more wine and kept his head down. Clearly the evening was something to be got through because she wanted it. Simon had watched how their elbows chapped off each other, the way they said sorry, and wondered if that was his son's vision of marriage: a healing operation, a minimum of disaster. They didn't face into each other as he and Jinny had. They sat side by side like houses in an orderly terrace.

Bairns? Is there room for them in your career?

A third bottle of wine question, he regretted it soon as it came from his mouth. David looked down, then to her but she was concentrating on peeling her grapes.

We'll see what happens, she said.

David glared across at him. Since when are you concerned about children?

No, it's a fair question, from the fiancée. It's just not high on the agenda right now.

Bloody nosy if you ask me.

Another pause. He lifted his glass and drank more blood-red wine and watched the pair of them. Something was happening and not happening there. He drained his glass and poured another.

You do intend to have a sex life, eh?

The girl had reddened but laughed.

For God's sake, Dad. Get a grip.

The boy's right hand shook with his fork and the colour was high in his throat.

Just asking, Elliot said. There's the estate to think on.

Give what's left to Tat, I don't give a fuck.

The lassie put her hand on her man's arm. Let's not get uptight, she said.

It's tainted. The boy pulled his arm free. I dinni want it.

Elliot winked at her. You'll notice how the accent changes when he riles up.

David's the gentlest man I know, she replied. That's one of the things I love.

The girl was pale. She was that thin, those wee bony wrists, she was vibrating like a tuning fork at the raised voices. Elliot looked at her too-big eyes, her clever, quivering mouth, and felt something stir in his stomach. So his son wanted to give her the kindness he'd never had. And she was grateful and edgy with it, and more intelligent and focused.

Elliot raised his glass again. Projection, he thought. I'm just seeing my marriage again. He cleared his throat.

Aye well, I wish you luck. He swallowed, felt the redness rise into his skull and couldn't stop talking. Tell you this though, you can swear to be kind, keep your temper and all that. You can swear to be faithful and – he raised his hand – you'll make a better fist of it than me. Surely. Fine. But it's not love.

His son was standing up. The girl had gone white under that spiky blonde hair.

I'm not listening to this.

The girl was squeaking in her throat. Elliot put out his hand, clamped on the boy's arm.

Sorry, Davit. I'm just haivering. Too much wine, eh?

Too much dope, more like. I don't know how you live with yoursel. Give the fucking estate away.

Language, laddie. You'll frighten the lassie. Heh, you look like a reiver when your blood's up.

David's fist grabbed his shirt. The boy had a grip on him.

Gie the estate to Marnie, you auld cunt, if you want to keep it in the family.

The girl moving away from the table now.

I'll not have my . . . body . . . insulted.

She looked about to throw up.

Hold on a minute!

The girl stopped then looked to Annie Tat, come quietly in the door with a tray.

Hold on, Elliot said more quietly. What was that about family? Did she say that? It's a damned lie!

The boy looked straight back at him, said nothing.

Who's Marnie? Jo asked.

The woman staying in Crawhill Cottage, David muttered. I mentioned her.

Calm down the lot of you, Annie said. This is a stushie about nothing. Elliot, behave yourself.

David looked at her. He'd never heard her speak to his father like that. She shrugged, put the tray on the table and began gathering in plates.

The one you went to visit once? Jo asked.

Couple of times. I told you.

But who *is* she?

A long silence. Annie clattered with the knives.

Her name's Marnie Lauder, dear, Annie said. If you've all done, there's coffee in the sitting room.

So what's this about family? Is she a relation, David?

Better ask the old man about that.

Annie's hands stopped. The room was very silent. All eyes on Elliot.

If she said that, she's a liar and I'll have her out the morn. Did she, eh?

David hesitated, then shrugged and turned away.

No. She never said that. My mistake.

Elliot's head went down. Annie moved in and cleared his place.

Will you be wanting a dram with your coffee? Not you, Sim.

David put his arm round Jo's shoulders. I'm sorry, he said to her quietly. He winds me up something rotten.

Elliot looked up. It's true, he said quietly. She's no mine. Worst luck, but she can't be. If she was mine, d'ye no think I'd have gone to see her?

Forget it, Dad. I believe you. Sad old bastard.

Feared you fancied your half-sister, were ye?

Annie cut in quick.

Marnie is Jinny Lauder's daughter, lass. But it's ancient history now. Jinny was . . .

Dad's hoor.

Tsk, laddie. That's not awfy politically correct.

Okay. Adulterous lover, then. Though I don't know if love came into it.

Elliot rose from the table. He stepped round the edge towards his son.

Oh, so she's the woman who, uh, died, Jo said. You never said her name.

I didn't want to.

Yes, the poor soul's dead and that's an end to it, Annie said. Now are you all coming through or what?

Elliot leaned on the side of the table, still half a head taller than his son. His breath expelled then he looked old. He shook his head vaguely.

My, Davy, but you're a pious wee shite.

He straightened up with Annie's arm at his elbow guiding him towards the door to the sitting room. He shook her off and stumbled towards the door to the back stairs. He ducked his head, mumbled Sorry, and was gone.

Love, they heard him mutter as he went up the stairs. They ken nothing of it.

Annie looked back at David and Jo.

Don't heed him, she said. He's had too much. He'll be right sorry in the morn. He's not been keeping well, and this woman turning up . . . A thud then a clatter from upstairs. I'd better put the old fool to bed, she added.

Jo and David in the silent dining room. Scuffed old panels, spilled candlewax, half-full glasses. She moved away from him.

What the hell is going down here, David? What's the sub-text? Is it because of me?

He hesitated then took her thin hand and squeezed.

No, I think the old goat quite likes you. Private hell is the sub-text and we're getting out soonest.

Simon Elliot groaned again and reached for his morning pills, the ones that would keep his heart going a while longer, though the only part of it that mattered was long dead.

*

After that burning day on the moor, he stayed close to the house and the home farm for a week and went through the motions of his life. He even managed to make love – no, he managed to have sex, he knew the difference now – with Fiona. It was half-hearted, half-cocked, an embarrassment to them both. Little wonder she gave her time to wee Davy and the county set, and lately she'd begun to have a couple of gins before lunch and more in the evening.

Perhaps because of the booze one very hot afternoon she found him up by the dyke and sat down in the bracken by him. She said how hot it was then unbuttoned her shirt. She said she might as well get a tan and took the shirt off.

She sat a couple of feet away in her heavy nursing bra. Her

feet weren't bare and she would never not wear a bra like Jinny. He rolled back his sleeves and a minute later agreed it was bloody hot and took off his shirt. They sat on for a while then his hand went out and touched hers. She squeezed his hand, slippy with sweat, till her ring pressed painfully against his knuckle. Speech had become impossible. He put his free hand on the knee of her new lime-green linen trousers and tried to want her. There are many things can be willed in this life but a hard-on isn't one.

Her other hand came into his crotch and he willed himself, a fraction too late, not to flinch away.

You're jumpy, she said.

Sorry. He laughed the worst phoniest laugh of his life. It's these sleepless nights with the bairn.

But it's worth it. Isn't it, Simon?

He patted her hand, hoping she would stop scratching at his leg before he jumped away. Well, it's reality, he said. That's got to be worth something.

It's what you wanted?

He hesitated and knew himself lost. He couldn't lie, he couldn't tell the truth. The silence went on too long, her fingers were still, her shoulders very set as she didn't look at him.

It's what's happened. I'm glad about Davy, you know I am.

A long pause in the afternoon before she nodded. Her fingers fiddled with the strap of her bra. He wished she wouldn't do that.

I'd hoped it would be better, she said. And because her voice was low and hopeless, not an accusation or a plea, and it was the first true thing said between them for months, he leaned across and kissed her ear. Her hand came up and held his head to hers and for a time they seemed to be consoling each other at a funeral.

Then she lay back in the bracken. I know we've not been very adventurous, she said.

His heart lurched. He had no choice but to lean across and slip off one heavy strap then the other. As always she lay passive, waiting. In the early days he'd once or twice suggested she could lead. So you don't fancy me, she'd said. You're a man, I shouldn't have to excite you. Jinny slid sideways into his head, her fingers running over him like blown leaves, stripping him root and branch. His erection lasted through him lowering the cups of the bra. He saw the blue veins and tried to like them. He bent to suck. Ouch, she said. That's not nice.

Then it was too late, though he tried. It seemed his cock was the only part of him that couldn't lie. He tried to perpetuate enough hard-on as he unzipped the lime-green trousers. Tried to move himself so her fingers brushed his cock. She was trying. He was trying. There is nothing sadder than two people trying.

Trousers round his ankles, he lay on her, a sad remainder of an erection pushing at her dry entrance. He even tried thinking of Jinny but that was disgusting. His wife's face was red, she pushed and pulled and made small huffing sounds. He tried to find her clitoris, which was small and temperamental and prone to hiding, but she pushed his hand away.

Not that, she said. Just do it.

They rocked back and forward in silence for a while. Silence was about the only thing they shared, and they didn't even share that. God knows what she was thinking. He tried again to will himself hard again. Think of anything, anyone, anywhere else but here.

She stopped moving. He slowed and stopped. His cock slipped out of her.

It isn't going to work, she said. Her voice was flat, resigned. His heart went out to her and to himself, lying foolish and useless in the bug-ridden bracken. She sat up briskly, brushed bits and pieces from her hair. Oh well, she said. Better get back for Davy. I always thought it only happened in films anyway.

Tenderly, he did up her bra, straightened the collar of her shirt.

Sorry, he said. Let's try again later.

She stood up, smiled briefly back at him. You know it's not very important to me, she said. I think it's overrated, actually.

You could be right, he said as a bit more in him died. He turned away from her and pulled himself together. Hid away his prick, good only for peeing and once or twice in a lifetime making a baby. He'd always known he was unlovable and unloving. Only with Jinny had that been untrue.

They set off down the hill together. He took her hand in sympathy and need, she squeezed it once. After a while they began to talk about the estate. After all, they were a good team. God knows what she was thinking. He was trying to tug himself away from a black tarn that had opened up somewhere in his heart. This wasn't going to work.

*

What the maps call Breckan Hill is known in this isolated corner of the Borderlands as Creagan's Knowe. It is a well-known beauty spot, with a fine outlook from the top of its high red escarpment. Down below, in mixed woodland, a stream settles in shallow linns then winds down to farmland. It is a place of Sunday picnics, for the rest of the time visited only by the odd solitary walker. The low round green mounds are not Iron Age forts but ruined sheep fanks (pens). The bigger green hillock by the lowest pool is the remains of an old mill that was sacked one time too often in the Border wars.

The local legend is that one Neb Creagan, fleeing a hot trod pursuit, came on his horse to the top of the crag with a pack of bloodthirsty Grahames at his heels, looked at the drop before him and the men behind, then jumped his hobbie down the cliff. By some miracle he made it to the bottom, turned and gestured – we may imagine how! – back to the riders crowding the top of the cliff, then rode for the Border and safety.

It is probably nonsense, you might think as you stand looking down the knowe. Or maybe not, for on closer inspection from below, the cliff is not a sheer fall but a series of ledges and drops. Someone desperate enough might roll his *weird* (fate) into one ball, launch himself off and make it to the bottom unharmed – though unless the horse had wings, that part of the story is surely impossible. As so often in the Borderlands, it is impossible to separate history from myth; so much is forgotten and only a name and a brief tale remains.

Curiously – or is it purely by accident? – this spot was in recent times the scene of a family tragedy that led to a trial still talked about in the area . . .

The wind keens and rolls the drum on the window frame as she puts the guide-book aside then settles down again with the rose plate. A thin line of briar curls towards the scene her eye has been avoiding, to the fatal place: the high bluff, the pine trees above, the woods below. This is where it happened. She stares until her eyes unfocus and the light grows thick in the morning kitchen.

*

In the dale we used to cry it Creagan's Knowe, but for the last while folk call it simply Murder Hill. The morbid wifies all went for a look, to point and gasp, imagining Jinny Lauder bouncing and breaking, crawling to the edge of the ledge and falling again. But only a tractor orra-man, two drunks from the pub, Elliot and myself saw it, and I was closest. I'd followed Elliot and Jinny to their last tryst, saw them arguing at the brink, saw his arm come out, her break away and go down.

I've no need to go there again to see her fall and hit each ledge then crawl, stand twitching and jerking like a daftie, then waver and fall again. It wasn't canny. I couldn't believe she wasn't deid. It looked as though, like Creagan, she would make it down alive, and I was on my feet and running from the trees till she fell the last thirty feet and burst open at my feet. Her thrapple opened, her shattered jaw moved, then as I hunkered down at her head I heard her last tiny wind move through the darkening grass.

It's much in my mind of late, as I think it will be with Marnie Lauder holed up in Crawhill. She's been to the town and read through the old papers. She may have found the court transcripts and read my say. As the day goes on and she doesn't set foot outside, I'm wondering what she's about. I work here at my bench by the window, keeping an eye out for her stirring, and from time to time I have a wee grue, thinking I feel her mind stroke over me.

*

Elliot made himself a sandwich and wandered through the empty house. Annie wasn't in today, David and the fiancée had gone off early in the Land-Rover, he'd heard the rev and rattle fade and been relieved. He'd apologise later, but for now all he was fit for was to drift through the house hearing the wind circling round it. Quietly opening the doors into room after room as if he was already his own ghost, listening for the voice he didn't expect to hear again, then closing the door again on silence. Time there was when Jinny could reach him wherever he went. The first time she did that, he'd thought he was cracking up. Even now, he has no explanation for it.

He'd left Ballantyne's one morning feeling solid and responsible. Now he and Jinny had done the right thing and called a halt, if nothing else there remained duty, decency, the estate business. He had to spend more time with Davy and try to love him. So he bent his neck like an iron bar away from the rusting blue caravan two fields away. He was about to step into the car, even wrapped his fingers round the door handle, when her voice said *Sim*.

She spoke clearly. Her voice, not his, right in his head. He looked helplessly round the yard. Mid-afternoon, the long hot spell beginning to fray in the wind from the south. No one there.

Meet me.

His fingers dropped from the door. He tottered slightly, suddenly weak as water. This kind of thing didn't happen. Sex so glorious the bodies flared like magnesium strips then disappeared into spirit light, that didn't happen. He didn't believe in it. Joy didn't happen, the world wasn't made for it.

You'll know where.

He stood in the yard feeling a breeze running over his palms. He stood with his arms out like an aerial, turning this way and that, willing to hear Jinny again. Nothing. He looked to the caravan. Not there, he'd wager the estate on that. He looked up to Crawhill Woods and shivered, they'd always been unchancy.

It was a nonsense. He needed to clear his head, get away somewhere. He found himself going uphill to the west, away from Crawhill. He crossed the dyke, followed the old drove road round for a mile into the next glen. The road dipped, twisted back on itself, and he came round the corner at the bottom of Creagan's Knowe.

He leaned back against one of the oaks and looked up the stepped cliff and the long smear of water whispering down. As a boy home from boarding school he'd spent hours and days exploring here. After his mother drowned this was the special place. Something to do with the great stepped drop, the dark rock and the red ledges, the crown of pine at the top against the skyline like an Indian head-dress on a high forehead, and the small plootering burn dropping in stages, rubbed out when the wind gusted, reforming at the bottom to curve under the silence of the oaks and hazel and sycamore. He hadn't been back here since Davy was born.

Simon!

Her voice this time not in his head but above him in the sky. He'd finally cracked up. He didn't even bother looking.

She jumped down from the tree. She seemed startled as himself, smoothing her skirt back down over her hips.

How did you know I was here?

I didn't.

Oh. This is one of my special places.

Sorry, he said. I thought I heard your voice down at Ballantyne's.

She laughed. Oh that. What did I say?

My name. And to find you. You said I'd know where.

She looked down, nodded. Hair rolled and unrolled down her white neck.

The astral telephone, she said. Well, it happens. Only I can't do it to order. But that's exactly what I was thinking to you, oh forty minutes ago.

The stream ran by her feet, dusty summer leaves made light cancelling gestures above her head. His first thought had been disappointment: she looks less bonnie, not so special. (You weren't as tall as I remembered, she said later. Though I still liked you, you seemed just another person.) Now she looked up. Her lips moved and everything around her began to glow.

Oh come on. He laughed nervously. Suddenly he wanted to run away. This spooky stuff made him jumpy. Hippie-dippy haivers, Jinny.

She shrugged. You heard it. You came. You explain it.

He stood distracted by her eyes. They'd swollen, he could see the yellow flecks wavering round the black centre. His body was starting to crawl and buzz, a high singing in his head.

I can't. He stood helpless, unguarded. I can't explain any of this.

She looked down. He couldn't focus on her face or even her body. His eyes seemed to slide off her. She wouldn't hold still, bits of her floated off, reformed. Swarming, the voice said in his head. She's swarming. So am I. Nothing's what I thought it was.

She hadn't stepped towards him. In fact she looked ready to run or burst into tears. Her toe was rubbing a stain into the grass. He put his hand in his pocket.

I forgot to give you this back.

She stared at the worn coin. She stepped closer, put her thumb onto it. His palm dipped, she kept pushing down. When his arm was pointing straight down to the ground, she raised her head and kissed him and he was falling like a satellite into the sun by the banks of Creagan Water.

*

This is only the fourth plate. I may yet decide whether I'm a recluse, a mystery, or a straightforward person on the mend after a difficult time. I like to keep my options open. Yet I want to know what happens next, and sure as Fate, something must.

I could be frightened but I'm not. I could be anyone at all, and of all the people in a story, there is always one who cannot come to harm. But I must get out for some air, I can't stay cooped up here like Elliot. I see him so clearly, skulking in the tower with only his guilt for company. He lies sweating on his bed, reading or dreaming. I can see the off-white sheet, the tall thin window pane, darkness beginning to silt up outside in his garden.

Time to rattle his cage a little at the end of the day. If I climb out the back window and keep low behind the dyke, I can make it to the woods without creepy Tat seeing me.

I light the lamp and put it at the bedroom window though the gloaming's only begun, then lift down my cloak and fix the clasp high next to my throat. Rub the coin one time for luck, then ease the window open.

*

Living yet, Jinny reached up, tilted her head back and opened her mouth to him. From up on top of the knowe they could see way beyond the Border to the blue-green distant rise of more hills. Wind blew through the grass round their feet, the trees behind sawed and groaned against each other.

I love high places, she said. I can see why the Devil took Jesus up.

He nodded, still panting from the climb and her nearness to the drop before them.

Heights scare me witless, he said. The trouble with being tall and that, is no one sees how wee and feart you feel inside. I can't always be in charge and strong.

Her hand closed on his. Then don't, she said softly. Let me make love to you. It's your turn.

He was on his back looking up at her and the pine branches as she moved over him opening his shirt then his chest then his heart. No one had ever touched him like this, like he was precious. She looked down at him, holding his erection in her hand. Every other part of him felt soft and open. Her little breasts swung like clappers over his face.

Go slowly, Jinny. I want to remember for ever.

It's all for ever, she said. Then smiled, opened her legs and settled down on him, inch by lovely inch. There was a thin ringing somewhere, like from bells no one has struck. He felt himself huge, disintegrating, full of space. She cupped both hands behind his neck and pulled his head up to her breasts.

Baby. Oh my baby.

He gently pulled the tufts beneath her arms in time to the branches moving overhead. Perfect, he thought. Everything.

So the first time wasn't a fluke, she said quietly. We had to find out.

Jinny, I've never . . . I mean I've had sex but . . .

Wheesht. Later.

You've never?

She looked down at him, serious now.

Never like that, even when I'm really stoned. We were made to do this.

She sat up suddenly, looked around. Just the trees and the grass moving to the invisible wind, yielding and bouncing back. She relaxed, her mouth softened as she looked down on him, held him in her hand.

Is this for me? Again? It's not scientifically possible.

He looked down at his erection, her fingers swirling lightly over the tip. She didn't seem to find it ugly, or ridiculous.

I'm just a mortal man, he said. I don't understand what's going on here.

Mysteries, she said. The breeze made a low moan over her mouth. Mysteries and energies.

He rolled her over onto her back. She opened her legs wide about his hips, took his cock and guided it in. When she was almost there she opened her eyes and saw Tat's pale face through the branches above, eyes wide open seeing everything. Elliot mistook her cry, moved deeper and her eyes clenched shut, she had no choice.

When she was able to look again, the boy was gone.

The worst of it isn't the sex, the staring eyes and bodies folding each into the other in every imaginable way (and several you hadn't known of before). The worst of it is what cannot be shown in the plates but you know was there: the tenderness, the joy, the souls rising from the body like trout plucked from water on a tight line.

Jinny was speaking about love. Elliot cannot imagine now what excuse she must have given to get away for a whole weekend, but he can see her lying diagonally across the bed in his flat in the city, surrounded by nightlights flickering floating in saucers. She's wearing the electric-blue crushed-velvet dress. He must have taken her out somewhere posh to impress, because she's right dressed up, blue eyeshadow and stockings.

But none of that matters. All that matters is the gap between them closing. He is quite spaced out, not used to her long cigarettes. Her eyes are huge. Their centres open like a camera's lens and stay open for a very long exposure. She is whispering now as his hands talk inside her and he too is talking without thinking. Between her legs his thumbs are opening her up as in his chest rusty doors have painfully squeaked open. As she kisses him, an ancient portcullis squeals and rises. He bends and sucks open another door. Her palms rest against his chest, pause then slide apart and open his heart. Now there are only thin curtains between them. She is locked into his eyes as she parts his heart. His fingers find a secret button and she is telling him she is down to the last veil now and he is too. As she rises in the bed they are staring direct into each other's core.

The city has vanished, they are way beyond where taxis run and police cars wail. He is in a conservatory of the night and all the glass is flaming. She reaches and shows him a thorned trunk stretching up into the stars, and as her moment comes she reaches up crying and plucks a rose from the end of the branch. Between her fingers it is black and radiant as the centre of an eye. She hands it to him with a glittering smile as she falls away . . .

Simon Elliot lies sweating, still clutching the tent-pole of his hard-on. Outside the curtainless window of his bedroom it is near dark and his estate is a barren place. But twenty-plus years back he saw a night rose, rarest of all blooms. It rests still on an unreachable shelf somewhere, for Jinny Lauder is dead, but from time to time he still feels another petal fall.

He sits up on the bed by the window, chin clasped in his gnarly hands. The whole house is silent, just a faint wind brushing at the window. Down in the mirk of the garden, something stirs in the willows. It's Jinny. He blinks salt away. No, too tall and strong and dark for Jinny. The willows bulge and part. The Marnie woman, surely.

He shouts and presses his face to the glass but she's gone. There's no one there and he knows that he must die soon. His heart won't take much more of this.

That's enough excitement for tonight, another little shake to Elliot's tree.

Take off your muddy boots then trim the lamp and brush your hand across that Lovers' Plate as though to close it. Time for bed and whatever dreams may come. Put the plate under the others then run water through your hair and shake all these imaginings away.

The Lovers' Plate (Red)

The second Lovers' Plate has flecks of red, near-crimson red that hasn't faded like the other plates. Perhaps it's made of different pigment, or else has seen the light of day less than the rest. Certainly there is much to be kept hidden here. A figure hurries from a little hut with cloak raised over its head. Another slips into the forest. More secret trysts, and the watcher there in the background. In this panel the woman has either put on a lot of weight or . . . Yes, you follow clockwise round the rim and there she is holding a baby, with one shadowy man at her side and another in front of her. Husband, father, lover?

The plates are neutral and ambiguous as oracles. You read into them what you need to, sure that is their only power.

She washed in pale light in the cold cottage kitchen, standing shivering at the sink. Jinny must have done this often, she thought. I wonder whose seed she washed away then.

Snow had fallen sudden and unexpected through the night, the last kick of winter. Outside was a ghost world, even the corbies' nests were white in the tree tops. The top of the dyke was crusted and sparking in the low sun. Water was already dripping down from the roof, falling past the window, bright and distracting.

She dressed quickly. The doubt had grown bigger each time she woke in the night. She'd always assumed the affair had started when Jinny was living here in the cottage with Patrick, the baby already born. Thus the photograph. But more and more she thought on the rusting shell of the caravan overgrown among the trees. No mention of it had been made at the trial. In all that testimony, confession and cross-examination there was not one suggestion the daughter wasn't Patrick's.

She stared at herself in the mirror propped on the shelf, looking for Elliot, but he wasn't there. Not much sign of Jinny either. Perhaps one could imagine something of Patrick in her heavy straight eyebrows. She had seen the same look *Are you her?* when she'd caught first Tat then Annie checking her out.

She didn't know nearly enough about the order of events. At the trial, the prosecution had focused on Jinny's pregnancy and Elliot's fear of the affair coming to light as his motive for pushing her off Creagan's. Introducing doubt about Marnie's parentage would have muddled their case, even weakened it. By then Patrick was too drink-sozzled to think straight at all, and Fiona too . . . gullible? Furious?

She had breakfast and thought it through to the sound of snow-melt running from the roof. Her stomach was jumping and her jaw tight. She couldn't spend another day dreaming over the plates when there was a mystery more close at hand. And she wasn't ready to talk to the organ-grinder, so it had to be the monkey.

She picked up her notes and shopping bag, pinned her cloak and set off down across the soft white fields towards the Tattersall house.

*

Leave before dawn, Simon Elliot. Leave the tangle of her arms in the narrow bunk of the caravan. Whispers in the halflight as you pull on your shoes, drink water, wash your face in the little sink. Dry your hands and sniff your fingers and know your life has become impossible.

Two embraces at the caravan door. The first one slays you, the second resurrects. There's nothing more to say, you must leave now. Hurry home while you still have a home, while your wife and child are still sleeping, before her man returns from the South.

This is the worst you've ever done. *I'm so alive it feels like dying* she whispers as you squeeze her breathing ribs into your chest.

Hurry through the thin dawn chill. Grasses bend before you, dew soaks your breeks and a sharp moon rests upright on Hunter's Rigg. You cross the burn, loup the fence and come up through your own garden.

Go canny, Sim Elliot – in your shaky hands you carry a lamp that burns no fuel, a bowl that's always brimming. Bear it carefully, let nothing spill, even Jinny's last words whispered at your left ear. *This must end.*

Bear it carefully through this world. As you hurry through the garden and fail to see the sleepless city child crouched at his window, and circle round to the back door, you know you have already begun to pay. You are not the man you thought you were, the responsible, decent, dutiful and slightly dull man who never had to sin or suffer. You have no idea who you are now, only that you are alive.

As you prepare to make noise in the kitchen and pretend you have been up for an hour, you feel coarse hair tickling your face, see her grey eyes expand to enclose you, and know for a few moments in your unexceptional conventional life you have lived. As you stand lost over the toaster, the kettle appears to be boiling in some other universe.

Let there be no tears, not a drop.

Sim Elliot lies awake in bed waiting for his heart to slow or stop, but it doesn't. The light is pale and ghostly on his ceiling. He turns his head and sees the black branch across his window has been limned in white.

He closes his eyes, but that ends nothing. He hears Annie drive up but he doesn't want to talk to her, not yet. There had been snow then too, early winter snow, the second time Jinny had summoned him in his head. Her voice urgent, shocked. *You must come. It's terrible.* And he had had to wait and pace outside the house where he could watch the caravan until he saw Patrick leave and then ten minutes later the centre of his world hurry across the dazzling fields towards the bottom of Crawhill Woods.

*

She banged on the door and waited, thinking on the netsuke figures and what they said about the man who made them.

It's yourself. Tat looked her up and down, pausing at the clasp about her throat, taking his time but she'd already seen his first involuntary backward step. What can I do you for?

Have I taken you from your netsuke?

His pale blue eyes unfocused, yet now he seemed to take all of her in.

What's your interest in them?

She smiled and shifted the bag over her shoulder.

Only that they're strange and beautiful, Tat, she said.

The flush went to his ears. He looked down and his elongated bare head gleamed in the snowlight.

Ta, he said. But Annie shouldna have shown you them. He looked up. So you're needing a lift with your gear to the bus?

No, she said. I'm not leaving just yet. But if you tell me what I need to know, I might well be.

He put his hand up to the door frame and waited, his eyes winter-bright.

It's about the caravan, she said. Jinny and Patrick's caravan. He looked past her so intently she turned to glance but there was nothing there. Where the affair started, she added.

His head swivelled fluid as a hawk's then he grinned through his beak.

I suppose if she was your ma, you'd be entitled.

No suppose about it, she said. She paused. It's my father I want to be sure about.

He blinked once, then reached down and lifted his shotgun from the shadow of the porch. She stood firm on the briggie-stane. I can always ask David, she said quickly.

Again that little snapping grin as he stuffed his feet into wellies.

The laddie kens nothing, Tat said. Though I'm minded he has doubts he can't admit to.

I can ask Elliot. Or go to the city and get the full transcripts . . .

Let's take a daunder, he said. I need to check on the pheasants.

He shrugged on his jacket, pockets weighted down with cartridges, then stepped past her into the thin snow and sniffed the air.

Fine day, Miss Lauder, he said. There's no doubt about it. I'll tell you what I can about Elliot and your father, and you'll see there's nae doubt at all.

Sim Elliot goes down the tower stair carrying his boots. In the passageway he can hear Annie and his son and the fiancée, but he turns away and opens the big door very quietly, puts his boots on then out the back door.

Today is white all around, the snow squeaks under his boot heels. The willow branches are stiff as spears as he heads down through the garden then across the wee bridge. He puts one hand on the fence post and loups over, into the lower paddock. For a moment he's almost young again, in full vigour, whole-hearted. He dreamed Jinny last night, she seemed happy and excited, and though he sets no store by it that always makes him feel better. She's not gone, not entirely gone. Within him she is fresh and green as these grasses cased in icicles. When he dies, she truly will be gone and there will be some peace.

He stomps past the snow-dusted remains of the caravan with scarcely a glance.

I'm very late, Jinny said. I don't know why I took risks. Sim, I've never been this late.

They were down at the bottom end of the woods, half-hidden from the road by spindly trees. It was winter, a first snow was running off in sunshine. There was brightness everywhere, he had to bend close to hear her she was speaking that quiet.

It's ten days now. She raised her gloved hand to his cheek. Hey, you make the snow look grey.

They stood in the flat grass with meltwater running over their shoes. Through the water the grass was sharp and clear, each blade.

It'll all come out if I have the baby, she said. I don't know if I can bear that. Or if I can bear not to have it. Or lie to Pat.

No, he said. I doubt if I could bear it either. He was amazed his voice still worked when his heart had stopped. Would Patrick know it's not his?

Her face coloured as she looked away to the road then flinched as a car went past.

Maybe, she said. He's been mostly away or drunk, and we've scarcely . . . Maybe once or twice. Even I'm not sure . . .

He didn't want to think about that, nor why he'd always accepted her call on the condom. Our biology is working to betray us, he thought. It knows what we want.

It could be a false alarm?

Yes, she said. But it's made me see everything differently. We thought it was beautiful and it was, but it's all so sordid. The better it is, the worse I feel.

Another car, and they both swayed back into the trees.

I ken, he said, whispering now. This is the best and worst thing I've ever done. So what do we do?

Hold me, she said. I had to tell you, I probably shouldn't have.

He held her head to his chest, felt the warm splash on his wrists. He looked back up the fields, checking no one was coming. If this came out, they'd have to leave. Leave all this, leave with nothing.

She put her hands to his chest and pushed.

I must be getting back, she said. Just wait and let me think what's for best.

Jinny –

No, she said. Please say nothing more. She stepped away from him. Let me sort this out, she said. I'll call you.

You don't have a phone, he said foolishly.

Since when have we needed one? I'll think to you – but to be on the safe side, I'll also hang out washing when you should come down.

Then she was gone, heading up straight across the fields. She looked great, going away, head down across the winter field, so strong and forlorn, leaving him with the melt running over his shoes, terribly cold and clear.

*

Here walking by a river, his hand straying out towards her. Or here, lying among heather, looking up, her hair tangled into his. Or sneaking from a barn in the gloaming, faces averted from each other. So much secrecy, so much pleasure, so many eager ambushes, the lovers

setting out on different trails by night or day, by moon or sun or
through the heavy slanting rain, along secret paths that twist and
turn to finally deliver them to each other.

I saw them trysting, couried as I was high in the craw's nest of
the Scots pine. I saw Jinny greit, Elliot's arms round her as
they stood in the melt like they'd gone simple. They hadn't
come for the usual. This wasn't the haybarn, the Land-Rover,
the moor nor the caravan, all the places I'd seen them at it.
They'd never gone back to Creagan's Knowe since she seen
me that one time. Never a mention made of that, though we'd
both taken a redder when we clapped eyes on each other
again. I loved her for that, and she'd been douce and gentle
with me like I was sickly.

Then Jinny pulled free, said something to him and hurried
awa up the brae through the snow-wreath, hand over her face
and head down. I waited on, looking down at the top of Elliot's big shaggy head as he hunkered by the burn for a long
age, scooping handfuls of snow out into the water and watching them grey and be gone. I saw him walk by under my very
tree, muttering, shaking his head, chuckling. Laughter and
greiting, I didn't get it.

When he was gone, I slipped down out of the tree and stood
picking needles and crud off myself, watching the corbies rebuilding in the scraggy birch. School and home were worse
than ever, even I couldn't dodge all that was coming to me. I'd
do near anything not to be sent back again at the end of these
holidays.

I set on after Elliot. It was an unchancy time but it could tip
my way yet.

*

Sim Elliot kicked the snow off his boots and left them dripping
in the scullery. Flesh of her flesh, he thought. Jinny's bairn.
The last living piece of her. What have I to be feared of?

He came whistling into the steamy kitchen. The fiancée was
pouring David coffee.

Grand morning! Got enough there for me?

189

David looked incredulous, the lassie smiled uncertainly but poured him some. Then he sat at the table by them, warming his hands round the mug.

Sorry about the other night, he said. I was ill-mouthed and rude.

You were pissed and disgusting, David said.

Aye, well I was. Truth is, son – he looked up into the boy's blue Fiona eyes – I was jealous. He glanced at the girl. Jealous of your happiness. Take it with both hands. He lifted the mug to his lips in the silence. It doesn't last that long, he added. Least, mine never did. I wish you better.

The girl Jo put her thin-boned hand on his arm, slid it down to his wrist and squeezed. He hadn't been touched like that in a while.

Thank you, she said. We needed so much to hear that.

Silence from the boy but he nodded. Outside the window water was running from the eaves, steam hung over the fields like they were breathing.

Thinking of visiting the lassie in Crawhill? he said.

Not really, David muttered.

Jo glanced at him and adjusted her glasses.

She sounds interesting. I might like to meet her.

Not many kindred spirits round here for you young ones, Elliot said. She must be perishing up there.

Well, she survived the night, David said. Annie saw her walking in the low field by the burn. Didn't you see her?

Elliot reached for another biscuit with a hand that scarcely shook. He was better the day.

Too busy thinking about . . . other things. Anyway, if you do call in at Crawhill anytime, give the lassie my regards. He hesitated, crunched the biscuit and coughed the crumbs. Tell her to call by for tea if she wants.

·*

Now Tat can lie as easy as me, but this time I think he was speaking true, or at least true as he knows, as we walked among the corn bins in the snow and on under the trees.

Mid-story he waved me still, then walked on so silent and

light I was surprised to see footprints. He stopped by a holly bush, bent down and picked up a stone from the snow and lobbed it into the bush. A rustle, a flicker, a shotgun blast. I was impressed as much as sickened as he dragged the mink out from the bush, and he didn't seem too happy either, just stood with his head bowed looking at the blood drip into the snow.

We've pine martens in the wood, he said, and that was all the explanation I got or needed.

My boots were leaking as I trod beside him, his head turning, turning, not missing a thing. And I think he told me it as best he knew from what he'd seen and heard and what Elliot had confided later. He gave me something of the order of events, when it started, where they went. I asked few questions, it was more important to listen and let it sink deep. It's easy to obscure it takes two to have an affair, and I winced every time he showed me Jinny's part in it. His eyes jumped on that.

Are ye wanting to hear this, lassie? Is this what you're wantin?

And I swallowed and said it was the truth I was wanting.

And you'll leave when ye hae it?

Put it this way, Tat – I'll not leave till I do.

Where the trees thinned out near the road he stopped, put his hand on the rough scaled bark of a Scots pine and told me how he'd sat up there watching Elliot and Jinny have a different kind of meeting, and I thought I saw what was coming next but I was wrong. There was another turn to it yet, and it's left me sure of nothing.

And now I trail home across the fields from the village with my shopping. The sky is darkening, the low moon's shredded through the bracken. My feet are freezing, cold burns my fingertips and scrunches up my lung-sacs like empty crisp packets. I shift my shopping bags to the other hand and put my fingers to my cheek. It's like wood touching wood, no feeling at all.

An owl slides by over my head, silent as conscience as it enters the wood. I turn away and walk on through the moonlight towards the cottage, knowing this will hurt like hell when the numbness wears off.

In his study in the peel tower as evening comes on, Sim Elliot locks the door and takes out his old journal. He glances out the window: a white world now as it was then. He flicks the pages, lingering awhile over some of the records of their love-making. He wrote down most everything then, certain it would never come again. Even now he feels the heat of it, or perhaps he is blushing. So many times, so much surrender and in each surrender a life regained. Nothing in his class, his background, the frozen nursery of his childhood, the beating-rooms of boarding school, nor the fumblings of sex that lead to marriage, had prepared him for that joy.

But he's not here for arousal. It's Marnie in Crawhill that's on his mind. Odd he didn't see her by the river this morning. Maybe he can't see her. That's an old tradition, eh?

He turns more pages till he gets to the part that matters: the child. He hugs his knees and looks down at the white space.

All my life has added up to this, he thought as he crossed the wee brig over the burn, went through the willows stiff and white with rime, across the rough grazing where the frozen tussocks exploded like meringues under his feet. *Come now, come now* still in his head, and her blanket hung up on the lines strung by the caravan. I've borrowed against my life – the estate, wife, child, everything – and gambled it all on black.

His breath was short and stiff, white clouds going back over his shoulder as he put his fist on the fence and jumped over. Three days now since they'd talked, a long weekend made exhausting by the effort to concentrate on anything but waiting for Jinny to come and say she wasn't pregnant. Or that she was. His life had come down to this: the red or the black. She was or she wasn't.

He stopped abruptly in the middle of the field with a clap of corbies over his head. Let it be so, he thought. If she is, we'll have to leave all this. We'll tell the truth and take the shame and the consequences and the disgust in the eyes of those we care for. Be ruined and free. He pictured a horse-drawn caravan, a dusty road in another country, Jinny and the baby sitting up beside him . . .

He laughed and swung the bag of tools over his head, once, twice, just for the swish of it. More likely a striplit engineering office in a Portakabin by the docks. Why not? That's what he'd always wanted, to be out in the world making things, not buried alive in this ancient glen. He felt the readiness gather in behind his ribs. Whatever it took, he could do it. They could do it.

He stood, letting revelation sift through him as his toes went numb. Let it happen. Let it all come out. Once he'd spoken wildly of what he'd do to keep it secret, and it really had felt important enough to kill for. Suddenly that seemed nonsense. If it was fated, it was right.

Lose the estate, of course. Fiona wasn't forgiving and why should she be? And Patrick had been looking funny at him of late, scowling and muttering under his breath. Tat knew something, Jinny had hinted as much and for sure the laddie was getting cocky. Lose wee Davy. He'd cheated the boy, his heart had been elsewhere no matter how often he picked him up. These days his son squirmed to get away. Somehow he knew.

I've never loved like this, he thought. I want that baby. David just happened. If she wants to, we can do it. I hope to God she's pregnant and the bairn is mine

He looked up across the river, the white Border hills. He'd have to leave here, go south and start again and that would be the end of the Lauders and Elliots in this corner of the Borders.

The craws criss-crossed the fence and into the trees, carrying twigs, and for minutes in this life he saw everything perfectly clear.

We've done wrong, he thought, now let some good come of it. He didn't look up at the caravan side-window as he went by, she'd have seen him coming, she always did.

He pushed open the door, felt the paraffiny fug. She was

standing at the sink washing something. Her face turned but her body didn't. He dropped the tools and stood behind her, waiting for her to fold back into him. He put his arms round her waist, smoothed his hands over her belly. She held up a dripping clot of white and pink and began to scrunch it between her fists.

It came last night, she said. I was just late. A relief, eh?

He couldn't speak, still clinging to a vision of that gypsy caravan as it dwindled down an empty road. She picked up a brush and scrubbed at her knickers.

No one need ever know, Sim.

Her pale neck had flushed red. Still she wouldn't turn round, nor her body soften against him.

There's Tat.

He won't tell Fiona. He adores you, he likes me. She hesitated then wrung out her knickers, knuckles rising white. Still there may be a price for his loyalty. I'd suggest you pay it.

She swilled the water out, shook in some powder, added a kettle of hot water. As she moved he was forced to back off. He sat down to be out of the way, helped himself to one of her roll-ups. The harshness felt right, he sucked it past his tonsils right down into his chest and for once didn't cough. He was starting to get the habit.

What's going on, Jinny?

She bent over the sink, scrubbing wildly. Held up the white material, stain nearly gone.

This whole alarm – this false alarm – has made me think. About what we're doing. She glanced at him, he saw the flush move up the side of her neck, her eyes brighten. He knew what came next.

No, stay there, she said. Please, Sim. She wiped the back of her hand over her eyes. You know it, I know it.

Jinny, I love you like crazy.

She nodded, sniffed. Crazy is the word. If I had been pregnant, with your child, it would have destroyed your world and ruined two other lives. Three, counting David. You've touched me deeper than anyone since my mum . . .

Now she was crying openly and he was on his feet holding her into him.

I can't do that, she said.

He put his thumb gently to her eye, wiped it and looked at her looking back at him.

I don't want us to stop, Jinny.

Her mouth opened so he kissed her. Her lips were salty and gave inward. He was near shaking with relief he hadn't lost her. Her hips moved into him as they had a dozen times, he could remember every one of them. His hand under her skirt. She let him feel the soft pad under her knickers then her hand closed round his.

Don't, she said. Please. I really am too bloody. Anyway . . .

Anyway?

In her pause, red head turning from him like a fox slipping back to cover, he knew fine. Outside the window frost dribbled from the crowns of giant hogweeds. I've no idea how far there's left to fall, he thought.

Her head came up like it was very heavy. Her eyes focused on him and held. He giggled, something he did when he couldn't cry.

So it's nevermore, eh?

Her hands came up, clasped the back of his head. She pulled him down past her lips and carefully kissed his forehead.

Not in this life, my dear man.

He seemed to be on his knees on the narrow floor. His head on her breasts, soft under the knitted waistcoat. He smelled wet wool. He must be weeping.

He came in the scullery door, put down the tool-bag, straightened his shoulders and went through to the kitchen and all the warm familiar smells of Raeburn and child and cooking. Fiona looked up from a seed catalogue, the bairn on her lap.

Did you get it fixed?

More or less, he said. Enough to let them get on the road.

So they're leaving soon? Before Christmas?

He shrugged. I think that's the general idea.

She turned another page.

Must be nice being young and free, she said. In a way I'll miss them, and she was always very good with babysitting. Ah well.

He reached down and lifted David from her lap. He seemed startled, his hands went back towards his mother but she'd got up to get another pre-lunch gin. Sim watched her go, her heavy solid shoulders, the sensible expensive tweed skirt. He held Davy tight. He had to learn to value all this again, it was all that was left him.

The child whimpered, he gently stroked its back, consoling as he would wish to be consoled. In his pocket he felt Jinny's note crinkle against his leg, he must hide that with the journal. Hide everything, no one must ever know. *Read it*, she'd said. *I tried to explain.*

I expect you'll miss them too, Fi said. Cheers.

*

Round the centre of the second Lovers' Plate everything seems white. Images of winter, freezing winter, and a tall man hurrying across snowy fields sends a cloud of white into the air. The moon behind his shoulder is white as bone.

At night in Crawhill Cottage, she checks her notes and makes new ones. She replays Tat's replies, fills in his gaps, hesitations, the moments when his empty-sky eyes turned from her. Times when he could have been blushing and she'd felt the urge to squeeze him like a stunted flower for its juice.

She shakes her head as she circles names and dates, draws double-headed arrows connecting one to another. She's trying to make them hit the target, but they don't quite. From time to time her eyes stray to the plate.

There's a puzzle here, a sleight of hand. She can sense it like the blur that passes under the magician's patter and distracting movements. But who's the magician – Elliot? Tat? Or Jinny herself? She can't do anything till she's worked it out.

Keep your eye on the man who matters. She looks up but of course no one's there. That thought was not one of her own, nor was the voice. Spook is busy again and it isn't obeying her.

She props her head on her hand as she lets herself sink towards the centre, the heart of this mystery. She has to get it all in the right order, move scenes around till the dates fit and the sequence is clear. And where there are gaps, she must listen to the wind and the voices that whisper still in the corners of the cottage.

And that note Tat mentioned then clearly wished he hadn't, the one Jinny had given Elliot when her period came, slipped into his hand as he left the caravan, spied on by Tat through the gorse. She wants to see that piece of paper so badly it burns like hard frost. Just to see Jinny's writing and know her hand once moved there. Perhaps something was there even Tat had missed, for she thinks he spoke the truth as he knew it. He'd absolutely refused to pinch it for her and she hasn't the levers yet to prise it out of him.

But it's hard to see another way of getting that note, short of burgling the big house, which is getting into the realm of fantasy, and she tries not to dawdle overmuch there.

When there's nothing else to trust, she must surrender to Spook. She turns back to the plates, her notes, and her beating heart. Outside the moon is on the rise, the Hunter is mid-leap across the northern sky.

*

Simon Elliot lies on his back in bed, lifts his journal and an old piece of paper falls onto his chest. The only note he has of hers, they were always careful not to put things on paper. It's written on the back of a shopping list, he's memorised that too. He turns it over. *Domestos, library? green beans* . . . She'd tucked it into his pocket as he'd left the caravan. He'd put his hand on it, turned and young Tat was snooping by the gorse with his queer long head and very sharp eyes like there was a hole in his head clean through to the horizon. Some things don't need said. The boy knew.

Matches, aspirin, Tampax. She had headaches, yes. The Tampax, yes, once she'd known she wasn't pregnant. It was just a shopping list. The real message was on the other side. The shopping list and the note – in which order did she write them? Did she write her brief explanation and apology then turn over and calmly jot down *Potatoes, butter, candles*? How the candles had tormented, knowing how she liked to make a ceremony of making love, and these candles weren't for him

197

now. She must have known he'd read it. *I've had to think for both of us.* She must have known.

Sim Elliot lies back in his sweat-wreathed bed by the moonlit window. He can follow the fleeting thought no further. He can hear voices downstairs, laughter of the young. His heart is thudding, missing beats. He really does not feel right.

*

A long brambly briar winds from one winter scene past several others you cannot bear to look at for they are too tender, to end inside a cave or little shed. The near-naked woman is standing over a bearded sleeping man who doesn't look like her secret lover. Outside the thorns are huge but there are no leaves or berries, so it's still winter. For a moment you forget to breathe. Shiver, for the stove's going out and you don't know what the date is or even what year you're in, but like an eye opening in your forehead you begin to see how it might have been done.

In the little caravan Jinny rose from the mattress and stood a moment at the window. She has tried to make love with her husband with more attention and it has nearly worked. She pulled on her knickers, thinking of the precautions that didn't get taken. Patrick lay wrapped silently in the blankets, only his beard showing. Soon it would be time to have another smoke and let the silences overflow into sleep. Nothing useful could be said now.

As she hung the blanket across the window she knew she'd done what was right for everyone. *This is how it must be.* She stared down into the valley where the power lines crackled and fizzed into dusk, then let the curtain fall.

Simon and Fiona Elliot stood together by the edge of the trees at the end of the shortest day, the very howe of winter. She had wanted to keep walking, into the wood and across the brig, maybe call in at Ballantyne's the way they used to before David was born, but something has thickened about them and it seems impossible now to go into the trees or say what needs to be said.

She stops, helpless. She cannot continue whatever she was saying about her hopes for their son and the estate. The weave of her sweater tickles his cheek as he suddenly holds her. Her breath is hot and moist in the hollow of his throat, and it is impossible to say whether they are holding up or letting go each other.

The last of the light still shows above the long riggs that ride down about the dale and cut it off from the world. The moon has already set, the first star is in place and the rest will soon follow. They stand loosely linked looking round the fields of their estate. For a moment he thinks If this isn't love, I do not know what is.

But he does know what is, and it is not this pained, shameful tenderness, this joint acquiescence. He looks at his wife, her face and averted eyes so familiar it's hard to see her or feel anything at all. This is the life that has happened to him. He has chosen only one thing in his life, and it was wrong. And now it has ended. He and Jinny have sworn on that.

It's very cold, the grass is stiff and crunchy at their feet. Skeins of geese stream over Ballantyne's Farm repeating *So what? So what?* The moment when he should speak, or she could speak, rises like darkness from the ground.

But nothing is said, only a pressure on his arm and her throat clearing. They feel the lines of their ageing deepening like furrows cut across the winter fields. They turn without a word, her arm loosely through his then back into her pocket, and set off home to where their duties and responsibilities wait behind the yellow lights in the valley below.

*

Sim Elliot wakes, at first not knowing time or place. Hazed moonlight spills like low-fat milk, thin and grey, over his face. He is unstoned, sober, and helpless. He's in his chamber in the tower and his chest hurts somewhere about the lungs or heart. The doctor has warned him often enough – with his family history of heart disease, father and grandfather both gone well before their time, he must stop smoking if he wants to live long.

He reaches out to his right, grips the packet and papers then rolls a thin cigarette on his chest. How clear his lighter flame rises in the half-dark! The cigarette kisses his lips and makes the long watches of the night pass quicker. He is waiting for someone, and until she comes all he can do is remember.

Congratulations, he said and briefly kissed the side of Jinny's cheek as it turned towards him. He shook Patrick's hand and somehow looked him in the eye as Fiona opened the champagne.

It'll be terrific to have another child on the estate, she burbled. I'm sure they'll get on.

He looked to Jinny but she looped one arm round Patrick's and reached out with the other for a glass.

Just a drop, she said. I'm already a bit queasy.

So, he said, where are you moving to now? A missed beat. He looked around but couldn't find it anywhere. Hello, he said, have I missed something?

Fi handed him a glass. It was very cold in his hand.

They can't have the baby in the caravan, Simon. Not through another winter like this.

She glanced at Jinny who nodded on cue. Patrick shuffled his glass against his beard and muttered they'd been saving but not much. The forestry work dried up in winter, but at least there'd be planting in spring.

So, Fi said.

They stood grouped round the fire in the sitting room. Simon Elliot felt the blaze warming his arse but the rest of him was frozen. No dusty-road caravan, no new life, no second degree in engineering. Above all, no perpetual adventure of passionate engagement with another human being. Just more of the same till the end. And now this, so soon after the false alarm. Her and Patrick's baby.

Jinny glanced at him, quick as a touch on an electric fence and he felt the quiver up his arms.

I want our baby to be born in the Borderland, she said. We could move, but . . .

Another pause. They were all looking at him like he knew what to say. He began to giggle. Fi grasped his elbow and squeezed. He was deafened by the things he mustn't say. He felt the pressure build in his chest like hiccups. He opened his mouth and knew with horror and relief he was going to say it. *We've been having an affair. She thought she was pregnant and now she is – isn't that hilarious?*

He swallowed. Jinny went pale. She could always read his thoughts. He opened his mouth again. This time it would come out.

So! Fiona said. I was thinking about Crawhill Cottage now the Maxtons are leaving. Jinny can help me out here by way of rent.

He closed his eyes. Weighed the horror of seeing Jinny day after day with her new bairn against never seeing her again. He felt the arms of the balance buckle under the weight. He opened his eyes, looked at them all. Saw Jinny's tiny nod, the twitch of the mouth he'd never kiss again. Or maybe he would. He had no idea what was being set up here.

He lifted his glass, lowered it again. Fi smiled encouragingly. He forced himself to look at Patrick.

Please, Patrick said. We're pretty desperate, man.

Those lips on Jinny. Then the anxious eyes on him. He'd wronged this boy so badly. No one must ever know, ever. This secret went to the grave, whatever that cost.

Sure, he said. Have Crawhill. Why not, eh? Why bloody not?

He clicked his glass off the other three, saw Jinny's slop and spill. Tiny bubbles fizzed and burst about the hairs along her forearm. He saw meltwater over grass where they had walked just weeks ago when she might be pregnant by him. He saw himself lap the champagne from the delicate pool between her finger and thumb.

No nay never no more! he shouted.

What are you on about? Fiona laughed. You can't be drunk already.

Wild rover, he said. With the baby I mean. There'll be no more of that.

Oh I don't know, Jinny said. She glanced at Patrick. We don't want to go entirely straight.

Aye, Patrick said. I told Jinny once the baby's old enough we'll move on. Just the first few months while I get the bread together.

They drank to the future. Early twilight outside, snowlight settling into the valley, ghost hills on the other side of the Border. Elliot drained his glass and felt the fire and the cold. Christmas cards still hung on ribbons down the walls, the uprooted tree shed dried needles onto his father's Malay carpet. At least the old man had had his adventures before settling down. He'd had the war he never talked about, then years in the rubber estate, dawns in Rangoon, night boats across the Straits, women too most like. Sim suddenly wanted very much to find young Tat and go with him on long expeditions into the snowbound hills and valleys, trace the tracks of foxes and rabbits and the delicate-stepping deer, see the steam rising from sheep sheltering behind the dyke and hear as they moved the tinkling from all the teeny icicles stuck to their fleece.

That's what they would do, stay out all day. He let his glass be filled again, heard Fi invite Jinny and Pat to stay for lunch. He and the boy would dig snowholes. He would dig into a snowbank at the edge of the woods, curl up and close his eyes and fall asleep under the pale cawing trees far from all this.

So – was this a happy accident? Fiona asked brightly.

He opened his eyes onto his own little corner of hell where Jinny had one hand over her belly, the other round her husband's waist.

Yeah, Patrick said.

Sort of, Jinny said.

But it's cool.

It's worked out for the best.

He went to the window and stared out down the valley at his estate, his life. He'd never leave now. Soon Fi would start the campaign for a second child and in time he'd go along with it. He would carry on with nearly friends, neighbours, the county set and people in the estate- management business. Even with his wife he'd carry on making the right noises a fraction of a second too late, smiling after the joke, nodding to the pompous remark before following it with one of his own. He'd carry on as he had before, miming to his own life. There'd been only one brief time when he'd spoken and acted from the heart and not been on his own. Now it was by with. Whatever happened to everything that mattered? He heard again his exasperated cry. Gone, he thought vaguely, buried under winter snow, and around his neck for good measure the deadweight of estate and title and family.

Fi nudged him. He smiled at her.

It makes me think, Simon, isn't it about time we . . .?

Her hand ran down the side of his leg. He worked very hard not to shift away, to smile down at her again. Presumably in time he'd be able to touch this woman again. She'd done nothing wrong. She was a better person than he was, and no duller.

No hurry, he said. We're both still young yet.

He drank and felt old. It would have been kinder if he'd never met Jinny, never known a life other than pointless.

*

What the hell are you up to, Jinny?

She panted as she put the big box down on the kitchen table in the empty cottage. It was the first time they'd been alone together since she and Patrick had made their big announcement. Somehow she had taken herself away and left someone else in her place, and that person caused him mostly pain and irritation.

I know it's a shock, she said at last. Coming so soon after our . . . scare.

You didn't waste much time getting pregnant.

I had to try with Pat once we'd finished. And, um, this was the result.

He was already walking away, dragging the mattress into the bedroom.

By the window? he called.

Yes. I like to see an out.

And you found it.

Hey. Her voice was soft from the kitchen, personal for the first time in two months, and he had to strain to hear her. I had to think for both of us, and that's what I did. It's for the best, you must see that.

He sat heavily on the mattress and put his hands over his eyes. I'll never get through this, he thought. Never.

I'd hoped you could be happy for me, she called through.

Did you love me? Was it for real?

Then there was no sound but the wind snuffling at the window. He opened his eyes and she was standing in the doorway, arms folded around herself.

Sim, please. That's not fair.

Nor is this, and you know it.

She bowed her head.

Pat wanted us to stay. He's got work and friends here. It wasn't my idea, but I'm trying to make the marriage work, so I'm going along with it. She looked away, sounded unconvinced, almost shifty. Then she thumped the door frame with her fist. This dale is as much mine as yours. I want to stay and it's not to hurt you.

Let me put it another way, he said. Do you love me?

She hesitated so long. She dropped her arms and for the first time looked at him directly.

From my heart, she said simply. But it must stay shut in there. He bowed his head. Does that help?

He got up quickly.

I've something for you, Jin.

Me too.

She was smiling as he fumbled in his pocket.

I kept it from the first time, up on the moor. I've had it made up so you can wear it close.

He opened his fist. She came nearer and looked down at the dull-glinting pewter brooch. Her thumb stroked the worn silver coin, emperor's head at the centre, the VIIII scratched at the circumference. The only one of its kind ever found. She hesitated then her fingers brushed his and she was pinning it on her sweater.

I'll treasure it always, she said quietly. You too.

Then she turned away and padded through to the kitchen. He followed her and watched as she crouched to rummage through her box of household gods. He remembered everything of the person she'd been with him, the light of dawn spread across her cheek, the secret shadows beneath her arms, her moist words in his ear. His palms were prickling as he reached for her. She turned round and he stopped, waved his arms like he was just loosening up.

Mum gave me this before she died. It's the most personal thing I have.

She held out a small flat stone disc. It had a circular hole in it, off-centre. He picked it off her palm. It was cool, smooth, speckled, very dark. Meteorite, he thought. It's been polished and worked. He tilted it to the light and made out faint grooves, lines that could be a formalised pillar or tree with, yes, a serpent twined round it. Yggdrasil. The world tree. Knowledge of eternity. He stared at it, feeling the weight grow, feeling it brand into his hand.

He squeezed his fist and opened it again. Ran his thumb over the faint feathery markings along the rim.

Family tradition says it first came from the neolithic burnt mound up on the moor, she said. The one near where we . . .

He nodded.

It makes the Ninth Legion seem recent. I've never seen the like.

She put her hand formally over his, slipped her other thumb through the hole in the stone disc then looked up at him, eyes shining.

A draught went round them and young Tat was standing in the kitchen, shiny head angled like a radar disc picking up invisible signals.

There's no one to hear the sleeper's breath quicken. She begins to turn over, her arms come protectively round her head. A moan starts in her chest and rises in pitch as it expands in her throat, then from her mouth bursts the howl of something that knows itself abandoned for ever. Outside in the night small animals edge away from the cottage.

Her cry stops as though a guillotine has dropped. She is awake. Her lighter rasps then the candle spits and sways by her bed. She is, as at all times, utterly alone.

She won't dare sleep again tonight. She hugs herself deeper into the blankets and stares at the candle flame. I am awake, I am awake and in my right mind – she repeats it over and over so it may be true. Gradually it becomes so, her breathing settles, and she again passes into a summer dead but living yet.

She stood on the bright grass headland, wind in her hair and the sea behind her – my childhood pal, my other half, my first lover, back in my life again. She surveyed along the coast as I lay looking up at her, blessing the minor fracas that had led to my picture in the papers and her finding me again.

No one coming?

I'd say we have twenty minutes in each direction.

So let's not waste it, I said, like we've wasted the last ten years.

She knelt beside me, put her fingers lightly on my mouth.

Are you sure about this? she asked.

I grabbed her by the waist and yanked her down.

Sure I'm sure. We never did it outdoors. God there's so many things to do!

But, she said, we must talk.

I rolled her over, pinned her like a wrestler with my weight. She always used to love that. She tensed then went oof! and was soft under me.

Twenty minutes, I said. Whatever you have to tell me, give me twenty minutes first. Give me everything.

She looked into me for the longest time. Then a quick grin, the one I remembered, the devilment that made her never boring, never defeated.

Okey-dokey, she said. You're the boss, guv.

I sat up on her groin and began to unbutton her shirt.

I want you mother naked, I said. As the day you were born. The watch too. And those girly earrings come off.

And when I had done I looked at her sprawled dazzling on the salt-coarse grass. She stared back like she was memorising me for a future I wouldn't be in. I kissed her so she wouldn't look at me like that.

Beautiful her shoulders, her neatness against the blue sky above as she opened me to pour the love in. Then beautiful her tanned skin against green grass as I gave it back to her. She rolled like a surfboard on the sea of grass, so responsive and buoyant as I rode her all the way in.

Now me you, I murmured into her shoulder. I licked her salty skin. Now me you, darling.

She sort of laughed. I guess, she said.

She turned slightly, began reaching for her clothes. In her stirring I felt time about to resume, with all its shitty, restless normal service. I clung onto the last of heaven in her shoulder.

I'm going away, she said, very neutral and casual. That's why it's so lucky I found you again in time, because I had to tell you. She paused. New Zealand.

I've often wanted to go there.

There's a man. He's waiting for me.

Oh, I said. I picked bits of grass from the sweeter parts of my anatomy, the ones she'd seemed to love so well. I hope he's broad-minded.

I don't think so.

She sat up and my head slid from her onto the coarse grass. I kept my head down and watched an ant struggle through its forest world as she pulled on her sweater and explained she wasn't really bi, she just loved me. The usual guff. How there'd been no other women. And no other men now, just the one, for it was time to stop floundering and start swimming.

New Zealand's a long way to swim, I muttered. Then she held my head as I cried, stroked the spot on the crown as she used to when we were lost babes in the bad girls' home. So I cried some more and watched the ant struggling past my gluey tears.

I don't expect you'll tell him about this.

I have to. He'll understand it's a last time. He knows about my past.

Her voice was soft and low, almost soothing. She was my twin, I was her other half.

I'm not your fucking past. I'm now!

Someone's coming, she said. Some twitcher. Please get dressed.

She pulled on her knickers then jeans. I lay on my back.

Let them come, I said.

Please, she said.

Our promises, I said. Remember those? All the things we were going to put right.

I'm sorry, she said. Things change.

Not in my world.

I gripped her hand. I forced her hand between my legs, began to push her limp fingers against me. Please, she said. Don't do this. He's coming.

I'm not. Then I pushed her hand away. Forget it. Pass my jumper. As I pulled it over my head I added Fuck off to Kiwi-land.

I'll always love you. Don't spoil it.

I felt the thump and swish of footsteps. The ant put on a spurt to the top of its grass. I stretched my jumper down over my waist as the man walked past our heads, hesitated then moved on. I reached out and squished the bug between thumb and big finger to put it out of its misery. She looked shocked. She was always too tender-hearted, except when it really mattered. Then she was unbending, hard. Not as strong as me, but harder. There was no point arguing.

I pulled on my knickers and looked around at our headland, the sea folding the shoreline, grass bending in the wind. It should have been paradise.

I won't forget.

Nor will I, she said. But I'm letting it go. You understand? I'm letting go all of it.

Socks, trainers. Straightened my hair. I never let go, I said. I never forgive. Take away anger and there's nothing left of me.

She shook her head, bent forward to lace her boots. I would

never see her naked feet again. Never her belly melting into mine. Never her hands in my hair. In this world everything is never again. No wonder I prefer to live in Spook. In Spook everything is now for ever.

I stood up and looked back the way we'd come. The wind was stronger now and my knees were trembling. She stood beside me, put her arm round my waist despite the man twenty yards away. Leaned her sweet cheating head on the crook of my neck.

Please come and see me off when I go, she said. I want you to be the last person I see here, you're that important.

Let's go, I said. We'll miss the boat back to the mainland.

She grabbed my hand as I moved off. Please, she said. For us.

And because the water in her eye seemed salty, I said yes. I rubbed the smudge off my thumb, smelt her smell on my lips and said I wished her well, and then we scrambled down from our headland and never returned.

I didn't wash my face for days but kissed the smell of her into my pillow before I punched and hugged it through the nights that followed. Sad event that I am, I wake to find I kiss and hug it still.

*

Now the Lovers' Plates rest unread on the table in Crawhill Cottage where a woman curls like a dark tadpole on the mattress by the window, uncurls and is asleep. In Ballantyne's Farm, Smiler slumps in the big chair by the range, scowling yet as he dreams of the wife who drove off. Elliot, his son, the fiancée, all lie in their separate beds in the big house. It is the dead hour of night, when even weasel, owl, and lover rest. Of all these only one blinks his eyes open in the dark.

The Tarot's influence is strong in the plates, Jinny was explaining to young Tat as they all picnicked by the river one day that summer. Do they tell us the future? he asked, wide-eyed. I'd like to ken that. Jinny had smiled briefly over at his head and Sim lying nearby had to draw on his roll-up and look away. Some folks think so, Tat, she said. But I think they show what we nearly know is happening now.

And so she spread her pack of cards on the grass that hot afternoon as Sim lay trying not to look too much at her. Most of what she said travelled inside and disappeared like summer rain, but as he lay resting in the shade of her voice he glanced over and one card jumped out at him and he knew at first glance it showed himself.

Simon Elliot lies awake in the tower, long after midnight, thinking of questions he'd let slumber for years. The card comes to him now: *The Ten of Wands*. By God it truly showed that summer.

A man is kneeling inside a cage of burning oars. Behind him on the shore his ruined boat lies beached. He's still young but clearly exhausted. His voyage, his adventure is by with. Nearby his wife and his heir play in the grass. His boat can never sail again, his adventures are over.

How do his friends see him? As someone come to man's estate. A serious, responsible, mildly prosperous man with a family and a title. He has been around, he has travelled a little, and now with his father's death he has come home. The rest of his life is mapped out. He is a fortunate man, no doubt, though his hair is getting long for someone in his position.

His friends see the big house and the conservatory, but they do not see the burning cage of oars he kneels inside. They see the Land-Rover and the Volvo, but they cannot blink and see the ruined boat, the threadbare tattooed sails, the bowsprit splintered on the sand.

Even his wife knows nothing of it though perhaps she sometimes senses the deep fatigue in the arms that hold her, and for some mornings last summer she was mystified to find sand gritting the sitting-room carpet. But her father died young and was sometimes distant too, and for the most part she has got what she wanted. She has the estate and a child of her own. She has told her husband that seeing Jinny growing bigger, her hand resting on her belly as she sits cross-legged on the grass, makes her rather keen on having another, a girl would be nice. For the time being she keeps busy and makes sure her husband does too. Time passes, everything vanishes, that's her motto. She pours another glass to help it on its way.

Sim looks to Patrick helping himself to more wine, rolling another cigarette. This is one of several weekends since the Crawhill house-warming that they have hung about together. People in the village are beginning to blether. A smell of burning seems to hold in Elliot's hair and he speaks slower and mirky, but the drug helps him kiss his wife goodnight and turn away to live again the time that is past.

Sim sneaks a glance at Jinny as she talks quietly with young Tat. Perhaps she can't see the ruined boat or the burning oars or the exhausted man in the Ten of Wands. She seldom looks directly his way these days. She just smiles a wee secret smile and slidders her hand over her belly again. But Sim doesn't have to look up to see everything, perfectly well. He can see wee Davy restless in his mother's shade, smell the burning behind this high summer, and on this bonnie afternoon he can see brown floodwater creep over the grass round their feet.

Fiona has another glass, Patrick chucks his cigarette into the river. Jinny is sitting smoothing her bump and it is her that Elliot is looking at from inside his burning cage. Then he sees Tat's sharp eyes jump his way then flicker towards Jinny, and Sim knows he has seen everything.

Elliot stretches and sighs, leans over and puts his hand on the boy's shoulder. His hand is heavy but his voice is low and soft.

Fancy a spot of fishing?

Tat must know it's way too bright for fishing.

Eh, sure, he says.

Downstream, at the head of the beat, the two lines flick out, drop and drift slowly sinking.

The bairn's no mine, Tat. Canna be. Take my word for it. Women's stuff, I'll explain to you later. It's been over since that time you saw us at the cottage. Since before then.

Elliot's eyes drop on him, looking for a response.

Eh, right.

The tip of Elliot's rod rises, then Tat's. The two lines whip back, run out again, settle to the current.

Appreciate your silence. Me and your folks have been talking. He teases the line back, lets it run on. All things considered . . .

He retrieves and casts again, notices how his knuckles whiten on the rod.

Would you like to stay on here and finish your schooling?

Tat keeps him waiting now. Says nothing.

I mean, we like you being here. Gives me an excuse to do things like this, eh? And you can learn how the estate runs, help keep an eye on things. But not a word, not a hint.

Tat waits on till the end of the drift then brings the line back with wrists suddenly supple and canty. He kens it now. He has the feel of it, Sim can see that.

Aye sure, Sim. I'd like that fine.

Elliot's cast quivers then runs out and plops a bit heavy. They fish on a while for the look of it, but everything has been recast atween them.

Now below Ballantyne's Farm the Tattersalls snore in unison and even Sim Elliot is finally still. Woods and moor are silent as the snow melts. Only weasel and owl stir again, and small creatures shrink deeper in their hiding. The night becomes mild in the Borderlands, a change is coming with the dawn.

Plate 6

In this plate a readiness gathers. It is taut with movement, partings, hurried meetings, sudden changes of direction. You run your fingers over images of lovers, spies, the dreamers and the betrayed, wondering who to identify with next. Like a pond-life water-skater you skitter over the surface of Spook, and only the thinnest of membranes keeps you from falling through.

By the river, sunlight falls on bright green winter wheat. In the wind-bleached grasses below the cottage the last wads of snow slip and are gone. Late ewes move ponderously, bulging with the unborn. High on Creagan's Knowe the piny woods bend and spring back. A force gathers in her hips as she rises and works through her wake-up routine, pummelling kicks and blows at invisible assailants, moves learned long ago in the bad girls' home.

If this is God's hand at work, she thinks, it conceals death in it like a magician palms the black ace. Warm wind flows over her hands as she stands blinking and panting in the cottage doorway, looking down over Ballantyne's fields that once were Elliot's and before that belonged to the Lauders. In her mood today, she wonders if it really makes much difference whose name is on a deed. Some days just to wake and breathe and be here now is enough.

A change has come, silent and unexpected. Perhaps her time here is almost done. Spring has come, and with it she'll be leaving.

Bright flecks of colour and decoration here, especially round the framing borders. Green buds force through black-ended twigs of thorn hedges. Blue-and-yellow birds mate and fight in the beech coppice. A kestrel hangs high above the corbies, its russet wings tremble like rapid eye movement, as though it too were hunting in a dream.

This new season brings dew in the morning, a chain of glitter clasped round a bare anklebone. In a tilt of sunlight, a grey-silver cloud of spiders' webs streams from the hawthorn bush, visible for a moment. They coat your wrist and palm as you reach to touch the first struggling bug of the year. In the top corner a tiny spider waits. And any day now the quick light birds will be back to gorge themselves on bugs and spiders alike, hunters and prey moving as if deep in love, so complete is their complicity.

Henna-red smooth willow twigs, and soft on your fingers their furry ends. The beech coppice twigs are bone-grey and seem entirely dead. But look closer, hold one in your hand and see along its length tiny red pointed eruptions pushing from their sheaths.

You worry about Nature sometimes. It's not a pretty thing.

*

She sits so still against the dyke she could have been there for centuries.

Light scours out the dark hollows round the eyes, her shoulders relax and drop in the new warmth. As she reads, her hand comes up and undoes the top button of her shirt to let heat into the hollow of her throat. The first lark of the year is moving up its scales. Smells of turf, heather, moisture rising steaming from the ground, and the faint sweetness of rabbit-shit all black and glistening.

The first sudden warm day of the year. She'd forgotten what it's like. It's been a long cold lonely winter and at times she's been near the edge. She feels at home here though the plates are more disturbing than expected, the voices in the wind so easy to receive and so hard to turn off. Too many days and nights of listening to the corbies pour rumour and memory into her ears, as though she were an empty space old forces could at any moment inhabit.

But today it's possible to hold a book loosely and flick back through the past. Today she's in her right mind, relaxed and clear. Today she can tell the difference between inside and out, between fantasy and history, the past and the present. Perhaps she'll leave soon, just take the plates and return into the mist while that's still possible. The moments of intersection still bother her – Elliot with his torch going by at night as though she'd summoned him. The details Tat has confirmed to her. The things she invented that turned out to be true. The voice that has just spoken so clear and amused. *You know how this must end. After all, it's traditional.*

She lifts her face to the sun, feels the warmth at her throat, the half-conscious fumble of her fingers at that button, the warm roughness of the page under her thumb as she turns it and drowns that dead woman's voice.

> Descendants of these passionate, cunning, desperate men known as the Border reivers, would include two American presidents (Nixon, Johnson), the best known evangelist (Graham) and poet (Eliot) and astronaut (Armstrong) of the twentieth century. It is worth taking a moment to study the physiognomy of any of the above and compare it with the portraits of the notorious, charming and ingenious Johnny Armstrong, any of the sleek predatory Elliots, the bloody charismatic Wat Grahame, the duplicitous jowly Nixons. More than the set of a brow, pendulous ear-lobes, a fearless stare or pale long-fingered hands, seem to be inherited down the generations.
>
> The Border reivers were no ordinary bandits or tragic remnants of the dispossessed and war-torn. These were the ungovernable who in many ways thrived on the shifting loyalties and dangers of their age. Bold, passionate, cunning and creative, they exploited the tensions of the Border, that interface between two related but very different realms, and made it their own for three centuries. And in many ways it suited the two countries to have this buffer zone – a place where even map-makers refused to enter.
>
> These were the people that gave the world *black-mail* or *black rent* – money paid on a regular basis so that one's cattle and house and person would be left alone. In other words, the protection racket. And

from the reivers getting together and riding out to, in the phrase, *shake loose the Border*, we get the word *gang* (from the Scots, *to go*).

Though Walter Scott and others considerably romanticised them, the reivers did have codes of honour (along with a tradition of treachery, ambush, back-stabbing, rape and abduction). They wrote and gave rise to much haunting poetry. They were peculiarly classless, unlike say the samurai – an avenging reiver could be equally a lord, a small farmer, mercenary soldier, miller or outlaw. On market day in a prosperous town, a Warden of the Marches might meet and play cards with two leading reivers, discuss politics, the price of cattle, the news from the continent and the latest weaponry – each knowing well that the next night all three could be engaged against each other in a deadly struggle among the secret ways of the debatable lands. And the women were by no means helpless pawns (e.g. the implacable Jean Carey, arsonist extraordinaire, or the supposedly beautiful and tender-hearted Liza Hume, who killed three prisoners in cold blood while avenging her equally bloody brother. *See Appendix: Violent Femmes*).

She smiles and nods as she comes to the end of the page, at ease for once. Surely this is what she came here for, days like this and a good read, history held comfortably at a distance. Things are looking up. Today she can keep the voices in their place, enjoying them without being carried off. She can feel the stirring in the earth, in her core and in the birds and beasts on the go all around, feel the stirring but behave herself. She feels real and ready now to turn the next page.

A call from down the valley. Two figures are walking up across the grazing from Ballantyne's. A man and a woman, stumbling arm in arm, a dog sticking close by them. The man waves, he shouts something that could be her name. She hears the woman's voice, high-pitched, accented, sees her face turn to his.

It could be Sim and Jinny come visiting, happy and in love in a world next door to this one. It could be young David and his Jo and his hound called Hawk.

She waves, picks up the book again and with her head back against the wall in the warm light she waits.

*

For the first time you realise just how complex and incomplete this story is, even more than the ballad – which is itself terse and corrupt. More than ever you ponder the central implausibility: how does a woman kill a fully grown man by daylight in the open air? In those days hand-held guns were huge, impossible to conceal, and in any case there is no sign of one in any of the plates. A knife then. Here and there a blade flickers – in the young man's belt or in a kitchen scene. Still you're not convinced. How would she find him defenceless? Could she really kill him with one blow?

Motifs from the earlier plates are here again, for it's a story of constant foreshadowing. Here is the splayed, falling figure. Now that, you think, is much more possible. Already you can think of two deaths by falling, there may be more to come.

I leaned protectively over the plates so she couldn't see them properly, not sure about this.

Think of them as a Borders Willow Pattern, Jo, I said. It's a story of lovers, adultery, betrayal and death – the archetypal drama. Plus a bit of Spook.

David said these came down your family, she said. Wow!

Yes, you could say they're family history. Mine and his.

I'm sorry, she said. I don't follow.

She's winding you up, Jo, David muttered as he poured the coffees. It's nothing to do with us.

She peered past my shoulder at the first plate. She leaned closer, she leaned against me and this time I let her look.

These plates, it's a see-what-you-want-to-see thing, right?

I looked at her wee sharp squared-off chin, her thin white wrists. This woman has never harmed me, never could. I looked into her eyes and smiled.

Something like that. I took the second Lovers' Plate from the bottom of the stack and placed it on top. Have a quick peek, I said.

Her eyes were quick, I'll say that. A vole, I decided as the flush rose in her throat. A little alert vole scurrying between predators. I glanced at David but he was too busy fingering my clasp, opening and closing the catch, frowning. Pair wee brave timorous beastie with her red-rimmed glasses and clever brain and sweet pale hair short on her blushing neck.

I put my hand on her thin shoulder and felt the hause-bane lift.

Wowee, she said. These are pretty horny! Like, very sexual.

I glanced at the many images of lovers there, all manner of sexuality in every known mood.

See what you wanted to see?

I guess, she said. Someone should do a paper on these. It's some kind of archaic gender karma, right?

I smiled and lifted the plates away. Her trusting blue eyes, darker yet more pallid than his, followed me as I stretched to put them on the top shelf beyond her reach.

Trouble is you also sometimes see what you don't want to, I said. You'll stay for some lunch?

She turned and glanced at David hunched over the table flicking the catch on my clasp. Her flush was sinking but restlessness was in her hands and tiny hips.

That would be neat.

Come back another time and I'll maybe show you them properly.

Her glance ran to me and scurried away very quickly with a little nibble between its paws. I knew then how it could be, if I so desired.

What you must do here isn't what you thought.

Go away, go away, little voice. But still my heart softened. It must have been the warmth outside, spring and all that. Out on the grass, Hawk rested his head on his paws and gnawed the bone I'd set aside. He'd be less trouble from now on.

Hey, what's this?

He'd pulled out the carrier bag where I'd put the broken bits of the third plate. He crouched over it, fussing and clucking.

I broke one, I said. Dropped it. My own fault.

That's such a shame, Marnie. You must be really upset.

I shrugged. Well, yes.

He sounded so natural and sorry I couldn't take offence, even as he started fingering around in the bag, turning over the pieces.

It's a right shame, he said. They're beautiful if somewhat grim. I mean – his blue eyes flicked to me, twin blue darts across the kitchen table – this could be our families' story, right?

With her watching I said, Not really. I mean, it's an old story and everything comes back in time. As Jinny would say.

My words went out in the sunlit kitchen and were preserved in the silence that wrapped around them, like a card sealed in plastic. For a moment none of us said anything. The untouched blue mug of coffee at the head of the table seemed to tremble tinily and glowed more blue. Spook. I felt its power everywhere focused on us.

He coughed, she laughed like I'd said something clever.

You mean the Eternal Recurrence, she said.

I don't mean anything, I said and was surprised to hear my voice sound normal if pressed flat. I just open my mouth sometimes, I said.

You must do something with these, Marnie. David prodded the shards, still looking upset. You could bury them out in the garden where she was in that photo. Or set the bits in plaster, or stick them back together again. Not just leave them in a bag.

For his unforced concern and his imagination and his thick wind-thatched yellow hair, I could have loved him. He acted as a decent loving young man, even if he'd linked himself to a woman who had problems with her own body. He just didn't know his true nature yet.

I tried to close myself up again but he looked and grinned at me guilelessly.

You'll think of something, he said.

I put my hand on his shoulder as I leaned over to take back the bag.

I'll work on it, I said, and cursed my voice's tremble. I could never cope with unaffected kindness. Fancy going out for a walk with Hawk after lunch – maybe into the woods and across the bridge and home that way?

The voices in the wind come in whatever language you need, like the voice in a headset guide. It could be Silver Latin, or Norse, or the lost language of the Picts – but as you are not so fluent in those you will not hear them save in a fleeting murmur below the rattle of leaves or in the burble at the bottom end of the river sound. Like infra-red and ultra-violet they are in the air but outwith your range. So you are left with degrees of English – and Scots, the remnants of that speech of both sides of the Border once known confusingly as Inglis.

We are back with our faithful voyeur, the lovers' shadow, jailer, protector. Glimpse him skulking in the bushes at the side of one scene, padding low behind the wall in another.

So I hunkered down ahint the dyke, took out my piece and ate while I waited on. I was thinking more of the fine wee hobgoblin I'd put aside on my work-bench when David and his Jo called in that morn – an eldritch crittur half-sprung from an old sheepshank bone with his whang erect. A private collector's piece, that one. In time I'd give him ruby eyes. I like working in bone – it's free and comes to hand everywhere. From bone I make beasties real and imagined, so small so vivid so illdeedie that folk hold their breath.

But a fine morn and warm. The first laverock up, and horned peewits tilting black-white as they jouked by the drove road. Even the craws caaking over the high beech by the heuch sounded melodious, sweet in their wersh way. I had nothing to worry about here. I'd watched the lass rise from the dyke and greet love's young dream and all seemed right and easy, even when she led them indoors.

I was half-dreaming in the sun, hearing their laughter from the cottage and minding the times when Elliot and Fiona would call on Jinny. As her belly grew, Patrick was aye away working for money for the bairn to be, at the tree planting or behind the bar in the village then staying late and sozzled when the doors were closed. But there were no shenanigans going on, I was sure of that. Elliot never visited alone but always dogged along one pace behind Fiona, looking pale about the gills and breathing shallow for all his smiling.

That was the good time, with me now living in the big house. For all I walked mostly on my tod, I was happy with that. The loons of the village were nothing to me and after a few run-ins they let me be. Queer Tat they cried me. Also langheid or langneb. The rest of the time I was with Elliot, learning the estate. He worked hard on it then, spending on the farms, improving the fishing and the shooting, rebuilding dykes and hammering in fence posts like a man trying to drive himself deeper into the earth.

I watched and I learned, never happier than at his shoulder or steadying the stakes for him as he bashed them down. He was a power in those days, stripped to the waist and swinging the big hammer and the posts dirling in my hand when they hit bedrock. Or sitting nearhand while he did the accounts and explained the living in the estate, which wasn't grand but enough. Enough to raise a family and get by, Tat, he'd say, and what more can we ask, eh?

No answer to that but the one that lay unspoken atween us.

I was finishing my sandwich and thinking it was time to get back to my goblin when I heard the door open, then their voices. I thought they were saying fareweel but the laughter and crack began to fade. I stuck my head above the dyke and saw the three of them and the dog walking away down the track to the woods about the Liddie Burn. Marnie was in the middle between Davy and his Jo, a bounce to her step and her arms waving. She put fingers to her mouth, the whistle came back to me, high and shrill, then the hound ran on ahead and disappeared into the trees like it had been skelped.

I louped the dyke and sneuk into the cottage. I stood in that kitchen where Jinny used to make me tea and scones and when her belly grew round I'd help her out with any heavy work. We never spoke of what I'd seen pass between her and Elliot, but it lay accepted between us, more a brig than a dyke. She kent the kind of laddie I was just as I kent what she'd done.

The used bowls and knives, spoons and mugs were still on the table. Three places but on the fourth side of the table was a bright blue mug still brimful of coffee.

Man, I just gawked. The signals I was getting were all mixed. What should have felt wrong was right. The room seemed to approve of this morn's wee gathering. I felt Jinny was all for it, had I set store by such imaginings. But what should have been right, the laughter and Marnie's raised spirits and the hound leaving Davy, felt all wrong and agley.

I ran out the door and lifted my binocs, picked them up just as they ducked and entered the wood. Marnie up front. Then Davy. Then the blonde lassie Jo. And then – no, it was impossible – for one moment I glimpsed a long dress and wink of white feet that went into the mirk below the trees and was gone.

I ran after them with a tremmling in my gut, though the day was blithe and bonnie enough for anyone.

*

I've not been silent all this while. I have been walking and talking with Jo above all. Also Annie, Tat, some semi-friends in the village. Even with my father when he comes downstairs and tries to talk though his eyes look somewhere else, somewhere not in any room I'm in. I try to pray first thing and last, and I still believe my Maker and my Friend is listening. Trouble is, when it counts I'm not speaking. My lips move, I smile at Jo, words come out of my mouth but I remain dumb.

This morning I got off my stubborn knees, looked out at the bright day, and knew my heart was beating the big drum because we were going to call on Marnie.

I cannot talk for fear of what I'd say.

She led us through the tunnel of trees, ducking under piny branches, her strong dark head disappearing in the gloom and Hawk barking faint. Jo behind her, chattering all the time, faint flickering fair hair standing up like a bog-brush. I should have been pleased the two of them seemed to click after some preliminary sparring. Jo's eyes were bright, Marnie was sardonic but kindly for her. And I felt shut out and sulky like a child whose best pal has a new best pal as I followed them towards the fall at the heart of the heuch.

*

I was closing in ahint them as the branches began to drip. Had to jouk aside as the Marnie woman stopped sudden afore the brig and looked back my way. Her head didn't budge but I doubt she couldn't spy me in the mirk. Then she waved young Davy on.

She stood aside by the first plank, put her hand on the fiancée's arm, bent and said something in her lug and the two heads bobbed a bittie. Davy stopped with one foot on the brig and glowered at them. He hesitated, looking ahead at the plume falling grey-white through the gloom, the roar and stramash of the waters wheeching under the hanging brig. I dinna blame him. I haven't muckle imagination but I've never liked the place. Even when Elliot took me there, or standing by Jinny while she laughed and chucked twigs out into the flood, even then I couldn't settle to it.

David walked slowly out onto the bridge, hand over hand on the rail. Then Marnie gave Jo a wee push, and the lassie pushed her back then cut in ahead of her with a bounce onto the bridge. I was too far away. There was nothing I could do to stop it even had I kent what it was.

I did what I aye do. I keeked out through the branches and waited.

Marnie glanced at me over Jo's head as we stopped in the middle of the bridge, raised her heavy straight dark eyebrows like a hawk's wings before it drops. She knew how the place made me feel. Tiny rainbows lined up and shook on my lashes as I tried to breathe slow and deep. I wasn't prepared to walk off the bridge and leave the two of them plotting together.

So I winked back and got a wee hint of a grin before she looked away. Her near-black hair clung at her neck. I saw the side of her cheekbone, the twitch of her strong mouth so different from Jo's pale clever lips. One woman's non-existent hips and tiny arse had always aroused tenderness in me, the desire to be very gentle, for Jo was afraid of male force as she was afraid of many things. And still she fought her corner, pushy and determined in her way, and how I admired that courage. And next to her, Marnie's more solid curve in jeans, at once more male and more female. More potent. She had virr, Tat would have said. Smeddum. She walked like no other woman, that loping mannish slouch. Head up, challenging all comers to take her on or leave her alone.

She spread her legs and leaned further out over the rail and the shake in me wasn't fear of the place any more. Behind the roar of the fall, the multi-voice going down that rock throat, I could at last hear myself perfectly well.

I closed my eyes and called on my Friend and Maker but in that place I couldn't call loud enough. I put my hand on Jo's soaking crew-cut, felt her damp scalp as she jerked away for she hated having her hair touched.

Sorry, I said into her ear. Past her head I saw Marnie's mouth twitch again, saw the gleam of the teeth that had gripped my lip.

Maybe it was the falling water of the linn through that dark place, but I felt queer as I keeked out at Elliot's son and Jinny's daughter standing either side of wee blondie like they were competing to guard her.

I told myself Jinny liked this place for all that her ancestor had met his weird here. I'd been sitting with Elliot in his study one dreich afternoon some months after the bairn was born. We were going over bills and VAT when his head came up and he sniffed and turned like a hound that's heard a call beyond human ears. His head went down again and his pen wandered down the column, but I kent it was only a matter of time.

Sure enough and soon enough he'd muttered about a headache and going to get some air and would I check over his sums till he got back. I watched him in the yard, turning this way and that in his welly-boots and tatty Barbour, raised but vague like someone caught up in a dwam. It had been near on a year since I'd seen him like that but I minded the signs well, and when he set off on the path to the woods I left the life of sums behind, sneuk down the stair then ran up to the higher trail and shadowed him on his way.

He came, as I knew he would, to the bridge over the Liddie. He paused there and gazed about. I stayed still as a stookie by the whiskery lichened trees but he wasn't looking for me. To this day I don't think he kent what he was looking for, he'd just felt the call and he had come.

She came out of the mirk at the far side of the brig in Patrick's long army coat. She half raised her hand and it could have been a wave or a warding-off. Then she dragged her feet onto the slidderie planks, then he did, and they closed towards each other.

They met in the middle. Her lips moved. His hand came up slowly, so lightly on her shoulder, then she laid her head to his chest and was hidden from me.

There was no snogging nor foolery. They parted and stood next to each other, hands on the rail looking down into the drop. They stood there a long time and I know not what they spoke, but I saw that though what was atween them had been buried near on a year it wasn't dead and could yet walk again.

At last he put his big paw on her white hand then turned away and walked back off the brig and his face was more distractit than joyous. She stood a long time, her bonnie head bowed, then turned and set off with slow dragging steps back to the cottage, her bairn and her man. And I ran to get ahead of Elliot, my eyes still full of falling and mirk, and my heart sair in ways I couldn't understand.

Elliot came back into the study pulling on a roll-up like he needed to eat it. He put his hand on my head and shook his fingers gently in my hair. Most times I liked that an awful lot.

How's the estate doing then, loon? Are we still in business?

I looked up from the figures. His eyes weren't on me, his hair was wet and sleekit down.

Dinna ken yet, Simon, I said dead cheeky. I made a mistake and had to start over. You ken how it is.

Aye Tat, he said. Aye I do. And he looked away past me, so lost and gone I can see that pale wild look yet.

And still the three stood in the middle of the brig. The two women were scraping big dods of moss off the rail and lobbing it out aiming for the black pool at the bottom. Davit had let his hand drop from his fiancée and stood staring out at the trees. I'd seen Elliot stare that way after he and Jinny started trysting again, fixed on a black drop like it was tar dripping from another world. Now Elliot's son and Jinny's daughter stood above the drop with only the skinny foreign lassie coming between them.

Why not? I heard myself think. Why not? But as the dark one bent to put her mouth to blondie's ear, I stepped out onto the planks towards them.

Tat! I said and nudged Jo. Marnie didn't blink but I knew she'd felt the vibration of his feet on the bridge. She didn't move a muscle but her hands whitened on the rail. She became dense, a dark star. For once I was pleased to see the wee ferret, for he broke the unholy feeling that had settled around us, hanging on our shoulders and hands like the fine spray. Otherwise I don't know what would have emerged from someone's throat.

He nodded to Jo, had a long look at the back of Marnie's head then pivoted very light on his feet and came up to me.

Aye aye, laddie, he said dead friendly. He put his arm up on my shoulder and spoke near my ear. I'm away to see Elliot – you'll chum me along?

Sure, I said. We were just going that way.

I followed him, very carefully, off that creepy bridge. At the far end I looked back. Marnie and Jo were leaning over the drop talking, but I couldn't hear for the torrent that rushed below their heels. A grue went through me. I just wanted out of there into the light of day, but Tat wouldn't budge until they finally straightened up and came to us across the planks and onto solid ground again.

A hand parts the alder saplings and Tat steps out of the wood. He holds a branch back till David emerges. It's still bright day, sweet smelling and some warmth in the sun. David shivers and Tat nods.

It's no a canny place, Davy. You'd do well to stay away.

I'll be leaving in a few days anyway.

Glad to hear that. Your dad's pleased to see you and the fiancée but you can see he's no well.

David nods and looks down. The two men are standing close together waiting for the women to emerge. A certain sort of silence settles in. David looks down the trail towards the big house, but there's no sign of Hawk. Odd.

Eh, about the estate, Tat says. Is that settled?

David shakes his head.

I really don't want it, Tat. Most of me wants shot of all this. To be honest, it's a millstone. But he looks off down the dale to the river and the Border, breathes in and stands taller. Then again, it's a bonnie enough place and the family have been here for ages.

Along with the Lauders, Tat says quietly.

David laughs and looks up to the sun. The two men aren't looking at each other, that's how they know it's intimate.

Yes, it's been a right old tussle. Maybe it's time to let it all go.

Or settle it once and for ever.

In the silence they can hear the women's voices in the wood, a high laugh and a low one.

Tat, tell me true. She's not my dad's kid?

Now Tat looks at him. Holds him in his colourless eyes.

Davy, your faither's told me everything when he's been fou. The precise details are a bittie embarrassing – women's business, ken – but convincing enough. And mind I was mostly thereabouts keeping an eye on them, I ken when they got thegether and when they didn't . . .

He stops and swivels his head without moving his shoulders, an owl's trick, a hawk's.

She's no sister of yours, Davy, take it from me. Elliot's sure of it, and short of a DNA, that's the best you'll get. But there's no need for that unless you were planning on jumping the lass yoursel . . .

The voices of the women in the wood are getting clearer. High flapping laughter wrapped like ivy round the dark trunk of Marnie's voice.

Don't be fucking disgusting, Tat.

Tell me you're no tempted.

David turns to look him full on, breathes deeply and forces down the fist he yearns to smack into Tat's grinning face.

Temptation's one thing, acting on it is another. You'll know that, Mister Tattersall. Those jaunts to the city? And what exactly does Annie do for Dad these days?

He hears the hiss through Tat's teeth. It had just been a poke in the dark but he'd hit on something. His heart is thick in his neck. He needs to say something irrevocable, unforgivable. He needs to do something to quell this roar in his ears.

Jo pushes through into the light, twigs in her hair and looking flushed. She holds back a sapling branch then releases it as Marnie comes through. Marnie's hand comes up in a blur, gripping the branch inches from her face, breaks it off with a hard snap of her wrist and starts chasing Jo round in circles, beating her on the head and shoulders.

The two women are laughing and flushed, playing like bairns. David watches, thinking he never does that with her. It's always gentle or serious. Good to see Jo being loose, playful, physical. Pity they can't do that with each other. Pity he has to hold back so as not to frighten her.

The estate, Tat, he says more gently.

What of it?

If it becomes mine, you stay on as factor. But I don't want it. It's up to Dad and Lord knows what he's up to.

Jo grabs his arm and hides behind him. Marnie looks David full in the eyes, then grins and lowers the branch.

Peace, she says. Pax vobiscum.

The four begin to walk the path towards the big house. The warmth is just starting to go from the day as David passes on his father's invitation, loud and clear for Tat's hearing. Marnie is asked to eat at the house tomorrow evening.

Why does he want to see me?

You're his lover's daughter, aren't you?

His *dead* lover's daughter.

They have all stopped at the stile into the garden.

Please come, Jo says. I think he really wants to see you. He said it's time to put things straight.

Tat is standing very still at the edge of the group. David twists one foot into the hard ground. Marnie looks away the way they've come, back into the woods as if her answer hides there.

On one condition, she says. Her voice is flat and expressionless as though she is passing on someone else's message. You two come down to the pub in the village with me afterwards and get rat-arsed. Then she looks up at them and smiles. It's my birthday. See you.

David and Jo wandered up through the garden in search of Hawk while Tat hurried to the back of the house to find Elliot. But the tower door was locked against him and no matter how loud he banged on the door he got no answer. He ran to the side of the house and lifted his binocs, picked up Jinny's girl at the entrance to the woods. She stopped. Turned to look back towards the house. Her right hand came up like some sort of salute, then she was gone.

High barred clouds turned pink over the hills. Tat's shadow stretched long before him as he thought about it. Birthday. He sniffed the air. Had it been much this turn of year yon afternoon he and Elliot and Fiona had driven the old drove road to see Jinny back from the South? She'd gone back to her family for the baby, though she seemed to have no further connection with them and they never visited. She must have been away a couple of months.

He tried to remember that drive. The smoky guff off Elliot – no, more than that, there'd been fire on the moor. Sim silent, Fiona chattering away to wee Davy on her lap as they bumped and shoogled along. Through the gate and up the garden path. Patrick and Elliot had gripped hands at the door then they all went inside. But he'd looked back to see the smoke and flames where the men were firing the heather.

Jinny in the kitchen folding her shirt over her breast as they came in, then looking up at them over the white bundle in her arms. Tat wondered yet at her expression, still can't read for sure the flight of Jinny's glance over them all before her head went down over the bairn in her arms, all proud and protective. Defiant. But heather is fired in autumn for the next year's grouse. The woman at Crawhill had lied again.

He hesitated, looked up at the peel tower then down the drive that led to the road and the village, then over to the woods where the mist was beginning to rise as the mirk came on. The signals were mixed, no doubt about that.

He went round the back and picked up the bike he kept in the lean-to, then pedalled off down the drive. Elliot had taken a turn and wouldn't change his mind. Tat hunched over the handlebars like his own netsuke goblin, the wind reddening his eyes. The faster he went, the more sure he was. The lassie who cried herself Marnie was lying again, about her birthday at least, and what for would she do that? He'd need to check with Annie. If she agreed, there was only one thing for it, and it needed done right soon. It needed done tonight. The woman had to go.

Who's betrayed, who is betraying here? The plate is crawling with figures, flights and pursuits, hurried whispered conferences, babies and drunks and even what may be a ghost from the expression of the man confronting it. Here a bright bird, perhaps a kingfisher, jerks upriver, sewing the opposite banks together. Here a room full of heads bends towards a fight.

There is more here than you bargained for. It seems the time for bargaining is over.

I pick up another razor-sharp blue shard very lightly between three fingers and thumb. Interesting to see the skin fold in minutely but not break. You can handle the most dangerous things if it's done lightly with no hand shake.

When Tat left an hour back, I couldn't have done this. I'd have cut my palms in many places and let blood pour from my cuts like that girl whose name I've lost. She'd hold her hands out like Christ and let blood drip onto the wooden floor, which wasn't clever because she knew the staff made her scrub it later.

I press the sliver lightly into the plaster of Paris, stand back, adjust it with slowest pressure.

When Tat finally left, loose in the hips and his head swivelling for unseen watchers, I was exultant and exhausted. It had taken all my powers and even as I called my last instruction after him my knees began to quiver and that old metal taste was bitter in the runnels of my mouth.

I knew what I had done and why, but Spook knows what it will lead to. The evening air is soft, the light is going in the bedroom as I select a large sail-shaped fragment. It shows, or hints at showing because so much is maddeningly uncertain and shifting here, two lovers strolling through a wood arms linked. Behind the next tree a man waits with something silver in his hand. Already the woman's glance is going towards him. I look at how her arm is linked round her lover's, and now it looks like she is not his follower but his leader, she is leading him like a gentle sacrificial bull to this appointed place. When that assassin steps in front of them in the gloaming I do not think she will protect her man, nor plead or bargain for his life. I think she will smile in recognition and step away.

I press this fragment into the hardening plaster and twist very very lightly. Two layers of skin peel back, but no blood. This kind of work is my therapy, it's how I put myself together again. Reassembling this broken plate and making new patterns from it takes such healing concentration. I am trying to heal by doing something well, hoping to be guided.

I'm putting the exploded fragments back together, laid into plaster on the wall beneath the window by the devastated bed on the floor, the screwed-up sweaty sheets. As always there is something lost, some ground to dust, some vanished pieces. Despite this, the plate ends up bigger than it was before, an exploded diagram of itself, an effect of all the tiny gaps between each piece.

I too have grown in this way. Each time one cracks up and reassembles in time, one is bigger than before. If one were not a person but a focus of forces, an instrument of Fate, would anyone know it? Would I?

If Tat hadn't threatened me I might be sitting on my doorstep on a pleasant spring evening thinking about my pleasant neighbours, the pleasure of my young visitors, and feel happy-sad that I must refuse Sir Simon Elliot's invitation and leave this place soon. But I respond well to threats. They bring the best of me out, like an indolent preening lifeguard jerking upright then suddenly sprinting across the beach and slicing into the undertow.

I lift another broken piece and twist it gently into place.

He stood in the doorway with the light behind him. She kept her eyes on the plate and blue mug by her hand.

Top of the evening to you, Tat.

It's your last here.

Her hand shook the mug very gently. He was in the room now like he'd slid in on grease.

This time I mean it, lassie.

She steepled her fingers and put them to her bottom lip. She nibbled her fingertips as she looked vaguely his way.

But I've an invitation to tea tomorrow, followed by a session in the village with my young friends. I was looking forward to it.

Tat said nothing. He was now at the dresser. His free hand ran over the plates there but he didn't seem to want to look at them.

So Elliot doesn't want to see me. He wants me out?

The man doesn't know his own mind. *I* want you to leave. Now. I ken what you're about.

Heh, that's more than I do.

This canna be your birthday. I was about when Jinny brought her bairn home, and it was autumn. You slipped up there.

She stared back at him, her hand resting on the plate before her like it was her Bible and she was taking the oath.

I lied, she said lightly. About my birthday. I'm a Virgo, though personally I think that's mediaeval nonsense. I just fancied a drink with my new friends, and that was the best excuse.

You're no getting your hands on Davy or the estate.

She glanced up at him, seeing he was no bigger than her but he was a man. He had the power and the assumption of it. He also had the shotgun hung loosely in the crook of his elbow.

She looked down and swigged some cold coffee. You're the boss, she said.

Aye, right. Get your things together the night. I'll run you to the village and put you on the bus with fifty quid in your hand.

Uh-huh.

She stood up slowly, both hands on the table and keeping her shoulders down and defeated.

Does it have to be now?

Right now. He glanced round the kitchen, through the half-open door to the bedroom. It'll take you half an hour to clear this lot.

Her head stayed down and away from him. Perhaps that was why he added Nothing personal, Marnie, if that's your name. But I've this howling in my gut says you should be away. Jinny was right special to me but I'm factor for the living not the dead.

You think it's that simple? The living and the dead and no passage between them?

Her voice was husky like she was about to greit. Tat shifted uneasily from foot to foot.

In the end, aye it is.

All right, she said. Her chin dropped to her chest and he had to come closer to hear her. If this is how it has to go.

He stood a little way behind her as she lifted the Corbie Plate and put it on the pile on the dresser. The sixth plate, she'd got that far. Tat shook his head. Those plates gave him the creeps. For a moment he saw Jinny Lauder's hands pass over them, her voice telling him the story.

Pass me the satchel, will you.

It was hung on a hook below her shawl. He looked at it, at her slumped shoulders. Jinny had been kind to the boy he once was. She'd never mentioned seeing him watching on Creagan's Knowe and he doubted she knew of the other times, what he'd seen through the cottage window or down by the river. Her thin pale legs wide open, the hairy darkness in between. The lips held open, flash of red. Much more than that, the long white pole disappearing into them. And then the cries, guttural as corbies. The huge prick of Sim Elliot withdrawing, her hands pulling him back in again. The boy had felt it deep inside.

He shook once like a dog casting off water, then put the shotgun across the table, reached down the satchel and held it open as he turned back to her.

The knife was very steady in her left hand. Young David's fishing knife, the reiver's dagger sharpened to a slicing edge.

Now back off, you wee bastard.

Dinna be daft, lassie.

Believe me, I can use this.

He glanced down. Her thumb was firmly along the blade.

The tip very very sharp and pointed at his gut and not shaking at all. Light was peeling off its edge. She had the fighter's crouch and no doubt whatsoever in her eyes.

He backed off, feet sliding across the floor. She followed him step for step with her eyes levelled into his. His back touched the wall, the knife-point steadied at his belly-button. He felt the scrape through his shirt. He felt heat radiating off her. In truth she was an outlander, a stoorie-foot, with nothing to lose and capable of anything. He smelled lavender and somewhere a smell like burning thatch.

Want me to cut your balls off, friend?

Something way back in his eyes flickers, is gone. She saw it. She knows. She knows everything about him. Her eyes are even darker than Elliot's.

You *do* want me to cut your balls off.

He doesn't move. Pores are springing open all over his body.

Tat, she says gently.

She puts her left hand, outspread, palm up on his chest. Possessively, almost tenderly, her hand moves across to his heart. Her hand pumps slightly to the beat. The tip of the knife still pushes against his belly-button as her fingers slip inside his shirt and close on the extended nipple. His breath hisses in the silent room as she squeezes. She stares into his eyes and almost smiles.

You poor love. All you had to do was ask nicely.

She squeezes hard between thumb and finger. Squeezes then tugs and looks grinning into his face and he is lost. Then the knife goes back into her belt as she half turns away.

You'd better come with me.

She leads him through the half-opened door into the bedroom. Mattress on the wooden floor, small silver-framed photo by the pillow, some books.

Lie down, she says. Open yourself.

She stands tall over him for a moment in the dim room, then she begins.

*

237

She did things to me no woman has ever done, nor randy callant in city parks at night. She did things to me I didna ken were possible.

She did for me what I have aye needed done. She brought delirium and peace.

There's a stang and a saftness where she has been.

Later I told her near all she wanted. The where and the when and the how. Of what I saw when the lovers closed on top of Creagan's Knowe, and what I minded of Elliot's secret diary – aye, I'd read that more than once with beating heart and stirring in my breeks – and Jinny's fareyeweel note written on the back of a shopping list. How her eyes flashed at that. Reive it, she said. Reive it for me. I want that in my hands.

And I'll do it, for she has me now. She could threaten to clype to Annie but she doesn't need to. The burden's off at last.

*

I rise from my knees, take a break and heat some soup then drink it walking in the darkening kitchen.

David's blade still lies across the table. I think of him, of Tat surrendering the soft places in his thin hard flat body, of Jo with the wounded mouth and huge needy eyes. Her light breathy voice and the tough clever things she said when she spoke of her work. Semiology, ethnography, portents, signs and contexts. Beneath her T-shirt, tiny breasts with swollen teats as she talked of the construction of gender and sexuality. Davy shifting in his seat, fiddling with bread in his fine right hand then dunking it in the stew. I watched his lips, the long Elliot mouth, the lower lip I'd sucked and plumped for him. Her mouth kept moving, sweet white teeth beneath her upper lip as she leaned to me, laughed then looked to him. She thinks she knows all the secret signs, yet she knows nothing of Spook.

We sat one at each side of the table and as the afternoon went by the presence of the one at the fourth side became so strong I put an extra mug of coffee at that end, a libation for the gods, a mug of instant coffee for the dead. Against my shawl hung in the corner Jinny stood on the border of visibility, a spring of red hair against the green. I felt she was willing us together but to what end I still do not know, and for the first time I wonder if her ends are mine.

In the silence of the evening the birds drop off one by one. With a short invocation to the kingdom of the invisible I lean over the table and spin the knife. It revolves like a compass needle that has lost its North, flickering by the places where each of us sat this morning. It begins to slow. The blade points to me, scrapes by to aim where Davit had sat. It wobbles once then stops, the blade pointed directly at the chair where Jo had been.

Let it be so. My heart is thumping but my hands are steady as I go through to the bedroom, flick on the light. I kneel by the window, mixing fresh plaster, and wonder when I last felt so strong, so sure, so far gone from the wee girl I was.

Whatever happens next, I will leave this much behind, embedded in the wall of the room where a woman once lay, betrayed, and was betrayed. It's been a long long day but I work on, remaking the ancient pattern. I select my next piece of shattered plate so delicately between thumb and ring finger and prod it into its soft bed.

Don't pass beyond this morning hour until you must. Shake your head and hear the tiny rattle like poppy seeds in your neck.

Too early in the day to give much thought to the scenes you must go through tonight, too late to dwell in yesterday. So look here, just left of centre: the meeting of waters below a red bluff where a body lies sleeping. Or dead. Someone is standing over her, if it is a her.

Even in sharp morning light through the kitchen window, it's hard to be sure what is happening here. This could be a scene where the young man stands guard over his sleeping lover. Or is about to possess her. His head is bowed as in prayer or thought or respect. Perhaps she has fallen to her death and he mourns her.

Perhaps she was pushed, or jumped because she could not bear . . . Bear what? Another child? The truth?

Your heart is chapping at your ribs like a demented woodpecker, and you haven't even had your first coffee yet.

*

What's your dad up to? Annie asked as she unpacked food.

Heh, not very much these days, David said. He felt high and giggly and not quite in control as he waited for the kettle to boil. Two mugs, oatcakes and cheese for two. A surprise for Jo, a little wooing. A kindness to cross the distances between two people.

Don't be too sure about that! Annie said.

For once he didn't like her laugh. He used to think her jolly. He kept his head down and waited for the steam.

I mean, why does he want to meet the lassie now? He owes her nothing.

David shrugged, tightened the cord of his dressing gown, shifted his cock under the pyjamas.

He's more likely to confide in you than me, Annie.

He'll not give me a word on her. Is it about the estate?

He looked at her then as she slammed tins and pans onto the work surface.

Why shouldn't it be?

If he thinks I've – She crunched the jaws of the opener into a can of plums. Strong brown-speckled hands, brisk and competent. He thought of her stripping her washing from his father's. No, surely the world couldn't be that iniquitous. There had to be someone honest, someone who wasn't at it. Someone like Jo.

Annie sighed and scooped out flour. Well, I only work here, she said.

And I'm only his son.

And they laughed, but it wasn't the same.

Don't heed me, dear, Annie said. I'm in a bit of a tizzy the day. Tat's been acting right queer again, prowling around in his workroom half the night.

So what else is new?

I reckon Marnie's not right in the head. You shouldn't trust her.

Oh really. David mashed the tea-bag and flipped it into the bucket. Why?

Annie looked uncomfortable as she hid her hands in the flour.

You've met her, and she's surely a bittie touched.

She's unusual, he admitted. She's also the most vivid person I've met in ages.

He put the mugs and oatcakes on a tray and squeezed past Annie's solid arse, outlined in blue stretch pants as she bent down for pans.

So it's breakfast in bed with the lass?

He stopped at the door.

We don't do that, Annie.

More's the pity, if you ask me. You should bed that lass soon before she gets other ideas. Her voice was muffled in the cupboard as she rummaged and clattered. Or you do, he thought she added as he left the room to bring some kindness to his intended. He hesitated on the stair then went on. Not worth making a fuss about, he decided. Soon enough they'd be out of here.

He tapped at the door and went in. Jo was lying on her side looking at him.

Hi, she said. That's kind of you.

She sat up in bed, her pale hair flattened to one side like a cornfield beaten by rain. She took the tea and coddled it to her white T-shirt, held it steaming in the low valley between her small breasts. He looked away, wanting some truthfulness in this world.

Sit down, she said. I won't eat you. She sipped her tea then looked straight at him. Unless you really want me to.

He said nothing, with his tongue swollen in his mouth. He'd known, of course he had. Known about Annie and Dad. Known in the tingle and rush in his head his own motivations for bringing Jo tea in bed, what he'd hoped for. He would pray but that's impossible now.

You do want me to, she said and put her mug aside.

He sat down slowly, knowing what was coming next and why he'd come up here. Her hand slipped inside his dressing gown, fingers flickered through the fly of his pyjamas. It happened once in a while. Nothing in the Bible against it, she'd pointed out. Fingertips lightly under his balls. She was amazingly expert at this. The rules were he mustn't stroke her head or touch her or do anything at all.

He sat in the dim room looking down at the top of her head and the bulge along inside her cheek. If he held her they were both lost. She had to be in control, unthreatened. This was her kindness to him. He saw the movement under the blanket as her free hand began to move between her legs, and then he closed his eyes against everything. He'd wanted truth and this was it and it didn't feel much at all.

*

I stand blinking in the doorway looking out over two countries then walk out onto the grass, feel the cold dew hiss on the soles of my feet. Hold my arms out, palm upward to the sun, and listen to the messages streaming through me. There is vengeance and there is love. Which do I desire? Which does Jinny want?

Surely that's obvious by now.

I close my eyes and sway from side to side like the grasses bent in the wind and springing back. Because for the first time it has occurred to me I'm not bound by what she would want. I am not bound by the story I read in the plates. I'm not bound by anyone at all.

When I finally turn and go inside, it seems dim and ghostly in the kitchen. I put the plate on the table and lean over it. There seems a new urgency in all this frozen stillness, a speeding up like the river approaching the falls.

*

Jo sat back and swallowed tea.

Better? You'd been storing that up for a while.

He reached towards her, felt her flinch and swerved his hand onto her thin shoulder instead.

It's not right, he said.

Don't come here for sex then give me your guilt. She bit into an oatcake then made a face. Sorry, she said. Didn't sleep too well last night, lots of weirdo dreams.

Me too. It must have been the coffee or something.

Like to tell me about them so I can do my deconstruction trick?

Isn't that what you've just done?

She glanced down at him. Yeah, not much left of the young laird now.

They laughed. This was safe ground. They could always banter their allotted roles, and find a certain kindness there. He opened his mouth, knowing it a mistake.

I've never been loved, he said. My childhood was so cold that boarding school was almost a relief.

I know, she said. And my growing up was way too hot. The idea is we balance each other out. What are you trying to tell me?

He shrugged, looked away from the white crust at the corner of her mouth.

It's not right.

Hey, we've been right through your master text and found no prohibitions on blow-jobs.

I didn't mean that.

Oh.

A long silence. Her hand stopped moving. She put the oat-cake aside.

Just once, he said. Just once in my life I want to be passion-ately loved. I want to . . . He shook his head, swallowed. I don't know. Look into someone's eyes and see no distance. Something daft like that.

She sighed and shook her head as though he was a particu-larly dense student, cute but dense.

David, that's just romantic myth. The other is *always* other. A good relationship is like two people living in separate hous-es with communicating doors, and we always knock and ask and take our shoes off before we come in. We share for a while and then we separate. Above all, we respect boundaries.

Can't people ever be, you know, *inside* each other? I mean, eh, touch souls?

She clasped his hand and put it gently between her knees where they rose under the blanket.

That's not my vocabulary, David. Our hardware is animal, biological. Our software programming is socio-economic and psychological. And that's it. There's nothing else. I know you want there to be, but there isn't.

He looked away sweating, looked at the strip of light be-tween the curtains. Some days he wondered what was wrong with him. Some days his Faith was faint and he felt himself falling into chaos.

David, I know you want the absolute symbiotic oneness we maybe knew as infants, but it's not there. There's no ghost in the machine.

No ghosts, he said vaguely. I hope not. Wouldn't like to think my mother was watching me now.

She grinned and squeezed his hand.

That's better. Believe me, it's better like this. More sane. We can respect each other and help out and be kind. I've seen the other, and it's quite mad, all passion and possession and the heebie-jeebies. My wolf thrives on it. But we're adult and we can choose to walk away from all that.

He nodded, thinking of the little she'd told him about her

sexual past, and the wolf that always stalked her and moved in when she was stressed. Thought of his father and Jinny. Yes, it was a madness.

Do you love me, Jo? Want me?

He hadn't meant to say that. She looked down, smiled slightly. The favoured student was being particularly obtuse today.

David, you're not hearing me. What do these words mean, other than your own insecurity? Of course I do, if that's what you need to hear.

He took his hand away and stood up and then didn't know what to do so he went over to the window and pulled back the curtains. A fine-looking morning and something was terribly wrong with him.

Jesus, he said softly.

Look, don't worry about the sex. It'll be all right once we start . . . you know. You'll just have to be patient with me and always very gentle. You know why.

I know.

And – hey – it's not as if you don't enjoy this. We'll be good to each other.

He turned away from the window and picked up the tray.

Reckon I'll go fishing up by Cauldhame Rigg. Hope you enjoyed your breakfast as much as I did.

Get out of here, David Elliot.

As he closed the door he saw the movement of her hand under blue blankets like a mole burrowing. Her business, her separate business. Nothing in the Bible about it.

As he went slowly down the creaking brown familiar stairs, into his head slid a picture of Marnie barefoot at the cottage door, stretching her arms out to the morning, greeting the world of Spook.

Sinners who overcome will be given a white stone, he thought vaguely, and on that stone a new name written. He had no idea where he'd picked that up, nor what the name could be, only he carried that phrase with him as he took the rods, dirled the stone key-ring round his fingers and set out into the world.

As you touch each painted figure it seems to quiver then move and become what you need it to be. The solitary fisherman flicks his rod out over the ruckled water. The shaven-headed man bends over his work-bench, reaming out his latest tiny figure of bone. He gets up to check through his telescope, and the next panel shows the cottage and the dark woman sitting on the briggiestane, hands dropped loose over her knees as she stares out, giving nothing away. The lady fair sits at a desk in the study, her hand moving steadily over the pages she's studying. From time to time her legs squeeze tight together, then relax. Let your fingers drift on, and there she is going through to the kitchen where the housekeeper looks up from mangling dough. The two women talk for a while but you cannot hear the words that pass between them.

Pass through the heavy door into the oldest part of the house. Up the dark stone steps worn in the middle, up two flights to the room where Sim Elliot hides out. The door is closed and no matter how you concentrate it doesn't open up. But this evening it will, and then you'll see him face to face.

> As I was walking all alane,
> I met twa corbies making mane . . .

More than ever you wonder about that mysterious I. What exactly is I doing there on the moor, why is I alone? Why indeed. Is it just by chance that I turns up on the lonely moor where the young man lies dead? Is I in fact the real killer, or is I here for another purpose?

These speculations rise into invisibility like the lark outside. The shadows shorten across the flagged kitchen floor, the privy's rusting roof tips a groaning wing as you go in and make another coffee then lean over the plate again. The fisherman's rod dips and rises where the water slaps on Cauldstane's shores, the husk of the shaven man works on, and you like the rest of them must pass the day until the sun levels down over the long riggs and the evening's revels begin.

And when we die, Jinny used to tell him, it's only as a wee white dog enters the dark forest, all wary and excited and alert. The trees arch over, the dog trots on and is gone from view. It's simple as that. No one knows what his adventures are in there.

Sim Elliot sits in his bedroom, at the dressing table that was his mother's. He looks into the dark smudges of his eyes in the mirror as he inhales. For a moment he hears her voice *Come here, my wee darlin*. He puts the joint aside, lowers his shaggy head to the wood and sniffs. For a moment, the whiff of mother, something of lilac and bathsalts. She crumbles cubes into the bath and turns it blue. He is sitting in her lap in steaming water, her hands linked round his tummy. They are singing, her hot soft shakes against his back. *Where have you been, my blue-eyed boy?* He is held, embraced, at one. As with Jinny. *Where have you been, my darling young one?*

Just a moment then it's gone. He sniffs again but she won't come back. She has gone into the dark wood, the wood his mother and Jinny, Patrick and Fiona, his father and even the family's Jack Russell terrier have entered. That he will enter soon.

He pushes himself upright. He does not feel well. He really does not feel well. There's no particular pain at the moment, just a feeling in his core that he's about to fall down.

He does up the top button of his white shirt, feeling it pinch around his neck. He pulls a face, hearing Jinny's laughter as he tries to brush his hair into shape. She'd been looking forward to dressing up and going out on the town that last weekend. She'd started to become impatient with the enclosed world of the dale. Lately she complained Patrick seemed content with casual labour and living day by day without ambition or direction. But she talked of the Open University and a chance to use her brain, to get out and do something in the world. The baby, home-brewing, gardening and endless jam-making, pickling and preserving, were no longer enough for her energies.

Her electric-blue, velvety dress, stockings and lace-up boots – she was changing under his eyes. Her figure had returned but some of the lightness, the insistence that life was an easy adventure, that had gone. She seemed to him preoccupied, even when they were together, even when she looked into his eyes there seemed to be some question being asked. Or maybe he was asking it: Have we deluded ourselves? Has all this shame and wickedness been for nothing but a few fantasies and spasms of pleasure?

They were walking below the castle in the old town in silvery drizzle. Her face lit up then was swept with shadow as they passed another lamp and she was starting to talk about Patrick. Sim sees himself in top hat and tails but that's nonsense. He would have worn the near-black linen jacket. White shirt, dark tie of his Border riding. Clean-shaven in those days but his hair getting long enough to raise eyebrows in the dale. You should have a ponytail, she said. You already smoke enough dope for a longhair.

She'd stopped with the gleaming wet cobble street at her back and said like it had occurred to her for the first time that she'd married Patrick for the same reasons she dropped out of college – because she wanted to, and to piss off her parents. Now she found it impossible to care much about any of them. She was going through the motions, she and Patrick had grown far apart. Marnie was the only thing they had in common and even that . . .

She'd sooked in her breath and was silent, very far away from him. Marriage as rebellion, he'd smiled ruefully at that. He keeked sideways at her, wondering if he was included in her plans or if he was still ready to be. She was no longer glowing when he looked at her, the light on her was only the streetlight. Then she looked back at him quite objectively, hesitated and he guessed he saw the same doubt, the same unspoken question in her eyes before she smiled and put her head to his chest, her arms around his back and palms flattened against him.

I know it's not the same as before, she said. He looked down, relieved and terrifed to hear her say it. But if this can't stay special, we've thrown away all decency and peace of mind for nothing.

She'd finally voiced what he'd scarcely let himself think.

He'd clasped his hands to the back of her head, remembers yet the coarse dampness in his palms and the tearing feeling in his chest and the wetness on his face, and pulled her head against his heart. Her voice was muffled when she spoke again.

If this isn't special then love is a delusion and we've hurt good people for nothing and I'd rather be dead.

They'd stood in the mild dreich night, pressed to each other and the collar of her coat wet in his eyes and her hands now pressed to his arse, and it seemed like neither of them knew where to go from here. Then a group of lads passed, one of them laughed and made a remark about the wee drookit hoor, and Sim broke from her, seized him by the throat and put the fella's head a few times against a convenient wall, ignoring the blows starting to thump in on him.

He smooths out the ridings tie, flips up the collar of his shirt and tries to remember how to do this. Left over right, under, back up through the loop. He remembers yet how good it felt, the relief of turning from Jinny to a fight, the blood rising in him and all his ancestors at his back. The relief of rage, of blows given and taken. The blow to his kidneys was nothing to the hurt of the question she'd begun to voice. He stotted the wee thug's head one more time off the wall, dropped him and turned at a crouch to face the other three, ready for anything. No kick in the balls could compare to the sickener when she'd announced she was pregnant with Patrick's bairn. He heard her scream a warning, put up his arm to catch the blade of the Stanley knife in his sleeve, smashed the hand into the wall of the close, kicked the legs away from the bastard, felt himself being bundled to the wall and knew he was in trouble.

He straightens the knot, smoothes down the tail of the tie, tightens up his gut as he prods another beta-blocker down his throat then settles the linen jacket over his shoulders. A bit tight now, but it will see him out. A city rammie broken up by the police, it had served its purpose. Once he'd washed his face, put ice on the swelling, they'd gone into the restaurant and somehow never finished that conversation, never resolved whatever it was that had been hanging in the balance between them. *I'd rather die . . .*

He will die soon, he knows it, he feels it. The thought calms his hands, for it would be a relief. But first he must face Jinny's girl, the daughter they never had.

His son believes in resurrection of the body. Jinny had her

daft notions of meeting again in many lives, over and over. But he has never seen Jinny since that last unfathomable look as she fell away from him on Creagan's Knowe, and their unborn child died with her. Death is an end, thank God. Only for one brief time had his life been worth living. He had known joy, long syne. Perhaps it's better not to have, but on the whole he doubted that.

He straightened the jacket, pulled the comb through his beard. The man in the mirror looked tall but stooping slightly like a bigger man deflated. But the man in the mirror looked almost amused, had perhaps some spunk in him yet. He could have been going out on the town with Jinny, for maybe their twenty-fifth anniversary and trying not to get into a fight this time, instead of going downstairs to meet her daughter.

His belly was quivering. He really felt he could shit himself. He had wanted and feared this moment for so many years. It was almost the only thing he wanted or feared. Almost the only thing left to do other than get the estate settled.

He squared his shoulders, took a quick drag and exhaled. He opened the door and stood at the top of the back stairs. He could hear the voices now. Davy, the high-pitched Canadian, then a deeper murmur. Her. Marnie. Jinny's lassie.

He closed the door behind him and set off down the creaking stair.

And when we die, he thought dreamily, it's like a woman pulling off her summer dress and walking to the edge of a river pool, feeling for the last time the earth beneath her toes before letting go and diving out, away, into the current.

He almost knocked before going into his own sitting room, hearing at some great distance a muffled barking. The doorknob was slippy in his palm. He turned it and went in to meet whatever.

The man and the woman stand looking into each other across a room gone faint. She's all in black, a greenish shawl about her shoulders and something glinting at her breast. Both have cheekbones and eyes like flint arrowheads. They stand, frozen, mid-step towards each other. His hands are coming up empty as though he was offering her

something invisible. Her left hand holds a glass, her right hand is
bunched behind her back.

Stare till your eyes ache.

The man who killed Jinny is a handsome charred devil. I
should have been prepared for that. We were all on our feet as
he stood in the doorway. I said and did nothing, just waited,
feeling the shake go through me like lightning ripping down a
trunk.

Dad, David said. Dad, this is Marnie Lauder from Crawhill.

The power is in the waiting and I've waited long for this. He
stood with his dark burnt-out eyes set on mine. His hand came
up, palm open towards me. Powerful hand, broad palm, long
fingers strong to love or kill. The mouth that once kissed Jinny
opened and I felt myself falling away from everything known.
His voice was deep and slightly slurred.

It's been a long wait, lass, he said. I'm right glad you've
come.

His hand shook slightly as I stepped towards him and
looked up into that face. My hand came up of itself. Heat of his
palm on mine, then our fingers wrapped tight. The shock went
right down to my feet, earthed through my soles. He leaned,
turning his head like trying to see past me to someone else. He
looked so hard into me that for the first time I doubted myself.

You dinna look like your mother.

I thrust up a laugh. So who do I look like? My dad?

He kept his eyes on me, so close now I saw myself tiny in his
pupils.

I never saw Patrick beardless, he said carefully, so it's hard
to say.

Still he clung on to my hand. I gripped back and felt the
pulse of his thumb. Anyone else in the room had gone faint
like in the plates. Burned out though he was, I felt the heat and
the sex in him as I stared him back. For a moment it seemed we
stood in a high place, just the two of us, with the green stir of
trees on one side and the death-drop on the other.

He loosened my fingers and our palms slid apart.

You're welcome in my house, he said.

And you in mine, I said, and let the shawl slide back to show the brooch pinned high on my black sweater, and had the pleasure of seeing him turn pale as moon on snow.

*

Annie Tat brought drinks then they went through to the dining room. Shifting yellow candlelight, meat on the table, pasta for the lady fair, wine red in the glasses. The grouping was as foreshown – the young man silent next to his intended, the father opposite, staring into his glass. The two women bent towards each other across the table.

No one will remember what was said that evening. Only Annie Tat heard the faint creak above as her man went soft-footing up the backstairs to the study, and she banged crockery and joked as she served until she heard the footsteps descending. No one talked about the past nor asked about the future. There was only the women laughing and the candlelight stirring deep pools around the eyes, and the pale glimmer of the ancient coin set in the brooch's heart.

Shifting groupings at the back door as the young ones make to leave. Sim Elliot drapes the shawl round Marnie's shoulders. She nods acknowledgement but her eyes are fixed on the stone disc and its bunch of keys that David dirls from his index finger. She crosses to the kennel and crouches down. Hawk growls low, rises to his feet.

Careful, David calls. He's not usually violent, but . . .

Her hand comes out slowly, waits, then drops firmly onto the dog's head. Hawk subsides, his head turns and he licks her palm. She squeezes his ears then gets up.

Nor am I, she says to David. As she walks to the Land-Rover, Tat drifts from the shadows and slips Jinny's old note into her palm. She pockets it, and then there is waving and thank-yous.

Go canny, Sim says, you're all half-pissed already.

He holds out his hand to Marnie but she raises her arms and clasps his shoulders, pulls him down to whisper something in his ear. He jerks back and bumps against Annie Tat who steadies him with her hand flat against his back. The engine grunts and catches, white lights stab into the trees. In the dazzle only Tat sees Marnie's hand come out the window to drift pale as an owl, and how her palm angles as with her little finger and thumb she signs for him alone the gesture he thought had long vanished from the Border country.

And then they are gone. Tat shivers as he steps inside. *Revenge hot trod. You may not hinder me.*

Annie is clattering plates in the kitchen, Elliot has already vanished up the back stairs. Tat stands in the doorway and lights a cheroot as he watches the headlights swing down into the valley. None will get much sleep tonight, that's for sure.

Plate 7

The second-last plate is the most vividly coloured and detailed of
them all. Here is action, scene after scene, linked by drove roads, the
flight of birds, brambly briars, drystane dykes laced against the sky.

Even at first glance this plate is one of fatal meetings, final part-
ings, fights and ghosts and resolutions. At the centre are linked per-
mutations of sexual meeting, skeletons white in river beds, bairns
held defiantly. Around them salmon leap from rivers at the end of
arcing rods, lovers turn into birds, fly into the sun or rise to meet the
arrow's flight.

In the cold hard angular metal of the Land-Rover cab, Marnie
and Jo are squeezed in beside David. They're giggling and carrying on, pushing him against the door as he struggles to steer
between ruts. He tries to listen to them but his head is floating
high alongside the white moon above the dale, pierced by sliv-
ers of blackness then clear again.

The dirt road twists downhill and the moon is lost. At the
edge of the headlights' onrush he sees bushes sway back like
gasping crowds as they lurch by. He winds the window down
and feels the cool and fragrant air wrap round his face.

It is too long since he's been out in the country at night, his
senses alive to the mystery and the danger. He wants that
again, to feel young, alert, on the loose, his life hanging by the
speed of his reactions, each moment sharp as a blade drawn
across the skin.

Perhaps it's the whisky and then the wine and the raised
state of his companions – and how long is it since he's seen Jo
like this, so aroused and vital? – but he has a parallel vision of
them moving through the darkness under the trees on their
trusty hobbie horses. Moving near-silently towards the village, the crouched houses and darkened corrals, as they re-
hearse the fell business to be done there . . .

He feels the heavy leather jerkin stitched with metal, leather boots and breeches, the steel helmet pressing down on his forehead. The lance, the short sword, the coarse rope coiled on his pommel, the fire-making kit in his saddlebag along with bannocks and dried meat. They are moving in single file with no need to speak, taking the secret ways through the woods and mosses. Flurries in the undergrowth where weasel and fox pursue their ends. A white owl moves through the gash in the clouds where the last light holds, banks and is gone into the ruined keep and its song of stone.

We could die tonight, he thinks. One mistake, wrong turn or hesitation and it's over for ever. That's what lights this fizz in his belly and lets him see in the dark. That is the cause of the love he feel for his companions who ride alongside. We are reiving, he thinks, reiving into the unknown, and for this hour we are alive.

The wheel jerks and nearly breaks his thumb. He smothers the blasphemy that rises in his throat and he slows as they pass by the shallow linns at the bottom of the woods, still shining grey in the night. The women have dropped some argument about feminism and art in favour of tickling each other. He has never seen either of them like this, so wild and lit up.

Even as his pulse beats in his neck, he shakes his head at his fantasies, the ones that warmed his frozen boyhood. He had forgotten so much. Above all, though he'd always known reiving was business in stolen cattle, kidnapping and protection rackets, at times the sole economy of these lawless parts – he'd forgotten it was *exciting*. Sin and sex make us glow like coals in the dark. That's why we do it, to burn. Though the night is all around and in us, we are on fire and we like it. We like it. We choose it. That's why it happens, over and over.

Jo stabs her fingers into his ribs. He jerks and jabs her back. Squeals of laughter in the cab as he swings onto the winding narrow road into the village up ahead. So this is why Dad had that affair, for the burning wild feeling. We aren't so different. I too want to feel like this more often, to burn my life instead of stolid sullen smouldering.

Lord pluck me from this fire.

He swerves into the car park outside the first pub, aware

that somewhere along the way – and he's never quite been able to pinpoint exactly where – they have passed through that invisible doorway out of the dale. They're now in the recognisable world. They pile out, Jo jumps up and crooks her arm around his neck, clasps the other round Marnie, and between them they carry her to the front door. Through small dirty windows the lights burn too white and hard. The place is packed with young locals scowling round the pool table, jabbing the jukebox and shaking the electronic bandit, pushing for pints at the short dark bar.

A word, he says, and puts Jo down. This isn't necessarily a nice place. The women hoot with laughter. Not nice! No, seriously, he says, we must tone down a bit. I'm from here but I'm not. We're from the big house. I'm supposedly posh and you're two uncowed half-pissed gorgeous women and that's not common round here, right?

Right right right! So let's get rat-arsed!

Marnie already has her hand on the door. Fine, David says. Just remember this is their village, not ours, so we go canny.

You make it sound like Dodge City, David.

Put it this way, Jo – just a few years back one cowboy here killed another because he took the last chicken supper in the chip shop after the pubs had closed. Unfortunately I'm not joking. So we just keep our heads down in the corner, right? I'm not wanting to get into a fight on your behalf. I'm no fighter and anyway it's against my religion.

Hmm, Marnie said. As she pushes down the handle she looks back at him, eyes black tarns in the shadow cast from above. Are you sure about that?

There are of course scenes of drinking on these plates. You never paid them much attention before, that not being your weakness, but certainly you'll wince in the morning and avert your eyes from the trio staggering down a country lane, one waving down the moon, the second raising a squat bottle to his? her? lips, the third turning away to throw up over a wall. You'll look away but still glimpse the fourth one, the one who waits behind the tree, weapon drawn to cover their passing.

The challenge came as it had to. Since their entrance David had met and nodded to certain eyes and taken care not to meet others, shepherded the women into a corner table out of the ruck and tried to keep them from being too loud and outrageous. A round of pints went down without incident, he went for another and started to relax. He turned from the bar with three full glasses, stepped round a foot that happened to be sticking out, swerved away from an elbow jabbing back by chance, and made it back to the table.

Marnie and Jo were arguing about borders and frontiers. Nationality. Born in one country, living in another, educated in both – what is David? Does it matter? Where exactly is the border, and does that line divide a unity or connect a diversity? David suggested the peoples of the Borderland had more in common with each other than the rest of their own country, then drank and listened while monitoring the situation around them. He wasn't a stranger, faces turned their way, mouths moved, muttered, turned away. The lads with women weren't a problem as a rule. The ones to watch were the teenage drunks though they mostly fought their own. Worse were the ageing nutters, the ones whose pals had settled, leaving a lone bewildered belligerent, the one whose violence and fearlessness the girls had fancied in their teens and as women now kept well away from.

Or masculine and feminine, another kind of borderline, Marnie was saying.

Well there's all kinds of trespass can go on there, Jo said quickly. Mucho ambiguities and ambivalence.

Marnie glanced at her over the rim of her pint glass then nodded. So the outstanding question is, she said, whether you like borders or think we'd be better without them.

It's all one to me, David said but no one took much notice.

For myself, she went on, I like having these lines drawn – Scotland, England, male, female – so I can raid across them. Much more exciting.

That's terribly unsound, Jo said, but I like it.

Thought you might.

Marnie grinned sloppily, tilted her pint again to her face. David took his eye off the bar.

It was only the Border that allowed the reivers to operate for so long, he said. Like crossing the Rio Grande or the state line in westerns. That's what made it ungovernable, and it suited both countries having this buffer zone. With the union of crowns it all came to an end very quickly.

How did they end it? Jo asked.

By hanging a few hundred and deporting the rest to the New World, where some of them did pretty well. Once the Border no longer signified, they had nowhere to run to. The Border made it all possible. You may well be descended from them.

The chair squawked as Marnie got to her feet.

I'll get this one. She looked over at the bar then down at them. There's a strip of forest just along the road from here, she said. Not a wide one, just a belt of trees. But one side of the forest is England, the other is Scotland – right, David?

Aye, right enough. He must be drunk, his voice was starting to echo in his head and his tone to change.

Jo stared at Marnie, apparently riveted.

And inside? she asked. Inside in the middle of the wood, which country is that?

It's . . . debatable. I think they're still arguing about it. I took a walk there the other day, right down the middle of the wood. It's . . . an interesting place to be.

Jo drained her pint, eyes shining.

I'd like to check that out, Marnie.

Then we'll do it. But right now I need a drink.

She moved easily through the ruck towards the bar, turning sideways, meeting some head-on, not pushing but not yielding. David watched her go, feeling he'd missed something.

This is great, Jo said. It's good to get out of the glen and I really like her, you know? I can see why you kept hanging round her place.

I did not! Twice at most.

Jo put her hand on his, splayed her pale thin fingers.

I'm not jealous, she said. In the least. That's what I'm telling you. If Jinny was anything like Marnie, I can see what your dad saw in her.

A stir, a cool draught as the door opened. Tat slipped in

with his bike padlock and chain in his hand. David hadn't thought Tat socialised in the village, raised his hand in greeting. Tat nodded to them then his head twitched as he stared hard across the room towards the bar, and it was only then David picked up the vibe. He stood up to better see Marnie with a group of men crowding her and a couple of lassies looking on.

He moved quickly in on the group, heart thumping. She'd got herself into an argument about the boundary ridings that had split the town over women riders. Daft to have offered an opinion. The two girls were sneering at her, one flicked ash into her drinks. Though Marnie's accent was mongrel and hard to place in country or class, she wore black wool trousers, shawl, tan boots and no make up. She was definitely not one of them.

It's all fuckin lesbians causing the stooshie, the curly-haired man crowding her on the left said. Anybody kens that.

David was still trying to push through. With her hands full of pints, she was vulnerable. Blessed are the peacemakers, he thought, but I'm ready for a fight. I want to hit somebody.

The other man knocked her elbow and drink slopped onto the nearest girl's dress.

Look what the bitch has done, the girl said. You'll be paying for the cleaning.

The smaller man, one David minded as one of the village nutters from his time, said You'll be a lezzie and all, eh? You and your pal wi the bog-brush hair.

As David edged in, he saw her eyes flicker. He was sure she was choosing between putting the drinks down to free her hands, or making a joke, or chucking the pints over them. Then anything could happen.

Hey, we're getting thirsty over here, he said and tried to make a gap for Marnie to get away from the bar. But she stretched up and whispered something into curly's ear. David saw his face go red, he even moved back a step, and they might have got away but the wee nutter's hand clamped on his arm.

You'll be here to push another of our women off a cliff, hey Davit?

David blinked, saw the other arm come up to go behind his head. He knew this move: the head butt, the Glasgow kiss, and he felt the energy rush through him as he stepped sideways, clasped both hands across the back of the man's head and slammed his face down into the bar. The crack was not pretty, the fella began to slide down to the floor, the girls screamed at blood on their dresses as two more bodies were moving in and he had no room to back off. Three to one, oh Jesus. Then there was a whirling glitter and a louder crack on the bar as Tat slammed down the padlock chain and retrieved it in a flash to face the group in a fighting crouch.

Out, he said. On ye go, man.

A way opened and he and Marnie walked through it towards where Jo was sat round-eyed, her lips bloodless. Marnie put the pints on the table and seized her hand to pull her up.

Time to go home, my dear, she said.

David looked back at the bar and hesitated. Wee Tat was facing three big men. The other was stirring on the floor. The rest looked undecided, it could go either way. He couldn't leave Tat, not while the adrenalin still shook through his body and a fight was there to be had.

Aye, away hame, young Elliot. That's enough shenanigans for one night.

The man who spoke was still sitting down but indefinably in charge of the room. Big red amiable face, thinning curly hair. MacIver the local policeman, off-duty but still a presence.

Let them go, he said calmly to the crowd. They didna start it.

Marnie pushed Jo towards the door. Then she lifted her pint, took a look round the room with her head high, and folk fell silent where she looked. She smiled and drank deeply then smacked the glass down on the table.

Come on, Davy, she said, and tugged till he followed her out through the door.

In the rattling silence in the Land-Rover, David checked in the mirror but no lights were following. The excitement ebbed and left him shaky.

That was just disgusting, Jo said quietly. She was sitting well away from him. I couldn't believe that was you. You know how I feel about violence.

She was shivering. David swung onto the dirt road but said nothing. He thought it was pretty disgusting himself and he was frightened and exhilarated by this stranger that had been born, fully grown and dangerous, inside him ten minutes ago. Marnie put her arm round Jo.

Davy was right, she said. There was no other way out. It was my fault – should have kept my mouth shut but it's hard when people talk shite.

Horrible, Jo whispered. Is this deliverance or what? I thought this was a nice quiet place.

Marnie smoothed her hand across Jo's rigid neck. In the cab dimness David saw her fingers stroke and knead.

Nice? she said. It's anything but that. What do you want, Jo? Me just to accept insult humbly and know my place? David to be humiliated – and believe me, he'd had to have grovelled. It's not in Elliot blood. Nor Lauder, she added.

In the blood, Jo said. I can't believe I'm hearing this. What century are you living in?

But her head began to drop and her shoulders slacken.

No, Marnie said, believe me the boy did right. If you've got to do violence, it must be quick and total, it's the only way. Did you hear the sound his head made!

David winced in the dark. It was not something he cared to think of. He heard it again, crack of bone on solid wood. Worst, he caught the retreating savage joy of it. Tomorrow he must pray. And then leave here, leave this place which seemed like a dark mirror reflecting back things he'd rather not see, leave and never come back.

Tat saved us, he said. Without him we'd be mince. I must thank him rightly the morn.

You must. Our guardian angel, eh?

Marnie reached into her pocket and drew out a half bottle of whisky. I think we all need a wee medicinal, she said. For the shock.

She cracked the cap, held the bottle to Jo's mouth until her lips opened and she swallowed.

Good deep swallow. And again. She stroked Jo's head then held out the bottle. Here, Davit.

Somewhere along the way they crossed the invisible frontier and were back in the different atmosphere of the dale. They crossed the bridge by the hornbeam, still passing the bottle as they went round the hill, and by the time they were bumping along the drove road towards Crawhill they were singing loudly *In Scarlet Town where I was born, there was a fair maid dwelling.*

As Marnie led the singing, David had a whisky vision: bright morning, a dusty drove road, a dark young man on a horse singing. And then a woman stands up from behind the dyke, young woman in a long green dress, fair hair and a good voice high and clear as she sings the response *And her name was Barbara Allan.* The rider stops, looks down, and David sees the young man is Marnie, and knows the woman as himself and it feels good to have these hips, this body, this triumphant heart and a voice so pleasing to herself and to her lover looking down smiling in the morning of the day.

*

He stood alone in the dark by the Land-Rover, swaying slightly as the stars drifted and swirled overhead. Somewhere in the valley a barking dog grew hoarse then stopped. The women's voices faint from the cottage, a lamp coming on at the bedroom window like a reiver's signal. It was time he went home. It was time they all went home. There was something he had to say to someone, it had been just off the edge of his mind all evening. No matter. He felt warm and muzzy and tall under the night sky. He looked up again and saw the Hunter midleap across the northern sky, the scalp of another galaxy hanging from his belt.

Bonnie fight, my Lord Elliot.

She was at his shoulder, a darker blackness, only the gleam of the brooch and lavender in the night air.

It wasn't one I sought.

But it found you just the same.

A long pause. She passed him the bottle and he felt the burn on his lips. Fact was he felt challenged and complete with her standing there. He thought again of the young man rising and the woman behind the wall. It made a secret warmth in his chest like whisky going down. It could have worried him but it didn't. If that was part of him, so be it.

Spook, she said quietly. The night's full of it. It can be beautiful.

You're of the night, aren't you?

She laughed quietly, stirred in her black sweater and black trousers. She touched his arm, lightly, once.

I love the night, she said, but I'm not of it. Not entirely. I just like to be in it sometimes.

A long echoing pause, big and intimate as the night. Yes, he said at last. I understand. The distinction she was making seemed to illuminate all that was rich about her. What was it like seeing my father?

She stirred at his side, made some deep sound in her throat. Again the silence, faint singing of Jo in the cottage.

He's just a man, Marnie said, though once a sexy one. Her voice was low, deep brown but clear, like the burns coming off the peat moor. He looks pretty wasted and worried and not happy. But I still believe he killed Jinny.

You can't know that, Marnie. If he loved her, why should he kill her? Come on!

To keep the estate. To keep the affair secret. Because he'd tired of her. She sounded doubtful. Oh I don't know. Maybe I should let it drop, go back to where I came from.

Where was that anyway?

He waited. She didn't reply.

Why don't you ask him? David said eventually. Ask him about Jinny.

Maybe I will at that.

But first ask yourself what she would want.

He heard her breath cough out in the dark. Then she breathed in deeply at his side.

Thank you, she said. It's time I did that.

Talking of time, he said. I'd best be getting back.

What, and leave your lady fair in my clutches?

Don't be daft. We'll head off.

You're in no state to drive, she said. And certainly not for walking the brig over the falls in the dark. Jo's put the kettle on. Here, have a cookie – made them myself this afternoon.

He felt in her hand and took the biscuit. It was crumbly and earthy in his mouth, with little chips that didn't taste like chocolate. Nice enough, but.

*

A long night and it wasn't by yet, not for me anyhow. I'd a notion Davy was coming to his end once I heard the door bang and spied him veering across the garden, birling slowly round like a falling sycamore seed. He found the gate, couped over it and got up again, still mumping away to himself. Dad, listen to me, eh, right? Something to say to you, you gotta hear this. Important, canna wait.

The loon was far gone, right enough. I seldom seen a man so fou, if that's what he was. I kept my head down and scried over the dyke, watched him wave his arms up as the moon tummled from the clouds and he thumped into the Land-Rover. Curses and blasphemies I'd never heard from him afore. He got the door open and fell in.

I stood up, minded to loup the dyke and stop him. I couldn't let him drive like yon. More sweirs but no engine starting up. I jaloused he couldn't find the keys or one of the women had taken them off him.

I hunkered down by the off-side wheel and waited and wondered what for the best. The boy was raving away but seemed quite blythe. Best for who, anyhow? Best for me and Annie, best for young Elliot, old Elliot, Jinny? Or her that I was in thrall to? Even crouched behind the wheel I felt yet the soft heat she'd left inside me, the peace she'd brought when she opened me up like a whelk. In the bar – I did that for her as much as young Elliot, she kent that and the flash of her eye made it worth. I never much liked drinking there anyhow.

So I crouched and waited, trying to sort my thoughts and strategies while the laddie haivered on.

*

We might not really exist – that primal terror we wake to in the night. When she was really guttered my mum could look right through and not see me. As a boy I was scared to pass mirrors in case I looked and saw no one.

But it's not that. I certainly exist, this consciousness in this body in this cold cab and mind spinning out among the stars and the black night.

But what if David Elliot, forester, fiancé and stuffed shirt, is the fantasy, and the brawling callant in the pub and the young woman I was behind the wall are at least as real? Perhaps it's true and Spook exists, invisible but ever-present as the air and the Mercy, and the dead lean into us.

We were sitting round the cottage table blethering then I was looking at Marnie and saw a host there, flickering and shape-changing in the bones of her face. Saw the young man riding and my dad and all the women and companions I've ever wanted, the sister I never had. Saw all the people she had met and been in this lifetime and others.

She looked back into my eyes, smiled slowly and it was clear she didn't exist, and she knew it and that was the source of the glow that hung about her. That was what made her different or plain mad.

And I felt myself plunging into her eyes like twin peat-dark lochans set on a pale moor, and I didn't know if she wanted to destroy or have me, and just for a minute I saw she doesn't know either. And then I had to be out, get some fresh air, drive home and talk to Dad. Leave Jo and Marnie, they'd know what to do.

It's cool in the cab, some stars are out now, the Hunter is keeling into Lang Rigg and something is snuffling around my wheel. Above our heads a shooting star stravaiges and I wish that all might be redeemed. Consciousness isn't so much a stream as a falling weir, silvery and dark. I feel myself on the edge of a great freedom, some great knowledge, and then I am falling and I go with it without fear, for all is fated and is good.

Silence from inside the cab, the boy had passed out at last. I stretched my shanks and listened to the great wheesht of the night blowing over the moor. Then the cottage door opened and blackness came out.

I heard her footsteps come over the grass, heard the cab door clunk open. Imagined her looking down at young Elliot, wondering what to do. I read and hear signs like no man, but I didn't know what she would do with him.

A soft rustle. I keek up round the wheel, she is spreading something over him. And she is crooning like a mother to a bairnie *Where hae ye been, my blue-eyed boy? Where hae ye been, my darling young one?* Then she was gone, back to the cottage. She'd happed him in a blanket. She may mean well.

I would serve a cause and have done most of my life, but I am lost not knowing now whose cause I serve. What will the woman do now, whose cause does she follow? The breeze reishled one time through dry grass as I padded up to the cottage.

The lady fair was dancing alone to the radio, arms wrapped round herself and thin hair like cut grass, shaved short into the soft of her neck.

He's passed out, I said. I put a blanket on him.

She giggled. The hash cookies were too much for him, Marnie. She pirouetted past me. Looks like it's down to the hard core now. I'm blasted but not tired.

Me neither, I said, and put the kettle on again.

I was standing at the sink waiting for the boiling and washing up the morning's bowls, very aware she'd been peeking at the plates while I was out. The silence was like after a bell has rung and faded. I glanced round. The pink plates, of course. People always go for the Lovers' Plates. Her small fair head was bent over them. She'd taken off her sweater while I'd been out and was just wearing a skinny white T-shirt. With the stove blazing, the room was very warm.

These are like icons on a screen? she said. You feel you could kinda click on them and it would all open out and there'd be action.

Then she was standing beside me. An owl hooted outside, the room was quiet but for the pulse in my ears.

You were very brave, she said all throaty. I thought it was

wonderful the way you stood up to them.

I shrugged like it was nothing. I'll not be bad-mouthed, I said, or have women be. Actually it was very stupid.

Very strong, she insisted. I wish I could be like that, brave in my body, but I'm not. She laughed. Not when it comes to a fight, anyway.

She was leaning against me now, her hip fitting in below mine. I stopped the washing and stood with my hands in the water. Her hand stroked my forearm, the dark damp hairs there, and I shivered from the hashish sensitivity.

Strong, she said. I always want to be close to women's strength.

And when I didn't move one way or the other, she ran her hand up my arm, paused on my shoulder. She let her hand drift down onto the brooch above my breast. As we looked at each other, she opened her eyes very wide. Her pupils were huge, her nervous swollen lips parted. It's a long time since a woman looked at me like that, and no man, for that is not a man's look.

Her hand came up slowly to my cheek. Such a soft touch, I had forgotten. She touched my lips, my mouth opened of its own, a little finger slid inside my upper lip.

I let her think it was all her doing, for that was the only power she had. I let her lips come to mine, then closed my eyes.

She was stronger than I could have guessed. Thin limbs smooth and hard as carved wood, the only woman I've known with a flat stomach, a runner's legs, tiny breasts with long nipples that embarrassed her and delighted me between my teeth.

She was fierce in her way, my first Canadian, my little Jo. She sucked on my mouth till my lips swelled, and then her hand in me pushed and turned, and her other hand teased so lightly I was near pleading for her, then her wee red tongue spreading brush-fires through the undergrowth. My little seductress looked up at me through the bedroom lamplight, big-eyed and pleased with my state, sure she'd made me hers. And I let her think it awhile until I grasped her head and clamped her there till she had drunk off all the sweetness within me.

Which is a lot, by the way. And to some extent renewable.

We lay awhile, her head damp on my belly. Now me you, I said, and pulled her up alongside me.

I began at the top and worked down. Good her cries and hands gripping in my hair. I gave her the pleasure once then put my legs between hers, turned her over and started in on her again. I wanted her to remember this, and it had been so long I was greedy, and I was savage from trying to punish by magic the lover who has me.

*

The cries of women mating mind me of hawk and weasel with their claws into each other. Thin high skreeks mounting up and up the scale to a final squeal, a long tearing from the throat. With the blanket hung across the window, I couldn't see them but I could hear, and picture well enough. Then it began again, the cheips and groans deep in the thrapple. They have sic stamina, women at their loving. And me, I hunkered down with my hands at the laich of my belly, and burned and burned for her uncanny force.

*

There came a time I realised she was not moving, that thin body finally slack and soft. Fair stubble hair on my pillow, her mouth open, passed out or asleep. She looked a child and I held her for a while for sake of all the children needing held.

I drank some water at the sink, scooping it up into my mouth. We'd been somewhere out among the galaxies, and I had almost forgot myself and lost my name. But not quite. I splashed cold water over my head. Great sex, raw and subtle, long and even tender, but I had not lost nor found myself in it, and I stood at the sink and wept.

*

At last, no soun. I saw her shadow at the window where Jinny had stood lang syne, waiting for Elliot to dress and slip away to his rightful bed across the Liddie water. Then she fuffed out the lamp and I saw no more.

I stood and stretched, wakeful yet though the dawn wasn't far off. I could rouse young Elliot on a ruse, get him into the cottage to see what was sleeping there. But I couldn't figure the outcome of that, nor what way it would fall, nor even how I'd want it to. So I checked he was still away with the fairies, and set off for some early breakfast. Let it fall as it will, I thought, or maybe as she wills.

I jigged down across the loaning in the half-dark, thinking again of Jinny and Sim Elliot. To this day I ken not exactly when they started up again. Some time I think after that meeting on the brig when she turned away so tired and dreary. It's hard doing the right thing and it makes us weary. It's like an alkie off the bevvy, it's the right way to live but in a world so dreich that often as not we reach for that fire again. I ken, I ken.

But Elliot and Jinny began trysting again in the year afore she died, I'm sure of that. You'd have to be blind not to see the distracted dwam in Jinny's eye as she dandled the bairn on her knee and taught me the pattern of the plates, head and eye aye cocked towards the door. Deaf not to hear the waewan in his voice when he talked to Fiona or Davy, and the desperation in his song as he went about the yard.

It couldn't go on. The lovers were peelie with lack of sleep. Not fou with joy and randiness like before, but weighted down like their trysting was a penance. Fiona was drooping or sarky, right tired. That's when she took on Annie as a school wean new come the village, evenings and weekends, and we first set eyes on each other. And Annie saw my position here and what it might lead to, and I saw what she had in herself.

Sense it has made, good enough. We each turn the blind eye to the other's wee fooleries. I dinna mind. It keeps her happy, and whiles it rouses me to lie aside her and think of Elliot's cock moving atween the douce braes of her arse, and then sometimes I can do it and that seems to please her. We shoogle along fine and we raise the kids. Only lovers dream of mair.

As I louped the last gate I thought too of Jinny's note for Elliot round the time they thought she was with child, and wondered what Marnie would make of it. Then in for a right good bacon buttie and a quick lie-down in the workroom, surrounded by my latest netsuke goblins, their beady siller and ruby eyes winking in the mirk.

Here in a panel off to the side, so discreet you have to peer and wonder, are two heads in a bed, one fair one dark. It was foreshadowed in the early plates too. Thirsty and hungover in the halflight, you rub them lightly with your thumb and wonder what next.

Go back to the bedroom, naked and shivering, very fragile. There's a man in the Land-Rover who might wake anytime. There's his lady fair curled up in your bed. There are many many options here.

Now the moment comes, you are divided and unsure. Revenge, yes, but on these innocents? They have not harmed you. Just who and what do you want for yourself?

The cold decides it. You pull on jeans and sweater and go back to bed. She stirs once, her arm comes out your way and rests across your breast. Let it be so. Let the world make of it what it will.

David woke up and banged his head on the steering wheel. Grunted, grasped the blanket to his face, studied it. Jo must have laid it on him. Kind of her. She must have crashed out in the cottage.

He half fell out of the Land-Rover. The weather had changed again, brisk wind from the east shaking the corbie nests in the flayed beech trees. That woodland was in poor shape, it should be coppiced, thinned, replanted. Though it wasn't his problem it bothered him. Grey cloud shrouding the dale, cold wind through dry branch. Spring postponed.

He walked cautiously towards the cottage, feeling he'd missed or forgotten something. There'd been some kind of comprehension last night, some momentary understanding of how things were and had to be. Or maybe just hallucination brought on by whisky, wine, beer then hashish. Of course he'd known perfectly well, had recognised the taste immediately from student days, but because he was pissed and greedy had gone for it anyway.

He went into the kitchen, half expecting to see them slumped over the table, or else brisk and hideously cheerful making breakfast. No one around, perhaps they'd already gone out. The bedroom door was ajar. He hesitated, tapped on it, went in.

David looked for a long time. With the blankets askew, he saw more of Jo than he'd ever seen, her naked back, one little pink-tipped breast flopped over, her hand across Marnie's chest like a child clutching her teddy. Marnie facing away, still in the black sweater from the night before. Jo clinging to her.

He looked for a long time and he didn't know what he was seeing. Surely this was innocence, a lovely picture corrupted by his dirty mind.

He stepped closer, his eyes adjusting to the curtained halflight. He saw a breast that he'd kissed only once in a moment of weakness, he saw new livid streaks on Jo's back scored across the old pale injuries. He could see nothing of Marnie's face, just the side of her cheek, her ear, the dark hair parting over its lobe.

He could be looking at innocence or wickedness. At everything he wanted and all he couldn't have. At love, ambiguity, betrayal. Spontaneity, accident, calculation. He could as well be looking at his own soul.

Or perhaps it was just two women asleep together.

As he left the room, Marnie opened her eyes again and waited.

Room service!

He stood in the doorway holding two mugs of tea, a plate with toast and honey. Marnie turned her head to him.

You're an advanced life-form, Elliot, she said. Thanks.

She sat up and Jo's hand slid off her.

I'm afraid we were all rather bad last night, she said.

She reached out for her tea and as she stretched David saw the waist of her blue jeans. Jo's head swung round, eyes opened, stared up at him. Looked to Marnie.

Marnie raised her mug. Top of the morning to you, kid.

I think you need this, David said and held out her mug.

Jo didn't move. She blinked. Far as he could tell in the poor light, her face darkened. Then she sat up. Two brief white slopes he might have sledged down as a whooping joyous boy, but never had. She pulled the blanket up with one hand and passed the other over her eyes. Silence in the room, somewhere a faint creaking of corrugated iron.

I'll leave this with you, David said, put down the mugs and toast and left the room, closing the door behind him.

Great, honey! Marnie said and reached across Jo. Jo put an arm round her shoulder, nuzzled against her neck. Marnie sat more upright and bit into her toast, swigged the tea. God I need a pee, she said and got out of bed.

Marnie?

Yes?

Jo let the blanket fall.

Last night . . .

Just one gaudie night, Marnie said. Don't think about it. She paused at the door. Maybe you need to review your options, but I'm not one of them. God I need that pee.

She went through into the kitchen. David was standing looking out the window at the morning.

Nice one, she said. You're a star.

He turned and looked at her. Black sweater, blue jeans, bare feet. Hair sweat-sculpted, sticking up in little horns. The dark and the fair, he thought, sometimes we have a choice, or think we do.

Can't have too many nights like that, he said.

She nodded, almost grinned, glanced sideways at him as she made for the door.

I wasn't planning on another for a while, she said and was gone, leaving him remembering that last night she wore black trousers not jeans.

*

A hungover breakfast once Jo had come through, no one saying very much, pale faces and eyes down. A brief chat about the scene in the pub and Tat's intervention.

I'll not be going there for a while, David said. Anyway, we're leaving in a couple of days.

Marnie looked up at him.

Me too, she said. I just need to settle something with your dad then you'll not see me here again.

Then there seemed nothing to say. Marnie stood at the door and waved as they got into the Land-Rover. A long pause, then David got out again. He walked back to her. A long moment of blue eyes looking into black. Then she held out her hand, the keys hanging from the stone disc. Her fingers uncurled slowly and she dropped it into his hand.

Thanks, he said. See you.

Uh-huh.

Then they were gone down the drove road, grey dust rising and settling in grey light.

*

Elliot lay alone on his back in his bed in the tower, stretched out full length, feet sticking up, hands clasped over his belly, eyes not opening as the morning light grew. All he needed was a small loyal dog – or perhaps Tat – curled by his feet to look the effigy of a mediaeval knight in a forgotten corner of a church, the image unchanging as the body below collapsed slowly into goo and bone then powder. But he hadn't had a pup for years, and Tat had abandoned him – why else would he have stolen Jinny's note?

So his last loyal follower, his shadow and accomplice, had deserted. Sim had known the end was coming when he finally lay down the night before and closed his eyes on visions of Jinny's daughter. The last time he'd seen her she was a little girl in someone's arms as he came out of the court, staring round-eyed at him with a wooden parrot clasped in her pudgy hand. She'd stared into him and he looked back, even opened his mouth to speak – then Patrick had broken away from the police and started swinging blows into his face, and Sim let him hit till the men in blue separated them. He'd looked then to the child but she'd already been whisked away, and the small crowd around the courthouse turned away from his eyes and bleeding face as though to look at him might be contagious, as though he were already dead.

But he wasn't dead, not yet. He unclasped his hands, wiggled his fingers, stretched his cramped toes. Nothingness would have to wait a bittie longer. On the whole he was looking forward to it, he had been since the moment on top of Creagan's Knowe when his arm came out and Jinny fell away from him with that last look. Since then life had been one long crawl over broken glass. Enduring the trial, Patrick's death months later, the poor drunken sot wandering in front of a bus, the dale condemning and mocking, Fiona's rage. The divorce and half the estate gone, his son growing up a sullen stranger. Waiting for one thing only: the boy to grow up and Marnie to return so he could explain. Or was that two things?

He almost smiled as he swung one leg out of bed. A spiked fist squeezed his heart then released it. He lay panting. Not yet, please God, not yet. I'm not ready. He saw again Marnie's bottomless eyes fixed on him. Worst, he heard her last whisper in his ear the night before. *Justice, Elliot.*

Justice she would surely have. He cautiously rolled out of bed, set both feet on the cold cold floor. He knew now what had to be done.

He swallowed his pills and began to dress. Then the Land-Rover snorted into the courtyard. He stood at the side of the window and watched the fiancée jump out, head averted. Then Davy, slow and stiff-legged.

So. So. He watched them cross the yard. No sign of last night's high spirits. Not a word atween them. David swung the keys from the disc, Elliot wished he wouldn't do that, but when he'd given the stone on the laddie's twenty-first he couldn't explain what it meant for him or the boy would have flung it back in his face.

As David stood back and let Jo pass into the house, Elliot studied his face and saw everything he needed to know there. He'd sensed it the night before in the raised, hectic feeling round the table. Had half known they wouldn't be back that night. It didn't really matter exactly what had happened at the cottage, though he could make a guess. The boy wasn't entirely cool-blooded. David stared where Jo had gone, and looking down at his son's frozen, despairing face, Elliot felt another hot wire across his chest.

He left the window and dressed in the city clothes he'd worn last night. Then he took a small suitcase from under the bed and began to pack the few things he'd need, the clothes, the documents, registering the silence from downstairs that spread through the house like the chill of the tomb.

*

The cold in here is my hangover and the chill left by departed lovers. I put on another sweater and take out at last the note Tat slipped into my hand as we left for the village last night. Yellowed lined paper, torn from a wee notebook I'd say. Written in green biro, faded but legible. I'm suddenly tearful, knowing Jinny's hand moved over this paper. Her mind must have been birling. Certainly her writing is a hurried scrawl.

> Matches, candles
> Aspirin
> Tatties. Beans (green)
> Milk, butter. Domestos
> Library? Brew shop. P.O. (cash)
> Tampax

Well, yes, a shopping list. Innocuous enough. The important part is on the other side, surely. Turn it over, heart thumping, a sense of presence hovering over me. I glance up and for a moment almost see her clear.

No, she does not appear for me. But Spook has brought me here to unravel this. So put assumptions and sentiment aside, be open and empty like Tat's eyes and look at what's in front of you.

Dearest – you seemed so stuck when we first met, far too old too soon. I wanted to tell you it wasn't so bad, life isn't disappointing and we mustn't let it be. And now I wonder if it would have been better if we'd left each other alone.

I can't quite believe that. Everything we felt was real and

279

lovely and in my heart still. You're part of me, always.

But I feel such a shit towards Pat. I'm coming to hate my-self. When I'm not exstatically (sp?) happy, I'm miserable. You too, Sim. And now this situation . . . I said I'd think for both of us and I have. This is the only way it can be – please if you love me don't try to persuade or ask any more, whatever happens. Please. It's been very hard but this is the only course of action I can live with and is right.

Love – J.

ps I was going to chicken out and just leave you this note, but now I've just seen you crossing the top field I know that's wrong. I have to tell you to your face – but I want you to have this anyway.

I'm still sitting here, open and waiting. Odd that the note itself looks less rushed than the shopping list on the other side. Only the postscript is the most scrawly of the lot, as though that were added at the last minute, even as Simon Elliot ap-proached the caravan . . . But according to Tat, Elliot had con-fided in his cups that she was washing her knickers when he came in. She must have finished the note then jumped to the washing. Isn't that a bit strange? Or was she just nervous, or wanting to appear occupied when he entered. Or?

Don't hurry. Circle high above it, look at both sides once again. Picture what this piece of paper asks us – asks Sim Elliot – to believe.

It's meant to look like she wrote the shopping list first. Maybe she did, though why then give it away? Because it was an old list, a piece of paper she happened to have around. But why is it written in such a hurry, at least as scrawly as the postscript? Because she's writing the ps even as Elliot jumps the last fence and approaches the caravan through the snow. Then she crosses to the sink and starts washing . . .

I still myself, then my mind folds its wings and drops.

The shopping list is part of the message, perhaps even a half-conscious clue. *If you love me don't try to persuade or ask any more, whatever happens.* What happens is Jinny gets pregnant, almost as if she knows she will.

I'm not shivering any more though my breath raises clouds. I turn away from the note and look a long time at the penultimate plate. The ambushes, deceptions, betrayals there. Then look at my notes, the order of events, the information I screwed out of Tat. The tryst by the river among the snowmelt, Jinny's late period. Elliot visits the caravan. Jinny washing out bloody knickers as he comes in the door.

Think it through. Lean again over the table, the note, the plates. And then the day stirs, the corbies raise hell in the high trees, and at last I see it clear.

Oh men, men, masters of ambush and plot, so gullible when it comes to a lover's sleight of hand.

Tat hesitated in the hall with the phone dead in his hand. Annie had called from the big house, her voice sharp with excitement. So it had come to that, and so quickly.

He went slowly up the stairs, hearing still the women's cries, the hawk and the weasel. Only one would win that fight, and she had. He crossed to his work-bench, picked up the new hobgoblin, part human part creature of the mind part force of nature. He checked the blind empty eye-sockets. But does she even ken what she's about? he wondered. He looked down at the two tiny rubies that would let the netsuke see, then felt something rustle across his mind like someone had crinkled paper at his ear. He crossed to the window and looked through the scope, trained on the cottage door.

And there she was, standing in the doorway looking directly his way. Her arms came up slowly over her head, slewed down then waved back up again like a dark bird in flight. And again. He felt damp deep in his bowels, and knew she was waving him her way.

She met him by the rickety gate and almost dragged him into the kitchen.

The note Jinny gave Elliot! she said. Her colour was high in her cheeks but mirky under her eyes. The shopping list isn't an accident, Tat. It's part of the message. Elliot was *meant* to read it.

What – she had tae tell him she was getting beans and tatties? Dinna be daft.

No, you donnert wee bugger! Tat blushed. She took his hand and prodded his finger down on one item. *Tampax*.

This is the only item that matters, she said. That's what the list was written for. Just another wee clincher. One too many! Elliot was *meant* to come in and see her washing. And you told me he told you how Jinny pushed him away, but only once he'd felt the pad under her knickers.

She cupped her hands like she was holding a world in miniature and stared at Tat. He felt himself take a redder. She was too oncoming to let him think straight.

Come on, Tat! Isn't it all a little heavy-handed, a bit too pat? Wasn't Jinny supposed to have bought tampons? And then the real pregnancy . . . Oh can't you see!

He saw she was vibrating like a dark struck bell. But he looked and blinked once, emptied his mind and then he saw. Oh he could see well enough.

It was all set up, she said. Elliot had to be convinced Jinny's period had come. That's why all the business with the washing, the shopping list, the pad she let him feel. That's why she wouldn't let him come closer – because then he'd know she'd never stopped being pregnant. The baby was supposedly a bit premature, right? *Wasn't she?*

Tat looked past her out the window at the moor, the clouds coming apart. The woman's possessed, he thought. She's gripped by a notion she'll no let go.

I've nae idea, he said. I swear on it. That's women's stuff and I was but a laddie, and there wasn't so much frank talk back then. She went away to her folks for the baby.

Yes, the family she'd cut off all connection with! Doesn't that strike you as convenient? And then she comes back, what, a couple of months later?

Tat closes his eyes and plays again coming in the cottage door with Elliot and Fiona, Patrick standing dead proud and Jinny, Jinny sitting in the chair holding the bairn and her eyes flicking over them before her head came down.

The bairn was big, he said slowly, I'll grant ye that.

Well! Big *and* premature? Come on!

It's no impossible, Tat said stubbornly. My Laura was that-aways.

Huh! She ran her fingers over the topmost Corbie Plate. If I hadn't assumed Jinny was hundred per cent honest, I'd have worked it out sooner. She said she'd think for both of them, and she did. Oh she did that. No wonder she said it was hard.

She turned away and stood at the window, hands jammed in the pockets of her jeans. He looked and felt the force of her, and aching knew it wouldn't come his way again.

It's possible, I'll grant ye that, he said eventually. No likely, but possible. You spend too much time alane with these plates, they'll turn your brain. Jinny never took them out much and she was richt.

Man, the truth's in them staring at you! The baby was Elliot's and he doesn't even know it.

For a moment he looked straight back into her eyes. It minded him of looking down into his shotgun barrels, so round and black, and he turned away thinking her not well.

If you want to be sure of the faither, you can do yon DNA, he said.

She went over to the window and stared out. She began to chew on her thumbnail, seemed so lost in thought she'd forgotten he was there. He looked at her, wondering, while he let his brain cast around.

So is it the estate you're after?

Her hand rose up as she turned, and for a moment he thought she was going to clout him.

You daft gowk! she shouted. Don't you know anything? She went to the door and pulled it open, pointed for him to go out into the world. I want Simon Elliot and I want justice. I want you to send him here.

Tat stood with his back to the table, not moving.

I canna do that, he said.

You'd damn well better if you want our wee secret to stay that way.

He shook his head slowly from side to side, like it was a worn clapper tolling out the wickedness of the world.

Old Elliot's awa – left this morn. Annie phoned and tellt me when she got to the big hoose.

She was absolutely still, bordered by light as she stood dark in the doorway. He felt something streak across the room like a comet, frozen and fiery and full of dark space.

So, she said. So. The old man's done a runner. When's he coming back?

He didna say to Annie.

Her hiss carried the length of the kitchen.

So where's he gone, Tat? Where can I find him?

Tat put his head down, thinking about her last gesture the night before: the thumb and crooked pinkie touching, three fingers out stiff. *Revenge hot trod: don't impede me.*

Nae idea, he said calmly. Could be the city. Whiles he takes aff and goes on the ran-dan there, then comes back all douce. He never says where he goes and he could be weeks and that's the truth.

She advanced on him across the kitchen, seemed bigger with every step. A fighter, he thought, but more than that. This one can't stop.

You don't know? She stood in front of him, right hand on the shaft of the gutting knife where it lay on the table, but there was no need to threaten. Swear you don't know where Elliot's gone.

He gave her his thoughtless look. He reached back and put his right hand on the seventh plate.

I don't know where Elliot is, he said formally, staring back into her eyes. He left no word. Speir with Annie, she'll tell you the same.

She stared into his soul, such as it was. His fingers quivered on the plate as he stared her back.

I will that, she said softly. I'm going to the big house to see what Davy knows.

He's gone and all. He's taking young Jo to the station, she's offski. You're no having much luck the day. Tat's breath reishled through his teeth. Nor is the fiancée lass, pair thing. According to Annie, she looked knackered and he was distractit. Looks like you've done for them.

Her shoulders came down, the force in her burned out and she seemed to him a very tired young quine.

So it's happened, she said quietly. Maybe it's for the best.

Aye, best for you.

Me? She seemed genuinely astonished. You still don't know what I'm here for, do you? You've no idea at all.

He took his hand off the plate, rubbed his damp fingertips together. Forgive me, Jinny, he thought. I hope I've done right.

She caught up with him at the gate. She gripped him by the arm as she looked down to the distant Border, the blue-green hills riding through the haze, then round at the ridges that enclosed the dale, and he felt her longing to be gone.

I didn't plan it like this, she said at last. And I'm not after the estate, so you and Annie can set your minds at rest.

What are you after?

He saw her fingers move unconsciously into *that* gesture and was right glad he hadn't told her about the city flat. He still owed Elliot that much.

So, she said after a long pause for a question unanswered, you know about last night. Did it turn you on?

Tat's giggle as he freed his arm.

Not as much as it turned you on, I'm thinking.

She made no reply but kept looking down the valley, so hungry and lost. Then she shrugged and turned back to the cottage.

She stopped at the door.

Goodbye, Tat, she said. Thanks for saving our skins at the pub.

What will you dae? he called, but she had gone inside and closed the door. He felt like a smoky room that had been fugged up for years till she'd cam by, smashed the window and entered and gone again, leaving him clear and bereft.

*

Once at a circus you saw the man in the costume of the clown of Fate, spinning plates on top of long bendy wands, hurrying from stick to stick to keep the plates whirling. You think of him now as the story spins towards an end, the end you cannot bring yourself to foresee or enact.

Here's the dark powerful man sitting in a coach, hand before his face. He could be shouting, or keeping the dust of the roads from his eyes. Where is he going, Sim Elliot, where has he gone? He has gone off the map, taken fright. You should never have whispered those words in his ear but you got carried away by this passion play. You've been carried away further and further from whoever you once were.

So the old man is gone. As is the lady fair. Now only the son and heir remains. Before you lean in closer to study the last panels, glance round this familiar room and know your time here is almost done, and hear behind the wind the lovely song again.

> Farewell, farewell, to you who hear,
> You lonely travellers all,
> The cold north wind will blow again,
> The winding road does call . . .

Tat held a ruby in the tweezer's jaw and twisted it gently in the socket. Removed it, picked up a tiny riffler and worked deeper into the bone. His conscience was clear, he'd owed Sim Elliot that lie. Sure as Fate the old man was off to the city flat, and Tat minded the plates well enough, minded the last plate and a panel there of a man dead in a room with spires and tenements out beyond the window. The Marnie woman meant Elliot harm, but that didna sit with her obsession that Sim's her father. Same went for Davy – if she believed him her half-brother, she'd surely neither harm nor mate with him.

The eye fitted tight. Tat dabbed a fleck of superglue and screwed the ruby in. There you go, my bonnie wee mannie-beastie. But he was uneasy still, can't settle. Something didna fit right. He closed his eyes and saw again Marnie shrug and turn away as though who her father was suddenly wasn't so pressing to her. As though it was only an interesting puzzle. He glanced up again through the binocs, still no movement at Crawhill. That *Goodbye* had sounded more than casual. As he picked up the other ruby eye, the phone skirled in the corner.

Tat, David's back.

Without the lassie?

Of course. Annie sounded impatient. He's been sitting here all white and moping and fidgeting and looking like he's about to greit. But now he's just put his boots on and is on the path for Crawhill.

Tat felt his breath puff from his lips like Jinny's last breath at the bottom of Creagan's Knowe. This must be stopped. He can't stop Marnie, but perhaps he can turn Davy aside, whatever the boy has in mind.

He checked through the binocs, still no movement up at the cottage, then he was out the house, hurrying with the sun in his eyes towards the Liddie Woods.

*

Annie Tat put down the phone, sat and took Elliot's note from her slacks. *Marnie Lauder* written big on the outside, just above the wax seal imprinted with Elliot's ring. No one uses wax these days, she thought, someone ought to tell him. Doesn't he trust me?

She frowned, held the note up to the light but could read nothing. She knew from experience it wasn't possible to peel off the wax without breaking it. She also knew it was possible, with care, to remelt the broken wax. Give this to Marnie soonest, he'd said on his way out the door, the taxi waiting.

Kiss my arse, she muttered, and broke open the letter.

Dear Marnie Lauder – I have waited long to see you in my house, and now you have come I am somewhat overwhelmed to the point I could say little to much purpose last night. What you think of me I don't know, though I fear the worst. I fear you have been misled by rumour and gossip. You are owed a true account of Jinny's death, and I would beg of you to meet with me again and that's what I will give you.

Your mother was, and remains, the person I have loved above all others. I expect you long ago guessed the anonymous trust fund payments that ended on your 21st came from me – I only regret there wasn't more to give without tipping the estate into bankruptcy. But I have turned the matter over all night and am now going to my lawyer to will you half the estate upon my death. The other half – apart from some considerations for the Tattersalls – will go to David. I gather his engagement may be at an end, and I

287

will not deny that I have hopes the two of you will find a
way to keep the estate whole – and at last heal and end this
ancient, ruinous feud, as your mother would have wished.
But that is up to you.

I will explain everything at greater length on my return,
and hope to get better acquainted with you who are at once
a stranger and dear Jinny's only remnant in this world.
This note is to ask you to remain at Crawhill till my return
in 3 days time.

Sincerely
Sim Elliot

Annie stood up, walked over to the stove, then to the window.
Back to the stove, head down thinking hard. Shagged the auld
sod for six years – not that he wasn't good at it, a sight better
than Tat anyhow – listened to his girnings, wiped the sweat off
him. Not to mention Tat and herself working for a pittance. All
that to let him give the estate away to the first bold chancer
that comes along?

She opened the fire door.

Best not mention it to Tat, couldn't tell which way the wee
devil would jump these days. Anyway, it was her job to protect Elliot and sure as potatoes have eyes, the Marnie woman
meant him ill. She watched the note turn brown on the coals,
crisp through and curl up wings, then suddenly like a tiny
bird bleeding the red wax ran out and the note whirled up the
chimney as she hitched the fire door shut.

Back in the sitting room she paused with a duster in her
hand and for a moment felt she was looking at a children's
puzzle-picture. Can she see the cat hidden in the vase? Or can
she see a slender woman hidden in the green cushion covers,
dispersed among the red tulips, smell her lavender beneath
the woodsmoke?

Annie sprayed with the can and followed up with the
duster. Three days till Elliot returned . . . She rubbed her itchy
palm on the hip of her slacks. Itchy palm, money coming soon,
she murmured as she sauntered through to the scullery.

*

The young man with yellow hair is going into the woods like his father before him, without hawk or hound or friend. The trees arch and stir over his head. He looks straight ahead like a man going to the scaffold or the marriage altar, then he is lost among the light and shadow and you can see no more.

Move on to the panel above and find his father, stepping down from a coach by an inn. Behind him are pale scratches that could be spires, tall buildings. And though you suspect Tat lied, you saw in his eyes that nothing you could threaten would make him tell what he knew or guessed. Sim Elliot is fled, you cannot catch him now.

Elliot paid the taxi from the station and watched it scoot off downhill towards the city centre. The trees in the park stirred over his head. The day had changed, it was mild spring again. He was back in the city for the first time in two years.

He crossed at the green man, went round the corner and fumbled for keys at the tenement door. The sharp jab and twist like a corkscrew in his heart, but it's maybe only memories of Jinny standing beside him on this same worn step. Stone lasts so long, he thinks, yet even it wears down to our passing.

Then he's inside in the fousty dimness. He climbs the stairs cautiously, noting the hollows worn in the centre of each step. There'll be time to wash and collect himself before lunch with his lawyer. He comes at last to the top landing, to the dark green door, the old brass plate *Robertson* he's never seen fit to change. In the city he used to feel like Robertson, whoever he was, free from his position and his place, his marriage and the estate and all the deadly suffocations of his upbringing, free to be Jinny's man.

Inside is chill and smells faintly of sweat and booze. He ignores the blue door, her room, not ready to face that yet. In the other bedroom everything's tidy, the bed stripped, but it has a whiff of Tat and semen, the dirty wee bugger.

He puts down his suitcase, then the slim briefcase with the documents, and slumps for a minute in the worn winged chair by the window looking out over the city's spires, the castle, the hill, the distant firth. All that hard clear rational East Coast light clears the head of bogles and fanciful imaginings. In a moment he will wash and sprush himself up, but not yet, for in this seat there lingers still the whiff of lavender.

So the clever, skittery fiancée is gone, fled back to the South, leaving David and Marnie. He smiles at the possibility, feels the rightness of it as pressure coming off his chest. At feud – and God knows the Elliots and Lauders were at it long enough – often ended this way, in marriage. All may yet be well.

But it may not, he is not God almighty. So he must do this and give the lassie justice. *Justice not cash* she'd whispered hot breath in his ear under the stars. The note will keep her there till he gets back and tells her to her face how Jinny died. Then she will have what justice there is in the world, and cash for what there isn't. Adam Crozier will purse his lawyer lips, he will not like it, on the phone he certainly didn't like it, but when Elliot gets to the offices the documents will be there for signing. Then he can sleep.

He twists his neck and inhales the musty seat covering. The smell slips inside him, sweet and painful as a day long gone. Jinny would approve, he thinks. My boy and her girl, surely that is what she'd want. And then another bairn to replace the one that died with her.

He sits back and closes his eyes, imagining Jinny coming up the stairs to him, her standing ringing the bell, all raised and flushed, some answer still in her eyes. But the bell doesn't ring, of course it doesn't, he isn't soft in the head yet, and she can never come again.

*

Tat flickered up through the trees on the far side of the Liddie Burn, came to the path from the big house to the falls and checked his watch. Seven minutes dead. No way Davy could have passed by yet.

He hunkered down with his back against a rowan, facing the way young Elliot would come. He let his breathing slow and empty out his mind, then it would come to him what to do when the laddie came through the trees towards him. He knew fine why Annie wanted to prevent this tryst, she'd long had hopes of the estate. His reasons were his own. Jinny's bairn had possessed him, but deeper than that he was Elliot's man.

He waited. No one waited better than Tat, eyes fixed on the path. The day had changed utterly since the morn, and the afternoon was very still. Not a whisper in the tangled firs, not even a hiss of breeze over the bare oaks and alders. It really was awful close.

Twigs blurred along the way, a branch twitched. He blinked. Blinked and looked again. A flicker of gingery-red in the dim tunnel of the path. A fox, surely, though byordinar in full daylight. He crouched unmoving, feeling sweat tickle under his arms. Movement and colour again, coming closer, coming his way.

Then Tat is pushing himself upright, leaning back on the trunk to stop himself falling over. For a woman is coming along the path towards him, and it isn't Marnie. She is not as tall as she should be. Her hair is too long. Its red lights flicker in the still air . . .

Jinny walks towards him, the same rapid light steps he remembered, same dancing hips under the long green dress. The day starts to go dark round the edges, his fingers are freezing but sweat's running into his boots.

This is not possible, he thinks. This is not on. He shakes his head, blinks several times, and she is standing right in front of him. She grins exactly her grin. Then she smiles, dead natural.

Hi Tat, how's it going? she says.

He gurgles. She's wearing sensible shoes but nothing else is sensible in his universe.

I miss you too, she says. Pleased about your bairns, though. Congratulations.

This is no Banquo's ghost. She isn't covered in blood, head caved in, last breath hissing from her battered mouth. She is just his friend Jinny, nodding to him to follow her as they start to wander slowly down through the trees. He can't focus on what she's saying, can't retain a thing. She chats away like they haven't met for a week or so. She smiles to him again, almost slyly, like there's some secret joke he hasn't got yet but soon will. He can't feel the air. His whole body has gone numb. Maybe he's dead. Jinny's dead. He clutches his mind round that.

But you're dead, he says.

Did he say that aloud? She stops, one pale hand on a scarred oak. Her fingers spread then are still.

These things happen, she said.

She turns and steps gracefully downhill. He follows and finds himself confessing how he'd watched her and Sim at it all those years ago – down by the linns, in the cottage, on Creagan's Knowe.

Her head bobs, copper coils and russet lights shake loose through the forest.

I know that, she says gently. Don't worry about it.

But there's mair, he gasps behind her, his voice going wee and bairny. What I said at the trial . . .

Don't fash yourself. Don't worry about it. Her voice floats back to him. You thought it better to defend a living man than a dead woman, and who's to argue with you? I know you only wanted to be me, he thinks she adds as she moves further away.

He hastens to catch up with her, suddenly panic-stricken she'll just drift away and take the last of his right mind with her. The ground begins to level out, she hunkers down by the linns and trails her fingers in the water.

Let them meet, she says carefully. That's what I want.

Davy and Marnie?

She lifts her hand and watches, seeming fascinated as the water streams, trickles, forms single drops. The last pearl shakes and falls and is gone into the wide water.

Let them meet, she says again. Her head moves down then to the side as though both nodding and shaking her head. Or perhaps she is listening to something beyond his range.

Tell me, he says then stops, but he must know. Is Marnie – is she Sim's child?

She looks for a long time at the smooth gleaming water. That's not for the living to know, she says at last.

Then she looks up at him, all easy and smiling. She hasn't touched me, he thinks. She casts a shadow, she's breathing, but she hasn't touched me. If she did, would I feel anything? Would I die?

Here, Tat, she says. Mind we used to play hidies before Marnie was born? You were always good at it. I want you to play it with me now.

Now? he says. Here?

She nods like it's great fun, a game between pals. I'll hide in the world, she says. You sit here, close your eyes and count a hundred, then try and find me.

He does as she asks, feeling some inevitability press down on his shoulders as he sits back against the nearest tree.

No cheating, she says. Promise?

Aye, he says, and closes his eyes. Promise.

Plate 8 (Broken)

You should be getting ready to move on for the finish is certainly nearby. Instead you've fallen into a deep dwam over the last plate, your eyes open but not seeing anything else around you. More and more you find yourself falling into that other world.

The rider jumps down from his horse, the woman rises from behind the wall. They lie together and life sparks. A man falls off a brig, a woman lies broken at the bottom of a cliff, a figure in the shadows draws a dagger from its sheath. The man and woman lie down again. And through it all the wind blows over the moor, wearing even the stone away.

But you stop and sit up straight, for you've felt or heard something just beyond human range. Though you could have read it in this plate, you did not expect this. And though you may have desired it, you dread it deep. He's coming.

She secured the sheath onto the belt of her jeans, slotted in the dagger. She paused to glance in the little mirror, didn't see Jinny's face in there, then hurried out the door. She stood with a cup of cold coffee, waiting for him in the late afternoon sunlight, the air full of unseasonal bugs, the corbies near asleep on the dyke as he came from the woods.

He put one hand on the sagging post and easily jumped the gate and strode towards her, strands of lichen in his yellow hair. He stopped at arm's length and stared long at her. A fine hardening, she thought.

Did you have to? he said. Of all the folk in the dale, did it have to be her you had?

He was panting. The ends of his hair were shaking, coarse and yellow. She couldn't meet his eyes but watched only his mouth and his right hand flexing by his hip. She said nothing.

Christ, Marnie! Jo and I have waited a year and a half, then you two have it all in one night.

David, she said, and now she looked in his eyes. David, I didn't exactly seduce her. She's an old hand, believe me.

This is the moment, she thought. Now we see.

He ripped the cup from her fingers. It hurt, she panicked, reached down for the knife but he grabbed her wrist in a flash. His other hand blurred forward, the Willow Pattern cup whizzed past her head and shattered on the wall.

Shit! he shouted. Shit shit shit. You bastern Lauder!

She looked back at him, denying nothing, open to anything. At last he let go her knife hand and stood before her like he could burst into tears but resolute yet. Yes, a fine hardening.

Of course I knew she used to . . . He looked over her head, down the drove road. I mean, we both had things to put behind us. That was the deal.

She put her hand on his arm, felt it flinch. She gripped tighter.

Love's no big deal, she said and leaned towards him.

You've nothing worth telling me, Marnie. Cynicism's cheap.

I mean it's not a *deal* at all. His head turned slowly back to her. His horizon-blue eyes locked onto hers. Davy, love exists way before you agree to it and way after you end it. She paused. Ask your father about that.

It was a rotten thing to do.

I know.

He stared at her, waiting for something.

It's no excuse, she said, but I've been alone for a long time. I have my needs, I wanted her and she wanted me. Jo thought she was seducing me. It's the only power she has.

He looked down at his hands like the answer was there. Hands broad-palmed, long-fingered. A larger version of her own. She reached and took his hand.

But I hurt you, she said. And for that I'm sorry.

Her voice was ragged, she said the words like they were foreign to her. But she gripped his hand tighter till he had to look her in the eyes again, and maybe he saw moistness there.

Perhaps I wanted to hurt you, she said. But I don't now.

What's with you, woman? What have I ever done to you?

Jinny. Patrick. She paused. Your father. I couldn't get to him, so I got you.

There was nothing he could say to that but let it sink down and down through the silence of the afternoon. At last he loosed his hand from hers and stepped back. He looked at her standing so ready, one hand on the hilt of his knife, the other still held out towards him.

There's one thing I have to know. Are we . . .?

Related? She smirked like it was funny. I don't think so.

She stood square on, poised on her feet, alert, black hair swinging across her forehead. So alive, so there. So not all there.

I must be off, he blurted. I've no more business here. It's been . . .

With each step back away from her the tugging forward in his chest was stronger, like there was elastic strung between them.

Davit?

He stopped like she'd run him through. Davit. So personal, no one had ever been so personal. He looked at her with the cottage behind, remembered the old photo, the plastic sword, the little girl pushing herself up from the ground, Jinny smiling as she moved from light into shade.

There was another reason, she said. Her voice faltered then her head came up and she said it clearly. I was jealous. I'm very jealous and insecure.

Jealous of me? Come on!

No.

Now he couldn't move. They were frozen like figures on a painted plate.

Jealous of her, she said. And I think now you are too.

Her eyes came up, she almost smiled. It wasn't *her* we wanted, she said and came towards him across the overgrown garden. He couldn't pretend not to know her meaning as she put her arm through his like they were old fellow riders.

We're both tense and confused, she said. I think we need to take a walk. Just a little walk.

They crossed the dyke and set foot on the drove road and walked along it, heads bent towards each other as they talked. They walked unconscious of time or distance, empty moor on their right and green pasture on the left. They walked till the road dipped and then they were facing over the next glen to Creagan's Knowe, the red bluff and the stream and woods below.

He stopped dead, with the tug of her arm pulling him on.

No, he said. No!

She halted, came back. Lips warm and strong, the tip of her tongue burning in his mouth. It felt like nothing else in his life.

We've put this off too long, my blue-eyed boy, she said. We'll be able to see everything better from up there, believe me.

*

Tat came up from somewhere dark and comfortable, still counting. He opened his eyes. No Jinny, no smothered laughter through the trees. Of course there wasn't, she'd never been there. Just a daft dwam on a close afternoon, come to a mind shorn of sleep from the night before.

He rubbed the back of his hand over his eyes and looked for David coming along the path through the woods. But Tat wasn't by the path any more. He was sitting by the bright murmuring linns of the river, four hundred yards further down the hill. And – check the watch – he had lost an hour and some.

He was on his feet and running back up through the trees, already too late.

The lovers climb higher and higher through the green light under the trees. They're silent but panting, their faces pale and set. The path kinks round the back of the knoll and then they step out from the last of the trees, and stand to face each other in their appointed place, at their appointed time. Late blue sky above them, the dizzying fall to the valley before, the coarse turf of their bed at their feet.

*

Sim Elliot slowly climbs the tenement stairs. The meeting is done, the new will witnessed and signed and filed in Adam

Crozier's safe, but now the air in the stairwell is vile green and hard to breathe, and he's weary unto death. The ancient steps go up and up. He pauses on the second landing, feeling for a moment Jinny swinging on his arm, seeing her run barefoot down the dusty stairs that last weekend to greet him though he was late. Her smile, her vitality, banish all dinginess and dross and doubt. Whatever comes, it will be worth it for this moment as she wraps herself round him and her belly melts into his and he says in her ear *Love you for aye*.

He smiles now and murmurs to her shade then sets his foot on the next step for all the tingling in his chest. I have lived, I lived in those hours, he thinks. The rest has just been existence.

He climbs on and up, near the top now, letting his memory run ahead with Jinny into the flat to fornicate lovingly, desperately, the way one does when every time could be the last. Now the endorphins had calmed, the receptor sites sated and all that had permitted their bodies unprecedented energies and their hearts to open like prison gates – now that was done, what was left? Each time they looked at each other, the unspoken question was reflected in the other's eyes: is it worth it? Where do we go from here? Does this mean anything?

He scratches and fumbles his key into the lock, seeing her tumble up and over him, the ragged edge of her laughter as she settled down to ride him, gripping his hips between her knees and his hair clenched tight in her small fists.

The door lurches open. He drops the keys on the hall table and hesitates outside the other bedroom, the one with the blue door he keeps locked. She'd said it would be safe – had she lied or just been mistaken? In any case, his seed had found her and their bodies got what they were straining for, and even as they lay cooling on the bed the way had opened up to her last summons and the final tryst on Creagan's.

Elliot grinds the heel of his hand into his forehead, picks up the keys and opens the blue door.

*

They weren't on the brig over the falls. Thanks be to the gods of the North for that. I leaned over the rail and peered down into the louping water and the black still pool at the bottom. As my een strained in the mirk, at last the knowledge rose up through the spray and stramash: *Marnie isn't Marnie. This one has come in her place. She's a step-in.*

I blinked, went empty. The waters stopped falling and I saw clear how it was. She was something far more queer than an imposter. And Davy wasn't protected by her notion Elliot was Marnie's sire. And because she wasn't Marnie – and Lord alone knows who or what she might really be – she could do anything she wanted with him.

Then I hurried at a lick across the greasy planks, through the woods towards Crawhill, still hearing at my back the Liddie roar to its rest.

I keeked in through the bedroom window. No bodies there, no lovers yerking or lying still. The mattress had been stripped bare. In the kitchen, the books were in a cardboard box with the silver-framed photo on top. Clothes lay folded by her backpack. The woman was set for a flittin.

The plates were stacked on the uppermost shelf of the press. I reached and took down the top one and gowped at it long. It was as I'd minded – the tryst on the high place, the lovers raxed about each other, a body falling without end.

Jinny, Jinny, I muttered, what are you about? You must ken she's no the one.

I stood outside, not knowing which way to go. The dale was empty in the low yellow light, only the sheep, and Smiler Ballantyne slouching down the lane. I raised my glasses and scanned the muir, found nothing but a hawk hung high above the old stane. It was as though the woman had taken David off with her, back into the mystery.

I looked down the drove road, kinking round the shoulder of the hill towards the next dale and Creagan's beyond that . . . And then I kent. I went back into the kitchen, came out with the last plate in my hand and in a bleeze of anger and fear, smashed it agin the hind wall. Then I was running straight for the low sun settling over the knowe.

*

They emerge from the last trees at the crown of Creagan's Knowe and he follows her towards the edge, a narrow strip of turf and then the drop. His chest is heaving from nerves and the other. He knows what she thinks happened here but he's never allowed himself to think on it. He'd pushed it away with a lot of other things he didn't want to look at. He just called it *Sin* and thought that dealt with it.

Now she stands on the very edge, faces out over the drop and spreads her arms wide like she's greeting some old friend, he sees he never knew much about anything – not his dad, not his mother, not Jo, certainly not the woman who has brought him to this place. All this comes too late as she looks round and holds her hand out toward him.

Come on, she says. Take a look.

He steps towards her but stops just beyond her reach. She's right on the edge where the grass peters out to some crumbly rock. He looks into her unfathomable black eyes and thinks of the Devil taking Jesus up to a high place and showing him the kingdoms of the world. That's what she can show him, the kingdoms. They're locked in her eyes, in the mouth he's felt on his, in the force of her hips. She is not of the dark, he tells himself, not entirely, and we can both be saved in ways we'd never expected.

Come on, she says. Hey, don't you trust me?

The kingdoms are the secrets of her heart and they can be his. He takes another step forward and stops, a yard back from the edge.

No, he says. Since last night I don't trust anyone.

She laughs quietly but her eyes go down.

I've taught you something then.

Least of all myself, he adds. So I'm staying right here. If you want my trust, you have to earn it like anyone else.

Her chin comes up, something flickers in her eyes. He doesn't know this woman at all. He's known her since he was a wee boy. Then she shifts slightly and the setting sun makes it hard to see into her any more.

Fair enough, she says. She holds out her hand to him again. Her voice drops low and quiet like there's only the two of them left in the world and no need to talk loud. Come here and stand with me. No more games.

In the end it's not what she says, nor the look in her eyes which he can't see rightly anyway for the glare, but the tone of her voice that decides it. It resonates somewhere round his breast-bone. He's been waiting for it for years, that buzz in the bone: her absolute kinship with him.

He steps up beside her, holds out his hand. They're standing together at the lip of the drop as her fingers knit round his. Her knees flex, her shoulders come forward. So be it. If she wants to take him with her, so be it. He's lost everything anyway. He's nothing like he thought.

She's breathing heavy. The burn glisters way below, the fields and woods hump down to the Border and somewhere cushie-doos are calling. At this moment he's prepared to go.

Her fingers squeeze hard.

Thank you, she says all throaty. Then she turns to face him, puts one arm at his waist and the other round his neck like they're dancing, and together they take one step sideways away from the edge, and then another. She looks up at him and gives a near giggle.

Let you into a secret, she says. I don't know myself at all, so you taking a chance on me means one of us is crazy.

Her hands clasp together at the back of his head.

So here's our reward, she says.

I saw them from the valley, wee figures on the brow of the knowe, miniature and twisted as my netsuke. I stopped running, it being ower late to change anything now. I raised the glasses and saw them close on each other. I saw them clutch and graipple agin the sun and thought of the peregrine falcon, the blue gled we cry them, how afore they mate they link claws, fold wings and drop as one out of the sky. Trust. It's an unco sight, and most times they mind and let go, but years syne I saw a pair crash. Found the one deid, the other blinking up at me its black and golden eye, baith wings smashed. I put the pair thing away. Never made the same mistake myself.

So my bonnie pair linked on top of the knowe and I could only watch from half a mile off. Aye in my mind were the other lovers I'd seen up there yon afternoon twenty-plus years back, and what I had witnessed, and how I had forsworn my-self. It was that half-lie that kept me safe for all these years and now had brought me here as punishment to witness again while the lovers enacted their weird, helpless as myself.

This surely was what Jinny willed, even if she was just a whigmaleerie of my brain. I couldn't understand it. Then the notion came and made me grue – the dead may know no more than we what is to come, and their plans go agley as our own.

*

He had his father's mouth, but young and sweet. I matched my lips to his, the fit was perfect as I'd known it would be. A man's mouth but so like my own, and as we clutched together in that high place, each movement unlocked gates in me I'd thought closed for ever the day my lover left me at the airport.

We fell on our knees, still locked together, his belly burning into mine. Chill hands were on my breasts, he held them as if they were something wonderful. He was full of juice, that man. I felt I could lift the ripeness of the world into my mouth and crunch.

Then something broke somewhere and we fell over on our sides in coarse dry grass. The low sun lit on the blood-red stone of his family ring as he stroked my face over and over and my hands moved inside his shirt. He felt closer to me than any man I'd ever known, he was mine as our hands worked each other's belts, and with a groan deep in our throats he eased into me.

With eyes closed there was no-time, that place of peace. There was no-person, we were neither two nor one. Only him-and-me, and the evening air cool over the valley and through our open clothes. The world was young as in the early days, and we were gripped by nothing save each other.

Then there was no more but the pure doing of it. As the horizon sliced the sun in twain, I held him there for all time on the brink of Creagan's Knowe.

Behind the cottage the last plate lies smashed. Broken shards slip down in the grass. Some are face-down, others lie open to the conflagration in the sky. Here are the lovers embracing, over there is the woman falling. The watcher is lying on his side near where the barefoot woman is doing some kind of dance or perhaps calling for help. And here is the dark man in a room, broken clean down the middle.

Sim Elliot stood awhile in the little bedroom, sniffing the air that held her yet. Her crushed blue velvet dress, the one he'd bought for her that last weekend, was still spread out on the bed. Her little bottles and jars were on the sill, her green hair-grip crusted with dust on the bedside table. Her spare knickers in the chest of drawers, folded neatly beside her red sweater and the hairbrush he couldn't bear to throw away with her hairs faded in its grip.

And that was all that remained visible of her. He felt the tearing streak down his chest as he slowly laid himself down on the bed. His hand groped and tugged her dress to him. He tugged as he had tugged at her on the knowe. He held the dress to his face, felt it cover his nose and eyes, then he let go and wept as he saw.

Jinny tearful, wracked, almost possessed on the top of Creagan's where she had called him with her mind to tell him she was pregnant again. Talking of abortion, of telling Patrick everything. Telling Fiona. Or having the baby. I can't lie to you again, she says. He doesn't understand this, she's never lied to him. She can't stand it, she can't live with it any more. He wrestles with her, trying to stop her. Calm down, Jinny. Let's think this through. It can be all right. No it can't! she sobs. It never could be. We're not even sure how much we want each other. (Did she say that, or did he? He's no longer sure.) I can't bear it. Let me go. *Let me go!*

She pushes past him, he grabs at her, she pushes at him – and because he's much bigger she staggers back. One foot goes over the edge. The soft thin soil crumbles under her other foot. She looks down at it as though puzzled, then back at him. She says nothing, does nothing but keep looking at him as she begins to fall away from his grab. She drops, tumbles then hits the first ledge and lies still. He peers over the edge and calls to her. Don't move, dinna move lass!

She gets up onto her elbows, then her knees. She stands upright, swaying. She looks up to him, almost smiles as she steps sideways and falls again. A thud, rattle, the groan of her breath knocked out. She's twitching and jerking like a puppet with tangled strings. Then impossibly she's up again, staggers to the edge and falls one more time.

She's lying twisted on her back, a dark stain blooming at the side of her head, her blue eyes fixed on nothing. She seems calm, or just blank. Is she in her right mind or on another planet? He can never know as she twists again, rolls over and falls out of sight to crunch at Tat's feet and finally be still, herself and the unborn child dead.

And now, back in this room, it seems at last he can read the meaning of Jinny's last glance, the half-smile as she turns away. He'd thought it terror, accusation, even resignation. But in that slightest shake of her head, her mouth opening in a little O, her eyes widening, he can see acceptance. Even relief. She'd wanted it. At that moment, poised in the balance, she'd wanted out. And then he truly wept.

*

Don't know about you, Davy, I said, but I'm getting damp and cold here.

He blinked once, then grinned. Me too, he said, and began pulling on his breeks. Yes, he was a man who could yet turn out well. As might even I.

We stood a moment in the gloaming on top of that high crowning place. I shivered and drew my shawl around me, hesitated then unclipped the brooch, fumbled with it for a moment.

Here, I said. You have it.

He stood and let me push the long pin through his shirt then clip it.

To remember me by, I said.

His head came up at that.

You're leaving?

And so must you. Go and see Jo and get it straight.

Straight? he said. That's a bit of a laugh.

It can be a good one, I said. You'll know soon enough if it's right.

And if it's not? Where can I find you?

I linked my hand through his and squeezed.

I'll find you, I said.

*

I saw the two of them rise again and stand body-black on the knowe. My eyes watered with the strain, and the figures ran into Elliot and Jinny, struggling or embracing at the brink. I was young then, a loon, and a distance away hiding in the trees below – how could I ken the difference atween anger and desire? All I saw were arms rising, her turning, him reaching or pushing, then her slow backward fall. No matter how often I replayed it, I truly didna ken.

At the trial I lied, of course I did, and Elliot never looked at me aince as I testified how I'd seen Jinny step away from him and over the edge. And so I saved him because I loved him, and made my place siccar, and when we met outside the courtroom he looked into me, nodded once and turned away, his hair already growing grey, and we never spoke directly of it ever.

I thought this my punishment, to see his only son and heir fall and be able to do nothing. But at last the tiny black stick figures turned away back into the trees and I was saved. I shadowed them through the gloaming as they came down out through the trees, crossed the burn and headed for Crawhill. They walked the drove road and I jouked along above them on the muir, my heart burning like the sky ahint us.

*

And so I let him go, and so I let myself go. We walked in silence through the gloaming, for I was blown apart and he was soft and dazed as men are after love. As love it might have been. As love it might be.

As we rounded the drove road and saw the cottage up ahead, he began to sing very softly *In Scarlet Town where I was born, there was a fair maid dwelling*. His voice was pleasing to my ears and seemed to sooth the drowsy rooks in the tall trees above the heuch. And I answered him back, singing *And her name was Barbara Allan*, and in his glance at me I was pleasing to myself once more.

At the time we crossed the dyke the air was the colour of the stone of these parts, grey but lit within. The western sky was burning low and I was near at peace with no voices in my head save his and my own. I'd gone so near the border into the kingdom of Spook but stepped back.

He stopped and shuffled on my briggiestane. But I put my finger to his bonnie lips and bid him goodbye and good luck, needing now to sleep for a thousand years.

When young Elliot had gone back across Liddie into the gathering dark and she went inside and closed the door, I stayed hunkered down ahint the dyke awhile. So they had done the deed and she hadn't killed him. They had met and parted, perhaps would meet again syne. Perhaps this was what Jinny had wanted, she might have seen that far ahead. If not her daughter with young Elliot, then someone – I near thought some*thing* – who stepped into her place. About our meeting in the woods, I wasn't yet prepared to ponder oer long.

I got stiffly to my feet. There was only one thing left for me to do here. I chapped on the door, waited respectfully then went in.

She was standing in a dwam by the sink. The kitchen looked empty and the backpack was full by her feet, but the plates were still on the upper shelf of the press. She looked at me across the lamplight. She looked for an awful long time and her eyes had the shine of oiled whetstone . . .

I was minded to tell her I'd jaloused her secret, that she wasn't Marnie but one come in her place, and perhaps that was as it was meant to be. I was minded to tell her I'd let on to no one, and if she were to marry Davy and settle the estate and centuries of ruinous feud, well that was fine by me. I was minded to say I was both sorry and relieved she was leaving.

Instead I held out my last netsuke, my glowering thrawn wee goblin with the corbie at his shoulder.

This is for you, I said, wherever you're gaun. I doubt I'll make another.

She took it lightly from my hand into hers and we both looked down at the bone, the silver, the chancy ruby een winking in the lamplight.

I'll treasure this for longer than you know, she murmured. I blushed, she turned away and sat it on top of her pack for the morn. But I'm very tired, she said.

Aye . . . Goodnight.

She said nothing. At the door I stopped, turned to look back one more time.

Goodbye, Tat, she said. I hope you sleep better now.

Open your eyes on your last day here. Light floods again through the curtainless window, the wind murmurs its many voices. Your time here is spilled and done as an hourglass broken, worn out by the sand. And you are calm, released, for this is story's end.

She blinked, smiled up at the ceiling that Jinny must have looked to with Patrick or Elliot at her side. Then she rose from the mattress for the last time, stripped the sheets and duvet and left them with a note for Annie Tat: *It's all yours – M.*

She washed, she made tea and toast, quiet in her head and savouring these ordinary mortal things. After all, she thought, we're as fated or free as we believe ourselves to be.

She washed out the last dishes, looking out the window onto a day bright but with flags of mist clinging to the trees, drifting into hollows. At peace, she was ready now to kneel and pick up the silver-framed photo, her passport to this life she was leaving. She stroked the cool metal with her thumb then abruptly turned it over, pushed the little catch. She removed the back and took out the note she'd kept there, Marnie's last gift before she went through the security barrier and flew out of her life.

Have my plates and the photo with my love. Do what you will with them, but remember we're not fated. It's all bollocks, Carol. We're free! My love – Marnie.

*

Annie Tat stopped at the village shop to pick up supplies on her way to the big house. The bus to the city pulled up at the shelter and she glimpsed in the brief clear space between the shelter and the open door a small figure step rapidly. She saw a bounce of red hair, a flash of green dress then the woman vanished into the dimness of the bus.

Impossible. Annie shook her head. Ridiculous. She was getting jumpy as Elliot. She got back into the car and drove on, still thinking and planning. With Elliot's letter burned, the Marnie woman had to go before he came back, or they could kiss goodbye to the estate. That was the main thing. And according to Tat she was leaving this morn. Tat would watch to make sure she did, he was good at that. Though the wee sod seemed to have lost his grip of late, things looked to be working out fine.

She turned up the drive and thought no more of it.

The woman who'd called herself Marnie for long enough picked up the little radio and gathered her last gear together, keen now to be off. It had been the longest strangest time, she'd nearly forgotten on which side of the border she belonged, so carried away by isolation and fantasy, lust and those plates. Now she was in her right mind again, perhaps even her right heart. There was no Fate, no endless cycle, no unseen forces. Marnie was right. We cannot live with Spook, it's too big for us.

She placed Tat's eldritch goblin in the top of the pack and almost smiled. Here we go, back to wherever. The winding road does call . . .

The plates she'd left till last. She lifted them down from the shelf, all seven. No, six. She stopped dead. Her finger ran down the stack. The top plate was missing. Her eyes jerked round the kitchen, she went through to the bedroom knowing it wasn't there, just the exploded version of Plate 3 stuccoed to the wall below the window.

Unless she was losing her mind, someone had taken it. Perhaps to stop her. Stupid bastards, she wasn't stopped that easily. Who, then? Not old Elliot – he was gone. Not Davy . . . Then she thought on Tat coming to the door last night, offering his netsuke. She'd taken it in her pride as a tribute, and it was wickedly beautiful, but now she wondered if it was an apology. She stood at the front door in the morning breeze, looked to either side but there was only the silvered grass bending. The privy wing groaned quietly. As she walked slowly towards it, a bright speck caught her eye in the long grass breaking against the back wall.

She stood over the shattered plate, head bowed as if in mourning. Then she heard a dog barking from the direction of the wood. She knew that bark, and knew the man who a moment later followed his hound out of the trees.

You shouldn't have come back, David, she said. Goodbyes are hard enough.

I know, I know, he said. But it felt like I had no choice.

She stared back at him. If eyes are the window of the soul, today hers were smoked glass.

Yesterday was . . . miraculous, he said. I have to know it wasn't a fluke.

Her mouth tugged down to one side as though he'd said something funny.

Something to show you, she said.

She pointed down and half buried in the grass he saw blue and white fragments, knelt down as she stood beside him with Hawk licking round her feet. He picked up one piece of painted plate, then another. A falling man. A couple entwined.

Tat, she said.

He shouldn't have done that.

No, she said slowly. He really shouldn't have.

He started collecting the pieces together. I'm really sorry, Marnie, he said. I'll skin him for this.

Leave it, she said. It doesn't matter. As if you can break a story by breaking a plate.

She seemed that unhappy he closed his arms around her shoulders. Her dark hair blew up in little spikes and he wanted to protect her from everything bad that had ever happened. He wanted her to demand anything of him, something impossible like protecting her from everything in the future. Then her eyes came up, dark as a tarn on the moor.

All right then, she said. One more time. She swayed in, her hips fused onto his. Do you prefer the mattress bare, or a bed of bracken?

I sheathed my knives one last time and looked at all the fan-kled wee things I'd made, my beloved creatures of bone and seeing, the whigmaleeries of my brain. If I make anything more, they'll not be so crabbit and confined.

I keeked out the workroom window and saw movement up by Crawhill. Then through my glasses I saw young Elliot come near, saw her point down to the grass aside the cottage. He knelt and when he stood again she closed on him, and all the while the hound ran circles round them.

I wasna happy and blithe about this tryst, and I'm not sure she was either. Aiblins I should have set off up the brae but couldn't face her, not now she'd found the plate.

I settled down at my sill to watch the lovers as they tacked across towards the dyke. I thought they'd go back to the knowe but she stopped by the bracken this side of the dyke, at the very spot where she'd first couried down to wait for him the morning after she'd arrived. I reached for a cheroot and lit it, drew the bittersweet nothing into my throat and waited.

Send the hound away, she said. I'll not lie with you while he's around.

He looked down at Hawk. Home! he said. Away you go.

Hawk trembled, whined but wouldn't budge. Sorry, David said, he won't leave.

She held her right arm out, two fingers rigid towards the dog's eyes. Go, Hawk! she said and he turned and ran back to the forest and was gone.

There was a pause between them. David Elliot's knees were shaking with wanting her but she put her hand flat to his chest.

Is Elliot returned? she asked.

He shook his head. No word of him, no one knows when he'll be back.

And your Faith?

He spread his hands, suddenly tearful.

No one knows when that'll be back either.

She smiled, then tramped down the bracken and spread her cloak. She looked down the dale then gripped the bottom of her sweater and peeled it off over her head. She stood before him, strong and pale and proud.

You're right, she breathed into his ear. She bit his lobe then licked the pain. We have no choice, Davit. Lay down, my bonnie man.

She kent fine I was watching as they lay ahint the dyke. She turned him so I could see everything through my shoogling glass. I saw her nakedness, even the flicker of his whang afore it went in, as I had seen Elliot's lang syne. I saw her wrap hersel around him like a net. The phone rang and rang downstairs. I let it ring a long age till the lovers shuddered or my hands did, and it was done.

*

He lies beside me in the bracken below the dyke, shirt half-off, pulled back over his shoulder and angular hause-bane. The clasp glitters dully round the emperor's coin, it would be so easy to pocket it again. His eyes are closed, the long lashes stir as he breathes. We could have fallen from another planet, like this one but much greater than ever suspected. It could be mine. It could be ours.

I look again at his calm face. I look at the lie of his rumpled yellow hair and then against the hazy sun see in his hair cornfields parting on horsemen riding in ambush. I see a man pushed off a bridge, a woman falling. In the drift of his golden hair are red tips of sword and lance, and the burning farms appear, the cattle reived, men going down, the mother raped and harried.

At my side his knife lies spilled on the grass, and I know at last how it was done. How a woman may kill a full-grown man in open air. It is this moment after love, the one time he rests defenceless. The knife is so sharp, he is near-sleeping as my hand reaches out for it and grips the cold handle.

His eyes open, so pale blue and northern as he stares into mine. He looks into me and I can never know what he sees. His eyes flicker to my hand on the knife and he almost smiles, as though he accepts everything. His long Elliot mouth moves.

I believe in the Mystery and the Mercy, he says slowly. I even believe in Spook. But I'll never believe we're fated.

Staring still into his eyes, I lift the knife and slide it back into the sheath.

*

The city street is loud with rush-hour traffic, no one would notice if her feet made no sound as she crosses at the lights. She is slight and light-footed and no one bumps into her as she slips like a salmon up along the grey river of the pavement. As she moves through the evening crowd, uphill towards the crossroads and the tenement, the wind blows crisp packets and papers about her ankles then passes on. She rounds the corner smiling slightly and stops outside the tenement door. Her index finger alights on Robertson, *then she's in and moving up the stairs.*

They stand up, pulling bits of bracken from their clothes. He lifts her cloak and puts it round her shoulders. She kisses him lightly on each cheek, and as she kisses reaches in his pocket. She stands back.

This is what I want from you, Davit, she says.

He stares down at what she's holding.

My keys? he says.

No, the stone disc. It was ours once, long time syne.

He stares but makes no objection as she carefully prises the broken metal circle from the stone. She clasps the disc with its off-centre hole in the curl of her palm, breathes on it, runs her thumb round then puts it into the hole with a low sigh. When she looks up at him, her face is radiant.

This is so old, she says. You've no idea.

He shrugs uneasily.

So everything's returned that was owed, he says. What happens now?

Nothing has changed. Then she smiles and a little colour comes to her cheeks. Except we know the first time wasn't a fluke.

Marnie, about what we did back there . . . I assume you had protection.

And her voice is not so pleasing as she turns away.

Don't worry, you'll see no bairn. I'll walk you back as far as the brig then we go our ways. And when he hesitates, she adds We can't part like this, not yet.

She takes his hand and with her other clasping the disc she walks him into the forest.

*

I watched them go and thought there time left to chase after, but the woman who'd come from the mist birled round and looked directly down the dale to me, her white face agin the dark green of the woods. She made a very simple gesture that forked me to my goolies and I sat down winded on my seat at the window. I wasna just feart – thinking on what I'd done to her plate and of all the keeking on lovers I'd done over the years while looking for what only she had given me, I was affronted at myself.

If she wanted young Davy, she could have him. Whoever she was, she wasna his sister. And if it came to marrying, she could have half the estate when Elliot passed on. If meeting Jinny among the trees was anything other than a dozent dream, this must be what she wanted, one who came in Marnie's place, unless the dead are unkennin as ourselves.

I felt near at peace if a wee bit chittery as I waited on.

*

Inside the flat, Sim Elliot opens his eyes and stares into the blue cloth of her dress. He must have been asleep all night, or passed out. He can't remember when he last ate. Eating doesn't matter. He hugs Jinny's dress to his face and goes through the blue into paler blue. It's very calm among the blue, no pain in his chest at all as he goes in.

Their last day out together, some weeks before she'd summoned him to Creagan's Knowe. They'd driven south across the border and finally out along the causeway onto the tidal island, parked and walked past the ruined abbey till they came to the water's edge and could go no further.

They sat on the beach in hot sun and felt the day grow full around them. Past her shoulder, sand dunes rose and marram grass spiked the sky. The tide was very full. Near-in the water was flat calm. Beyond that, three dinghies swung lightly together at anchor. Further out, beyond the tidal islands and the two strange obelisks, the open sea was ruffled and much darker blue. Someone somewhere was ringing bells. Her dress was blue, the sky at the horizon was platinum, her eyes were very bright as she turned to him. Her small square chin, two uneven white teeth, the little mole on her cheek moving as she spoke.

This is Heaven, she said. Here, now.

Yes, he said and put his arm around her waist, and his hand on her hip-bone fitted. She was familiar now, not strange. The light seldom quivered about her like the air over a hot country road.

Right now I love you without reservation, he said. With all my heart and soul.

Breath came from her mouth, he heard a faint puff, the kind that could fill a silk sail and push a ship across the sea.

I know, she said. I feel it. She leaned her head on his neck and closed her eyes. Me too, she said. Whatever happens. Always and for aye.

Always and for aye. Lying across the bed, Elliot's breathing is thin and erratic as breeze up on the moor. And he smiles because at last he knows that their doubt was unfounded. Since her death she'd never left him. He had ached every day and never ceased to mourn her. Love arises and is gone, that's for sure, but it has one foot in that other world, the one Jinny believed in, and lives there still.

If only she'd believed a little more. If she'd waited.

*

David Elliot led the way through the dimness under the trees, put his foot on the first plank of the brig. He looked back at her, she nodded and he went on. She followed, the upblow of the water settling on her hair. It was loud by the fall and she had to call on him twice before he heard her and stopped.

She came up to him in the middle of the brig and said she felt dizzy. The rocks above them were grey with falling water, deep green from slabbering moss. She freed her arm.

You're white-like, he said. Don't look down.

She nodded, looked back and on. Her fingers closed on the disc, she slipped her thumb again through the hole and felt herself wed, avowed.

Was that a kingfisher down there, Davy?

Where?

She pointed down over the wooden rail, into the heart of the fall.

Where the moss stops. I've long wanted to see one. Look!

He leans and looks carefully over the thin moss-eaten rail.

It's too dim to see much, he says. I must be getting back home.

He starts to walk on.

Wait for me, she calls. I'm feart.

He stops then, turns round half-smiling.

Down there, she whispers in his ear. Look again.

He sighs and leans over the rail, then one hard push with both hands on his back and his body falls spread-eagled through the mirk, into the grey falls without a sound above their gowling.

The neighbours will agree they heard no one come or go on the echoing stairwell. The entry-phone wasn't buzzed and the outer door had stayed locked. There was no sound of feet mounting the stairs, no quiet singing. Only the faint seep of tea-time television voices, and then the bell began ringing at Robertson's door at the top of the stair. It rang on and on and on.

Sea and sky weld blue on blue behind her and everything is seamless, inside and out. Sim and Jinny sit on the shore just watching and breathing until the light begins to go. Seagulls skreek, a curlew pirl-pirls from the grasslands, a bell is still ringing in the distance. On their way back to the car in the gathering dusk, they pass a ruined window arch empty against the sky where birds fly through. He thinks to say something but she stops him, smiling, after the first three words.

I know, I know, Jinny says. I feel it too.

They're standing watching the birds fly through the ruined arch in the dusk, and there is peace at last. Somewhere a bell is ringing and under his hand her dress is blue crushed velvet. The oddest thing, Sim thinks, the very oddest thing is that a ruined arch is so much more bonnie than a whole church – the way it gives out, the way birds fly through the ruins of his chest, the bell ringing on and on, then her voice speaking clear among the relief of falling night.

*

On the tenement stair someone finally got fed up enough with the bell to go up and complain. Thumped on Robertson's door but got no reply. Through the keyhole the light was shining, a small suitcase lay in the hall. And still the bell rang on till someone sent for the police and they came, opened up the door and in the back bedroom found the big crumpled man lying on a blue dress, his eyes wide open until the senior officer closed them gently with his thumb then wiped it on his trousers as if that could keep his own death at bay. Makes a change to see a peaceful death, he said, though it's hard to tell, eh?

*

I saw her walk alane out of the misty wood, and thought to leave the house to meet her. But something in the glower of her and the bright haze that limned her head and shoulders kept me down on my arse. She glanced aince my way across the gulf atween us then went into the cottage.

She came out carrying nothing but her pack and the satchel, and with her back turned held her right arm straight above her head pointing at the top of the sky and the world stopped right there.

Even the corbies by the heuch held their wheesht. Then she dropped her arm, the satchel gave a wee dunt on her back, and she was sliding over the dyke. She strode long-legged down through windlestrae and loaning without hesitation on her way.

I sat on and on in my workroom, pulling sweet wersh smoke into my lungs, knowing it too late to change anything at all as I watched her pass down into the mirk. A mist was poosking from the river, I strained my eyes as the haar clasped about her, then she walked into it and was gone.

*

Long may the lady pine and long may Sim Elliot wait for his only son and heir to come riding home. In the howe the hassocks wet my ankles as I enter the fringes of the mist. Warm in my right hand the stone disc and the coin. In my belly the future grows already and will in turn act out its fate.

We are who we believe ourselves to be, and I have done what I was made to do. I regret only that the blood-red family ring must lie for ever about a white finger-bone in the depths of the Liddie Burn.

In time there will be made another song, another story. And in time that too will be half-forgotten, doubtful and misread. Then there will be only the old road, a rickle of stones where a cottage once was, and the wind keening over the dyke for evermore.

The mist clasps about me by the Border. I walk into it and am gane.